BEYOND THE SPIRE OF NAVARENE

BEYOND THE SPIRE OF NAVARENE

M. WARREN ASKINS

Beyond the Spire of Navarene
M. Warren Askins

Copyright @ 2019 M. Warren Askins www.mwarrenaskins.com
Cover Artwork & Design by Jonathan Myers
https://myersillustration.wixsite.com/myersillustration
Map by Josiah Moore

The characters and events in this book are fictitious. Any similarity to real persons, living or dead, is coincidental and not intended by the author.

Second Edition: 2025

ISBN: 978-1-7341200-6-6 (paperback 2nd edition)
ISBN: 978-1-6972012-2-2 (paperback 1st edition)
ISBN: 978-1-7341200-0-4 (e-book)

Books by M. Warren Askins

Through the Thorns
Ian
The Dead Men are Dying Saga
Beyond the Spire of Navarene
Martyr for Cowards
Orphan's Rite
Ghosts of Halodwyth

For Gina

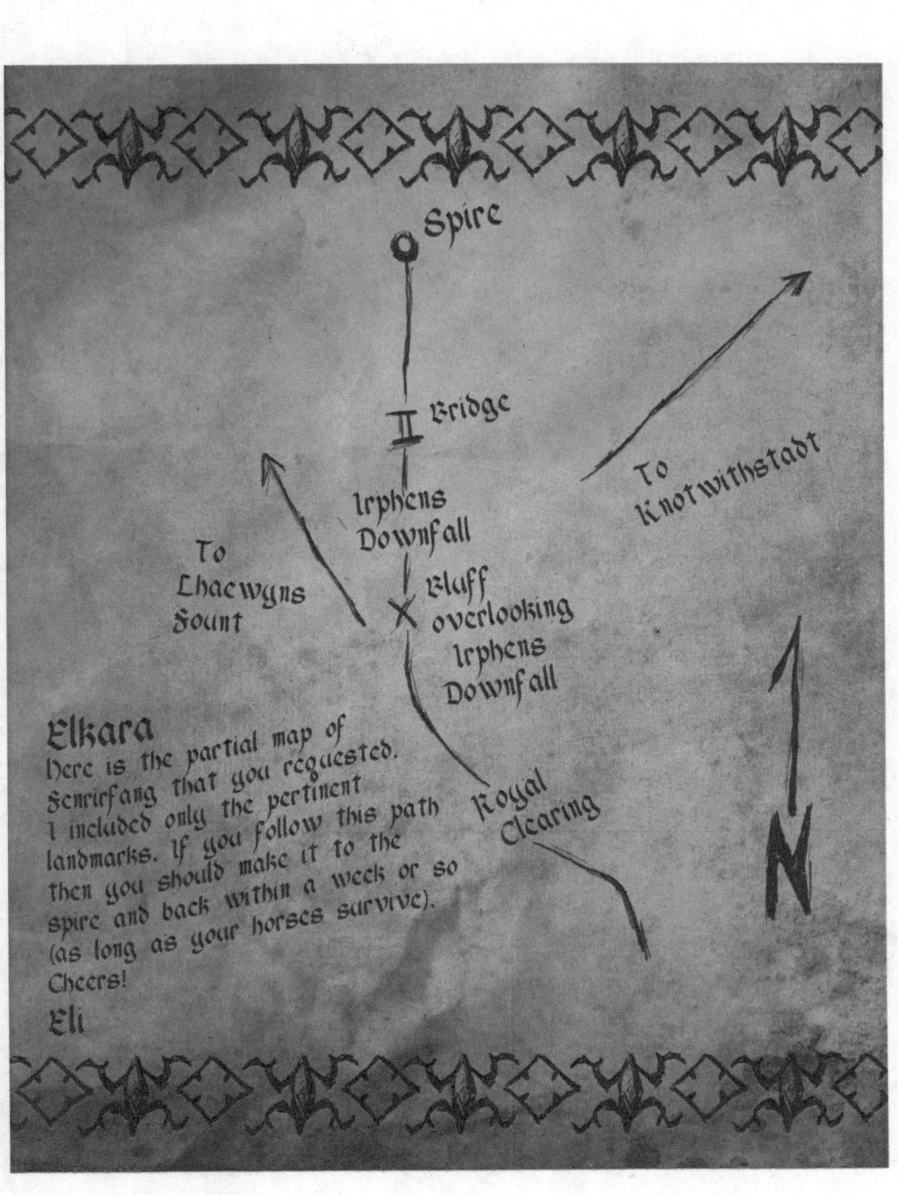

Spire
Bridge
Irphens Downfall
To Knotwithstadt
To Lhaewyns Fount
Bluff overlooking Irphens Downfall
Royal Clearing
N
Elkara
Here is the partial map of Fenrirfang that you requested. I included only the pertinent landmarks. If you follow this path then you should make it to the spire and back within a week or so (as long as your horses survive).
Cheers!
Eli

PROLOGUE

Lord Amyr,

I recount to you these words while the memory is fresh and the ink is damp. Though I may be reporting everything in person, in your wondrously ever-shifting and morphing chambers, the desire to scribble the details lays heavy.

An ample amount of time has passed since your divine edict was bestowed upon the people, and most have held the wisdom to accept it and abide. But there were some who simply ignored the new rule and continued to live their lives as if nothing of significance changed. While I fully and completely understand that when one in authority needs to remind those under him who is in charge, the punishment for disobedience is not only severe, but must also be a clear warning for those treading upon the transparent sheets of ice.

Others, I am sure, will criticize, demonize, and decry our actions this day. They will point out that the village of Knotwithstadt is out of the Church's dominion, and that possibly the news had not yet reached them. They, of course, would be incorrect in these assumptions, as the Church holds all the dominion. You know this and I know this. And when the dispatches assigned to Knotwithstadt returned to the Skyrend Basilica bereft of pants having had them unceremoniously stripped from their bodies, I believe that it summarized the people of Knotwithstadt's feelings concerning you as a figurehead wielding any semblance of authority.

As you well know, when the laives of Knotwithstadt accepted humans to dwell among them, clearing that patch of forest so they could assemble homes better suited for both races, by doing such an act, that village became absorbed by the kingdom. And thusly, absorbed by the Church. What concerns the kingdom concerns you. You already know all of this, and I most humbly apologize for stating the obvious.

When we approached the sleeping village, well before dawn's first gasps, I overheard an older knight talking with a much younger knight, or perhaps a squire? I did not bother to turn in the saddle to get a look. He stated something to the effect: "You'll learn in time that when it comes to most matters, especially ones with heavy consequences, announcing your plans is a good way to hear the Creator laugh." It went along those lines, obviously not verbatim. Regardless, I believe the statement was as appropriate summation for the day.

I only wish more would have heard it. I also wish I would have gazed back to behold the orator's face, to see if he is counted among the survivors.

We sat mounted behind a single band of soldiers, their numbers stretched across the outskirts, rubbing up against the boundary of the village. There was no front gate to funnel through, so in order to overtake them, we only needed to press straight ahead.

I gazed down the line to see mercenaries filling most of the standing ranks, rubbing elbows with some of the finest Holy Knights in existence. Steamy breaths emanated from the eye and mouth slits on helms. The rough faces were battle hardened, and honestly, a bit over-enthusiastic for what was about to take place.

Your instructions were quite simple: every person of an age to carry a weapon in attack or defense must die. Quite straightforward. And concerning the children, you left that to our discretion. Any surviving children were to remain unharmed upon their escort to the orphanages inside the city, under the Church's purview, slaving being strictly forbidden.

I am glad to report that we have a number of children amongst our ranks currently. I know this because the pitiful creatures will not stop wailing. As to be expected. And a few minutes ago, a particularly pungent sellsword decided to take it upon herself to cram almost an entire loaf of bread into a weeping child's mouth, nearly choking the little wretch into an early grave. One of the Holy Knights nearby took direct offense to this, and stepped forth and separated the woman from her spine. You would think this would shut the child up, but no. Once the thing regained its breath, it renewed its wailing with even more fervor!

A relative state of calm was achieved after a handful of knights set up a perimeter around the newly made orphans to prevent any of the disgusting brutes from laying another hand on them. Very odd to me, the men that created the very state that the children find themselves in (a mere three hours ago?) were placing their lives in jeopardy to defend them.

Anyhow, today is a day that I will never forget. It was the first day I watched a man die. And no recounting in any book or anything I ever heard or saw previously would adequately prepare me for the dreadful horrors. I only hope that time will act as a salve and heal my mental eviscerations.

When your acting field general issued the silent signal for all to advance, the plan began to unfold seamlessly. Well, as seamless as such bloody business could attain. Not even a whisper was heard when the first wave of houses was engulfed by the soldiers, the occupants silently slaughtered in their sleep. Knights and mercenaries alike exited the little homes with blood dripping over their hands, torchlight reflecting whatever steel was found on their persons, as they weaved in and out of doorways like synchronized phantasms.

It was rather brilliant, I must admit. At least for the first part.

Not even the dogs detected the invasion. After perhaps fifteen or so houses, some unremarkable man awoke to relieve himself on a nearby tree, and the glowing torches and glittering armour speckled with blood was a clear indication of foreign aggression. He began screaming for the village to rise and defend itself, emitting less than a sentence worth of words before being set upon like a goat bathing near a school of piranha. And suddenly the simple plan was elevated from "swift justice" to a "screaming, bloody slaughter."

That's when the begging and pleading and hand wringing and groveling began. Spittle ropes splashed from panic-stricken lips as the people screamed, with voices cracking, for a second chance. On their knees or running away, the results were all the same. Faces plastered with tears, of all ages, begging upon begging for a stay of execution. Deaf ears, Amyr. Our knights are afflicted with deaf ears.

I am not certain which corner of the earth breeds such filth, but I'm making note of a particularly cruel mercenary. He slowly bled out a man with a gut wound in punishment for the man's wife chipping his sword with her teeth when he sloppily decapitated her. I was not about to join the melee, but if I were a man of such bold savagery, I would have ridden forth and eased the man's suffering as he lay propped against the side of his home. He wailed and hollered for such a pitiable amount of time. That is a vision that will haunt my inner eyelids for certain. I shiver now just thinking on it.

The smell from the carnage still invades my nostrils. Actually, I believe that all of my senses have been molested this day.

As you instructed, I passed along the warning that we may experience some light resistance. Knotwithstadt was home to only a handful of warriors with any sort of renown. There were reports that Sir Palomides had been seen traveling to and from there recently, but I made certain that he was in the palace when we saddled up last night.

The village held a few skilled archers that acted to very meagerly thin our ranks. Hardly a drop in the bucket, honestly, in comparison to the losses we sustained when Sir Rebekah (known as "The Lithe Stone") emerged onto the dark pitch. Many fled before her, seeking easier prey, and where she walked became an empty circle as the knights and soldiers willingly gave ground. Your general took notice of this and signaled for the archers to rally to him. A concerted volley brought the great knight down, a considerably pitiful end for such an honorable knight. Even I must admit such things.   Though the Lithe Stone did considerable damage, it was at the rear gate, near a section of the wall, which extends beyond the shores of Lake Patreka, where we experienced some *discomfort*.

As you know, the village employs a pair of archers at all times to patrol the towers overlooking the vast body of water, day or night. You are also well aware of the purpose for such surveillance: Kapreta. The lake is veritably overflowing with the nasty horrors. The sounds of the slaughter and the stench of people dying and all the nasty business associated, drew the teeming masses of kapreta attention. The heavy reinforced gate was billowing as the horrid wretches clawed and slammed against it, desperate to enter the fray. I imagine that all of their senses were activated working them beyond a frenzy.

I will always wonder if it was an act of heroism or an act of cowardice that drove the archer from his post. His partner was felled only moments before, after exchanging several volleys with another archer who proved to be superior. I did not see this play out, but was told the details, and only witnessed the aftermath.

Somehow that fool archer managed to release the mechanism that, in tandem with the mechanism opposite, would activate the gate's opening. After he slapped his side, the sound of the clank was joined by a great heave of the gate as frantic limbs from the teeming mass beyond became visible between the crack in the great doors. Before the quivering gates, the last archer guard bolted across the divide to strike the mechanisms' twin, and our archers definitely proved their worth this day.

The sheer force of the man's momentum brought him to his goal. He was dead on his feet, resplendent in fletchings, collapsing in victory looking like a bloody deflated hedgehog. At least that's what I was told. They even went on to tell me that some of the arrows splintered upon others as they stacked into his throat.

Take it as you will. Yet it is not as noteworthy as the torrent of fangs and claws that spewed forth when the gates were flung open, as if the hinges were submerged in oil. Though I did not see this occur, my palfrey reacted in that moment, and the sounds soon reached my ears.

Every person that was touched by those monsters was devoured before their limbs even reached the earth. Holding ground against such a force was entirely fruitless, and we had no other choice but retreat against such a bloody, unforeseen circumstance.

I have never seen such grave warriors tremble so, and I believe some of them are still trembling in their tents as I now place ink to parchment.

The heaviest casualties sustained were from the barbaric mercenaries you employed, which as a whole is not a great loss as far as I am concerned. Their over eager blood lust sent them the farthest into the town and thusly placed them at the vanguard of the kapreta bloody onslaught.

This was fortuitous, in fact, as they became meaty shields for our hasty retreat, and as a result, we hardly lost a third of our numbers. We survived and succeeded, thus in two days' time I should either be delivering this report, (if I decide to) or will be making an account orally in your presence.

Not one villager escaped, aside from the captured children, and I have just poured myself a third cup of wine and will be enjoying it now, so I will put away my quill and vellum for fear of spilling (any more) of my wine.

With my humblest and most sincere regards,
Your Truest Servant,
Schroederstall

Post Script—The red droplets along the margins are wine, not blood, so please do not be overly concerned.

6 months after the slaughter at Knotwithstadt...

"You believe that this year's harvest will be enough to cover your family's debt?" Sir Dryden asked, setting her chestplate down on the table. "It has been consuming you for as long as I have known you."

Sir Galahalt paused, ceasing the circular motion he was using to apply oil to his left pauldron. "It must," he said, his eyes sweeping over the pond before them. "The first payment was made five years ago, and we have one final installment to make, then my sister is free."

With a solemn nod, Dryden spoke again, "It's a sad state of affairs when those without marks are offered as collateral," she said softly. "I'm not saying that Margot is not..."

"Aye," Galahalt assented calmly. "She has more to offer than most blanks, at least from what I see. She toils endlessly in the fields, and the quality of the crops she produces would make you think she had been born with a gift...with *some* sort of mark."

"I agree," Dryden said, holding a vambrace aloft to admire the article's integrity, the sunlight reflecting a glossy patina. "She is a special girl, your sister. I give you that. It's difficult for me to imagine her married to that toad of a man." She lowered the vambrace and squinted at the pond, speaking hastily, "That is, if you don't pay the debt—which you will, of course...I'm only saying..."

Galahalt's shoulders rose and fell under a heavy sigh. "Schroederstall." He uttered the name with such frigid contempt that it was a wonder his breath was not surrounded by a winter's fog. "I pray that it never comes to that. I could not forgive myself."

"Imagine what their children would look like," Dryden mused. "I would hope that they would take after their mother."

Galahalt cocked an eyebrow at the knight. "I cannot entertain such notions," he responded sternly.

"Would you run?" Dryden asked, sneaking a glance at her companion. "Run away and start someplace fresh?"

"Not an option," Galahalt replied. "Removing Margot from our land would be akin to plucking a fish from water."

"Poisoning Schroederstall's wine would be off the table as well?"

Galahalt blinked as if someone had spat in his eye. "I would consume the poison beforehand to avoid living long enough to see such a dishonorable act play out."

"What if it wasn't poison—" she began.

"No," Galahalt interrupted, his voice hewn from stone. "As deceitful as Schroederstall is, this business between us is sadly above reproach."

"I'll never understand how that worm has been handed so much sovereignty over church affairs. You know that he began as the headmaster of learning? And now he also oversees the census," Dryden remarked, dropping a gauntlet onto the table in frustration. "Someday, maybe, we will have squires that will take care of these tedious chores for us."

Galahalt held little interest in discussing notions of added responsibility, and waved at her dismissively.

Furrowing her brow, Dryden stared at him in disbelief. "You do not wish to have a squire? They're basically free servants?" she inquired.

"There are more important matters that occupy my mind."

"Ah," Dryden said dryly, rolling her neck toward the clear skies. "Your thoughts are still endlessly shifting from duty to fantasy?"

Galahalt winced at the calm accusation.

The knight continued, holding her hands open and offering an exaggerated shrug. "It has not gone unnoticed that you have mentioned seeking out the Questing Beast. An impossible quest for certain, but I do agree that it would change your family's fortune. If it wasn't simply a myth, it would be an excellent contingency. The amount of coin that'd yield could buy an entire kingdom. It would secure your family for every coming generation until the end of time. It could fund an army that you—"

"It would broker a future," Galahalt cut her off. "A free one."

***

5 years in the past...

"ONE LAST THING," THE ARTIST SAID, the back of his legs bumping the chair as he stood, and the ensuing crash startling the young woman who was making her way towards the door, intent on departing the shop.

"One last thing," he repeated, passing under the doorway.

"Yes?" She turned to him. Her nerves were nearly shot, and she was wholeheartedly looking forward to going back to her chambers at the estate and sleeping until she recognized some semblance of this world.

The artist held one hand up with his thumb to his forefinger. "The curvature of the fellows' nose?" he asked. The young woman nodded expectantly and he continued. "Was it a gentle slope cascading from the forehead, or was it more bulbous like a ripened tomato?"

She closed her eyes though it pained her to relive that dreadful scene.

Sir Connor Duncan's killer ran off, leaving the old knight to bleed out in the cold mud alone and unarmed. When Eulba felt it was safe, she ran to her lord and cradled his head in her lap, screaming for help over the sound of the pouring rain. She clutched his head to her chest and wept pitifully as his light grew dim and faded.

She opened her eyes, returning to the present. "Sloped, I guess. It had a ridge on it between the eyes. Like it had been broken before."

"Oh excellent, excellent! An important detail to be sure." The artist folded his hands in a prayerful manner before speaking, "I am at a loss for words to describe the sorrow I feel for that noble knight's passing. I will not delay you any longer."

"I won't feel sorrow for the coward who did this to my lord, if your sketchings prove their worth," she responded, her eyes hardening thinking of the murderer.

He crossed the room and held the door open, standing aside with a reverent nod. Smiling faintly, she strode past him and stepped down onto the stoop as the crisp spring air greeted her. The long winter was clinging with icy fingertips and the gentle spring breeze still had more of an edge than was welcome. Eulba was irritated by the weather. It felt like a guest who overstayed his welcome and had just poured another fresh pint before settling back into her favorite easy chair.

As she headed back towards the manor, Eulba decided to forego attending the outdoor funeral service. With each step, the beckoning song emanating from her bed chambers gradually increased in volume. Even though rumors swirled that members of the royal household would be present for the dreary days' festivities, the welcoming silence of sleep was a much more powerful draw.

Clouds spread across the skies, restricting even the faintest strands of light from punching through to the earth. The scent of bread baking and meat roasting permeated the atmosphere as food purveyors prepared for the public wake. The private service, reserved for the knight's relatives and close friends, was usually held within a smaller sanctuary, but for Sir Connor, the main hall of the Skyrend Basilica had been rearranged to host the proceedings. The judgments scheduled for that afternoon had been postponed until the following day, as the Arbiter himself would be at the service.

Eulba worked her way along the cobblestone street and found herself barred by a crowd that was moving in the same direction, but plodded at a snail's pace, blocking the entire lane. Eulba turned at the sound of hooves clicking from behind to see three women in royal livery trotting past on regal-looking palfreys adorned with dark gray and ebony fabrics. Their stern faces were pinched into pained expressions, and Eulba heard one official sigh loudly as the throng gradually parted down the center, allowing the horses to pass. The first official waved her palm dismissively as she entered and the people tightened away from the horses as best they could, widening the gap a few more inches.

A teenage girl in a drab woolen cloak took advantage of the extra space and sidestepped the incoming horses, cleanly extricating herself from the roving congregation. Eulba caught the girl's eye from under the drawn hood and the two exchanged a smile of recognition when their paths crossed.

I hope Margot is not traveling far on her own. After glancing over her shoulder, Eulba shook her head and stepped into the crowd following a swinging tail adorned with black ribbons. Raising her eyelids was pure labor and each footstep felt like she was trudging in a mound of oatmeal. The distant warmth radiating from the crackling hearth and the feathery soft blankets in her stablemaster's quarters were now shouting to her...and she held little interest in any other matters.

GAZING OUT THE WINDOW OF HIS SHOP, the artist watched the crowds trudge past on foot, each with an eye open for the occasional mounted rider, as they plodded their course toward the melody of a dirge now playing from inside the Basilica. The faint notes sailed on the breeze, reaching his doorstep at a volume just louder than a hum. A few of the passersby recognized the tune and quietly sang with heads bowed.

"You should know this one, Pietr," he said to himself, rubbing his eyes. The mental exhaustion was taking its toll. He heard the song over a hundred times throughout his entire life, but he could not recall the title, or even the lyrics. Leaning closer to the window he began humming along, matching the pitch, when suddenly the answer plunked into his mind like a tossed ball into a waiting hand.

"*The Knight's Elegy*," he exhaled. "Such a basic name for a basic song." He placed his thumb and forefinger on the bridge of his nose, squeezing his eyes shut, then walked back into the studio. Setting the fallen chair upright with a groan, he placed his arms behind his back and stood facing the cluttered desk. Pietr often spoke to himself when he was alone, and when a person interrupted, the artist would continue the audible thought without a hint of embarrassment before smoothly transitioning his attention.

Being born from a family that was renowned for producing strong fighters and warriors who more often than not became distinguished knights in service to whomever they swore allegiance, ensured *The Knight's Elegy* would serenade them...*but not Pietr*. Very rarely was a Revelle born without the Warrior's Sign and such an occasion was highly remarkable.

The Revelle Estate resembled more of a training ground than an upscale dwelling for a wealthy household. For example, the tiltyard sat adjacent to the primrose garden and the servant's quarters were inaccessible if the gauntlet was in operation. Any tardy member of the house staff held that excuse ready on the lips.

Pietr was born a disgrace to his family when he exited the birth canal those nineteen years ago without the familiar Warrior insignia etched onto his neck. When the attending lampyr held up the tiny body, dripping with fluids for all to admire, he nearly choked on the words upon proclaiming that the babe was born under The Architect. The room emptied quickly with Pietr's father the first to press through the old oak door muttering curses under his thick beard. Pietr's mother was left behind while the lampyr held the screaming disappointment in an otherwise vacant room. The story, as told by his grandmother, went that his father, Lord Hakon Revelle, marched directly to the stables and selected the closest mare, and mounted while ignoring the dissenting young stablehand's advice. He attempted to ride through the night on a horse that was not properly shod to offer his newborn son to a trademaster somewhere in the southern reaches. Pietr was always grateful that his father's arrogance prevented him from heeding the hostler's advice, for the return trek to the estate in the clear night air allowed Lord Hakon some time to contemplate his hasty decision as he humbly lead the limping animal back home. Once the fires of indignation dwindled to ash, his father realized the potential of a family architect and argued whole-heartedly against kin in favor of raising the newest Revelle, although not a warrior, within the confines of the estate.

Pietr's frame was scrawny and meager in comparison to his siblings and relatives, preferring the ink quill to a steel blade. His lack in skill with a sword was painfully apparent when he reached the age for sparring, though he never gave up, even after being overthrown or disarmed repeatedly.

The family was ill equipped for raising an architect, and it was not until he reached the age for apprenticeship that they made the decision to employ a tutor that would open the boy's mind to vastly new worlds. The bumps, bruises, and calluses from the training yard soon faded as young Pietr buried his face in books and scrolls, soaking up all manner of knowledge, but focusing mainly on the subjects of fabrication, art, physics, geometry, carpentry, and most important to his father, blacksmithing.

As the years of study under the guidance of his tutor continued, Pietr became proficient in several trades, but above all, he favored the sketch pen. It was no secret that Lord Hakon was grooming Pietr to become the estate's engineer, so when a mechanism went awry on the gauntlet or a pulley shifted out of alignment in the tiltyard, his father would no longer need to seek repair by various tradesmen as long as his son lived in their halls. For a while Pietr dutifully repaired the broken swing arms and secured the winches on the contraptions, and did so with minimal downtime for his grateful warrior kin. Sometimes he even exceeded expectations.

One morning the Revelle family awoke to discover their beloved training gauntlet in pieces, the blunted blades resting in the morning dew allowing rust to overtake them. The shouts of dismay carried beyond the garden walls, and Pietr was nearly throttled into oblivion when he admitted to the travesty. When Pietr, with trembling hands, produced a stack of sketches for an improved version of the gauntlet, Lord Hakon could hardly form the words for a proper apology as his eyes poured over the prints. Sifting from one page to another, the old warrior marveled at his son's prowess of mind just as he would if one of his warrior sons managed to unhorse a superior knight in a tournament. Pietr never forgot that look.

Now, some years later, Pietr used his tremendous skill with ink and parchment to recreate the faces of thieves and murderers using the accounts of those who witnessed the crimes, describing their features in detail, allowing him to sketch accurate likenesses to post all over the city. Or at least within the relative vicinity of the act. This was the primary function of his humble shop, but he was not above drawing the occasional lost kitty for heartbroken children that crossed his threshold giving descriptions over tearful shudders. But just as with the symbol on his neck, the Revelle family saw little value in the business. After the first year yielded a staggering profit for the young man, the narrative changed and his family quickly recognized the value such a unique service provided.

Pietr settled into his chair, his mind wandering to the floor as he began contemplating some sort of mechanism that would prevent his studio chair from toppling over every time he stood. After a few minutes of aimless moustache twirling, he decided that it would be much simpler to plane the floor instead.

Now that those moments were spent, never to be reclaimed, he rolled up his sleeves before lighting the candle overlooking his work desk. Shadows played all over the studio walls, cast by protrusions made by the contraptions and art pieces that his imagination willed into existence. Directly behind him, held aloft by a pair of curved ogre tusks, was a handcrafted horn bow that he designed and painstakingly constructed from rare and expensive materials over the course of several years.

Pietr was the first to admit that he was an embarrassing swordsman, but his precision and accuracy with a bow was nearly unparalleled. Perhaps it was his innate comprehension of physics and timing that provided such horrifying prowess at the archery pells, or perhaps it was the Revelle blood that coursed in his veins.

Several excursions into the wilds of Fenrirfang provided the necessary materials for the weapon. A handful of alpha ogre tusks and just a few pounds of faewolf sinew provided the bulk of the requirements, but the most important ingredient was the heartwood from an ancient guest. The latter was not only outlandishly expensive, but acquiring it also proved quite problematic and Pietr found himself in several uncomfortable predicaments, the least of which involved a bucket of carp and a handful of cockatrice feathers.

A remarkable quiver complete with a bundle of arrows hung underneath the bow, each one fletched by hand using plumage harvested from frosthale owls. The main housing of the quiver was comprised of tanned ogre hides, which offered a distinct shade of blue, and the buckles and base were forged with gilded metals. In the center, a medallion which resembled the Revelle family crest was pressed into the hide, but Pietr had made an adjustment to the design that caused some hurt feelings. He encapsulated the crest with the mark of The Architect, which was clever, but the seemingly small detail shot up a few red flags. For a family well known for stalwart and bold knights, it was funny how the softest slight could incur such controversy.

Pietr's desk was cluttered with sketches and measuring devices, calipers and rulers mainly, and a smaller table to his right held a short stack of notes he scribbled while the stablemaster gave account earlier. Shapes and calculations occupied each parchment and were kept within an arm's reach should he require reference. Pietr tucked a pinch of dried, salted meat into his cheek, saliva welling inside his dry mouth, softening the pinch just enough so he could work it with his tongue between his lower teeth and bottom lip.

"Hmmm," he reached for another pinch. "She wasn't certain whether his earlobes were attached or not, but did recall that the right lobe had a ring in it. Perhaps I should put a ring in both ears in case she was mistaken...that should offset whether his lobes are attached or not."

Folks passing by the window and the sounds of horses clopping on the cobble diminished as he worked through the afternoon. The public service for Sir Connor was well underway which left the streets nearly barren and the common areas uncommonly quiet. Opportunities that offered hours of ceaseless sketching were a rarity, and Pietr sought to capitalize on it. The goal was to have a handful of posters finished by the time the private service was dismissed.

A blunt knock lifted the artist's head from the vellum and he listened quietly for a few moments. Another round of knocks confirmed his suspicion and when he stood, the chair caught, sending it crashing as he stepped away.

"I really need to refinish that floor..." he muttered as he reached for the latch on the front door. His drawing pen was in his hand so he quickly passed it to his left then pulled the door open.

"Cousin!" Pietr's first cousin, Cahan, stood on the front stoop in armoured attire. A pristine crimson surcoat inlaid with silver passed under a brilliant set of plated pauldrons which met a gorget that clung just under his chin, and below, emblazoned on the chest, the royal symbol. Cradled under his arm was the helm of a guardsman, and a smile played on the man's bearded visage as he looked up at Pietr.

"May I?" he asked, slightly tilting his head toward the empty room.

"By all means." Pietr swung the door wider on its hinges and gestured a welcome with an open hand. "It's a bit curious to me, seeing you wearing the robes of a humble guard. Aren't you to be receiving your belt today? Am I mistaken?" he questioned, scratching the back of his head.

Cahan raised an eyebrow as he set his helm on the stand by the entryway. "That was the charge. But tragedy befell the house of Duncan so the ceremony has been put off for a week," he said, limply clapping his leather gloves.

Pietr placed both hands behind his back. "A most tragic turn of events for all."

"Yes, and as you can see," Cahan replied, looking down at his own garb. "I drew a short straw in the barracks."

"So you exchanged the prospect of knighthood for lowly sentry duty." Pietr clicked his teeth as he crossed the room. "For shame, my dearest of cousins. May I offer some wine or brandy to stave the chill that still plagues us?"

Cahan waved dismissively. "Stiff drink is forbidden while on duty."

"Such laws are overruled by the artist's code of hospitality," Pietr raised two wooden mugs. "You know this."

Cahan shook his head and raised a palm. "I must decline, as much as it pains me. A cup of mulled wine would serve to take the edge off, but I can't tarry long."

Pietr frowned.

"The family was uncertain as to whether you received the invitation to the feast. Your most *dearest of cousins* only gets knighted once."

Pietr opened his mouth to respond, but Cahan continued. "As fate would have it, my patrol led me past my cousin's art studio or shop, or whatever you refer to this place as, and I thought to myself, 'Hey, why don't you check in and see how old Pietr is faring in this great big city? And while you're at it, check and see if he's coming out tonight.'"

Opening his mouth again to respond, then hesitated, waiting for an interruption that did not come. "I have been so busy in the shop,"

Pietr said as his shoulders sagged. "That, well..." his writing desk peered back at him, strewn with parcels and unopened correspondence with the seals still intact.

Cahan's eyes followed his cousin's gaze and immediately understood. "You're a busy guy." He placed a hand on Pietr's shoulder. "I don't take it personally, but you know how the rest of the riff raff can be."

"Wait. Is the celebration still taking place?" With eyebrows furrowed, Pietr took in his cousin's outfit. "What do they intend to celebrate?"

Cahan laughed and clapped Pietr's shoulder then turned towards the door. "You're joking, right? The arrangements were made ages ago! Do you think the Revelle's will allow meat and mead to go to waste? Come on now." He placed his helm on his head then flipped the visor up. "We would celebrate a broken rake if alcohol was provided." Cahan opened the door and made to leave. Pietr walked to the door and held it while his cousin stepped outside.

"So we will celebrate an undisturbed pile of leaves?"

Cahan beamed from under his helm. "Ah, so I will alert the matriarchs! Dear Pietr will be darkening our hallways."

Pietr chewed his pen. "I have a substantial amount of work to do. You're well aware of the murderer on the loose."

"I have no doubt that we will have that bastard well in hand soon enough." Cahan took a step down.

Pietr nodded, hoping to close the door.

"We expect you before nightfall," Cahan turned and Pietr smiled, continuing to nod and placed a hand on the door, inching it forward.

"Oh," Cahan stopped and Pietr froze. "Bring a girl for once. You must have your eye on one of these city girls that are always flittering around the square."

Pietr stopped nodding and stepped onto the porch, but continued to smile. "Aye, as you can see, I have ladies lined up to the door." He gestured down the empty lane. Cahan wagged a finger as he laughed, then strolled toward the music of the funeral proceedings.

Pietr watched his cousin disappear around a bend. "Must have drawn an exceedingly short straw." Taking a deep pull of the afternoon air, he exhaled. "Poor sod wasn't even assigned a horse."

The dull quiet that surrounded him was a pleasant change from the usual buzzing outside the shop and the wholesome aromas wafting from the nearby bakery urged him to stay out in the overcast afternoon for a few more moments. He began to salivate as he remembered that the evening would bring several helpings of expertly crafted food.

"It's a shame you had to go and get yourself killed," he spoke towards the music. "Piss poor timing."
In defiance of duty, Pietr remained outside, ignoring the incessant nagging, contemplating the next course of action. Up until this point he was unsure whether he would go through the trouble of making a print of the murderer's likeness or simply recopy each image by hand. The process of print fabrication was time consuming at first, but in the end, more than made up for the time lost in preparation. Another deterrent for this process was the exorbitant costs involved but he remembered the cut he would receive upon completion of the bounty and that amount would more than cover any losses suffered from material. He had put in place a deadline for himself that functioned on a sliding scale, but he ditched the scale as he now had a defined end point for the evening.

He was calculating how many prints he could possibly produce, weighing both means before the sun set, "I should be able to fabricate the print and still have time to make," he rolled his head, "roughly three or four complete posters before dusk. This, of course, does not take into account the time necessary for actually going out and hanging them."

A chilly breeze swirled down the lane, tossing his hair, disrupting his concentration. He pulled a few stray strands caught on his stubbly chin and decided to make his way back into the office to see if it would be possible to expedite the process without sacrificing quality. As he turned and faced the door to release the latch, a high shriek carried on the wind reached his ears, freezing the man. Pietr was caught off guard by the not so distant sound of a person in peril and his mind began to rationalize it away, attempting to convince him that it was a rabbit snatched unaware by a fox or he was misinterpreting a joyful squeal for a panicked cry.

Ignore it and get back to work. His mind needled. He remained frozen in place, not hazarding a breath, waiting for another peal for help. His mind chided his instincts, urging him to release the latch and go back inside. After a few moments in silence, Pietr closed his eyes and released a breath, and upon squeezing the latch another scream burrowed itself up the lane, confirming his suspicions. This cry was cut short, the victim unable to complete it.

Dispelling all racing thoughts, the artist focused his mind while making for the horn bow on the wall. He lifted it from its rest, then snatched five arrows from the quiver below before turning a heel, making for the exit. As he passed the desk he was reminded of the dirk kept in the upper right drawer which caused him to pause for a moment before continuing. Shaking his head at the moment of indecisiveness, the architect set his jaw and dashed out into the streets.

Sprinting east with the bow in his left hand and the arrows in his right, not stopping for anything. Vaulting a fence, he knelt in the grass and passed the arrows back into his right hand, "Must be near." He craned his ears. The city was remarkably quiet, just as it was at the shop.

A harsh command cracked the silence from an alleyway ahead and Pietr narrowed his audible scope, tightening focus. Moving slowly now, temples pulsating as he crossed the lawn covered in a thick carpet of grass. The alley curved after about twenty paces or so, which hindered view and Pietr knew this. Back tracking around the houses in front of the alley entrance allowed him to approach at an angle that revealed the curvature.

An aggressive voice escalated in anger and Pietr surveyed the area for ample cover, knowing time was short. A dog-eared fence ran parallel with the alley on an upward slope.

"Perfect," Pietr breathed. He darted across the cobblestone street and slid head first behind the fence with careful abandon. The angry voice continued its tirade without suspension as Pietr made the move. He placed the horn bow against the fence for stability, and slowly rose while positioning his eyes between the pickets. A chilly gust whistled in his ears and stung his face, blowing some locks of hair over his eyes. He cursed silently, wishing for a hair tie as he tossed his head to clear the view.

"This is not good."

A thin teenage girl in a drab woolen cloak was struggling against two young men wearing scarves over their mouths. Judging by their builds, Pietr wagered they were probably fresh from completing their respective apprenticeships. Several feet from the confrontation a leather purse laid on the ground with its contents fanned out, soiled by the mud.

The angry man wore an olive tunic over a pair of trousers and his partner wore a tunic in a darker shade of emerald. Flailing frantically as the emerald man forced her to sit against the brick wall, smashing her hip with his knee while gripping her arms over her head. She tilted her head back to scream but the olive man dropped to a knee and punched her soundly in the gut. Tears burst from her eyes upon impact, and an inaudible squeak passed from her lips. The brick snagged her tunic as she sunk to the ground.

Pietr planted four arrows into the turf then notched the solitary remainder. The olive man was on both knees fumbling with the strings on his breeches while the girl kicked at him desperately with her slippered foot. After landing a blow on the man's knuckle, nearly striking his crotch, he inched back awkwardly beyond toe reach. In response, the emerald man squeezed her wrists and tugged upward, slamming her tailbone sharply against the solid brick. Struggling for a few more moments, the olive man finally succeeded in releasing his trousers, dropping them to the dirt. Pietr willed himself not to look. The man was now slithering toward the girl, pinning her ankles at the approach, avoiding another blow. He leaned close, their eyes inches apart. Pietr was not happy with their distance, but his instincts stayed his hand.

The scarf moved as the olive man spoke to the writhing girl, craning her neck, attempting to create a chasm between his nose and her cheek. The words falling upon her ears seemed to contain a freezing spell; the girl stopped and held the man's gaze, her chin bobbed as she took a dry swallow.

Pietr twitched to shift some loose strands of hair that danced in front of his eyes and focused on the girls' hands as they clenched and unclenched. "There is no magic here," he breathed. He rolled his jaw, popping his ears as he watched the olive man remove his left hand from the girl's ankle. She did not kick but her face was twitching as the man traced a path from her knee—to her hip, then up to her eyebrows, grazing the surfaces with the tip of his nail while his scarf moved inaudibly.

Recognizing the predatory patterns, Pietr felt his forehead growing warm as he anxiously waited for an opening. The olive man's mouth continued to run as he pulled the scarf below his nose. That was all

Pietr needed to see. He rose slightly, drawing the bow, its limbs tightening like a closing jaw as his back and shoulders pulled and released within the span of a breath. The nerves in his fingertips sizzled as he watched the pure-white fletching flash between the two faces; a gutted scream accompanied the sharp crack of the arrow terminating against the brick façade.

Clutching his face, blood flowing between his fingers, the olive man reeled in horror as his companion jumped, releasing the girl's wrists, then sprinted for the dark end of the alley. Pietr lined a second shot, cursing to himself as the emerald man somehow had the wherewithal to snatch the leather purse, his heels kicking up mud as he stumbled to renew his momentum.

The girl scrambled toward the bloody man, and reached with both hands to clasp his ears, using the man's head as leverage to stand. Tears intermixed with blood, running over his scarf, splashing in the mud as muffled howls escaped from behind his covered mouth. With both her hands firmly clasped, using every ounce of weight, the girl bashed her pointy knee into the man's fresh pulp of a nose. Blood sprayed from between his fingers, in all directions, splashing onto her face and tunic. Pietr blinked as he watched her seize the man's cap, clench the hair underneath with an enraged fist, then bring her face down to his level. "Never again!" She tugged violently, sending the man onto his side.

Pietr lowered his bow, resisting the urge to end the man's suffering. "Pathetic." Pietr clicked his tongue as he watched the buffoon stumble away while attempting to pull his trousers up with one hand.

Removing himself from cover and approaching, Pietr scraped a step on the cobbles to alert the girl to his presence. Bloody freckles covered her face and she shook when he moved closer. Her demeanor softened when she noticed the bow in his hand.

He produced a bundle of cloth. "May I offer a scarf?"

The girl, Margot, accepted the offering with gratitude in her eyes.

2

The Present

Propping her dirty sandaled feet up on the banister, Margot slouched comfortably in the wooden chair, gazing from the porch onto the recently planted crop of silver shadesgill.

Before sunrise she had carefully transported the remainder of the hibernating flowers from the cellars. When the spring afternoon rays cascaded from above, she could hardly resist the urge to take a break from the endless toil that seemed to occupy her entire existence. A single harvest was a monumental task for any competent farmer, but she decided to test fate and attempt a double yield this year. She was set and determined to make this happen, and when the only other laborer on the farm, Uncle Brett, questioned her sanity, she ignored him and spoke to her dog, "If dear Uncle Brett decides to get it in his head that he will gamble one solitary coin from this harvest," she ruffled the fur behind Elmer's ears. "Then I will burn him alive."

The winter months were stifling and oppressive, nearly transforming Margot into a mole. The shoots from the previous harvest were stored in the cellars below the farm, and they required constant attention. She prepared a makeshift bedroom down in the depths with minimal furnishings for comfort, the rest of the expanse was allocated for the care of the fragile, needy plants. When her uncle ventured down to see how she was faring, he would find her covered in soil, plucking and snipping amongst the shoots and stems.

Elmer, who would whine and glance longingly at the staircase, pleaded for a visit to civilization, encouraging brief reprieves. She would comply at times, welcoming a break from the doldrums. Uncle Brett would comment on how gaunt and thin she looked and she would reply by asking Elmer where he kept the tinder box and fuel.

Now that winter's grasp was loosened, peeled back by the approaching spring, Margot tested and found the soil was warm enough for planting. Unlike most crops, silver shadesgill's growing cycle could be manipulated. The tolerances, however, were tight and most farmers would not dare the attempt unless they were prepared to sustain great losses. Margot had made calculations based on the previous cycle and this double crop would only require a week to develop. After watching the little plants mature in the dank underground environment, tirelessly coaxing them from shoot to glory.

Margot released a sigh, drooping her arm from the armrest to give Elmer a good scratch over his rib cage. The dog lounged on the floor and stretched his limbs with a squeaky yawn.

Last summer while she was wandering about the property line near the forest edge, an adorable pup had trundled from the thicket and was drawn to her side like a magnet. Recently weaned and more than likely abandoned by his mother, the fuzzy creature had pawed her ankles until she reached down and scooped him up. Young Elmer's flat tail had pounded her hip when she cuddled him. His pointy ears were growing faster than the rest of him, folding and flopping over as she raised him up to inspect the furry body.

The canine experts in the city would not recognize this mutt, with the tail of an aquatic dog and the ears of a herder. He looked as though one of the neighboring farms' handsome shepherd dogs wandered into the forest and hit it off with a gorgeous swamp dog, creating this adorable outcast. But Margot couldn't muster any concerns over breed specific rules and the dog snobs inside the gates could get bent, she was in love. Ever since that day, the two had been inseparable.

The crop bobbed and danced as a spring breeze tangled itself between the blossoms, politely kissing the fragile plants as it meandered through. Gilded rays poured through the loaves of graying clouds, like seeds sprinkled from a closed fist. Where direct illumination struck, a shimmering aura activated flecks of silver suspended over the new petals hinting at the magical properties of the plant, highly valued by tradesmen and mages alike.

As rare as it was elegant, the silver shadesgill was a fickle beast, very particular as to where it took up residence. Many aspiring farmers shared tales of failure, waking to find a field of newly planted seeds sitting atop the soil after being planted the previous day.

When she was a child, Margot had attempted to replant one of the full-grown flowers after carefully digging it up from the soil. As she brought the stubborn thing toward a fresh hole, the roots had repelled upward, as if controlled by a puppeteer. To satisfy her childish amusement, she would hold the plant over her head with both hands, then thrust it down so that the spidery roots would tickle her wrist as they shot toward the sky.

Margot smiled at the memory, admiring the fruits of her hard labor, as she wiped her brow with a dirt encrusted wrist, replacing the sweat with grit. She kicked herself for not pouring a cup of water before getting comfortable, summoning the strength to stand proved difficult, but the overwhelming thirst somehow managed to remove her feet from their rest. Sitting up, she prepared her tired muscles for an inconvenience, when the front door swung open.

"At your service, ma'am," a much younger voice than Uncle Brett said. Elmer cocked his head at the awkward greeting.

"You read my mind," she said thankfully, accepting the cup from the outstretched hand of her brother, Galahalt, grateful to remain sitting. The young knight smiled and bowed as he brought the cup to his lips. A few stray droplets landed on his church issued training gambeson, its laces hanging loose. While Margot toiled in the fields all morning, he beat on a wooden sparring pell behind the stables, both devoted to their trade.

Having received knighthood four years past, the young man scarcely found time to himself; each week brought a new journey filled with errands. Some of his journeys lasted more than a week, keeping him occupied to near exhaustion. His employer, the church, provided the supplies necessary for the journeys; arrows, grinding stones, tack, armour repairs, etc., but concerning monetary compensation, virtue was mostly its own reward. A knight's wages starting out covered living expenses, but he was rarely home, so there was that. And the job consumed his life, so he did not have time to spend frivolously.

"I did not hear you arrive last night, did you make it back late?" Margot asked as she set the cup down, then brought her feet up against the banister.

"Arrived early this morning," he replied. The stool bounced along the floorboards as he dragged it closer. "Rode all through the night and couldn't sleep, so I hit the pell." Galahalt leaned back with his hair bunched up as he rested his neck and shoulders against the wall. This position proved uncomfortable, so he pulled the seat closer to the wall. He frowned and continued. "Lots of unrest in the city. That law has torn quite a rift between the cloth and the people."

"What did they expect?" Margot collected her loose hair and bundled it into a ponytail. "When you tell people they can't have kids without permission—may make people pretty mad." Galahalt leaned down and gave Elmer a solid pat on his shoulder then scratched his belly while the dog kicked happily.

"I have not seen Stutters today, where are you boarding her now?" she asked, looking around.

"Sold her." He continued to scratch Elmer's belly.

"When?" she demanded.

"Last night."

Elmer picked up on Margot's agitation and rolled away from the pleasing scrapes, uttering a low growl.

"Whatever for?" Margot palmed her face.

"For money."

She coughed. "Oh there has to be more to this." Leaning down, she snatched her cup in a blur. "That horse was a prize war horse of insanely good breeding. We sacrificed so much to get her and she cost nearly a third of a harvest..." she tossed her head back and took an angry swig. Elmer's hackles began to rise.

Galahalt's eyes darted from dog to sister, and he raised his hands, sensing the walls tightening. "Whoa, whoa," he said as his sister's eyes widened behind the cup. "*Was* being the operative word here. That old mare is...well, old. I don't know how else to phrase it for you. And, you see, the church has been continually sending me on assignments to the southern regions, extending over harsh terrains for many miles sometimes. Stutters was born and bred for combat, and is excellent at those things, I am sure. But she makes a lousy pack mule. The tourney grounds or a battlefield is where her she would best be suited."

Elmer's chin returned to his outstretched paws, the fur on his neck drooping and Margot leaned back and squinted, appraising her brother.

Galahalt continued. "I'll use the money to buy a horse that won't stumble on flat earth or lag behind."

Margot frowned. "Stutters was a good horse."

"I agree." Galahalt took a sip. "But not good for me. At least for right now. The Market Days are arriving soon so I'll see a horsemaster about a horse that will better suit my errand boy lifestyle."

"Very well," she agreed. "But I get to name it. You know the rule."

"I do indeed," Galahalt nodded and tugged on the gambeson's collar. "This coming harvest looks spectacular, sister. I cannot lie. And I must say, well done." The morning clouds moved on leaving the sky bereft of covering, and the unhindered sunlight set the crop ablaze in silver. Margot laughed under her breath, recalling the long months spent underground. Heartbeats of silence passed comfortably as Galahalt stood, walked to the banister, and leaned out, craning his neck. "Doesn't look like rain on the horizon."

"Excellent," Margot closed her eyes.

Galahalt turned and crossed his arms with his back resting on the wooden slats. "Wouldn't want the rain to drown the little fellows now."

"Ah, yes. That would be a problem," Margot said.

Elmer grunted a snore and a smile played on the young knight's lips, ignoring the urge to ruffle the dog's furry head. "Did you take all the shoots from last year and tend them all winter? In the cellars?"

"Yes," she replied, eyes remaining shut. Galahalt whistled and turned back towards the fields, his eyes formed slits against the brilliance reflected by thousands of silver petals swaying in the breeze.

With a yawn that broke at a whistle, Elmer stood and stretched, his rear held aloft. An odd musk awakened his curiosity and the pointy-eared dog hustled off into the spidery hedgerow which was the boundary between their fields and a wing of Fenrirfang Forest. Galahalt swung his leg over the banister, straddling it, as he watched Elmer disappear under the shade of the encroaching tree boughs. His sister was hovering somewhere between sleep and wake, not pinning a banner in either camp. A velikant owl sounded off somewhere over the treeline, and Margot's eyes shot open.

"Just an owl," Galahalt laughed. "A scrawny one by the sound of it."

"Where's Elmer?" She sat upright, head on a swivel.

"Yonder," he said, waving a hand at the trundling object beyond the sea of gilly.

The young mutt tracked a scent with his snout to the ground, fully invested in discovering its origins. He wound a curved line, tracing a course as his thin beaver tail slapped at the air, back and forth, while the aroma guided him.

A rush of relief swept over Margot as she watched the simple activity. She loved that mutt but the forest was a constant source of worry. A copse springing from Fenrirfang created a divide between fields, a neighboring farmer cultivated vegetables there. That was where she first caught sight of the little rascal wriggling free of the undergrowth. She often wondered how Elmer's littermates had fared and would often catch herself gazing over the treelines, half expecting a knife eared mutt with a familiar smile to tumble out.

"You have something..." Galahalt traced a line on his forehead.

"I've got what?" she rubbed three fingers over her eyebrows in confusion, then regarded the residue. "Oh." A few loose strands that escaped the hair tie began to swirl around her chin. "I'll be heading back out into the fields soon enough."

Galahalt looked into his cup then tossed his head back and drained the remainder. "You doubled the lines out there."

"Much doesn't get past you."

"What for?" he leaned down.

"Uncle is gambling again," she mumbled and turned her head, twirling a lock of hair.

Galahalt rubbed his chin. "I was under the impression that activity had come to an end."

"Consider it handled," she stated, sensing her brother's rising anger. "I already spoke to him about it." She finally looked his way, "And this harvest should be more than enough to get us free and clear of our debts."

"I am more concerned with getting *you* free and clear," Galahalt said. "Your birthday is coming up."

Margot was well aware. "Yes, yes, this yield will be more than enough to grant my freedom." A lump was developing in her throat. "Feels like ages since last we spoke and it's nice to have a conversation with someone that answers back with words that I can understand. Elmer is great company and all, but there's a bit of a language barrier."

"Must have felt like an eternity in those cellars, eh?" Galahalt got up and stretched, rotating his torso.

"That winter was abnormally long."

"I can only imagine." Galahalt pulled an arm across his chest and held it. "Living in the depths like some sort of fiend, tinkering in the darkness. It's a wonder you didn't develop night eyes like a laif."

"Night eyes would have come in handy for sure...and speaking of 'fiends,' what sorts of fiends has the church been assigning you to track down? Any exciting stories worth telling your sister who has been anchored to this homestead, toiling away in the fields for her entire life?"

Galahalt arched his back and released a yawn. "Let me think." As he turned his back to his sister, she considered his clean gambeson.

"New arming jacket?" she asked.

"Nope, same as I've had since the day I was belted," he replied.

Elmer appeared and plodded up the stairs, bouncing up the last on his way to the soft spot next to Margot's chair. He circled for a spell then flopped on the floor; a sigh escaped as he settled. The woman reached down to give the dog a hefty pat on his side, the force echoed by the bouncy floorboards underneath.

"It pains me to admit," Galahalt confessed, turning to face her with a palm to his breast. "I can't recall anything spectacular in the last year or more." He paused. "Can't recall anything worth speaking of."

"Well, what sort of errands are they sending you on? Come on," she asked and raised her eyebrows. "There has to be a tale worth dishing."

"Eh, mostly just messages from one cloth to another. I am no more than a delivery boy in a metal suit as far as the church is concerned. Although traveling south over the past winter was pleasant enough; folks there hardly see a pinch of snow at all."

"Their growing season must be never ending." Margot looked over her fields and scratched an eyebrow.

"One afternoon I did pass a meadow on the way to Touringuard's Cathedral that held a small ocean of golden shadesgill. It was brilliant. I even signaled the point man to halt for a moment, much to his irritation. Sir Palman is a one direction only sort. And I hopped off Stutters and picked one for you and pressed it in paper." Galahalt shrugged. "I misplaced it though."

Margot smirked. "I'd rather you bring me a lumpy rock than some fool's gill."

"That's easy enough to arrange," Galahalt chuckled. "I'll be sure to keep my eyes peeled along the crags for the perfect lump."

"A hunk of stone can serve a purpose."

"Most assuredly." Galahalt bowed.

Such a weird fellow. She regarded him, knowing full well that his mind was elsewhere. *Possibly making a list of the places to scavenge for a stone and at the same time, making a list of all the uses for it.* She was spot on with her assumption at the moment, but a sight that he had not noticed before interrupted his train of thought.

"For your friend in the city?" Galahalt asked and pointed at a worn gray pail resting against a column. On its side was a roughly worked spout with a yellowing cork stuffed into the meager opening.

She sat up and looked down. "Oh yes. It is. I'll be filling it once the sun drops a bit more; the flowers will be easier to milk."

"The friend is an artist, I recall?"

She nodded. "Yes, Pietr uses the juice for his trade."

"One of these days I will accompany you when you go to meet this artist friend of yours."

"He's not *that* sort of friend." Margot shifted in her seat. "But you are more than welcome to come along sometime. If the church lets you off its leash, of course."

The young knight stepped forward, kneeling to give Elmer a good scratch on his head. "Maybe we could pop by some other time? When it's convenient for us both."

"I'll try to pencil you in."

3

Bisecting the courtyard was a granite stone path that led to the Skyrend Basilica's census office, which shared a space with the coffer counters. On both sides of the walkway, young pages and squires sparred with blunted steel blades, training for a future within the church's Holy Knights. Only those who proved their worth would earn a belt, the honor was not a guarantee, and the clanging resounded from every wall.

Nathan worked his way along the pathway, careful not to trip on the uneven surface, and absentmindedly pressed a finger into his ear to muffle the sharp sounds. He successfully dampened the piercing high frequencies, but the tempest raging between his temples was a different matter altogether. A page with a slight build, wielding a too heavy blade, stumbled into Nathan's path, nearly crashing into his hip socket. Nathan was a capable squire, and with one hand on the lad's shoulder, he slowed the momentum.

"There is no shame in using both hands." The elder squire held the blade, determining its quality by peering down the length. "Not too badly balanced for a training stick. Stay on your toes and wait for a mistake, then make him pay." Looking across the pitch at the lad's partner caused Nathan to correct himself, "*Her*, I mean. Make her pay." The burly girl grinned and saluted Nathan with her practice sword, forgiving the error. "Remember, use both hands 'til you grow into it." He gave the page a slap on the back as he scampered back to the sparring circle.

Placing a hand on his neck, Nathan grazed the symbol that announced his status as a Warrior. It reminded the squire of his birth and gave him a brief moment of reassurance before his feet carried onward. Being born a Warrior did not bestow privilege nor ensure employment or status as a knight; that was entirely up to the individual. It did, however, bolster strength and reflexes, which gave the blessed recipient enhanced combat instincts which *always* exceeded those of the unmarked.

The two major employers within the kingdom were the crown and the church. Royal knights were mostly comprised of warriors born into families that held distinction: holding lands, titles, or banners. Those with lesser means, but who were still above the swamps, sought service within the embrace of the church. The church never turned a potential warrior away. That is as long as the child had obtained a wealthy sponsor willing to foot the bill. Errantry was, of course, always an option, but those who sought training outside of the established institutions were taking a risk.

Many a horror tale floated around concerning aspiring youths being taken advantage of by a clever "mentor" of an unseemly disposition. For those aspiring to gain renown and fame, the Royal Knights were the pinnacle; elite in every way, they were legends among the common folk. Always placing in the top ranks in tourneys. Songs were composed of their prowess in battle, and sung for generations. The annals were filled with accounts of incredible feats and heroic sacrifices that echoed beyond the halls of the ancestors.

Nathan dreamt of serving under the king's banner as Sir Nathan the...*something scary and powerful. Maybe Sir Nathan the Tall Bastard? Big Bastard? No, that doesn't make sense. My parents were married. I'll think of something later.*

It was rare, but historically the church personally sponsored squires who displayed tremendous skill, those who out performed even the finest of the breed. It was hard to believe, but the church would refuse coin and invest internally, on the promising knight's training. The last knight to achieve this honorable distinction was Sir Godfrey, the Hinter Knight, who died honorably several centuries earlier. The knight's name was invoked whenever a young squire was on the cusp of quitting and about to throw it all away. The deeds of the Hinter Knight created a spark within the youth that kindled into an inferno of inspiration. *Worked for me every time.*

Sir Godfrey's legendary claymore, *Vanguard*, was among the church's reliquaries. It was positioned in the foyer outside the armoury, as an inspiration. Growing up in the church, Nathan often found himself with his hands pressed to the glass coffin that contained the fabled blade. Comparing the massive red leather pommel with his own tiny hands, he was utterly disbelieving that a human could competently wield a weapon of that magnitude.

The church forcefully insisted that its knights make use of a long sword accompanied with a shield. Be it buckler or kite shield, it made no difference, but this was a crucial detail which must be adhered to. Most squires did not voice qualms over the arrangement, knowing that training with secondary weapons like spears and maces was always an option later on. Bearing a sword at all times was not only fashionable, but also gave class distinction. Nathan, however, found the use of a shield cumbersome and unnatural. When he voiced these complaints to his mentor, Sir Clemence, the veteran knight urged him to continue the training regardless.

"Strap the shield to your saddle," Sir Clemence said. "And once a melee is met, draw your claymore. The church will not be the wiser." She had reassured Nathan one evening as they rode toward the forest for a training exercise, but the particulars were foggy in his memory. *Ah "Nathan." Soon to be "Sir Nathan."*

He entered service within the confines of the Basilica at the age of nine, studied as a page for six years, then afterwards graduated into squirehood. Throughout the years, Nathan was unparalleled in the sparring circles and tiltyard, which caused the young pages to idolize him, but his peers regarded him as a prick. When he was a page, he had been insufferable in defeat, and exceedingly more insufferable in victory. After meeting Sir Clemence and receiving the wise older knight's tutelage, he had been inexorably changed and shed the scales of arrogance, revealing a fair and humble exterior.

Nervously accepting one stair at a time, he made his way toward the doorway leading into the Basilica. Nathan's nerves hummed behind his molars as he released the latch and entered. A pair of sentinels wearing azure tunics greeted the youth. Their armour was brilliant and well maintained without a speck of rust to upset the eye.

"State your business, squire." The man's helm was open, the visor locked upright, revealing a disinterested, unshaven face.

Nathan placed a hand on his chest and cleared his throat. "Business with Schroederstall."

"Right." Gesturing with his pole axe, he pointed in the direction of the census offices. "Move along." The other sentinel, whose visor remained down, spoke not a word until Nathan was six paces away, then uttered a muffled phrase that caused his companion to burst into laughter.

Jackasses. Not of the caliber for a knight's belt. Nathan scowled, his face stern, the anger surged, but he continued to walk. His wrath fueled him to mistakenly pound much harder than intended on Schroederstall's door. He listened hard for a response, but after a few moments, decided to strike again, albeit with less zeal this time. As he struck again, a familiar voice shouted from within simultaneously. The timing was awkward, and Nathan was unsure whether he heard "Enter" or "Hold on."

With a tentative grip of the latch, he opened the door slowly. The door opened silently on greased hinges, and the squire's eyes fell on Schroederstall, who stood behind a large desk across the room.

The young man glanced back at the door. "Wish it closed?"

"Certainly, yes," Schroederstall responded as he gestured with a pudgy finger at the woman seated next to him. "You, of course, know your mentor, Sir Clemence." He rotated to his left and pointed again. "And I believe you have met Sir Phillip?" The seated man gave an almost invisible nod.

"Hello Nathan." Clemence smiled warmly at her charge.

"Good day, Sir Clemence." The squire bowed, standing next to three chairs, which were heavily fortified with cushions.

"By all means, please sit." Schroederstall indicated the vacant seats, and continued on as Nathan selected the one in the center. "You are aware of why you are here, correct?"

Placing two hands on the sides of the seat, he straightened his posture. "This is to be my final council before I receive my belt and take the oaths of knighthood."

"And swear fealty to the church and all things therein," Schroederstall droned, waving a hand. "Would you like to begin, Sir Clemence?"

Coughing into her fist, the middle-aged knight spoke, "Nathan, you have served me well these past three years, and you know me as a woman of few words, so don't get too comfortable on that pillow."

Schroederstall frowned, rummaging a stack of parchments as the knight continued. "During your service, the church has not been involved with conflicts concerning man or laif, which is a blessing, but you have experienced many encounters with the evils that lay within the forest realms. Those evils presented perils unique to the particular locale, and during each encounter you proved yourself to be courageous and capable, displaying a level of poise rarely seen in squires sharing your age and experience." Standing with a smile, she locked eyes with her squire, "You kept my horses happy and your quarters clean...enough," Clemence turned to the seated Schroederstall, "I have no complaints."

Schroederstall struggled a bit, looking up at Clemence. "No complaints?" he asked, shuffling a few sheets of vellum. "There are no areas where the boy could stand to seek some improvement?" His eyes dropped down to the squire. "Surely you could indulge us with a few examples of where you feel lacking? Be honest. We won't judge you."

Nathan squinted, trying to come up with an adequate response, but his mentor spoke up, "In regards to service under the Church of the Culmination? No. He meets all requirements."

"Alright, alright." The clergyman raised a hand, watching the knight nod at her squire. "That's well and good. Which moves us along to assignments." Nathan sat upright, relief flooding into his limbs. "Should you accept the mantle of Holy Knight, is there a particular location or a particular office you would prefer? Know that your request does not guarantee the station. The church has the final say concerning its knights."

The possibilities sprawled before him, limitless and open. Nathan was content being a knight, but the business associated with the change in status was not something he had considered. "I would gladly serve the church in any way it saw fit." He balked. "Except," he began, rubbing his chin, as he carefully considering the next words. The three observers were not moving and the silence filling the space was stifling. "I would prefer not to work with the orphans." A roaring silence filled the room, and a bead of sweat formed on Nathan's temple in the space above his left sideburn. With a sleeve tucked into his fist, he reached up and wiped his face.

Schroederstall's mouth was gaping as he formed a response. "Such arrangements can be made." His words dripped with acid. "I am certain the church can accommodate such a simple request."

Not so bad. The air in the room seemed to drop a few comfortable degrees, and the squire settled back. Sir Clemence shot Nathan a wince and shook her head, causing graying hair to tumble over her eyes before being brushed aside.

"But!" Schoederstall piped. "We seem to be getting ahead of ourselves, are we not?" He swiveled his head back and forth between the knights. A large stained glass window overlooked the desk behind the council, and meager beams of light crept in. Tainted prisms of varying colors played along the walls, drawing Nathan's attention from the sober affair. An armoured laif raised a disproportionately large golden chalice over a crudely depicted faewolf; its tongue dangled freely as it gripped its chest, covering a gaping wound. The details of the chalice were painstakingly crafted to near perfection, while the faewolf was little more than a few brown and red pieces of glass cobbled together. *The things we tend to focus our efforts on.*

"In order!" Schroederstall began as he arched his back, snapping the squire from his reverie. "For a squire to achieve knighthood he must serve under a Holy Knight for no less than three years—" He paused to glance at Sir Clemence, who nodded. "And once these three years of service, training, chastity, and humility have passed, the mentor knight must decide when the final day of service has arrived before the squire may don the mantle of Holy Knight." The official steepled his fingers. "Then preparations must be made for the squire's commencement."

Sir Clemence shifted in her seat. Nathan was accustomed to seeing his ruddy mentor in armour, sporting weaponry, and being the pinnacle of authority. The woman appeared out of place with styled and washed hair, wearing the simple tunic provided by the church, answering to a toad like Schroederstall.

The churchman turned to Clemence. "I trust the lad understands what is at stake for his *final trial*?"

"He understands."

"Excellent." Schroederstall stood with a bit of difficulty, then walked towards the stained glass window with his hands behind his back. Squinting as he looked through the dazzling spectrum, he proclaimed, "*Every* squire must complete his final task of the commencement. *No one* is exempt. *No one* can buy their way past it. Believe it or not, others have tried." He held up a finger. "Speaking of sponsorships, your parents have dutifully paid *most* of the required payments." He allowed the words to hang in the air for a few moments.

Unsure of whether to respond, Nathan finally offered, "Most?" as he peered at his downcast mentor across the desk.

Schroederstall turned slowly to allow his eyes to adjust, then squared his shoulders toward the squire. "Indeed. It is most peculiar. I am the acting chair of the census offices, as you are well aware of, which means I perform a great many tasks daily. One of those being the oversight and management of the church's income; a daunting task, to be sure, but one that I thrive at accomplishing." His fingers drummed on the neck of his chair, noiselessly padding into the cushion. "The point is, I am still anxiously anticipating the arrival of your parents' final payment; it is several weeks late and has yet to arrive." Lifting his hands from the chair, he spread them wide. "Our coffers are bereft."

"That's not possible!" The squire was nearly in tears. "I spoke with my father last week and he made no mention—"

"No need to worry, no need to worry." Schroederstall clicked his tongue. "After much discussion and intercession, I managed to work a way around this. I have received the church's blessing to move forward and forgive your sponsor's indiscretion."

With heart pounding in his chest, Nathan tried in vain to manage the racing emotions. Controlled breaths proved fruitless, and he began to search Clemence's face for any indication of a jest, and Sir Phillip may as well been carved from stone for all the emotion he displayed.

That knight has the charisma of a box tortoise.

Nathan's mentor remained silent, and sympathetically furrowed her brow while distractedly grating her knuckles against her chin.

"You have trained *so* hard and served *so* faithfully for the last decade, it would be the greatest of shames to cast it all away, to discard that time as if it were week old refuse, based *upon* neglect brought *upon you* by forces out of *your* control." Schroederstall's words grated, even though they were uttered in soothing tones. "Good Sir Clemence and gentle Sir Phillip and I deliberated on your behalf *all* morning and we have seemingly stumbled upon a means to grant you a pardon. Free and clear. How does that sound? Now young man, I must make this *dreadfully* imperative: everything you are about to hear *must* remain within the confines of this chamber. No spouting off to your fellow squires or penning this in a letter back home to mummy and daddy. If you do, transgressions such as these will instantly disqualify you from potentially becoming a knight; the belt, sword, and spurs will be given to a more worthy member of your peers. But! If you agree to the terms that we will lay before you, then you will find yourself exempt from expulsion *and* your family will be granted immunity from the church's subsequent bilking." Strands of sunlight struck the top of the bald churchman's head, highlighting a few stray hairs that were clinging bravely as he turned back towards the window. "Now before I continue down this perilous path, I need to know *for certain* that you will not divulge *any* part of this discussion to *any* breathing soul."

Nathan nodded.

"I require solemn assurance on this matter." Schroederstall frowned. "I can not hear the contents of your head rattling, squire."

Sparing a glance at his mentor, Nathan cleared his throat. "The matters concerning this discussion will not leave this room by any deed of mine."

"Do you swear?"

"I swear."

"If correspondence reaches my office that you have broken this oath, then you will find yourself swiftly escorted into the presence of the Arbiter. You are well aware of the sort of justice that is found by those seeking an audience with him." Schroederstall narrowed his eyes and traced a line across his throat to emphasize the point.

Nathan uncomfortably swallowed with a parched throat and adjusted his collar as he awaited the details of his commencement.

WITH HEAD SWIMMING and nerves on edge, far worse than when he had entered the office, Nathan closed the door behind him. It took an excessive amount of focus to place one foot in front of the other, and to stride away without appearing as a shaking leaf. *Such a task.*

"Oi, Nathan." A familiar voice snapped Nathan's attention back to the present.

"Aye, Lucas," Nathan responded as the fellow squire approached. "On your way to the census master's office?"

"That's where I aim." The ginger haired lad placed a finger to his nose. "You just comin' outta your final 'sit down' with the tubby lord of parchments and numbers? In there long, eh?"

Nathan blinked while his mind processed. "It took, yeah, it took longer than I thought it would. Yeah."

"*Yeah?*" Lucas' eyes danced at Nathan's weird expression. "I was waiting with those sentinels for nearly a half hour before they let me pass. Said once you came out then they'd let me in. Said it wouldn't be long. Pair of twits."

"Well Clemence didn't really say too much and Phillip made little more than a peep. Well not even, the chap didn't really say anything, come to think of it. But, well, you know Schroederstall; long winded and heavy burdened, so I imagine that's what held me up. Lost all track of time, to be honest."

"You said Phillip was in there?" Lucas tilted his head.

Nathan leaned around Lucas and looked at the sentinels at the end of the corridor. "I did."

"Just why would my mentor be sitting in on your commencement meeting?"

"Can not discuss that. No way."

"Why's that now?"

"Sworn to secrecy."

"Don't you give me that—"

Nathan shifted his weight. "I have business to take care of, Lucas, if you'll excuse me. And I do not think it wise to keep Schroederstall waiting."

Lucas followed Nathan with his head, feet planted. "Will your knight be at my meeting?"

Slowing, Nathan spoke without sparing a glance. "Perhaps." He then continued his departure, attempting to manifest composure.

AS THE LAST SQUIRE OF THE DAY closed the heavy door, Schroederstall leaned back in his seat with a heavy smirk plastered on his face. Blood pumped from his chest and congregated in his groin, as his thoughts drifted, ignoring the existence of the two knights still seated in his office. A sigh escaped as he rested his head against the cushion of the ornate seat, while the sunlight played along the tops of the walls, ushering onward the late afternoon.

"Three squires. Seems like overkill," Clemence spoke dryly, seated upright, mirroring the other knight's posture.

Schroederstall waved a limp wrist above his eyes. "Lucas and Enzo are fodder at best." Catching Phillip bristling from the periphery, he added, "Nathan shows great promise, but it is imperative, as I have said before, that this task be completed without failure." He reached for the crystal decanter on his desk, which was filled to the neck with red wine, then produced a wooden cup from a drawer and gestured to it, caught the knights' eyes. Both shook their heads, declining the offer, but Phillip's face held murder.

"These boys are to be knights," Phillip began. "Not common foot soldiers and spearmen, or repugnant archers. I trained Lucas and Enzo. I know these boys. They may not be the brightest or most obedient, but they come from good stock..."

The churchman leaned forward as he gazed hard at Phillip, maintaining the stare with a scowl, revealing scarlet teeth. Phillip recoiled as Schroederstall spoke. His first words were slurred a bit, ejecting spittle. "That is precisely why I have tasked these boys with such an important mission." The wine seemed to be a strangely potent variety. "Do you think I would employ common soldiers or farm hands for a task of this caliber? Of utmost importance?!"

Phillip was taken aback by the grotesque display. "You called them fodder." His hand became a fist in his lap, out of sight, below the desktop.

"They must prove themselves better!" Schroederstall sat back and as he lifted the cup to his lips again, dribbles fell to his lap. "Lucas and Enzo," the words fell loudly, as if he was speaking to the hard of hearing.

"Have the proportions and bearing to be fine knights, fine knights for the church. *Holy Knights.*" He raised his cup haphazardly and the contents spilled over the lip. "Good stock you said. Would I lean on fools to accomplish tonight's task? Hmmmm? Answer me that Sir Phillip, eh?"

The grim knight sat still as stone, shadows seemed to pass over his countenance.

Schroederstall continued. "If they all emerge from Fenrirfang with victory in their little armoured hands, then I will have no doubt that they have earned those belts and I will welcome them with open arms, and I will eat my words."

"*When,*" Phillip emphatically stated. "*When* they emerge." Rising to a stand, he placed both hands on the desk. "I must depart in order to prepare my squires," he turned to his fellow knight, "I will see you at dawn, Sir Clemence."

Clemence nodded. "If not before."

"I take my leave." Phillip bowed dourly before making his exit, and mumbled well out of earshot, "*Let's hope this scheme does not end like the hollow victory that Knotwithstadt was.*"

Schroederstall paused as the latch secured with a thunk, making sure enough time had lapsed before speaking again, "Let's not delude ourselves, here, Sir Clemence. Your squire is capable of completing this task on his own. In fact, I'd wager hard coin on his success, if the church allowed such endeavors." Raising his eyes to the heavens and pressing palms together. "You grasp my meaning?"

"I do." Clemence rotated, facing the churchman. "I understand that you have no interest in failure and sending three senior squires to assassinate a rather freshly belted knight; a *Holy* Knight, does seem a bit much. I am confident in Nathan's skills but adding Enzo and Lucas will most assuredly guarantee the success you seek."

"The *church*," Schroederstall emphasized, gulping more wine. "Success the *church* seeks."

"As you say." Clemence stood and adjusted her belt. "I must take my leave as well. There are preparations to be made."

"Quite right, quite right." The churchman also adjusted his belt and nodded, gesturing to the door.

With both hands clasped behind her back, Sir Clemence strode to the door and paused with her hand resting on the latch. "In my years of service, battling hordes of evil and dancing the fine line between peril and sanctuary, I have come to several realizations."

Schroederstall furrowed his brow with both hands clasping his freshly filled cup as he silently waited for the room to finally clear.

Clemence went on. "One of which is this: there are two types of men that walk upon this world. Those that willingly fall upon their own sword." She paused, looking down at the solid brass. "And those that would push them upon it." Engaging the latch, the knight departed the office of the census magistrate.

Speaking hollowly to his wine, Schroederstall murmured, "Luckily, they only need to be pushed once."

4

The sun began to set, accented on all sides by plumes of whipped stratus. Daytime creatures began seeking sanctuary as the nocturnal scourges were now rising from their sheltered slumber. A fleeting veil of silence hung in the air, like a pregnant pause before the impending movement in a violent orchestration.

Margot shivered, a phantom breeze passed through her soiled tunic as she knelt among neatly placed rows of silver shadesgill. After squeezing the last drop of nectar into her little pail, she wiped the sticky residue on her thigh. Placing her dry fingers to her lips, she whistled into the creeping darkness, the shrill noise reverberated and bounced back. As the last echo of the note disappeared from earshot, a crashing in the brush responded. Elmer, struggling with a coil of a wild grandywine vine, nipped at the tendrils with focused aggression and freed himself.

She patted the dog's head as he drew to her side, shaking a tremor from head to tail, dislodging any straggling remnants of the vine. As dog and human began to walk toward the farmhouse, Margot pressed a thumb to the pail's floppy lid, reassuring herself that it was secure, having no desire to slosh any of the precious contents out.

"Gah!" Margot jerked her hand up after Elmer licked her fingers, breaking all concentration. After ascending the porch stairs, Margot opened the front door and gave a side step, allowing Elmer to press in first. The pair passed Uncle Brett on their way to the cellars; he was seated at the table with spoon in hand and a steaming wooden bowl before him, and Elmer hesitated at the scent.

"I made stew," he called after them.

"Thank you." The rhyme offended her, so she added, "Uncle," along the descent.

Set aside for this exclusive nectar harvest was a wooden keg that housed nearly a gallon of liquid and scratched across the warped lid was the word "Pietr." After filling the keg to near half, Margot smiled with satisfaction. This amount of nectar would fetch a tidy sum in the marketplace, but the farm girl was more than happy to gift this to her friend in the capital. It felt like the least she could do for the man who rescued her those years ago.

She placed the empty pail next to the keg on the dirt floor then turned to head back upstairs. The light and warmth that greeted her at the top of the staircase caused her to squint, and she faltered a step while her eyes adjusted.

"Ladle." Brett handed the utensil without looking up from his meal and she accepted it mid-stride, taking a step over Elmer, who had snuck back upstairs, drawn by the smell of cooked meat. The dog was heartily decimating a bowl of chow, hardly sparing a breath between sloppy mouthfuls.

"Looks good." She stirred the pot of meat and vegetables, unlocking the aroma.

"It's a right decent batch." Her uncle spoke after a swallow, wiping his chin. "Got some fresh coney in it. Snagged 'em lassnight and skinned 'em this morn."

"Oooooo, you hear that Elmer? It's got rabbit in it." She doled out a liberal amount of the stew into her wooden bowl, the spoon smacking against the basin. She carried the bowl and a trail of steam followed as she kissed the top of Uncle Brett's head, wishing him goodnight.

"G'night, Margot," he said, gravy clinging to his moustache.

She clicked her tongue without pausing in stride, and Elmer scrambled to his feet to join her, melding into the shadows. "Don't be up setting snares too late, uncle," she called. "We have a long day ahead of us."

Brett spoke into his bowl, "That is very true."

She heard the mumble, but didn't care to ask for clarification as she continued on to her room.

Years ago, the family employed two or three farmhands to tend the fields and maintain the outbuildings. The last few decades had proved to be trying for the family concerning finances, Uncle Brett's gambling problem being the primary source, with the last farmhand being dismissed over thirty years ago as a result.

A large room was designated as the servant's quarters, Margot had claimed the vast empty space in their absence, taking up primary residency. The room's large oak door was framed with black steel and Margot often applied oil to its hinges to prevent waking her uncle when she decided to retire, sometimes at ridiculously late hours. Her sleep cycle was constantly upended and changed between working the fields and tending the cellars, surrounded on all sides by delicate plants that withered at a stern glance.

With only the faintest creak, the door swung open as she pressed it with one hand, while the other held the hot stew. Opposite the door was her small bed on a dated frame, and she made her way towards the clean sheets with Elmer in tow. Glancing from the fresh bed to her soiled clothes, Margot elected to sit on the floor with her back against the solid footboard.

Gratuitously long beeswax candles rested inside sconces on three of the four walls, spaced an arm's length apart, flickering meager light. A shelf above the bed sported a few trinkets and keepsakes she had accumulated over the years. Javert sat prominently against the adjoining wall, the pointy-eared stuffed goblin gifted by Pietr, overlooked her bed, providing constant vigilance. Three bunks could fit comfortably, allowing room to move about unhindered, but Margot's belongings and single bed occupied only one corner, which left the appearance of vast emptiness. When Elmer barked, the sound would echo for a fleeting moment, disturbing the cobwebs, sprinkling feathery debris onto the floor.

It was true, the farm had seen many prosperous seasons over its lifetime, and the recent years after Uncle Brett ceased his excursions to the gambler's den proved very profitable indeed. But Margot was wary to spend needlessly. She allocated the extra profits toward more beneficial endeavors, such as replacing the old barrels and kegs, or sending the collection of harvest scythes off for sharpening. A fully stocked supply closet gave her the warm fuzzies and inspired hope that the family was finally working their heads above water, tasting gasps of freedom after hemorrhaging gold for so long.

"I'll bathe after I eat," she said, her hunger nigh overwhelming. The gravy was nice and thick, but not too thick, a credit to Uncle Brett's skill, and the meat was perfect. *Galahalt would inhale this*, she thought. The young knight loved rabbit. She stirred her brother from his nap on the rear davenport earlier, as instructed, when the trees tickled the base of the sun. Setting off for the church on foot, hoping to catch a cart on the road, Galahalt aimed to be at the Basilica by nightfall. Assignments would be handed out in the morning, and he was hoping to get them early. Any spare time allotted would allow him to return home to lend a hand with the harvest. He could not guarantee this, but he made it clear that was his aim.

"The church probably won't loan me a horse," he had said. "So I pray the roads be filled with carts laden with strangers willing to help out a poor knight like me."

*Oh Galahalt—that someday you will slay your questing beast...*With legs stretched, toes to the ceiling, she eagerly consumed every bit of the stew, even running a finger along the inside of the bowl, gleaning the final remnants. Elmer brought his snout within striking distance, earning him a sharp elbow and a "you-know-better." The young canine slinked away to drown away his sorrows in his water bowl which was a poor substitute for real sustenance. Margot made to stand with great reluctance, and groaned with the action as she watched her mutt lapping away, a deluge spreading across the floor.

Outside the servant's quarters, just a few steps from the side entry door, was a privacy fence surrounding a slate topped well. A bucket rigged to a rope and handle, descended the depths. The nearby access to fresh water was perfect for the young woman, and the privacy allowed her to bathe without fear of potential voyeurs.

Margot pried her sandals off without using her hands, then kicked them onto the rug before the hearth. The sound distracted Elmer for a moment, and Margot fled out the door, closing it right behind her heels. The mutt scampered to the door as it latched firmly, and he scratched the frame, whimpering, foiled again. Resigned, Elmer flopped at the threshold, exhales riddled with whines.

To his great relief, Margot soon re-entered the room unscathed, wearing a clean white shift with a damp towel wrapped around her head. Droplets escaped from the towel as her slippered feet slid about the room. Unfurling the top blanket revealed a welcome sight, and before easing in for the night, she selected a dry towel and draped it over the pillows. After extinguishing the candles along the wall, the only light that remained was the burning wick atop her nightstand. Several parchments of vellum and a thin booklet were all that took up space on the little table's surface aside from the candle.

After kicking off her slippers, Margot slid into the warm embrace of her bed, cocooning into the thick blankets. All those nights spent in the musty cellars on the bump-ridden cot caused her to develop an appreciation for such a simple commodity. She extended an arm over to her nightstand and slapped the thin book toward the bed. It was difficult for her to fall asleep without reading for a bit; when the lights went out, her mind wandered to all sorts of places, usually settling on the most cringe-inducing moments.

She ran her fingers over the flimsy paper cover, tracing the letters of the title, "The Kapreta Prince." It was a simple children's tale that was commonplace inside every nursery throughout the land. A prince is transformed into a monster, which evoked laughter among children, but underneath there was a deeper lesson reserved for a more discerning audience.

When a knight received his belt from the church, a copy of the tale was handed to the spouse or next of kin as a ceremonial reminder, as well as a tongue-in-cheek novelty. Galahalt was unmarried and the next of kin was Margot, so she had graciously accepted the gift at the ceremony.

Thumbing through the pages, she stopped at a dog-eared page, recognizing that it was where she had stopped reading previously. *Can it have been a year already?* she thought as she scanned the paragraphs. Deciding that it did not matter, she flipped the pages back to the beginning and started from there.

The tale is gleaned from centuries past, told and re-told over firelight and candlelight, following the path of a pure and loyal young prince, in a kingdom far from The Kingdom of Camelot.

One summer day when the birds were chirping and the insects were humming, a beautiful yet dangerous sorceress came calling on the king of that land. The only quality that exceeded the sorceress' unrivaled beauty was her mystical and mysterious prowess in the mystic arts. One could see the armour tremble on the most battle-hardened knight when they stood in her presence.

She came to the king seeking repayment of an old debt created many, many years ago. The unforeseen visit caught the king entirely off guard, and when he confessed that he could not repay, the sorceress decided to strike a bargain instead. She declared the debt would be satisfied and the contract burned to cinders if the king would give her one his beloved sons, body and soul, for her to retain ownership of until that boys' last dying breath. Asking a parent to disown one of their precious children, their own flesh and blood, was an insurmountable request and would have been dismissed outright, but the fate of the kingdom hung in the balance. With great woe and a helping of sorrow, the king retired to his chambers to confer with his wife, the queen.

Before the king's private discussion with his beau had barely begun, the tears still fresh on his beard, the chamber door still closed, his youngest and most fragile son stepped forward to accept the heaviest of yokes.

The sounds of torment, weeping and wailing, pervaded the entire kingdom as the sorceress escorted her new prize down the main road and out the front gates. Though all the citizens were touched by the turn of events, there was no debating who was touched the hardest and most viscerally. No, not the king or his queen, nor the other two princes. It was the daughter of the king in the neighboring kingdom. After brokering peace from ages of war and strife, the princess was betrothed to the fairest of the three princes. Their prevailing love had changed many hearts and minds, setting the land on a course for lasting peace and prosperity.

One night, the princess stole herself from her room, lowering a long braided rope onto the courtyard far below. She disguised herself as a common scullery maid off to fetch truffles under the light of the midnight moon, promising the guards at the gate that she would spare a few for them. She went many places and saw many sights, searching high and low, asking every person she could find for the whereabouts of the sorceress.

One day she came upon a dashing huntsman who sat upon a stump in a hollow, whittling the afternoon away, making toothpicks and drinking warm beer. When she inquired of him, he offered oddly specific directions, pointing where to go and sending her off with a smile and a wink. The forest was a maze inside of a maze, but the handsome huntsman's earnest directions proved true and soon the princess was standing on the shores of a great pond. All along the serene pool were trees, but a small crack in the chain exposed a quaint cottage with a brick smoke stack that puffed iridescent plumes into the clear skies.

Lo! And behold! Who was the young shirtless man with the chiseled features out front of this cottage, swinging an axe and hefting chopped logs? The prince! Her prince! The princess ran to her betrothed as swift as she could, and the falling footsteps alerted him to her approach. Neither could contain their excitement; weeping and laughing and kissing and hugging and kissing and laughing some more.

Unfortunately the reunion would be short-lived, as the sounds of rapture carried clear into the cottage where the sorceress sat upon a basket weaved from dried troll arteries. She emerged from her small home in utter confusion, unsure what to expect, the seclusion she had created deep in the forest was virtually impossible to navigate correctly. Her confusion dissolved into a frothing cup of fury when she took in the sight of the young lover's reunion, framed by the romantic backdrop of the sparkly pond bathed in soft hues.

As the princess snuggled into her prince's neck, she suddenly felt something strange. Her cheek began to snag as if caught on scales, and when she pulled back to see what sort of damage her nuzzling had caused, she was horrified at what she beheld. The once beautiful features of the prince were now those of a hideous kapreta! Where long flowing locks had luxuriously flowed, there were now oily wisps that clung to damp, dripping cheekbones surrounding a mouth filled with sharp teeth oozing with venom. Her back began to burn and throb and when she stretched her hand to check, it returned covered in blood. The prince's hands had transformed into clawed appendages as he caressed her, leaving a trail of bloody incisions, the flesh still dangled from the talons as he inspected his new form.

The princess backed away slowly, hesitant to make any sudden movements, fearing her love's mind had been altered along with his previously perfect body. When she was a safe distance away, she cut and ran, nearly falling over herself, scrambling inside the womb of the forest maze.

The trees and bracken seemed to open and part, creating pathways for her to tread safely, and she discovered another cottage at its end. She ran and ran, nearly wearing the soles of her shoes to nothing before fortune decided to smile upon her. This cottage was not nestled next to a pond, but was in a clearing surrounded by flowering plants, dancing wisps, and a chorus of laughing faeries. She collapsed upon the doorstep, nearly dead from fright and heartbreak. But who should open the door to this magical little home? It was the very same huntsman she met before, still quite rugged and handsome.

She awoke the next morning in her own bedchambers, somehow spirited there, not remembering anything after crumbling to the ground as the world faded to black. The trauma she experienced from the previous day had effectively sewn her mouth shut, and the princess refused to utter a syllable. Even when her family brought all manner of baubles and trinkets, hoping to illicit even the slightest murmur from the princess' sealed lips, she maintained her silence. They even managed to purchase a young unicorn for her to ride on as she pleased, but that gesture received a glazed stare as well.

A young wizard had recently taken up residence within the castle, having assumed the post after the previous mage passed away. The queen, nearly torn apart with grief, approached the newly arrived wizard and beseeched him for aid. He had never met the princess, yet he eagerly agreed and set to work on his first official royal task.

During his first visit with the princess, the wizard determined that there was no curse involved, and that the girl was simply lovesick. Knowing full well that a powerful sorceress had taken possession of her betrothed prince, he began to rattle off all sorts of scenarios that could have played out while she was wandering the world. As he continued to guess the source behind her deep sorrow, she answered each question with silence and a blank look. Therefore the wizard took his leave, deciding that he would pay the neighboring kingdom a visit to learn all he could about the stolen prince and the sorceress. After spending several days discussing the tragedy with the king and queen, the wizard felt that he had learned as much as he needed, and decided to head back to the forlorn princess' chambers.

The princess was still so heavily racked with guilt that she remained in bed, and refused to budge. Rolling a cart laden with books and scrolls before her, the wizard began speaking of the prince. He told tales of her love's early childhood, and spoke of details that only those closest to him knew. As venom is drawn from a snakebite, the princess' gloom slowly began to dissipate and soon she was sitting up with rapt attention. At first her voice was a raspy croak, but after the wizard offered water, her voice returned and she began to tell him all about what had befallen them in the forest. As the details arose, the wizard fumbled through the parchments, tracing passages with his finger. Before the princess even finished the tale, he made an exclamation of triumph and hurried out the door, nearly toppling the cart in his haste.

After a week of research he returned to the princess again, without notice and without his cart. Crossing the room at a brisk pace, sending the sheets of vellum on her dresser into the air, the wizard shook the princess awake with the promise of an antidote. Color immediately streamed into her cheeks. Clapping and shouting with pure joy, she demanded the answer over fits of giggles.

"True love's kiss will shed the scales from your beloved's face," he declared. "No longer will he adorn the coil of a beast to be hunted and scorned, but will be a man once again, to hold and adore."

Such a simple solution! She leapt from the confining blankets, freeing herself from their stifling weight, and sprung out to the stables to her unicorn. The magical steed ripped great holes in the topsoil as it plotted a ferocious course to that dreaded cottage beyond the maze.

The sorceress had banished the prince from the cottage the same day she cursed him, strongly suggesting that he seek shelter elsewhere, preferably amongst his own kind. The flavor he had brought to her life soured tremendously and she could no longer stand the thought of him, even if transformed back to his original form.

The prince traveled from lake to lake seeking acceptance within any kapreta clans he chanced upon. The monster lifestyle was difficult at first, but as time passed he grew wise and accepted his fate. Like the princess, the prince never forgot his love, and spent many moonlit nights lazing in rivers, dedicating the quiet moments to her.

As the princess rode on the unicorn's back, she had ample time for contemplation. "If only my sweet prince wore a monocle, it would distinguish him from the other ghastly monstrosities." She chuckled at the thought as the unicorn clip-clopped along the lane, passing under a great oak on which a lark sat singing an exquisite ballad. Nodding her head along with the melody, the princess was struck with a wave of inspiration, realizing just how she would find her charming needle amongst the smelly disgusting clumps of hay: she would stand on the shores of every lake in the kingdom and sing. Surely her beloved would recognize her voice and burst forth from whatever depths he was in, allowing her to bestow upon him a kiss overflowing with truth and love. She leaned forward in anticipation and hugged the unicorn's neck as they continued along their journey.

After many ponds, fjords, springs, rivers, and lakes the princess' ballad finally fell upon the ears of the cursed prince, who was lazing on a rocky outcrop just shy of a quarter league from land. He may have forgotten on which side of the plate the pudding spoon rested, but he did not forget the voice of his princess, though her face had become a bit blurry. The tones penetrated his ears and settled in his heart, sending a red hot surge of energy through his scaly core. Like a greased arrow, the prince bolted straight for the princess, nearly skipping upon the surface. Clouds parted and rays of sunshine poured down from above, the lake waters roared their approval and the lost lovers were reunited at long last. The wizard was correct; true love's kiss broke the spell.

In short order, the two were wed in a spectacular ceremony that took place in a glade between the kingdoms. Both kings spared no expense on this affair, and the kingdoms rejoiced as one with the return of the lost prince.

The young wizard received great accolades for his work and was placed in high regard throughout the two kingdoms. But in his haste and youthful exuberance, he neglected to research any possible side effects one may experience after being changed back from a monster. If he had dug a bit deeper into the research, he would have discovered that the person who was transformed will have one or two or maybe a dozen tendencies reflecting their previous state. For instance, a man blasted into the form of a bird may enjoy the occasional worm with his meat and mead. Or a woman converted into a wolf might be drawn to the full moon and on occasion be caught howling in its direction uncontrollably.

On their wedding night, the royal newlyweds enjoyed a private meal in a small lodge at the edge of the glade where they were wed. A choice cut of meat was laid before them as they sat on pillows before a roaring hearth. The princess encouraged her new husband to take the first bite, then she would follow after, anticipating the delightful sight of his enjoyment. He ripped a chunk and began to chew, then passed the meat to his wife. Joyful tears soon became tears of pain and loss. The meat passed beyond the princess' lips for only a moment before her eyes went dark and she collapsed, dead before she hit the pillows.

You see, though the prince was free of his kapreta carapace, the curse left its indelible imprint. While he no longer had fangs, his bite still contained deadly venom.

Margot's eyelids began to droop beyond control, so she rolled over, placing the booklet back on the nightstand without her head leaving the confines of the pillow. Gathering her last remaining ounce of strength, she reached to the candle and snuffed it between thumb and forefinger, its unseen death gasps emanating as a thin shadowy tendril.

5

Leaning back, Nathan watched the candle light flicker on the cream ceiling, shadows dancing along the surface. With neck tilted, he swallowed the mouthful of Gramercy red that had been trapped in his mouth while in deep contemplation for the last several moments.

Should I pour another cup? The wine he enjoyed was grown on the estate he lived and served on, and with that thought, he began to ruminate on the vast achievements of his mentor.

So many. Ah, if only I achieve half the things she has forgotten that she has done. He smiled, alone in his modest living quarters, as he recalled the account of Sir Clemence crowned tourney champion against many knights of the surrounding realms that were of great renown.

The church had pulled his mentor from a conquest deep in Karskill Wood, far to the east, sending five emissaries to reach her with the holy summons. Only two reached the knight, and they remained in the wild encampment long after Sir Clemence, with a laif ranger, returned to the kingdom to enter the lists. Sir Clemence was not interested in the *sport* of knights with its pageantry and frills, a zoo of prowess on display for the purpose of inflating the pretentious. Returning from the battlefield, blood still hot, Sir Clemence had bested every knight she had encountered with the aim of swiftly returning back to her men, back to her duty. With a focus unparalleled, she terrified a particular young duke taking part in his first tourney so exceedingly that when the young man faced her, he unceremoniously fled the pitch, leaving arms and mount behind.

I am told that the herald was not even finished reading the names of the combatants, Nathan thought, with deep admiration.

And when the victory ceremony began, naming Sir Clemence the champion, the hardened warrior had accepted the circlet scarf with a curt bow, and exited the yard at full rush to get back to her men. The trumpets blasted their adulations, but Sir Clemence was long gone, tearing up earth as she returned to Karskill.

"Ah, fack," Nathan cursed and lurched forward, chair creaking with disapproval, and placed his elbows alongside the letter that he was penning home. Writing this message was somehow much more difficult than he had imagined, perhaps the wine was not helpful in that regard. His thumb played a circle around the rim of his empty cup, *I have enough to deal with come sunrise. A skull-piercing ache would be a most unwelcome guest.* He looked at the nondescript bottle of wine, nearly half full as it lay next to its spent and sparse kin on the writing desk. *Sir Clemence's vines grow such excellent vintages, to be sure — the currants alone...*he mused, shaking his head, *but now I must focus.*

Placing his quill back into the ink pool, the squire aimed to complete the task he had begun.

"...next time I write thee," he spoke aloud as he scribbled. "Thy son will be belted a Holy Knight. My commencement begins on the morrow, so it is safe to assume that upon this letter's arrival, thy son shall be wearing the mantle of knight."

Furrowing his brow at the redundancy, he re-read the statements, eyes scanning the page with lips moving soundlessly. *Eh, good 'nuff.* Renewing his effort, he continued, "In the service of the Almighty Creator, and with deepest reverence for His assigned arbiter, Lord Amyr,

I must bid thee farewell. Thy son, Nathan." He rubbed his chin then placed the quill back in its well, "Soon to be 'Sir Nathan.'"

"Of that, I have little doubt." The voice startled Nathan, sending him twitching and looking for his blade. With hands up, Sir Clemence took another step into the small room with an arm concealed behind her. "Smells like oil and sweat in here, lad." Age lines shifted around the older woman's eyes as she grinned, "The familiar bouquet of a knight with his head above the clouds."

Running her free hand through the silver locks on her head, Clemence surveyed the room for a place to sit, deciding upon the rough-hewn bed. It was a simple design without post or tapestry. She placed the parcel that she was hiding at the foot of the cot, out of eye-shot, using the angle to shroud the view. The awkward exchange drew Nathan's attention, and when he moved to see what Clemence was up to, the veteran knight leaned forward. "Can't keep much away from you, aye?"

"That better not be another cat." Nathan lit a second candle with the existing flame. "The last scourge kept me awake every night, and I had the sweetest of dreams where I was throttling it into oblivion." Peering at the box, he curiously tilted his head, waiting for any tremors to indicate life inside.

"This is not something that will aid in killing the rats your crumbs attract, but will prove indelibly useful to your commencement." Clemence edged the box toward Nathan. "And beyond."

Nathan's eyes were alight. "May I?" and handed the candle to his nodding mentor. Wresting the envelope pinned to the top of the box, he began to rummage in the top shelf of his desk searching for a slim blade. Inserting the blade with care, he created a precise slit along the upper edge of the paper, then removed the small vellum square that resided therein. *From all of use at the Gramercy Estate,* he read aloud.

His fingers grazed the wax seal below the words. "Look, Clemence, the church endorsed this too." He flipped the square over revealing the distinct red blotch.

"I am aware, Nathan. I'm aware."

"Must've been expensive."

The woman rolled her eyes and waved away the accusation, then placed the candle on the nearby desk with a smirk. "What are you waiting for?"

Holding the gift in both hands, Nathan weighed it with a slight toss, and it barely left his palms. "Definitely not an arrangement of flowers," he said, giving it another shake. "Or a cask of ale." Setting it down on his bed and unfolded the flaps, then plunged his hands inside, feeling smooth steel covered with a thin sheen of oil. The squire bared his teeth in glee and Clemence chuckled, placing her hands behind her and reclining a few degrees.

Nathan removed the contents of the box with a heave, wresting free a glorious tourney helm. Such a piece of armour was reserved for the elite, and a squire of his station could merely dream of obtaining a helm of this caliber. The steel slid around in his hands, slick with preservative, as he admired the pristine craftsmanship. The lad was speechless.

Clemence stood. "There is a mechanism that must be pulled at that pin in order to open the visor and keep it open to prevent it from slamming down at an inopportune moment." She indicated the location as Nathan continued to gape. "When you bring the visor down, the pin will lock it in place. When a goblin horde is attempting to eat your face, they'll have a hekk of a time getting into the tasty flesh inside," she finished with a barking laugh, clapping her squire on the back.

Nathan was embroiled with emotion and he released a half-hearted chuckle, then placed the helm on his head for the first time.

"Keep the pin lubricated," Clemence's advice sounded further away and hollow. "Master Lorenz was adamant in his concern over the care of the assembly. Make sure to keep it clean and free from debris as well."

"Master *Lorenz?*" Nathan blinked. "Get out of the citadel!"

"You saw the seal. The same man who personally crafted the arms of Sir Percival and Sir Tristram, along with a great number of other famous knights, as I am sure you are well aware. You know I am not one to be swept up in the spectacle and ceremony of *knights* and courtiers and royalty, but even though they employ this armourer, there is no denying the quality of his work."

Nathan cleared a space on his desk and removed the helm, then placed the prized gift reverently upon it for admiration. A pair of candles played against the silver enamel of the helm, while the surface of the visor seemed to capture the light and hold it hostage. The visor was an organic material of a certain dark shade of green which appeared out of place, yet intrinsically mystical.

"The smith has been working on the notion of crafting a modified tourney helm for a while, and finally produced the final design which is what we behold now."

"A modified tourney helm," Nathan whispered, awestruck.

"I am sure a much more fetching title will be concocted; one that will catch the ear as well as the helm draws the eye," Clemence said.

"The eye slits are narrow enough to prevent splinters from peppering my vision," Nathan began. "But also wide enough to entertain a decent field in ground combat." He played with the pin joined to the visor, watching it recoil with the pressure.

Clemence rested her chin on her hand. "A helm that allows the knight to move the visor from a fixed place is nigh essential when seeking to engage in forest combat. You recall the open faced helm we gave you when we ventured into the hollows?"

Nathan nodded. "That was actually something I wanted to bring up. More about the commencement, actually, but we can speak of that later." He brought the candle close to the visor. "Lorenz really outdid himself when he crafted this face plate." Running finger tips over the shallow valleys and soft peaks, the material felt pleasant. "What do the symbols mean? Some sort of earth magic?"

"Good eyes." Clemence slid back and crossed a leg. "That particular portion was not forged by human hands exactly." She squinted. "Well, not forged, no. But crafted, yes. Only a master smith is able to produce such a piece from an unmalleable substance."

Nathan whistled, still tracing a path.

"That, my squire, is from the husk of an aelder terrapin."

Nathan stopped moving, his eyes widening while his imagination swirled into a jumbled mass, discarding nonsense and replacing it with more nonsense, the shelves laid bare then turned upside down. With searching hands, he found his chair and sat down, the floor rose and the ceiling curved like an upside down frown. A solitary tear emerged from his eye and cascaded over a scruffy chin, splashing down and absorbed in the wrinkled fabric of his night shirt.

The squire sniffed and wiped his nose, listening to his mentor continue her explanation. "It has earth enchantments and a myriad of other protective properties, but there is one that stands apart, penetrating water magic. This is evident on the shell of the ancient reptilians." Clemence rubbed her collarbone. "It grants the ability to avoid drowning."

"Water breath?" The squire wheezed in disbelief.

"I'll give you a few moments to compose yourself." Clemence laid back with her head against the wall, perpendicular to the pallet. "Then we can discuss the particulars of your commencement."

"I'm ready," Nathan said with a hard swallow. "We can hold a discussion."

"You are certain?"

"Yes."

The knight and her squire began to discuss the details, formulating a cohesive plan, fleshing the variables, refreshing clouded memories. After an hour of pouring over crudely scratched diagrams, Sir Clemence caught herself repeating the same idea, using different words. She rubbed her face from forehead to mouth, but the soreness behind her eyes was not alleviated.

"It seems night has overtaken us."

"Aye," Nathan agreed wearily as he stood and stretched.

"You will need quality rest." Clemence was on her feet as well, and she placed a hand on her squire's broad shoulder. "No mistakes."

"Aye," Nathan assured her. "I will use my head and will not allow emotions to blind me."

Offering a hand to the lad, Clemence spoke again, "Rest well."

"Do the same." Accepting the gesture, Nathan grasped the weathered hand of the veteran. *Allow some of her wisdom to transfer, Creator.*

Snatching the empty box from the corner of the bed, Clemence turned to walk out the door. Nathan looked around the room as his mentor began to diminish, eyes falling upon the correspondence on his writing desk, brushed aside earlier in haste. With a start, he realized his failure. "Sir Clemence, hold a moment!" A tinge of panic unintentionally infused the phrase.

I am exhausted. He softly knocked his forehead while the woman paused at the door. Quickly tucking the letter into an envelope, Nathan folded it sharply without bothering to seal it, speculating that the delivery would not see many hands. "For my parents. Can you see that they receive it?"

"Of course," Clemence promised, extending the empty box.

Nathan placed the letter inside, then nodded and turned back to his bed.

6

When she was able to see through the fog sifting into her room, Margot's breath caught. A roaring inferno blazed beyond the windows, belching dark smoke that nearly matched the backdrop of the night sky.

Uncle Brett was out there screaming, and she could just barely make out his frantic silhouette running back and forth. Ominous light spilled into the room, cast by the roiling flames, sending the shadows in unpredictable patterns. Elmer was now desperate to get out of the room, standing on his hind legs, impatiently scratching the door. He looked at Margot with a clear expression of urgency, and she flung the blankets aside and made for the door. It was now settling into her mind what was happening.

The harvest is ablaze!

The delicate crop was susceptible to catching fire at the smallest of sparks, and to prevent this sort of tragedy she would typically stagger the spacing, but this season she decided against it in favor of a double harvest.

Such an idiot! Such a greedy idiot!

Fumbling in the dark for a heavy cloak, her mind deliriously calculated the amount of water she would need to draw from the well in order to quench the blaze. Uncle Brett's voice now sounded markedly hoarse, and her heart sank. "Coming uncle!" she shouted, fastening the cloak.

An unexpected creaking sound drew her attention as she placed her hand on the latch. Looking toward the hallway door, she saw it swing wide sending the light veil of smoke swirling. A spectre entered the room, and her panic reached a fever pitch.

Elmer growled as he darted forward, brushing against Margot's ankles and causing the cloak clutched to her chest to billow. The dancing shadows created an erratic flipbook, the dog and intruder flashing in and out as Elmer charged. An unseen rebuff replaced the growls with a sharp squeal, and Elmer slid across the floor, defeated. His body came to a silent conclusion somewhere in the darkness. Margot froze; her better sense told her to run out the door, but her loyalty to Elmer demanded that she stay and fight. Before she could render a decision, a vice-like grip squeezed her wrist, the spectre pierced the smoke, spinning her around to face him. Pulsating illumination accented the masked face before her, his features coming in and out of clarity, and with each surge her memory struggled to solidify around the gaze that held her now.

The man shoved her onto the bed, the back of her knees scraping the footboard.

"Stay there. Don't make me hurt you." He pointed at her while scanning the room, clearly interested in something else. He gave a nod when his eyes fell on her dresser.

Not trusting the man's statement, Margot's eyes flashed over the room, seeking a potential weapon while calculating an escape to the door.

Elmer's lifeless form, some distance from the bed, shuttered in and out of view as she craned her neck, attempting to avoid eye contact with the intruder. The man stared at her, and she tilted her head, looking up at the shelf where Javert sat. Locking eyes with the little doll, she cast desperate pleas at Javert, hoping beyond hope that some residual magic lay inside him; that perhaps somehow he might spring to life and lay to waste this evil. To her grave disappointment, he did nothing but watch from his shelf.

As Margot stared at Javert, the man pulled down the scarf covering his face. "You think I would sully myself with a *blank* like you?" Disgust riddled his thin face, and he moved closer to Margot while he spoke, placing a knee on the edge of her mattress.

An aggressive scraping of claws interrupted the exchange and the man's head turned and Margot noticed something in the silhouette against the flashing backdrop. *That crooked nose!* That detail solidified his identity.

The man turned back to stare at her, seemingly oblivious to the on-slaught of fangs and claws that approached from behind. Margot gri-maced, bracing for impact as her most loyal friend snarled and hurled himself with complete abandon at the man. Eyes still locked on Mar-got, the man drew a glittering object from his hip and without sparing a glance, rotated the object and thrust it behind him.

Elmer did not have time to react, his body weight completed the blade's task. The dog fell onto the edge of the mattress, pitifully clam-bering, attempting to escape the searing pain. The frenetic descent sent blood flying in all directions as Elmer tried to reach Margot. She reached out for him, but the man twisted the blade and pulled it from the dog's flesh, dropping the animal out of reach.

A few whimpers came from the floor but after the span of several breaths, there was only silence. Margot shut her eyes, blood mixing with tears, as the murderer slowly and deliberately wiped his blade on the blanket all while continuing to stare at her. Though her eyes moved all about, his eyes did not falter, wholly fixated.

The smoke was thickening above them, and Margot coughed and shuddered, beginning to sob. Tears blurred her vision as the man returned the blade to the darkness and adjusted his position, moving closer.

The brief pause opened a window, and Margot snapped into action. Activating every abdominal muscle, she shot up and smashed her forehead into the man's snout, cracking the bridge. The man was shocked, putting his hands to his nose to staunch the blood pouring out. Using the scrap of momentum she had garnered, she began to claw at the man's exposed eyes, reaching as far as she could. Ripping and tearing at anything she could gain purchase on, she could feel her fingernails growing dull from the torn flesh accumulating underneath them. Suddenly the man leaned back, out of reach, then punched Margot full in the face, sending her onto her back.

"Whore!" he hissed, vehemently spitting a cloud intermixed with blood and sweat, spraying a mist over the bed. "I wasn't supposed to hurt you." A fresh blood trail ran from his left nostril, circumnavigating the thin mouth below and running over his stubbled chin before tunneling out of sight.

She desperately looked to Javert one last time before renewing her effort, but the doll only watched. *Always watching.*

She moved to repeat her assault, but this time the man was ready, and the dull handle of his dagger struck her between the eyes; bright light flashed under her eyelids at the impact. The dim room went completely dark as the disinterested universe granted a small mercy, and Margot fell back, unconscious.

MARGOT'S EYELIDS STRUGGLED TO OPEN through the thin film of blood that had congealed onto them overnight, so she used her palms to force them open, hissing in pain. The morning rays seared her skull and she groaned, holding her head, each heartbeat sending a wave of pain. Instinctively, her hand shot to her lower region, and finding her undergarments intact, heaved a sigh of relief.

When she became aware of her surroundings, she felt as if she had passed through a portal, waking on the shores of a nightmare. She slowly sat up, sucking in a breath upon noticing the blood staining her white shift. Sliding across the mattress proved painful, every muscle shouted at their activation. When her feet finally made their way to the floor, her eyes fell on a large pool of blood residing amid staggered rust colored smears.

"Elmer!" her shout escaped as a croak. Her mind filled with the image of her dog drowning in darkness, afraid and alone.

*If he is still breathing, then perhaps there will be enough time for a lampyr...*Her mind raced as she took in the rest of her room, searching it for any sign of Elmer. The blood trail ended at the threshold to the side door. Harsh light flooded her vision as she opened the door, cursing loudly and shielding her eyes, waiting for the world to draw into focus. Elmer's path was indiscernible in the dew-saturated lawn, and once her pain was manageable enough, she peered out for clues.

When the smoldering fields came into view, she nearly collapsed, steadying herself against the doorframe. Black tendrils of charred grass extended from the smoking expanse, the bright morning revealing the night's devastation. The entire crop was laid to waste, her entire existence for the last year completely nullified. *All those filth-wrapped nights in the cellars...*she breathed heavily through a covered mouth, unable to control the rapid intake of air, her chest heaved out of control and the fringes of her optics began to tunnel. *This was the year we were to tip the scales in our favor...*

"Margot!" a voice shouted over the din. "Sister?!" Margot turned to the voice, hand falling limp, revealing a mouth that was wide and gasping.

Galahalt dropped his sack and spear, shedding the burdens as he rushed towards his sister who looked to be at near collapse. She appeared as a vision of the undead: white shift spattered with blood, hair thick and matted. One eye was bruised a deep shade of purple, and the cheek below had swelled so much that it pulled her face completely out of symmetry. Growing closer, the many bloody speckles all over her face and neck became apparent, a few were large enough to create irregular crimson lines.

"Are you wounded?" he asked. Without waiting for an answer, he followed with, "Is that your blood?" He gripped her shoulders, looking over his sister as she stood stalk still.

"I don't know where he went," she mumbled. She tried to stand on her tiptoes to gain a better view, but toppled. The young knight went to one knee as she buckled, and with great care caught her in his arms, then brought her back to standing.

Margot's arms flopped over his steel pauldrons, but he was able to maintain her balance with both of his arms under her armpits with both fists clasped behind. Tears began streaming down her face, and as she pressed her cheek to his gorget Galahalt could feel the warmth passing between the steel and his neck, flowing downward, pooling somewhere in the fabric below.

"I can't find him!" she cried.

Galahalt lowered his head, attempting to make eye contact. "Who can't you find?" he gently asked, but she avoided his gaze and continued to sweep the landscape over his shoulder. "Tell me what happened." he stated, finally locking eyes with his sister.

"Elmer...last night...he...the harvest," she stammered, moving her gaze to the ground that was rising to meet her, but Galahalt held her firm. "What do you mean? What happened?"

"He had a dagger—" she defied her brother's hold and slumped to the ground.

Venom seeped into his voice. "Who had a dagger?" he demanded, but she had already slipped back into unconsciousness.

I can't lose everything I love so soon.

"Uncle Brett!" Galahalt called, stepping onto the porch. The older man was splayed in solemn repose, as if dead, black swathes of ash darkening his skin and clothes. He awoke with a start, sitting up straight with a look of utter surprise.

"I tried to rally the neighbors, but to no avail. Didn't see the sense in battlin' a blaze that plagued such a crop, s'what they said. Stuff goes up at the sight o' a spark," Brett explained, his eyes twitching feverishly with the confession.

"Did you manage to see who did this?" Galahalt asked brusquely.

The older man's eyes would not rest, and he continued without answering his nephew, "Figured I'd try an' save at least one corner of the flowers. I got as many buckets as I could and splashed and splashed 'em in one spot." He whistled sadly. "Didn't do no good. Lost it all." His eyes settled for a moment on Galahalt. "Every last petal," he emphatically stated, scooching toward the wall to rest his back. "Didn't get no help from no one. I hollered and yelled all night between buckets, I did, Galahalt. But no one came. Not even the dog."

The older man's chin rested on his chest, the sparse hairs on his head were singed and curled. Blinking back tears, he went on with his tale. "Your sister—" He thumbed the air and looked up with a sniffle, eyes widening in realization.

"Your sister!" Brett yelled. He struggled to his feet only to stumble into the wall, using an arm to brace himself. "I went to the neighbors and didn't bother her at first...I thought she'd be out to help—" He started to shake as his emotions welled. "In all the confusion and flames I didn't even think to—"

"She's sleeping, uncle."

Brett wiped the corners of his mouth, staring at the floor. "She slept through it all?" he asked, incredulous.

"No," Galahalt said simply. He did not have the proper words at the moment.

"No?" The older man's voice lilted. "Did harm fall—" He could not finish his question, beginning to struggle to his feet in a fit of sad anger.

"I'll sort it out," Galahalt promised. He helped his uncle gain stability, easing him into a chair. "She is fine." He went on to explain what befell Margot the night before and the young knight finished by asking, "Have you seen her dog?" He attempted to steer the conversation away from a possible heart attack.

The old man straightened, raising an eyebrow. "No. No, I haven't. Not since supper." His lips quivered under his bushy moustache, and he went on, "I didn't see anyone at all. Not all night. The neighbors spoke through their doors, didn't even have the courtesy to come out." He looked up at Galahalt through bleary eyes. "If I'dve known...I woulda...If I'dve known your sister was in peril..." The old man dropped his head and began to weep openly, his back heaving with each shuddering breath. Galahalt awkwardly patted the man's back.

After the sobbing no longer clenched his throat, Brett lifted his head. "I will ride to the city and tell the sheriff about this," he resolved. "They can find justice." He briskly wiped his nose on the back of his wrist.

Their conversation was interrupted by the distinct sound of jangling spurs, the men's eyes shot to the side yard, facing the common road. A rather majestic palfrey was heading towards them with two destriers preceding it along the lane. The lead riders were clearly from the Church, resplendent in the telltale azure and white.

The man bouncing along behind wore more formal attire, Galahalt and Brett immediately recognized the pudgy frame in the saddle. The horses' clicking hooves subsided as they cleared the even road and entered the soft lawn.

"Schroederstall," Brett exhaled darkly.

After dismounting their horses, the three men made for the porch, the last in line gaping at the smoldering ruins. "This is a tragedy!" Schroederstall proclaimed, his several chins wiggling along with the words.

The horses remained where abandoned, lowering their heads and chewing the grass, paying little mind to the light drafts of smoke wafting over. Schroederstall's palfrey was relieved to be free of the recent burden, pawing the earth and shaking her head, long glistening braids fluttering.

"I must know what happened here," Schroederstall said, removing his riding gloves and slapping them against the banister.

"Arson?" Brett speculated dryly, regarding the intrusion with disdain.

"Arson?" Schroederstall sputtered. "Arson?!" His voice rose in hysterics, neck swiveling all around, sweeping the surroundings. "Where is my dear, sweet Margot? Did she get scorched attempting to defend the crop?!"

Galahalt shook his head. "She did not go near the blaze," he answered.

"But her injuries weren't from the fire," Brett said bitterly, turning to Galahalt. "Someone broke into her room and roughed her up good. For no reason."

The church official abruptly stomped his foot. "What?!" he shouted, turning vehemently toward the pair of squires that accompanied him. "What?!"

The lads shrunk back.

"This act will not stand!" Schroederstall stomped his foot again, rattling the bolts that secured the porch.

The taller squire with flame red hair spoke. "We will report this to the constable as soon as we get back to the city, sir," he promised, straightening his tunic, pulling at the hem under his arming belt.

"You don't need to worry yourselves," Brett muttered, leaning forward, looking out beyond. "We don't need anymore trouble."

"Trouble? Trouble?!" Schroederstall shrieked, puffing up like an inflated windsock. "Nonsense! It will be our honor to perform this duty!" Placing both hands behind his back, he rolled up onto his toes with an audible huff, and looked over his shoulder at the squire escorts, then lowered back down onto his heels. He took a few rigid steps, the joints underneath creaking in protest, and put both meaty hands on the banister, leaning out to look at the fields.

"I journeyed here this morning to see how this particular harvest is fairing," he said grandly. With a loud exhale, he looked toward the skies. "My party and I decided to grace your humble farm with our presence in order to take a survey of the impending silver shadesgill harvest. My curiosity was overwhelming me, and when I opened my eyes this morning, I simply had to make the trek in order to satisfy it. You see, I have been growing most anxious to see the outcome of our arrangement..." He turned toward the men. "Allow me to cut to the chase, so to speak." Clearing his throat, the man continued, "Will you be able to pay the debt owed to the church? The obligation made in order to allow your nephew here." He nodded toward Galahalt and went on emphatically, "To train under the magnificent banners of the Church of the Culmination and earn his belt? By all accounts, the lad has proved himself most useful and honorable, I cannot lie about that, so it would be a most dreadful shame if this young knight's hard-earned reputation was tarnished by his family's inability to repay the debt accrued in order to gain the status that he currently finds himself delighting in." Turning his head, he looked from the corner of his eye at Uncle Brett. "It's safe to assume that you have no other assets?" he asked slyly.

Brett stared wordlessly while the churchman impatiently tapped his foot.

"There's livestock," Galahalt spoke up. "And the land we are standing on extends over a sizable area, dozens of acres running all the way to the edges of the forest."

"It's doubtful that a few cows and hens will cover the costs associated with bringing a young squire to full knighthood. If such an act were possible, then every hayseed from here to Seykland's Spire would be clambering for a belt. Those tiltyards would be just brimming with class. Can you just imagine?" Schroederstall grimaced at his companions who pursed their lips and nodded.

"We'll sort it out," Galahalt said, crossing his arms. "My sister experienced quite the ordeal last night, and right now that tops my list of concerns. But worry not, gentles, the church will see its second and final installment before the deadline."

Schroederstall flexed under his jupon as he turned and gripped the banister. "It pains me greatly that such a heinous act was delivered upon your meek and gentle sister. A most unworthy victim if there ever was." He gritted his teeth angrily as he spoke. "This action will not go unpunished! Mark my words." The banister groaned as he continued to grip and pull on it. "But understand this, men, if the gold is not deposited into the church's coffers by her birthday, then she will be taken into my care and be made my bride, as per our agreement. I do not believe this bears reminding, but I utter it anyhow." The churchman removed his black tricorn hat, revealing a mostly bald pate with a few sparse, sweaty fibers projecting at odd angles. "Furthermore," he started, hurrying his words, anticipating an interruption. "You mentioned a second installment?" He pivoted on a heel to face Brett and Galahalt, leaning back and working the rim of the hat between manicured fingers.

The young knight rested a hand on the pommel of his sword with narrowed eyes, and nodded assent while Uncle Brett shifted in his seat uncomfortably.

Schroederstall ignored the movement, and with deliberate light staccato continued his speech. "The church has no record of a first installment." With a smile that began to broaden into a grin, he went on, "So a second installment would *not* be the final. Unless my arithmetic is wrong? As I am sure it is not. Young Galahalt can attest to my aptitude with numbers. That was a favorite subject of yours, I recall." The churchman grinned widely, his teeth now apparent, jutting crookedly from a receding gum line like shaved tombstones.

"You must be mistaken!" Brett exploded. He moved to stand, but Galahalt placed a firm hand on his shoulder.

"Explain," Galahalt said.

Craning around Galahalt, Schroederstall spoke directly to the older man. "Rest assured, there is no mistake, my good sir. It appears that you have been operating under false pretenses. The impression that I am receiving is that you believe the church has been given compensation towards the debt?" He grinned, continuing gleefully, "The rather vacant look on your face clearly tells me that this must come as news to you? I was indeed born at night, gentlemen, but it was not last night," he concluded.

"My sister delivered the first payment five years ago."

"Your sister did no such thing. The church has no record of such a transaction occurring nearly half a decade ago, as you claim," Schroederstall delightfully informed them.

"Be clear," Galahalt insisted, his grip tightening on his pommel. The pair of squires took notice, but did not move in defense.

Schroederstall secured his hat with one hand, pressing it down, effectively obscuring the sunlight's reflection. He opened his arms, palms upraised in mock supplication. "I did not come to quarrel, sir knight, only to make an inquiry concerning the debt and our agreement. An early morning courier brought word that a field of silver shadesgill was devoured by flames overnight, and, well, you understand that I had to make sure your investment was safe. But..." he trailed off. "Seeing as this is the only crop of the precious flower inside the kingdom's purview, the odds were good that this would be what I would discover," he said slumping and exhaling a sigh. "However, the dispatch did not include any details regarding an assault. Such a pity. And only a scant few weeks from her wedding day. I do hope that any bruising dissipates by then," he clucked refusing to meet Galahalt's gaze.

Brett sat upright, his ash covered jaw set in a scowl. "There won't be any wedding," he stated.

"I beg to differ," Schroederstall said, and spared a glance at the squires.

Galahalt was still as a statue, not a muscle vibrated, his hand still clasped to his pommel. The squires changed stances, their eyes flitting from the sword to the knight's visage, keeping watch for any flash of movement. They remembered this knight who was several years their senior, and remembered how easily he held his own in the sparring circles.

Brett pinched the bridge of his nose. "You mean to tell us that we now owe ya the *full* payment?" he asked.

"*Now owe*? Let us be clear. Your family has always owed the church the full payment. Since its inception, until this very moment, as per our agreement, you were bestowed the liberty to pay in installments or simply pay a lump sum. Seeing as no installments were registered, a lump sum is expected."

"But Margot paid half already." Brett looked to his nephew for confirmation. "A few years back."

Schroederstall's face panned between the men. "Well, then, I suppose you should have a little discussion with your niece in regards to the whereabouts of the gold she claims to have delivered *all those years ago*. I fear you may not like the explanation," he said.

"How are we to conjure fifty thousand gold pieces?" Brett asked. Tears lurked around the lower rims of his eyes.

"I care not the *how*." Schroederstall chuckled. "And there are honest means to obtain such riches in a short time. Service in the church is *not* one of those means," he said, turning his attention to the young knight. "I fear that your nephew will be quite occupied for the foreseeable future, so I do not think it wise to rely upon him for salvation. Those messages or parcels or whatever it is he is tasked with, do not deliver themselves. Mighty responsibility for a mighty knight. Perhaps you might put your nephew's sword, that one he is squeezing ever so tightly, to good use? Maybe you could persuade him to leave it in your care? If you came across a wounded gargoyle, you could put it out of its misery, and that would, no doubt, fetch a handsome sum. Just as long as you steer clear of the gambling dens and other such caverns of iniquity."

Neither knight nor farmer took the bait, allowing a stillness to fill the space.

Schroederstall began counting on his pudgy fingers. "A barrel of troll horns, *or* a barrel of alpha ogre tusks would do, a few aelder terrapin shells, several stacks of griffin pelts, I already mentioned gargoyles, but a handful of gargoyle scales would do rather nicely. Each of these examples on their own would nearly settle the amount, or maybe even satisfy it completely. Oh! Yes! There's always the Questing Beast! Countless knights have set off and failed attempting to reach and slay the monster. *That!* Now that would put your family over the top. A single fang could change the whole world, upturn it, and settle it back." Walking over to his riding gloves resting on the banister, he finished his monologue. "So there are a few ways to secure fifty thousand gold, sir. Rest assured, I will not be sending out an invoice for a consultant's fee. I merely work for the census division." He clapped the gloves in his palm and looked over at the men, awaiting a response.

Brett settled back into his chair, watching Schroederstall signal departure to his shadows before turning back, his foot near the top step, and tipping the brim of his hat with a nod. The three men joined their horses on the lawn, then wheeled in the direction of the city. On the road, suspended in the air, the cloud of dust kicked up by their departure maintained its aura like a patch of bitters. Sir Galahalt wished for a stiff breeze.

With face buried in his palm, Brett spoke, his voice nearly muffled, "How are we to come up with that sum?"

"I'm going to follow his suggestion."

"That being?"

Catching his uncle's eye, Galahalt grinned. "Get a fang."

Uncle Brett slid his hand down over his mouth and laughed. "Ye can't be serious, lad? Everyone knows it's a fable. It's just a story we tell young nippers when we put 'em to bed," he said. "You heard that fat asshole. Hundreds of knights and foolhardy warriors set off to find the beast for centuries and come up with nothing. I'll bet more than half lost their lives in the stupid attempt. And 'sides you have your duties to the church sending you down south more often than not. They say the Questing Beast lives in some dark corner of Fenrirfang. The opposite direction!"

"See to my sister."

Galahalt was crossing the lawn before his uncle even had time to look.

* * *

THE TWO SQUIRES ACCOMPANYING SCHROEDERSTALL, Lucas and Enzo, did not exchange a word for the duration of their trek along the country road. Not even a smirk passed between the lifelong friends; the morning's revelations had sucked even the slightest remnant of humor from the atmosphere.

The tone became less dour after they re-entered the city on their way back toward the Basilica. Their course through the city led them down "the stray line," which was a name given to the stretch of dilapidated buildings that had been designated for housing orphans. Over the centuries, one great building was necessary to accommodate the number of children in need of a home, be it from war or disease or any other such means that would leave one bereft of parents. With the rising tide of orphans over the last decade or so, the church had compensated by purchasing multiple buildings to house them. As they passed the newly minted orphanages, the squires craned their heads to look inside the windows, while Schroederstall steeled his gaze forward. Shutters were left open, breezes gently lifting the skirts of the sparse drapes that ornamented a select few windows. The porches were empty, and the homes appeared vacant. There was not one peep of any children playing, as one might expect to hear when venturing close. Peeking from under the bottom sill of a ground level window was the crown of a child's head, and when her eyes became visible, quickly popped back down when Enzo fluttered his fingers in greeting. He grimaced at Lucas, and his mate covered his mouth to stifle a laugh.

"I will need a word once we arrive at the stables," Schroederstall said, not bothering to turn in the saddle. "Then after, you must promptly report to Sir Phillip."

"Should we seek the constable and have a word?" Enzo asked, lifting his eyebrows with the question.

Schroederstall raised a gloved hand dismissively. "That will not be necessary. We will talk more once we dismount." He was eager to avoid drawing further attention to their group, as the Church and those associated were currently undesirable with the common man. They had thus far only encountered a few scowls, which was vastly preferable to the recently popular lumps of dung being thrown at those wearing the colors of the Church.

Frequent traffic and consistent spring rainfall had created a sloppy mud pit at the archway leading to the Church's stables, which sucked at the horse's hooves, causing unnecessary strain. The destriers trod past the hesitant palfrey, and pulled through the sludge with only minor trepidation.

Enzo almost became unseated at the initial descent, but managed to quickly right himself with a sharp tug on the saddle's pommel. Once through, the squires turned to face Schroederstall, who was still on the street, anxiously eyeing the obstacle in his path. He cleared his throat and dug his heels into the palfrey's sides, urging her forward, but instead the horse lowered her majestic frame, urging the churchman to clear the saddle.

"Oh, I see how it is!" Schroederstall huffed. He dismounted onto the secure cobbles and watched as his horse stepped through the mud with relative ease. Looking around with his hands planted on his hips, from turf to sky, Schroederstall searched for an easier way to cross.

"Just go through one of the buildings and meet us on the other side!" Lucas shouted, then quietly added, "Wouldn't want to defile that evening gown, would we?" Enzo smirked and ducked trying to cover his laughter.

"What was that?" Schroederstall frowned in displeasure.

"Nothing!" Lucas replied quickly. "We'll meet you on the back side of that building." Lucas pointed and tugged his reins, in the direction specified, the palfrey following behind. Soon they were reunited and without a word Schroederstall mounted and followed the lads toward the stables.

Once near the stables designated for war breeds, the squires swung their legs and dismounted, leading their mounts the rest of the way. Schroederstall stopped and cleared his throat at the base of the hill, the tail of the palfrey underneath swishing impatiently, as if urging her rider to get on with things. The squires stopped and turned.

"A word, please, lads," Schroederstall began, looking down at them. "I would like to commend you both on a task well performed." The lads reflected smiles at their senior official but before they could express a return in gratitude, the man continued, "Please report to your shared knight-mentor that everything is going according to plan. I believe the young knight will disregard all sense and follow blindly on this impossible and absurd quest. Having taken the bait, we should expect him to be making the trek into Fenrirfang shortly." He paused, calculating the timeline. "Perhaps this afternoon, or the morrow? I cannot be certain, but be sure to prepare yourselves with haste. But Sir Phillip will advise you in those regards. We can not usurp the chain of command, now can we?" he finished dryly.

Schroederstall's mouth curled in a forced grin that did not match the dim expression held in his eyes.

Looking up, Lucas spoke, "Begging your pardon, sir, but me and Enzo have a couple questions we would like to ask."

"Yes?" Schroederstall replied impatiently, raising an eyebrow.

"Was it wise to have us accompany you today? So soon after?"

Schroederstall sighed. "Brett must see you in order to secure an alibi."

"Ah," Enzo said, squinting in confusion.

"Is this all?" Schroederstall's mount began to shift. "We have business to attend." His head remained fixed on the squires as the palfrey began to trot sideways.

"Oh, yes!" Enzo raised a finger. "Why won't we report the attack on the girl?"

The church official heaved a deep sigh and removed his hat, the stringy tendrils grasping at the sky as they became visible over his shiny head. "I suspect the old farmer is lying, making her seem as damaged goods or some other nonsense; taking full advantage of his victimhood. A desperate attempt by a desperate family."

"You give them a lot of credit, sir. Coming up with that on such short notice?" Enzo reasoned.

Schroederstall frowned. "It's clearly fraud. Makes no difference how it's concocted. And reporting a crime will draw unwanted attention. The less eyes on us the better. Surely you must agree?"

The squires nodded, Lucas more reluctantly than Enzo.

"Besides, the girl's condition is more Amyr's concern. I would just as soon allow him to sort it out." Smoothing down the thin strands of hair, Schroederstall placed his hat back on. "I know this goes without saying, but it is imperative that you not mention a word of this to anyone. For any reason. None of this *ever* happened. This conversation *never* happened," he emphatically stated. Wheeling his horse around, he shouted over a shoulder to the young men. "Report to Sir Phillip as soon as you can, lads."

The squires watched Schroederstall gallop across the yard before they turned back.

"I wonder how he knows that Sir Galahalt will be going into the Fang?" Enzo asked as they trudged up the hill. "How can he be so sure?"

"Shoulda asked that greasy git when he was in front of you," Lucas said with a smile. "Besides, we just do as we're told. At this stage, I leave the plotting and planning to our betters."

Enzo patted his horse's neck. "Aye, we just go where we're led."

7

Every year precisely on this day, she found herself seated in this exact spot on the very same ledge in plain view of the main gate. The carefully selected location was oddly conspicuous; her legs dangled at eye level to catch the attention of those walking on foot, and the rest of her body was in easy view of those on horseback. *Marketing. Everything has a price.*

Each spring, vendors and farmers traveled from the surrounding lands, some from hundreds of leagues away, in the hopes of turning enough profit to survive until the Harvest Days in the autumn. In order to provide safe voyage for the caravans, the knights of the realm would scour the fringes of the forest, slaying any beast or monster that might pose a threat. The weeks leading to the annual springtime Market Days were the most profitable for rangers as well. Humans rarely ventured into the forests without a laif ranger, and those who dared would not venture far. Laives, while similar in appearance to humans, were much more elegant and graceful, and their pointy ears were more attuned to the subtle sounds of the forest.

Elkara kicked her legs in the early afternoon breeze in a subtle attempt to draw attention. Finding employment early opened up the possibility for more total excursions in the coming weeks. More excursions meant more coin, *and so on and so on.* Looking down at her well-aged traveling boots, she noticed how dingy and dilapidated they were looking. The last trek she had led while wearing them was at the inception of winter, and her thoughts had been elsewhere as she hung them in her wardrobe, switching them for footwear that was better suited for the bitter cold.

I will most certainly allocate a share of my earnings from the very first trip for a new pair. She smirked, contemplating the prospect of dry feet. Without donning several layers of wool socks, the dampness would creep into her boots when treading near bogs and swamps, and draping the socks each night near a fire would be a necessary chore. *As soon as we get back,* she promised herself.

Rummaging in the satchel next to her, she searched for an apple, and pulled it free to inspect for any bruises. The ranger crunched down, and tucked a few billowing strands of hair behind her pointy ears, irritated by the invasion. Without looking, her other hand reached into the satchel and produced a second apple, and after playfully tossing it in the air, she passed it down to the waiting mouth of her laifhorse who greedily consumed the gift.

"Try not to take a finger next time," Elkara said dryly to her chewing companion as he warily eyed a large horsefly circling above his head. She gave it a swat with the back of her hand, the density of the insect registered with a decent sounding snap, and the bug was soon buzzing away in a twirling pattern further down the lane.

From one of the alleyways, a cat suddenly materialized and sauntered toward the pair with its tail held like a banner.

"She's got her eye on you, Error." Elkara laughed, nudging the steed. The laifhorse remained as stone as the feline weaved between his legs, brushing up and purring loud enough for the laif to hear.

Sudden movement emerging from the forest captured her attention. Patches of sunlight piercing the overcast sky glinted off the steel enamel of a hunting party. The clinking armour was out of synch with their movements, as the sound traveled quite a distance before reaching the laif. Elkara raised an eyebrow, curious to see which ranger was leading this particular cavalcade. She strained her eyes trying to focus on the approaching knights. As she took another bite of the apple while staring into the distance, a customer arrived and stood below, patiently waiting for her attention to shift. Error whinnied and stamped the ground, sending the cat reeling, tumbling over itself in its attempt to escape. This snapped Elkara's attention to the young knight who was dancing aside for a scurrying cat. Tossing the apple, she gripped the ledge with both hands, steadying her perch, and looked beyond the man. *Another puzzling encounter.*

"In need of a guide?" she inquired, leaning forward and scratching behind her knee. The young knight bowed, returning the perceived greeting. She gave him a once over, looking him up and down. *Meager amount of armour. Azure tunic; clearly a holy knight. A young and thin holy knight. Appears as if he earned his belt a couple years ago or so, give or take. A lone knight with that look in his eyes...yeah...he's going to be shooting fast and loose. I'll bet he wants to slay something immortal. Seen it a hundred times. Another Questing Beast or Abowraith. Typical. Quick, easy cash.*

"I am," he replied under her curious gaze.

"Where are you keeping the rest of your armour? In that sack?"

The young knight furrowed his brows. "This is all I require."

"Oh, ordinarily questing knights arrive fully armed and prepared," Elkara said, squinting. "And seeing as you only sport pauldrons and greaves, and maybe a helm inside that sack? You understand my confusion." Error snorted and Elkara looked down. "And where is your mount? You're going to need one of those."

"I was hoping to secure your service, then I would see to fetching one before we set off."

"Ah, that's quite the laundry list you have today. Well, I am glad I could help you check off 'find a laif.' And after you seek a stablemaster, then we go on your hunt?"

He nodded his agreement.

"Alright, I'll need a few silvers to hold my interest 'til the afternoon, at which point I will take the next charge that comes my way. Fair?" She leaned back, embracing the warm sun.

"Aye, that should grant enough time to acquire a decent horse." He scratched his chin. "Do you have a tack house that you could recommend? Or perhaps a breed that that would be preferable? I had an older destrier that proved—"

"No," she cut him off and closed her eyes. "Be back well before the sun begins its descent."

Clinking armour passing under the gate caused the laif's eyes to shoot open, and the young knight below exhaled, "Royal knights." He scanned the returning party for an empty saddle, not wishing ill on any man, but knowing that his search would be much shorter in that instance. Sure enough an empty mount with a full suit of arms on the saddle was at the rear of the two columns. Unsure of with whom to speak, the young knight looked from face to face, hoping to gain a foothold into a conversation that did not ring with disrespect concerning their dead comrade.

The twelve knights rode in parallel rows with their faces bare, helms secured to the saddles, and an iron demeanor. *May as well be wearing the helms.* The young knight found catching any of their eyes an impossible task. He looked to the laif, but before he could make a request, she spoke.

With her lips curled into a smirk, Elkara called out to the group. "Elithiel!"

A grinning laif led the knights, resplendent in a suit of light armour with a gray cloak draped over his shoulders, and wheeled his horse at the sound of the voice. The double column halted their movement, turning all attention to the exchange. Pulling back on the reins using his deadly looking gauntlets, the approaching laif stopped within speaking distance under the ledge. "Elkara."

The young knight, looking from laif to laif, decided to take advantage of the pause and went to beseech the nearest mounted knight.

"Been awhile, Dancer," Elkara returned the greeting.

"Has it been?" he asked, tilting his thin face at her. "I know time passes differently for those of us with consistent employment, but perhaps for you, it may have seemed like *awhile*."

"Oh, ha ha." Looking past the court laif, Elkara watched her latest charge locked in conversation with one of the royal knights, gesturing to the riderless horse. *He's resourceful. Not a bad thing.*

Elithiel brushed his shoulder with an armoured hand. "There has been a rash of unrest in the goblin community, in case you are aware. Just a little tip for you." He winked as he finished his statement.

"Amusing." Elkara's mouth became a straight line. "Does the king pay extra for wit?"

"He might." The ranger laughed and wagged a finger. "He just might." His horse pranced beneath him. Elkara's eyes roamed to the empty saddle. The young knight was standing nearby holding a debate with a heavily bearded knight.

"It appears you are a knight short," she teased, fluttering her eyelashes. "Am I to believe that all these royal engagements have dulled your reflexes, old man?" The clouds passing overhead cast a shadow on them.

Elithiel sucked air between his teeth. "Sir Gwayne lost a sabaton to a gremlin while he slept and the jackass tracked it to a river."

"So he abandoned his armour to swim after it?"

Elithiel smiled and nodded, tucking a few falling strands of hair behind his ear.

Elkara blinked. "Well then."

"He is a rather cunning fellow, and I'd wager good coin that he will survive on his own, pending the gremlin didn't take the stolen goods beyond a ward."

"Wager?" Elkara squinted as the sun appeared. "I'll see that."

Elithiel dropped his reins and folded his hands, leaning forward. "How would you like to play this out? Because I believe he will survive, so will this bet be in regards to his mortality? That's pretty dark."

"Let's not get so pessimistic. Come now," Elkara said as the cat reappeared from its alley. "I like to stay positive and admit all sorts of possibilities." Error groaned below. "I will be willing to wager twenty gold pieces that the jester knight will be back safe and sound, within the confines of the city walls of Camelot...with the sabaton in hand. Or foot. You catch my meaning."

Elithiel narrowed his gaze. "I'll take that." He urged his mount forward, removed a gauntlet, and extended his hand up to the perched laif who accepted it, but not before spitting in her palm.

"Sick!" The Royal Dancer waved his hand, recoiling. "You know that change is not painful under certain circumstances?" His mount retreated a few paces as he re-secured his gauntlet.

Elkara chuckled at his discomfort and looked over to see how the young knight in the azure tunic was faring. With the many gaps in his unremarkable armour, he unfastened Sir Gwayne's suit of exemplary plate from the horse and hoisted himself onto the borrowed animal.

* * *

"GALAHALT," THE YOUNG KNIGHT REPLIED to the question as they passed the old outposts, far from repair and centuries from use. He regarded the weather worn structures while seated in the comfortable saddle, compliments of the jester knight. This steed was a far cry from Stutters, *no disrespect to the old mare.* Plodding alongside the laif guide while being carried by the powerful legs of superior breeding only affordable to a Royal Knight, Galahalt was humbled and anxious all at once.

The road leading to Fenrirfang was well maintained but the meadows surrounding were unkempt and teeming with wildlife. Ages ago large structures inside the fields had been manned by sentinels who combated any sort of evil that revealed itself. A brilliant ivory birch sprung out from a roofless building, *a nice accent to a rather desolate aesthetic.* Galahalt nodded, lost in thought, not catching the question posed by his guide.

"Galahalt!" she spoke just beneath a shout, snapping his attention back to the present. "*Sir* Galahalt, I assume?" The young knight gave a thumbs up. "First time in Fenrirfang?" Error kicked a large pebble, shooting it forward. It skipped along the cobbles, but quickly lost momentum and plunged into a puddle.

Clearing his throat as the rock sent ripples along the surface, Galahalt replied, "First time."

"Splendid." The laif sighed. "Are you aware of the dangers so I can skip the tutorial?"

Galahalt was returning the stare of a devil horn owl. *Odd for you to be out and about during the day, friend.* "Yep, skip it," he responded dismissively. "Was that laif you were talking to the Royal Dancer?"

"He is," she replied.

"Good friends?"

"Kind of. Sort of."

"Becoming the royal court's exclusive ranger is quite an achievement. Must be a fiend with a blade."

"Oh, he's quite the daemon." Elkara waved a hand through the air, discouraging a stinging insect from its course. "Elithiel is very good at what he does, there is no doubt."

"Did you grow up together?" Galahalt ducked to avoid the wasp.

"He earned the title long before I was born." A prickly mass of tenrecs scuttled across the road and the horses slowed out of courtesy for the little creatures. "Anyhow, Fenrirfang has always been a wild forest, not quite as wild as some of the others, but for our purposes as long as we stay to the beaten paths and you wait for me to clear the wards, we should not experience anything too spooky."

"What I seek is not found on beaten paths," Galahalt replied as he watched a pair of man-sized birds stride through the meadow, their scimitar beaks glistening.

Oh boy. Elkara had been hoping that this would be a basic sort of excursion. *Slay a few faewolves and maybe a stray draconid. Nothing too fancy.* Every once in a while she would escort a blacksmith keen on harvesting an aelder terrapin shell, but that was rather infrequent as of late. "You have a specific game in mind, eh? Most young knights enter the forest to cut their teeth on a foe that means more harm than the tiltyard. Any sort of mortal danger will do for most. Within reason, of course."

"The tiltyard never held my interest much," Galahalt spoke as he regarded an eagle in effortless flight, navigating the updrafts. "I am seeking a salvation of sorts."

"A *holy* knight is seeking salvation? An odd day unravels before us," she mused and leaned down to scratch Error behind an ear.

Galahalt regarded his tunic. "The salvation I am searching for is not my own," he murmured.

"That's neat."

Galahalt raised an eyebrow when a sound closely resembling a giggle escaped from the laif's mount. "Is it true that laif bred horses are imbued with magic?"

"Yep." The ranger was not smiling and the conversation trailed off.

Soon the gates to Fenrirfang Forest were before them. Once they passed under, the pair was engulfed in shadows. The young knight's exposed skin prickled and his eyes strained, trying to maintain focus as they struggled to adjust. *Such a contrast. Wait, whoa.* Above their heads, amid the boughs, faeries and wisps danced upward, providing gentle light as they spiraled like a brilliant tornado in and out of view. Galahalt ran his fingers through his hair as he gaped, amazed by the spectacle overhead. His horse continued to keep pace with Error, whose rider was unsurprised by the business of the fae, and was even less impressed with the knight's dazzled expression.

The fee just inched a bit higher, Elkara thought with a palm to her face. "Let's get on the same field here, Sir Galahalt." The laif hefted her leg over the horn to ride side-saddle, facing the knight. "What sort of monster are we looking to slay? Daemonic, fae, ogre, eldritch, gargoyle, troll, hob, draconid..." She waved her palm encouragingly. "Chime in anytime."

"Keep going, this seems like fun."

Squeezing her eyes tight, she continued to guess. "Kapreta?"

"No."

"Carnal Shrike?"

"Nah."

"Gorgon?" she squinted.

He looked away, in contemplation. "No."

"We're not doing dragons are we?"

"Don't be absurd." His head tilted. "Think *one of a kind.*"

Oh, come on. Here we go. "The Questing Beast?" Her voice was brighter than intended.

He placed a finger to the tip of his nose and nodded.

Welp. Off to Fort Navarene. Seen this a hundred times.

THE AMOUNT OF PREDATION THEY ENCOUNTERED along the fringes was near zero.

"The Royal Knights just exited a few hours ago, so yeah, we won't be seeing much action until we at least get past the clearing." Elkara swayed in the saddle as her laifhorse loped along the uneven forest road, surrounded by ancient trees with tremendous trunks. "Seeing as 'knights' are at the apex of the kill chain, at least one knight, be they laif or human, man or woman, has felled at least one of every beast in existence." She continued, mumbling under her breath, "Except for the hurring vurst."

"What was that?" Galahalt leaned toward the laif with a hand cupping his ear.

"Except for the Questing Beast," she said, much louder with all emotion drained. The young knight nodded and opened his mouth to speak, but decided against it, and instead changed the subject.

"The road here appears well maintained. Are there creatures assigned to the upkeep?" The knight turned his chin from one side of the road to the other as he spoke. The road spanned just under twenty paces and was adequately wide enough for a large carriage to traverse uninhibited.

"Yes." Elkara faced forward. "They're called knights and horses."

"Ah, so the constant travel provides the clear pathway."

The laif tucked her chin. "Aye."

A scream of despair cut through the breeze, and Galahalt sat upright in the saddle, scanning the depths around them, his eyes falling on the scampering creatures that went about their lives, oblivious to their fellow in danger.

Elkara passively maintained her pace. "Wait for it."

The knight slowed his mount. The horse, sensing her rider's tension, began mentally coiling the springs in her legs, waiting to burst forth upon need, almost *wanting* a reason to surge forward. Galahalt felt the tension build through his legs, which was a unique and new connection for him. *Now this is a battle horse*, he thought appreciatively.

"Was that a crag lion with a—"

"Shhhh!" Elkara whirled back and glared.

There *it* was again, the same shriek, from nearly the same distance. It was somewhere above their heads, but perhaps a league beyond. The laif was laughing with a leather clad hand pressed to her mouth. Galahalt squinted his eyes, peering through the boughs of the forest, focusing on where the sound had originated, hoping to catch a glimpse of whatever may be in peril. "Alright, what critter's demise can be so funny?"

"Oh, nothing is dying." Elkara watched the knight reign in beside her, now keeping pace. "Well, *probably* not dying. Hopefully not dying."

The noise pierced the winds again, carrying over the sounds of the bird clutches, tittering and clucking at potential mates in their attempt to draw them in.

Over another bout of giggles, Elkara explained herself. "It's baby griffins tumbling from their nests, learning to fly."

Galahalt stood in his stirrups, looking into the dense, vast array of leaves. "You can see that?"

"They are so cute."

"But how can you see them?"

"I can't. I just know. I have witnessed the act a few times." *I wish I had seen it a hundred times.* "It's just like with birds; the parents shove the yearlings out, and the little bundles topple down and desperately try to float. Most can't, but one of the parents swoops in and rescues it before it smashes into the rocks below."

"Ah, I thought it would be a crag lion picking off a family of hares or something like that."

"We need not be concerned over crag lions." Elkara leaned down to give Error a pat.

"Something to be thankful for," Galahalt remarked.

The laif removed something from under her cloak, brought it to her mouth, and quickly tossed her head back.

"Is that a flask?" Galahalt asked, squinting at her as he caught a glimpse of the finely crafted leather armour peeking out from under her riding mantle.

"Aye." She held the skinny canteen out, and shook it enticingly. "Up for a swig?"

Galahalt wrinkled his nose. "No, thank you. That stuff rots you from the inside."

"*And* rots your insides," Elkara agreed as she took another draught from the tiny hole. "We won't see any dangers until we get through the first ward. And we won't reach that until tomorrow, I wager."

The young knight nodded his understanding, and watched a flying squirrel take a running leap to join her friends on a neighboring bough. The clan tittered excitedly, cheering their friend's arrival before scampering out of sight.

Their last hour or so of riding went unimpeded, and it flew by much faster than Galahalt anticipated, what with all the new sights and brilliant scenes unfolding before him. He passed creatures and beasts that he had previously only seen as sketches in books and in his daydreams as a child. Enveloped by the history of Fenrirfang, he marveled to walk where greater knights had gone before, their songs of valor still echoing amongst the treetops, chanting a song of encouragement for a young knight bent on vengeance.

A bend in the road obscured the view, but not the sounds of approaching riders.

"Friends of yours?" Elkara appraised the pair of knights that appeared, resplendent in azure, their visors open. She spoke quietly with her head turned, the words concentrated on Galahalt so the strangers would not hear. Galahalt cast a reassuring look at the laif before saluting the knights as they drew closer. The knights returned the salute, and the elder of the two nodded at Elkara with a pinched smile. Neither party reigned in for a chat, so the exchange dissipated with the sounds of retreating hooves and clanking armour.

"The scrawnier of the two was riding a laif breed." Elkara did not sound impressed.

"Like Error?"

"No, not quite. But still. That's not something you see every day." Elkara tugged the collar of her cloak. "Did you recognize them?"

"I did." Galahalt nodded, then continued. "Well the one, I did. I believe he deals with census issues. But the other I do not know."

"So the knight on the laif destrier works for the little number boys in the church? They looking to keep a tally in the Fang now?"

"That is not a discussion I was ever privy to. Nor have I heard any rumors. The church knows better than to press their boundaries any further."

"Very odd, indeed." Elkara's eyes were drawn to the young knight's spear secured to the saddle. *Those knights entered without a guide.*

A PAIR OF ANCIENT GUARD TOWERS matching those at the forest's entrance stood like crumbling soldiers in testimony to the battles of yore. Beyond the pair of weathered gatekeepers sprawled a sun drenched meadow, free of any tree, spanning several acres in a near perfect square. Four right angles sliced the corners of the expanse, and Galahalt imagined the tent stakes and staging areas for armies long ago, now barren, exempt of war.

"This is it," Elkara spoke as they crossed between the towers, shielding her eyes with one hand while she surveyed the unmanned landscape. "Looks like we have the pick of the litter." A river ran along the eastern border of the vast clearing, traveling north and south. She pointed towards the river. "I'm starving. Let's set up near the water and see if we can angle for a fresh catch."

Galahalt regarded the sun above. "You sure you don't want to press further?"

"No." Elkara set Error into a trot toward the river. "We'll make a long haul tomorrow and reach our first ward well before sunset, then press on from there. There are some excellent hunting grounds on the way, so we can split up for that before we reach the ward. If that is alright with you?" She looked at the knight keeping pace next to her, jostled slightly by the terrain. "Not looking to surprise you."

Galahalt raised an eyebrow and smiled.

The laif pointed at a remarkably flat plot of earth near the rushing waters and dismounted with a flourish of grace, while Galahalt nearly tumbled free of his mount. Ruefully pressing a fist into his lumbar, he thought, *If I ever believed myself to be indestructible.* As he began to unlace the supplies from Sir Gwayne's saddle, Elkara sniffed the air behind him.

"It won't rain tonight, so I would not bother removing your canopy."

Galahalt led the horse down the embankment toward refreshment, tossing the tent supplies aside. "Does no harm to lighten the beast's load."

8

⧟

Before closing his eyes to slumber for perhaps the final time, the last sound that the wounded dog heard was Uncle Brett collapsing in a heap on the porch above. *If I had lost more blood, then perhaps the crawling would have been an easier drag.* Delirious and alone, Elmer panted in an enormous amount of pain, soaked with dew and blood.

After sustaining the perilous wound, he had decided to seek shelter from the carrion-feeding creatures, and expiring in Margot's bedroom, below the chorus of horrid sounds was more than he could bear. His final thoughts as his body betrayed him were about Margot. *She'll find me. She always finds me.* With that, he was handed over to sleep.

In an instant, he found himself back in the Hold seated at a knobby wooden table of four amongst his three best mates, the night's atrocities left behind like a trail of road dust. Kiera was laughing at something Elrick said, but he had arrived too late for the punch line. Placing a hand on his, Kiera turned to him and said, "Welcome back, Lannor."

"Am I late?" Lannor asked, accepting the wooden goblet passed from the chair opposite.

"What makes you say that?" Kiera leaned close, nearly shouting above the din of music bursting from an ensemble on the stage.

The large cathedral was filled with uproarious spirits; shouts of laughter were carried on the breeze of smoked meats and fresh loaves, cleansing Lannor of the awful memories of the previous night. He briefly recalled the sight of a grievously wounded mutt slowly, persistently leaking his essence away in complete solitude under the porch of a farmhouse, existing in some foreign dimension. *Foreign yet familiar. Feels as if I have forgotten something of great import.* The fleeting melancholy swept over him, tugging at him, then dissipated.

"Staring at it won't put it in your gullet!" The laif across the table urged him to drink with a nod. Wrapping both hands around the goblet, Lannor took a deep draught of the frothy brew. *Oh I have hands again.*

"This is a solid ale, Elrick." Lannor dragged his wrist over his mouth.

"Aye! Glad ya like it, mate!"

To be back home again. Lannor leaned back in his seat, surveying the familiar sights. *To be back in this place.*

The Hold existed without the constraint of time, and its elect enjoyed the benefits of ageless living. Such a blessing, however, bestowed much responsibility on the bearer. Each member of the faculty had been carefully selected by the Creator, and would act as his emissary upon request.

The air was sweet and light, and gravity's grip was a bit more casual, which alleviated an assortment of unpleasantries. The Hold was a single, massive room: no entryways, no corridors, and no halls. Hearths spaced at even intervals along the outer wall contained roaring blazes that burned unceasingly, providing light and warmth.

Above, millions of glowing insects flew endlessly, swirling and plunging, chasing one another between the rafters and chandeliers. Elegant tapestries adorned the windowless walls, formed from exquisite fabrics and some from solid ore. The ore appeared soft and pliable, yet when approached was cold and unbreakable to the touch.

Lannor was now embroiled in pleasant debate, cavorting and swilling drink, but all the while, something continued to needle at him.

Every so often a sharp pain radiated from his shoulder, and Kiera shot a glance his way whenever he winced.

"That's not the way I remember it!" Kiera said, speaking just under a shout while holding a sideling look at Lannor. "And besides, faewolves and werewolves are different beings altogether."

"Well, they smell about the same!" Thorvil crossed his short, muscled arms. "When I was sent down as a dog that one time, it was at the peak of spring and whatever it was, *faewolf* or *werewolf*, kept looking at me with hungry eyes. And I don't mean *hungry* in the normal sense, if you catch my meaning?" The dwarf raised both eyebrows, crinkling his short brow. "Downright randy!"

A dog? Lannor was curious. "What sort of dog did you inhabit on that assignment?"

Thorvil tossed back another goblet, draining the remainder. "Ah, let me think." Combing his gnarled fingers through his bushy beard, he continued. "It was some sort of herding breed, I recall. Creator likes to use 'em whenever he's protectin' somethin' or someone." The hardened dwarf stood, which did not really make him much taller, and shook his empty cup at a passing maid. "Another bickle ale, if you please?" He flashed a toothy grin before taking his seat, returning to his recollections. "Can't recall the breed but it had a real nice set of chompers. Peeled the hide offa that faewolf or whatever it was, whenever it came around lookin' all rapey."

Kiera snorted a laugh into her mug, sending foam into the air. The conversation went on, but Lannor's mind began reeling, his friend's words became noise, a backdrop to the memory forming in his mind.

The Creator approached the table, just as we are seated now, the day he assigned me to that last place. It has been so long since I have enjoyed the company of these three, and yet somehow, not so.

I remember him kneeling at my side as I set my mug down, looking up at me with his chestnut hair pulled back into a loose plait, the remainder not locked in the braid cascaded over his shoulders.

He was in the form of a handsome laif with an ageless face like one of the Firsts. Exuding kindness and sincerity with one glance, he asked my friends if he could borrow me for a while. A while. I knew when he used that word this would be no side bar conversation, this would be business that would take me away. They all nodded at the request, spewing sarcastic words of encouragement that made the Creator laugh as he stood.

I blinked and found myself in the center of a small space surrounded by four blank walls; the room was immaculate, not a speck of dust existed there. Just below my chin was a scepter planted into the floor as a pedestal, and at its peak was a translucent orb.

I took a step back, having been transported uncomfortably close to it. A hand fell on my shoulder. "Are you ready?" he asked, his words escaped his lips without breath. The Creator stood beside me as we gazed into the orb. It swirled blazing shades of orange erupting into scarlet tints before flashing ebony, then white, then nothing. A crack issued from its depths, shooting a projection onto the blank canvas.

This was new.

A vast array of canines, organized meticulously, extended from one side of the wall to the other. The images tilted their heads and panted and scratched their ears as if drawing life from an unknown source.

"Each creation before you represents an experience you will undertake," he said to me with his hand still resting on my shoulder. I remember paying particular attention to one dog that wore a mane like a crag lion; sharp as razors and when he shook his head, the barbs bounced harmlessly off his fur. Another had the eyes of a serpent and another the tail of a beaver. "You have taken the form of a dog before," he continued. "Actually, many times before. You have a

gift for it." He smiled. "So I will need your expertise for a..." he trailed off for a moment. "Project."

I began to understand.

"You want to create another breed."

"Precisely."

"You have a purpose." I recall narrowing my gaze.

He looked back towards the orb's projection, and I followed suit. The images began to blur and fade, slowly disappearing, and converging into the solitary form of a young girl. All around her, creeping into clarity, was a vast field of steel plated plants that reflected every beam of sunlight. The light coat of dirt on the lass' pretty face was smudged a darker shade as she wiped the sweat from her brow. Sitting back on her heels, she released a sigh, surveying the surroundings.

"She looks kind," I said.

"She is that and more." He removed his hand.

For half a decade or so I wore the skins of over a hundred dogs, nearly losing grip on my identity, trudging through lives, each cut short. I died so many times. Some journeys I started as a pup, fighting for the nipple with my littermates, experiencing the formative years. But most I began in an adult body, needing a few hours to acclimate before treading out into whatever life befell me; be it as a pet, or a working mutt, or a nanny.

One skin was my favorite above all the others. I was a Cantotlian Shepherd; lithe and powerful with jaws that could crush steel wire, yet gentle enough to carry an egg without making a single crack. The range on this specimen was unparalleled, and this particular fellow's primary duty was the protection of an expensive flock of sheep.

The strange fuzzy creatures were sheared for royalty or some such nonsense, making them outrageously valuable, so the herders employed about a dozen Cantotlian Shepherds, which on their own fetched a hefty sum. When not patrolling the fringe of the herd, I laid around the campfire enjoying scraps of the finest chicken, lovingly tossed before me as I listened to tales of range life.

These tales almost always devolved into whiskey-driven shouting matches regarding such topics as tensile strength, or draw speed. Speech well above my station. Some nights on the farm with Margot, I would look up at the night sky, drenched in stars, and I would remember that chicken.

One day while the herd was passing through a stone-walled ravine, the cry of "LION!" suddenly reverberated against the pillared stones. A crag lioness was scaling the wall, nimbly managing her foot falls with expert finesse, and the first dog on the scene was wildly shouting and tearing up the dry earth, staunchly defending his charge. As she approached the chap, standing between her and a very expensive plate of mutton, she lowered her rear aiming to spring upon him. I recognized this movement, and not being one to hold any fear of death, I charged headlong into the fray. Well, before it became a fray at all. It was more preventative than anything else.

Which is really all a shepherd does, honestly.

Anyhow, my unexpected leap took the lioness unaware, and I clamped onto her spine as tight as I could before we toppled over, granting her razor filled maw free access to my vital bits. She chomped me good, and I burst open like an overripe grape, promising a swift end. I watched my mates tear into my aggressor, ripping her into sections, immediately neutralizing the threat with a hive mind of aggression. Only a few spared pitiable glances at me before returning to their duty.

I watched the red river, absorbed by the dirt, pooling below as I waited for that old familiar ending. I looked away, resting my head on the ground, considering the clear sky. A sad whine drew my focus away and I looked back to my wound as a female Cantotlian Shepherd licked the mess of small punctures surrounding the gaping crater. She nuzzled my head before laying down next to me, creating a barrier between myself and my killer.

I could not thank her for staying, but I willed the emotion in her direction all the same. I think she knew. The last I saw in that majestic skin was the forlorn dog and her eyes brimming with sadness before the agony overtook me.

Thorvil released a sharp barking laugh, snapping Lannor from his reverie.

"And that's the moment when I realized that I could tell the difference between a grope and a grapple!" The dwarf slapped the laif next to him on the back with a hollow thud, causing him to gag, nearly spilling his tankard.

Kiera leaned uncomfortably close to Lannor, oblivious to the raucous, inspecting his face before gently blowing a warm breeze across his eyelashes.

Lannor held stalk still as she passed gently behind him, resting a hand on his unmoving head.

Thorvil and Elrick were drunkenly shouting with their foreheads nearly touching, spittle flying between the pair, as Lannor sent pleading glances their way, hoping for a rescue from the awkward moment.

Her fingers running tenderly through his hair sent a shockwave of recollection into his cranium, and Lannor suddenly felt canine for a flash. Shaking his head, he knocked the memories away, dispelling them like baseless rumors amongst washer wives. A hot breath singed his earlobe.

"You are not yet finished."

A loud thump locked him into his seat, sending a second shockwave throughout his limbs. Shooting a look of desperation toward the laif and dwarf still embroiled in a heated debate, he felt gravity begin to sink its unyielding claws into his shoulder.

Within a breath, Elmer found himself waking in anguish, eyes opening to streaks of sunlight passing through the cracks in the porch. His head slowly drooped down, as if the knee it was resting upon suddenly dissipated, and the fur upon his crown felt disheveled. He fought valiantly against despair.

From above, a harsh unfamiliar voice was bellowing, or speaking, as it seemed this may be the speaker's regular timbre. Elmer craned his ears upward, a movement that thankfully did not send bolts of pain into his skull, in an attempt to distinguish the conversation that somehow he was alive to hear.

When the angry man spoke, Elmer's hackles raised instinctively. *That one is no good.* The floorboards groaned under the man's weight as he marched above, strutting about like an enormous turkey, his words dripping in condescension.

After the unknown men took their leave, Galahalt spoke up, and Elmer's tail began to stir, shooting pain up his spine, but he continued nonetheless.

Get a fang? The dog's ears shot up again. Uncle Brett sounded exasperated, and the hidden animal under the porch began to key in on the words. *The Questing Beast?* A dull pang of recollection shot to the outskirts of his mind's reach.

I will set out after nightfall. This will take time. I must reach him before the lad does. Elmer stretched out in the cool dirt, ignoring the sizzling in his shoulder, and surrendered to sleep...out of sight.

S ir Clemence reigned in, turning her horse to wave farewell at her
squire who was standing along the riverbank returning the gesture.
Rushing waters drowned out the sound of the clinking pair of knights
bouncing in their saddles as they returned from whence they came, disappearing amongst the wildwood.

Nathan adjusted the visor on his helm to block the sun, and suddenly the distant rattle of armour lurched into his ears, subsuming the
river's voice. He turned, expecting to see his mentor returning, but saw
only the thin, empty trail meandering under the overhanging foliage.
That talisman works like a charm! Nathan shook his head and urged their
packhorse into the waters.

"An excellent place for an ambush, eh?" Lucas bent down and
knocked the base of an oak as he passed, twirling on a heel.

His lifelong friend, Enzo, wiped the sweat from his brow under a
lifted visor, and whistled. The only flora occupying the clearing, aside
from grassy stalks, were patches of mushrooms and toadstools, dappled
all about, withholding all regard for symmetry.

Sounds of the surrounding forest invaded the space, converging in
a cacophony, twisting the squires' faces when a squawk from a nearby
partridge overtook all other noises, searing a sharp ringing in their ears.

"This magical spell will take some getting used to." Enzo hammered
the side of his helm with a fist.

"Aye." Lucas winced.

"Kinda freaky ain't it?" Nathan approached the lads in the uncannily flat clearing, dropping his horse's bridle to bend down and retrieve a particularly long strand of grass. Gently pressing the blade to his lips, he created a shrill note which added a layer to the chorus of birds and wildlife chirping and gargling all around. It was a trick his mother had taught him a few years before he accepted a life of servitude, when he was merely a child. He began to think of home, his mind swirling, fearful that he be overcome with longing. *Focus on the outcome. Do not dwell on this dreadful business. It will be over soon. After that, you will accept your belt, and bloody business like this will be behind you.*

"Say what you may about Phillip." Lucas took a stuttering step then booted a nearby toadstool. "But that crooked bastard knows how to make an ambush plan."

Enzo bobbed his head, following the toadstool as it careened across the ground. "That he does, that he does."

"Clemence found this spot," Nathan offered.

"I wonder how much that talisman cost the church? Must have set them back a bit, ya think?" Enzo looked at Lucas for confirmation.

"A trinket of *that* quality can't have been cheap," Lucas agreed with a shrug.

"I should think not." Nathan looked back and forth between them. "It was probably an internal job. The church does employ mages." Enzo and Lucas began to casually stroll toward the tree line, stopped at the packhorse to lift a few belongings, then made their way towards the site that Clemence had advised to set up camp. Speaking to their backs, Nathan continued, "But I agree, this is an excellent place for an ambush."

"You hear something?" Lucas looked all around and beyond his companions, regarding the landscape.

"Someone must have opened a window." Enzo chuckled, wiping the sweat around his upper lip.

"Wish that talisman had an extra spell to block out all those annoying sounds." Lucas parted the branches, entering the shade. "Let's get to the camp so we can be free of this armour. I can't wait to breathe again, like humans are meant to."

Nathan secured his duffel on their single horse. "That was rather impolite." He patted the animal's neck and looked up to see Enzo in the trees attempting to perform a chin-up on a low hanging branch. His armour rattled at the exertion, and he clenched his jaw, nearly grinding teeth into powder as his nose brushed the branch on the fifth strain.

Bent knees became straight and the squire dropped to the earth, greeted by sounds of derision. "My hero!" Lucas shouted. "You better be careful there, displays like that are likely to give me the vapors. And you know what that means!" He laughed and clapped Enzo's armoured shoulder as the lad stood upright, completely red in the face.

"Oh get bent, you git." Enzo straightened his pauldron. "Like to see you do as many."

Lucas' response was lost in the distance, as the pair pressed on, leaving Nathan the solitary squire on the pitch of their future battle. *More like pitch of murder.* Sweat was rolling from his back and permeating his undergarments. Standing in the lull of the forest, he grew more accustomed to the enhanced sounds, sparing a few moments to snag another stalk of grass to keep occupied as he absorbed the elements and dimensions of the clearing. He spotted a handful of gnomes rushing under the larger of the toadstools, their pointy hats brushing against the fleshy caps, jostling them almost unnoticeably. Ceasing the tune he had been playing on his makeshift grass instrument, Nathan placed his hands reservedly at his sides in order to better watch the little creatures scurry about the lawn.

I hope those two have started prepping the camp. The swamp developing in his nether regions urged him forward into the trees, following his companions' trail. Standing in broad daylight wearing maille and armour was catching up with him. *Remarkable, the difference between a glade and a shady forest,* he mused, holding a branch aside for the horse as it followed dutifully.

A pair of duffels and helms were all that accented the smaller clearing, and no actions to begin to build a fire or prepare food were evident. *Not surprising.* Nathan began to unfasten the supplies, giving the horse a few solid pats.

It was unnervingly quiet, even outside of the talisman's magic energy, and the squire sensed a humming tension that rattled his molars.

Lucas and Enzo were well-trained squires and fully capable in a scrap, when a commotion erupted, the lads were usually found at its epicenter. Nathan was looking forward to spending some quality time in the river with a bar of soap while his unmentionables hung to dry near a roaring fire. Looking to the sky surrounded on all edges by reaching branches, he sighed. *Only a few more hours, then I can be free of this armour. Now where have those nutters gone to?* He set a sack filled with pots and pans down, breaking the silence with the clatter of steel. A sharp hiss alerted Nathan to some movement in the brush overlooking a gully, only a few paces from the site.

"Oi! Nathan!" Lucas was on his knees, rising from a prone position, with a finger pressed to his lips.

Nathan raised both hands with a shrug and mouthed back, *"What?"*

Lucas looked over his shoulder, then turned back toward Nathan and signaled in a way that loosely translated, "get the fuck over here quietly."

Slowly, Nathan stepped into the thicket and dropped to a knee. "What is it?" he whispered.

"C'mere," Lucas beckoned, placing a hand on the other squire's pauldron. Nathan leaned in so closely that their faces nearly touched. "You have got to see this, Nate."

Nathan was torn. Half of him believed there was something amazing waiting for him, but his other senses anticipated a trap. *Better not be something gross...or dead, or dying.* The pair were infamous in the cathedrals for using recently deceased creatures for ill-timed pranks; ill-timed for those in authority, but perfectly timed for the spectating pages who found their dismay utterly delightful.

Sweat drenched Lucas' head and face, pressing scarlet locks tight to his chin and ears. "Follow me," he commanded as he returned to the prone position and began to crawl.

Nathan followed behind, navigating the bent tall grass, his elbows digging crevices where the coverage was sparse. The forest of thick shoots opened into the mouth of a hollow where the squires joined Enzo who was positioned on a shelf along the ridge, belly pressed to the earth, face fixed forward. He did not twitch until Lucas drew next to him, and even then, the sobriety on his features was apparent. *If this is a joke, then their acting has reached damn near professional.*

The hollow was filled with ancient trees. Massive trunks rose a fraction of their height from the squires' vantage point, terminating into the skies, twisted with age and countless seasons. Ten men would be unable to lock hands around the base of the average sized timber here. Their roots buried in damp soil, winter's thaw having departed merely weeks ago.

Nathan was staring at the snaking roots, unbelievably thick at their tightest diameter, punching through the earth and returning like a hekkbender, when Lucas exhaled, "Up higher." He pointed with an armoured hand, finger extending toward the crotch of a mighty white oak. Air escaping in a gasp, Nathan placed a hand to his chest. *Is that a bloody gargoyle?* This was certainly not a prank.

"I know, right?" Lucas wheezed. "Imagine if we could bring her down?"

Nathan shook his head, petrified.

The human-esque creature was seated with one knee to her gleaming maille chest, and the other leg dangled freely. When the breeze rattled the overhead branches, rays of sunshine broke free illuminating the scales covering the muscular curvatures of her body. Her feet were more beast-like than human-like, sporting heavy talons that curved menacingly and tapered to an extra fine point.

If the wild gargoyle was aware of the three young men on the ridge, she gave no indication as she rotated a round red fruit in her hands, selecting the next angle to bite. Nectar spilled from her mouth as she chewed, then brought a glistening forearm to her chin to swat the juices.

The chewing was not audible at the squires' distance, but the lip smacking definitely reached their ears. *This is crazy*, Nathan thought, trying not to appear rattled.

Enzo leaned awkwardly across Lucas. "Do you think it will attack us?"

Nathan scanned the concerned lad's face, trying to determine his sincerity before responding. "I have never encountered one before," he spoke in a much quieter whisper than his companion.

"You've never *what?*" Enzo squinted.

Nathan leaned closer. "Encountered them."

"*What?*"

"Encountered them." Nathan shook his head, then raised both palms. "You know, come across one."

With eyes wide, Enzo nodded, tapping a finger against his forehead in recognition.

Just to make sure Enzo comprehended, Nathan repeated, "Never seen one before. In the wild."

Enzo continued to nod, then gave a thumbs up.

"In my travels with Clemence we only—"

Lucas brought his face between the two squires. "You ladies think this is a good place to swap gossip?" he hissed.

Down below on the swampy surface of the hollow, a racket of crashing branches and footsteps drew all three heads to peek over the edge. The squires then immediately withdrew and tucked down, pressing as flat as humanly possible.

Nathan screwed his eyes into slits; the still image of a huge chicken pressed against the backdrop of his personal nightscape. *A cockatrice and its brood!* Peeling one eye open to check the gargoyle's reaction, Nathan hesitantly raised himself up by fractions. The beautiful creature crested into view. *Still eating that red ball.* Very slowly and very carefully, Nathan lowered himself back down, then gently placed both palms against the ridge and pushed away, sliding over the grass. His upraised visor prevented him from burying his nose in the soil, but its bottom crest scraped the top layer.

Catching a chill as a stiff breeze navigated itself between flesh and steel, Nathan shivered with jaw locked open, staring at the blades of grass in his limited field of view. He softly sucked in air from the back of his throat while his temples pulsated, gradually raising in tempo.

"Nobody move!" Lucas' advice felt redundant *and* suicidal.

Nathan braced himself, wishing to curse aloud. He expected to be overtaken at any moment now that Lucas had alerted their enemies.

Time stood still.

The forest creatures surrounding the lads were oblivious to the peril, and continued their usual afternoon routines as if a flock of extraordinarily deadly birds navigating the fringes of Fenrirfang was not above normalcy. A tree rodent over their heads fumbled a hazelnut, and its course through the leaves, smacking and bouncing, created a tense moment for the squires. Over the river, a heron squealed and a clutch of siskins tittered eerily as the breeze picked up again, Nathan's helm whistled tight into his ears, the trees groaned, and the gargoyle cleared her throat.

Enzo nudged Nathan, and the squire raised his head with a few cracks issuing from the base of his skull. He glanced sideways, afraid to turn as Enzo motioned to the left. Nathan's eyes swung down to the earth then pinned to his left, and filling his optics was the form of Lucas very slowly rolling sideways toward the makeshift camp. *He moves silent as a shadow.* Nathan was impressed.

Without looking at Enzo, Nathan followed suit. Activating stiff muscles, he shoved himself down the slope, propelling in reverse with a few prayers issued to the skies in regard to stray pebbles. When he felt far away enough to permit a few rattles of chain and steel, Nathan propped himself up on his elbows, then rolled up with his chin tucked above hands clasped in prayer.

THE SAFFRON FLAMES SPEWED from the blackened, crackling logs, licking and dancing on an upward path. The fire seemed to create more light than heat, and the squires sat huddled with heavy cloaks clutched to their breasts, spilling crumbs while munching on loaves of bread and dried meat. The proposal to roast game over the flames had been quickly dispelled by Nathan's advice against the activity. "The scent would draw unwanted attention," he had warned as he gestured to the hollow, and that was all that needed to be said.

The night air was brisk after the warmth of the day, though not unpleasant. Frogs and insects burped and buzzed nearby. A dozen fae played over the waters, bobbing and hovering, leaving colorful lines trailing in their wake. If they were laughing, the squires could not hear; such noises were drowned out by the rushing winter thaw of the river.

An uncomfortable silence penetrated the camp, the occupants deeply disturbed by reminders of their own mortality. Advice on stacking wood or questions regarding spatial locations were made, and the usual banter was set aside, taking up residence with other dismissed topics of conversation. The reason they were in this forest and the bloody business assigned began to congeal around its edges, hardening into a stark semblance of reality.

"Well, that was..." Nathan's voice started at a higher pitch, then he cleared his throat, looking through the flames. "Something."

The others were not as apt to begin a refrain. Lucas snorted and drew his legs from beneath the covering fabrics, extended his bare feet onto a toppled log, then leaned back against a tree. He settled in with his arms cradling his head against the gnarled bark.

Enzo bent forward with his cloak's cowl covering his head, so that only his mouth and dark stubbled chin were visible by the fire's radiance. Nathan took notice of the squire's seasoned appearance, and realized time's gradual pace had formed them into what they were. *We have aged.*

"How much you wager one of those gargoyle scales would fetch?" Enzo blinked while speaking into the flames.

"A lot." Lucas' eyes were thin lines. "Rutherford Vineyards started their business with a couple of 'em."

"Rumor has it that the old man stumbled upon a dead one along his hedgerow one morning when he was out for a puff on his pipe. Probably has an entire carcass worth of scales stowed away somewhere." Enzo brushed away a few stray crumbs.

"Ha!" Nathan laughed. "Never heard that before. I suppose that explains that picture of the gargoyle perched atop a pile of grapes on the bottle."

"That's the rumor." Lucas agreed and wiped the corners of his mouth. "Enz, you remember that wyvern we saw at Kendall's Crossing?"

Enzo sat upright. "Aye, I nearly forgot about that."

Lucas scrunched his toes and went on with his recollection. "The horses were acting all skittish and flighty, and we had a hekk of a time trying to calm them, then all of a sudden there was a huge lizard over our heads. It was soaring kinda like a bird, except it had to flap more often to keep in the air. Kinda like a bat, I guess. Anyway, it was green and gold and rather beautiful, if you are taken with such things. Remember when Sir Armand began to bicker with our elf about whether it was a boy or girl wyvern?"

Enzo laughed while breathing warmth into his bare hands.

Nathan rested his chin in his hands, his cowl falling back and asked, "Well, was it a boy or girl?"

"Dunno." Lucas shifted. "I wasn't looking for dangly bits."

Enzo barked a laugh while rummaging in his food sack, searching for more dried meat.

Lucas continued. "Armand was convinced the wyvern was female because of some discoloration between its throat and belly, but the guide said a bunch of elf nonsense that discredited everything Armand said. It nearly came to blows."

Nathan flinched at the repeated use of the word "elf" to describe the laif. Such a term had been virtually outlawed, and any laif that caught wind within earshot would more than likely take grievous offense.

"I remember that." Enzo tore into a meat strip, snapping his head back. "That elf woulda killed Armand. He was lucky those goblins came when they did, or else it woulda been his carcass we buried that night." He looked around restlessly, mouth full. "Did we bring wine, Luke?"

"No."

Nathan saw the squire's face wilt. "I brought tobacco," he offered.

The disappointment abated, and across the fire Lucas removed his feet from the log and leaned forward, teeth glistening in the firelight.

"Let's have us some then," Lucas said eagerly.

Nathan rummaged almost blindly in his satchel, patches of light created sections of clarity depending on how the sack was held, but soon his probing fingers found the small pouch containing the freshly cured leaves.

"Right on. Right on." Lucas tamped the overfilled pipe with a thumb, causing thin strands to fall like cinders. He passed the pouch to Enzo then ignited a strip of kindling and held it above the pipe's bowl, eyes following the gasping little flame as it darted in and out with each puff. After a healthy cherry was lit, he settled back against the tree, bunching his cowl between his skull and the stippled bark.

"What about you, Nate?" Lucas prompted as he propped his feet back up onto the log. "Tell us about some scary encounters. I'm sure Sir Clem didn't shield you from monsters when you went hunting for 'em?"

"Clemence and I once saw a strange faewolf," Nathan reminisced. "It was north and east of here. Much, much deeper in the wilds."

Lucas whistled. "It was only *one* of those uglies? Ain't it rare to see only one?"

"I think so. I mean, I've seen faewolves since that time," Nathan replied. "I was like twelve or thirteen winters old, but this one was different. It looked pretty messed up, and it was walking upright as they normally do, but this one was shambling across the road like it was drunk or something. Our laif ranger made us drop to the ground before we even spotted it, thinking we were about to catch a storm of 'em. We waited and waited, but that was the only one."

Lucas chuckled. "An elf would know."

"That's what we pay 'em for," Enzo agreed, exhaling a cloud.

"Spotting wyvern peckers from a mile away!" Lucas tossed a wrist sized branch into the fire, kicking up ash and dust. The guffaws from Enzo's corner seemed unnatural given their present location; the emotion seemed better suited for a tavern.

Watching their armour suspended from three separate tree branches, pendulating slowly in the night breeze, Nathan was suddenly reminded of a noteworthy encounter. *The lads may enjoy this one.*

"One time, Clemence took me to a graveyard to hunt ghouls."

Enzo's chuckling intensified. "Oh, whoa! Into a bone orchard to hunt some spooks? Please do tell!"

Nathan cleared his throat and wiped his mouth. "Well, as you know from the dispatch accounts, the monster population is growing far beyond our realm. Clemence reckons that's the reason why so many babes were being born under the Warrior."

"Or the other way around." Lucas twirled his finger.

Nathan pondered for a moment before opening his mouth. "That's fair," he concluded. The shadows played over Lucas' nose as he nodded, and Nathan continued, "Well, they were popping out of wombs left and right until the Church put that business to a halt."

"It was outta control," Enzo agreed as he clenched his pipe between his teeth. "People so scared of the dark and all the things that go bump in it, they decided the best way to fight it was to turn around and go *bumping in the night*, if you catch my meaning?" His eyebrows bobbed up and down.

Lucas laughed and tossed a clump of soil at the grinning squire. "Not too many people are excited about it."

"Oh *poor Amyr and his sweet Linette*, slain by the hands of that treacherous codger, Lord Ancel Something-or-other," Enzo began sarcastically. "Same old song and dance. Boo hoo. Old elf is just sore that he ain't gettin' it on anymore since she died, like what? A thousand years ago? Get over it, mate." Enzo spit into the flames.

Lucas uttered a one-note laugh, then spoke firmly, "You're lucky we are far from the church. A tongue like that is liable to get removed."

"Yeah, yeah."

Nathan swiveled his head, looking at each squire. "Anyway." They turned, and he continued.

"With the monster population out of control, well, out of greater control than usual, Clemence decided that I was ready for my first encounter with the eldritch. So when the Royal Dancer came knocking on our door to come out and slay some ghouls, Clemence obliged, but on one condition: that I come along. Elithiel was hesitant at first, but once Clemence heard that the other knights would have their squires, well, the laif had to agree at that point. Besides, he had no other choice. When it comes to eldritch horrors, Clemence is *by far* the most experienced of the Holy Knights."

"Whoa, whoa. Wait up a minute." Enzo fanned the air. "You slayed spooky monsters with the Royal Dancer?"

"Yeah, a few times. Elithiel and Clemence have a history," Nathan responded with a shrug. "My mentor has a specific skill set that happens to be in demand...when it comes to monster culling. Not saying that

Phillip is a dull blade or anything. I am sure he taught you both very well." He spoke quickly to recover from the possible gaffe.

After a brief silence, Enzo spoke up. "He's an alright, chap, I suppose. Gave us some good pointers when it comes to jousting and swordplay. Most everything he taught us was within the boundaries of the city. Not too many days spent afield." He looked to Lucas, who seemed distracted. "He is a right jack on a horse though. N'er seen anyone handle a battlehorse like he does."

Nathan sneezed. "He usually ranks within the top five in tourneys," he said, wiping his nose. "And he's not a massive brute by any measure."

Lucas finally spoke, unmoving, "It's all skill."

A pause settled around them and Nathan decided to continue with his tale. "The smell is what I remember most," he said, holding a finger firmly below his nose, fighting back another sneeze. "Even with the scarf Clemence gave me to block some of the stench. They eat decaying flesh and they also shit decaying flesh, so that should paint a rather clear picture for you. Ghouls are always female, and the males are called wendigos, but there isn't much of a difference between 'em to be honest, and I don't really want to get into the differences tonight. They are pretty closely related to goblins, at least that's what Clemence told me. They are more twisted creatures though, and much more sinister in their activities."

"Treacherous," Enzo translated.

"Aye." Nathan pointed at Enzo. "That and other things. But, yes, that's what distinguishes them as eldritch, I suppose. Goblins are not as angry, and they don't often fling themselves at you for no reason. Little buggers can be a pain, but for the most part they aren't too much of a nuisance. I saw some of the goblin resemblance in how the ghouls moved, kind of bouncy, like they run on their toes, but it's also a lot creepier. You see, they wear these cloaks that they fashion from the dead. I mean, from the dead folk's clothes, the ones they are buried in. It's not like they're draping themselves in skin coats or anything gross like that. And these cloaks, you know, they make it hard to make out a definite silhouette at night, so it almost looks like a bundle of laundry is darting for your shins. By the time you realize what's actually happening, it's too late, and you're all tripped up and they're already gnawing on your kneecaps. And they swarm like hornets, real fast, and their claws are like a reaper's scythe. I didn't actually see—Gnome!" Nathan pointed at his tobacco pouch on the ground next to Lucas.

Lucas waved a hand at the gnome as Enzo doubled over clutching his gut, bellowing laughter.

"Get! Go on now!"

The gnome, realizing that he had lost the upper hand, backpedaled, then turned with a hop, and scuttled away on tiny feet, clutching his pointed hat with both hands.

"Must have been hiding under those shrooms over there." Enzo wiped away a tear, laughter leaking into his voice. "Little blokes love to smoke, same as us."

Nathan watched the tall grass part as the gnome made his retreat under the cover of night. "Little fellows are harmless." He turned back to the fire with a shiver. "Where was I now? Oh yes, the graveyard." He placed his pipe between his teeth and rubbed his hands, hovering them above the flames. "We arrived several hours before dusk, riding along a slim road that divided the forest. Elithiel and Sir Bors set up a trap in the forest across the road from the graveyard, and the plan was to lure the ghouls into it so we could kill a great many with a simple flick of the wrist. It was a brilliant trap, really, and we brought a cart loaded with freshly dead people. I'm not entirely sure where they came from, now that I think about it."

Nearly simultaneously Lucas and Enzo responded, "The Church."

"A fair speculation." Nathan rubbed his chin before placing it beneath the warm layers. "We had to wrap 'em real good and tight to keep the stench from escaping, and Elithiel put some kinda incantation into the fabrics before we wrapped 'em, which worked great, actually. I didn't smell them at all on the journey, even riding behind the cart. Well, at least not until we unwrapped 'em, of course." He sniffed, brushing his nose with a sleeve and began filling his pipe, pinching the leaves between thumb and forefinger. Sitting back and taking a pull from the pipe, he continued. "So the trap was set and the bait was put in its place. I was assigned to be in the forest, away from the graveyard, in order to help Bors and the other squires with the trap. Bors' squire, Pence Pemberton, and I were tasked with unraveling the corpses once we heard the signal from across the road. Everyone else was positioned along the outer rim of the trap to pick off any stragglers that didn't manage to make it into the massive bow's death zone."

Enzo leaned forward with twinkling eyes. "Massive bow?" he asked. "Pence Pemberton? *Death Zone?* What sort of tale is this?"

Lucas exhaled a cloud. "I figured you would have just dug a huge pit and lured the ghouls into it, then just picked 'em off from above."

"Yeah, a pit would've held them real good, but the knights were looking to clean house on this trip using as little resources as possible," Nathan answered, slapping another bug off his neck and regarding his bloodied palm with a smile. "Arrows add up."

"Makes sense." Enzo shrugged.

"The bow itself was positioned in the trees just above my head, so I had to crouch slightly when I passed under it. None of the ghouls were taller than my waist, so we weren't concerned with any of 'em bonking their heads."

"They tall as goblins?" Enzo guessed, and pulled his cowl back to scratch the top of his head.

Nathan squinted. "I suppose they are. They hunch up when they skulk, but I'd say they were about the same size."

"Posture is principal, lads!" Lucas puffed up his chest as he spoke in a high pitched voice.

Nathan was caught off-guard by the sudden impersonation, while Enzo chuckled with shoulders heaving.

"You sound just like Schroederstall." Nathan gaped. "Spot on!"

"He said it so damn often." Enzo took another drag, the hot cherry fire in his pipe caused the tip of his nose to glow.

Lucas crossed his arms, his brilliant red hair gilded by the fire's radiance, and smirked, waiting for Nathan to proceed.

"Well, like I said before." Nathan straightened. "They are similar to goblins, but they're way more evil. Like, the way they move at night..." He shook his head as he continued. "Ghouls are unsettling creatures." Contemplating the next phrase with pipe tucked in his lips, he spoke quietly, "They somehow know your name."

A hush fell.

"What's that now?" Enzo squinted one eye.

Fanning away another invader buzzing behind his ear, Nathan admitted, "I don't really know how it works."

"Wait, do they shout it at you when they see you or something?" Lucas leaned forward, his pipe falling out of his mouth.

"I mean, I guess they can if they want to. Clemence warned me about it, said it was very disturbing at first, but once you kill a dozen of the suckers screaming your name the whole time, you eventually get used to it."

"Good grief," Enzo muttered.

"I wonder if that applies to those born without a sign," Lucas pondered.

Enzo pulled the cloak's cowl back over his head and drew a long pull from his pipe, contemplating the query.

Nathan shifted. "That's a good question, actually. I'll ask Clemence next time I see her."

"I'd wager no." Enzo took up a philosopher's air. "Our blood is different. Lots of magic in the blood." Tapping the bowl of the pipe to his front teeth, he spoke elegantly. "See if your glorious Sir Clem agrees with that."

Looking forward to having this bloody business done, Nathan found the prospect of having a conversation with his mentor infinitely more agreeable. *Can't wait for that day.* "I'll be sure to ask her, Enzo."

"I would be greatly obliged if you did, sir." Enzo continued to speak in a lofty tone, which Lucas found highly amusing.

When his companions settled down, Nathan felt that he could continue the story. "So ghouls are actually easily—"

"Continue!" Enzo snapped.

Lucas roared with laughter, and Nathan was taken aback.

"Please! I entreat thee!" Enzo commanded, rolling his wrist like a creepy wizard.

"Ghouls, well they—" Nathan paused, waiting for another interruption. "They are actually quite soft and easy to kill. They're naked under their cloaks, and the flesh underneath is easily punctured, very susceptible to any sharp edged weapon, really. A new butter knife could do some serious damage to them if handled skillfully with minimal effort on the wielder's part. Of course, subduing the little wretches is the tricky part. They're fast. Right and bloody fast. And the moonlight only seems to make the little devils more slippery, but good luck finding them during the day."

"So tell us about their plan. I want to hear more about that," Lucas spoke at the peak of composure, urging Nathan on. "I'm downright curious about this gigantic longbow and its killing fields."

"Elithiel wanted to schedule the slaughter during the new moon cycle, which sparked a debate with Clemence. The laif reasoned that if we were to encounter a pack of faewolves, which was highly likely, then they would not be at peak strength. But Clemence wasn't very excited about the prospect of chasing the ghouls around gravestones without much moonlight. When it comes to forest business, it's usually a good idea to defer to the laif, so Clemence relented and resigned herself to a dimly lit battleground. Bors and Elithiel set the trap in a glade so we had the palest light the new moon could offer, which showed great foresight on their part. Otherwise, it would have been darker than the inside of my boot if there were tree branches blocking the sky."

"Yeah, obviously," Enzo began. "But why didn't you just set a few sconces burning on the trees around you?"

"That would have scared the ghouls immediately." Nathan's lip curled fractionally.

"*Obviously,*" Lucas stretched out his legs, propping his feet on the log.

"They hate light. Repelled by it, actually. Even the dim light from a small hand torch would alert 'em," Nathan said.

Enzo took another long pull from his pipe. "You remember a lot of stuff about these creepy monsters."

"Well, remember who his knight is," Lucas pointed out as he exhaled a tight cloud with pursed lips. Enzo raised his stem from across the flames and nodded.

Nathan lifted his eyes as he attempted to recall the specifics. "There were five of us across the roadway: four squires, plus Sir Bors, positioned in the forest. And three royal knights, two red knights, Sir

Clemence as the only holy knight...plus the Dancer were set up in the graveyard. They were supposed to stir 'em up, get 'em all interested in some fresh meat then draw them toward us so we could spring the trap. We hoped the piles of rotting flesh would distract them enough to get them to break from their pursuit. Holdy and Scrant worked with Bors to adjust the bow's mast...not sure what else to call it...the curvy part?"

"The limb," Lucas offered.

"Yes, the limb. Anyway, they would position it so me and Pence could get out after we unrolled the dead, avoiding our own decapitation, then bring it back down to ghoul height. Does that make sense?" The others nodded and he continued. "Once we were free, Bors would release whatever the machination was, then the string would snap and instantly cull everything inside the killing zone."

With eyebrows raised, Lucas asked, "Was it successful?"

"For the most part. Bors and Holdy had to porcupine a few stragglers, but other than those, we pretty much wiped out a coven of ghouls in one night. Hard to say if we killed 'em all, but I'd say the death toll would rival the population of Drydentown."

Enzo whistled.

"We spent the rest of the night gathering the dead ghouls that didn't get killed in the trap; the ones in the graveyard and those stragglers that Bors and Holdy managed. The dead ghouls were surprisingly light when you picked 'em up. Felt like an armful of wet rags. But finding the dismembered parts was the hardest part—"

"How many did the knights kill?" Enzo burst. "Compared with what was nicked in the kill zone?"

"Oh, way more!" Nathan opened his hands. "Maybe a hundred or so in the graveyard and maybe sixty in the trap?"

"So why didn't your party just set up shop in the graveyard and slay the little bastards there?" Enzo questioned.

Nathan waved at another cloud of mosquitoes, or perhaps the same cloud regrouped. "Elithiel wasn't sure how many ghouls would be there. They had been dining on flesh, digging up the graves for weeks by the time we got to 'em. He estimated that the population would have swelled, but he couldn't be sure of the numbers, so he wagered for more rather than less. Better to have it and not need it, then need it and not have it, you know?"

Just beyond the hedge, a rabbit squealed in terror. Along with the rabbit, the conversation around the fire died.

"Well." Lucas stood and tapped his pipe against the tree, sprinkling crispy burnt bits. "On that note, I think I will turn in." Nathan and Enzo nodded in unison and Lucas continued, "Enzo, you want to take first watch, then wake me and I will take second?"

"Works for me," Enzo replied.

"So, Nathan." Lucas sat up and crossed his legs. "That means that I'll wake you just before sunrise, which means you are in charge of rustling up breakfast." With that, he flopped back and pulled his traveler's cloak around him like a blanket, tucking the cowl over his face, then shifted with his back to the flames. "Tend the fire," he ordered, speaking at the trees. "Make sure it survives until you wake me, Enz." He shuffled on the ground, seeking a comfortable groove among the roots.

"Aye, aye." Enzo gave a salute.

Fatigue hummed behind Nathan's eyes, and he was unsure whether or not he would manage to catch any sort of rest. *Tomorrow is a day of days.*

The forest played its nocturnal orchestrations; buzzing, belching, and crashing. All disturbing instances would be quickly explained away, rationalized with harmless speculations. Their blades provided the only sure security and their horse's attuned senses would alert them of any dangers.

Nathan swaddled himself in his azure cloak and traveling blanket, inching toward the fire. "G'night, Enzo," he said drowsily, pulling the cluster of fabrics to his chin.

"Pleasant dreams, Master Nathan," came Enzo's response, speaking in *that* weird voice.

Nathan rolled over and shook his head. *We're all going to die.*

10

Galahalt found himself alone on a bluff facing the lowered drawbridge of a stone keep. Before reaching the wooden surface of the bridge, damp tall grass faintly pulled at his ankles leaving his shins feeling uncomfortably wet.

He strode under the open portcullis and into a great dining hall filled with squires and pages, the volume and amount of merrymaking was unsettling to say the least. Glancing all around and over his shoulders, Galahalt expected someone in authority to step forward and bellow a demand for silence, but no one came forward. Unexplained relief washed over him as he turned around and walked past the children making an untethered racket, deciding that this place was not for him.

Passing back under the portcullis, he found himself under an unnaturally clear blue sky. The hill that the castle was on was angled at a substantial grade, and one could not help but pick up momentum when traversing the stairless decline. The feasting behind him penetrated the glassless windows, and shouts and laughter invaded his ears, even as he increased his distance from the keep.

A few other squires were flying kites in the knee-high grass, seemingly to be at the precipice of a great cliff, but he didn't know for sure. He did not go over to investigate. His attention was elsewhere: further down below, where the ground leveled off and became flat, like the bottom joint of an uppercase "L."

Looking back, the keep appeared much too small to contain all of the rooms and people inside, and it wasn't just the change in perspective that caused this effect. It was a stone walled cottage of a castle now hunched against the clear horizon, with parapets instead of a thatch roof.

Pressing on, the knight was exhausted by even the thought of going back and investigating. Another cluster of squires was in the flat meadow passing an overly large red ball around. They bounced it and attempted to wrap their arms around it. Whenever it came within grasp, careening toward one of the young lads or lasses, the huge ball would smack their faces just before they could contain it in a bear hug. Bloody noses accented the joyful faces, spraying red juices everywhere, propelled by uncontained laughter under dry scarlet moustaches. *Uncoordinated fools.*

Beyond them, playing by herself, to his immense confusion was his sister Margot at ten or eleven years, scraped knees and all, engulfed by a small patch of gray gilly. He was stunned as he watched her twirl about as if no one was watching, and he wanted nothing more than to reach her.

Tears dried against his face as he rushed down the hill to play with her like they once did when they were young. Before the armour and swords, and dirt and lances. Before the massive debt and horrible promises. Before the loss of innocence and the hunt for the impossible.

He was sure that he would take a tumble; his feet could not keep up with the overwhelming momentum, as he blazed past the blurry squires and their stupid game. Now the ball was in Margot's hands and her face was thankfully not bloodied, but he could only see from her mouth to her hair; the ball blocked the rest of her as she slapped its crown in an attempt to make it bounce. The ball gelatinously responded, only jiggling a bit from the meager force, and it maintained its position on the ground.

Suddenly his feet no longer registered purchase on the field, and he sailed upward. The open air created drag and slowed his pace tremendously, like a parasol carelessly tossed from a balcony. Margot smiled broadly at her big brother as if this was normal for him to be sailing overhead, then she bent at the knees to throw the red sphere up at him.

He tried to shout, but the gusts of wind were too strong, so he pantomimed, desperately trying to dissuade her from what she was about to do. Not a speck of awareness registered on her face, and she heaved the ball upwards with all her might, sending it directly into his stomach, blasting him up and away from all that he loved and all that he knew, orbiting endlessly somewhere above the strange castle on the hill.

A sharp stab below his rib cage shattered the dreamscape and vaulted him into reality.

"Wake."

It was Elkara.

"We must be off if we are to reach this Questing Beast of yours in a timely manner."

"HERE," ELKARA SAID AND LEANED IN HER SADDLE, handing Galahalt a strip of cloth two thumbs wide and elbow to fingers long. The knight accepted the offering with an upraised eyebrow. "Have you never had long hair before?" she asked as she watched him regard the offering with skepticism.

"Ah." pulling it taut, Galahalt wrapped the thin fabric around his knuckles like a brawler. "Thank you very much." Reversing the twist, the knight soon pulled back his long hair into a tidy knot. "I'll have you know that I have had my hair this length for the greater part of my life."

"Could've fooled me." *The way you were fussing and tucking and untucking your locks like a fumbling virgin.*

The pair broke camp before the first rays of light poked through the trees, giving them an excellent start, and Elkara was pleased with the young knight's readiness to press forward. *Much easier with one knight than a gaggle of them.*

The river guided them north, and the trail did not stray far from the rushing waters. Sir Galahalt proved to be an amiable companion, asking questions that required a few moments of thought. This ordinarily taxed the laif's nerves when traveling with newbies, but his queries helped pass the time.

He wondered how gremlins secured the armour in place when building their little cities, and how they prevent rust from overtaking the structures, whittling them down to steely powder. *All good questions.* It refreshed her mind, like a splash of oil on a dry bearing, as she had not considered such topics in ages.

Meanwhile, Galahalt was trying to shake the cobwebs loose in his head after suffering through a night filled with weird dreams that were not particularly scary, but presented such...weird situations. Recurring figments needled at him, just beyond his mental grip, fleeing like an army of ants scattered by a dropped torch. These unfamiliar, yet intimate apparitions plagued the space behind his eyelids.

He had been absentmindedly fussing with his hair while deep in thought, which revealed a brief glimpse of ire from his guide who offered a solution to a problem that he was unaware existed.

What was that castle on the cliff? And where the hekk was that hill? He rubbed the meat of his palm into his eye socket.

"There's a kind of fork up ahead," Elkara said, bringing him back to the present, as she regarded the bleary-eyed knight with an ounce of concern. "You alright?"

He nodded with a hand pressed to his forehead. "There's a fork ahead?" he asked.

"Yes," she replied, not altogether convinced. "We can water the horses and take in some food. Also, I want to pitch an idea to you, and if you're not completely comfortable, then we don't have to do it."

"I'm listening."

She straightened, looking ahead at a large break in the trees where sunshine poured down onto a sloped glade emptying into the riverbed. "There's a favorable hunting plot that I would like to hit while we're out in this part of the forest." She wrinkled her nose. "The only thing is, we will have to split up. At least briefly."

"Will you be sharing the harvest?" Galahalt asked, blinking above a cresting smile.

"Of course," Elkara promised as she eased her shoulders. "And the weather is perfect right now. Practically a guarantee that we'll have fresh meat sizzling over the fire tonight."

"I imagine that we will be parting ways where the path diverges?" Galahalt squinted at the penetrating brilliance as they passed under the shadowy trees, the sunlight bathed the clearing in a much brighter shade.

A line of large rocks dotted the river creating a footbridge which allowed travelers to meet the slim trail on the other side. The path to the left was more worn down, widened by frequent traffic, and Galahalt leaned forward to peer into the thickness of bark and branches, craning eyes upward at the near perfect canopy. "You'll be breaking right?" he guessed.

"Yes, and yes." The laif hopped down from Error and patted the laifhorse's rump as he strode toward the river without requiring any encouragement. "The paths reconnect after about three quarters of a mile. It's more or less like an oval shape. Should you beat me to the crossroads, I strongly suggest that you wait for me. There's a ward not far from that spot."

Galahalt stood on the shore and rummaged through a sack on his horse's saddle as she eagerly pranced into the waters, nearly pulling him along. He winced as a monsoon struck his face while he attempted to maintain his balance and keep his feet dry as the horse hastily positioned herself to drink. A few curses passed from his lips before he was able to retrieve the cheesecloth that swaddled a hunk of aged cheddar. He wanted to pull out the dried jerky as well, but decided to cut his losses after tangling near the water, having no interest in getting soaked. *A damp bum doesn't bode well for a day in the saddle.*

He walked up the grassy slope and took a seat on a flat rock that was carved at an angle parallel to the grade. Light reflected from the knight's armour caused Elkara to raise a palm over her eyes, casting shade from the stinging brilliance. Galahalt was munching on the cheese with the cloth pulled around it, preventing his grimy hands from tainting the flavor.

That cheese looks good, Elkara thought, selecting the food satchel from Error's saddle and retrieving a few strips of dried meat. As she walked past the knight, gnawing away, she stuttered a step. With his hair pulled back revealing his neck, the laif noticed that he did not have a mark.

Warriors bear the mark on their necks. She crinkled her mouth to the side, catching herself staring, then continued past the young knight who took no perceived notice. Every detail she had learned about Galahalt suddenly flew into question; *was he actually a knight? That would explain the lack of a horse and the sparse armour.* Standing behind him, she stared as she wondered if it was wise to split up after all.

"Elkara," Galahalt said, turning in her direction. The laif blinked and quickly looked up to the trees, admiring an invisible bird with a finger resting under her chin.

Taking a few more blinks, she lowered her hand, and registering his words, she replied, "Oh, yes?" *Nice save. He caught you staring like a clod.*

"Want to trade a hunk of this cheese for a strip of that jerky?" He held the yellow block toward her.

Act normal. "That sounds divine!" *For all that's deemed holy.* She separated a strip and handed it to the knight, who in turn broke a morsel and passed it to her. Raising the jerky in salute, the knight turned back toward the river and began tearing at the strip like a dog with a rope.

Watching the struggle, she mused, *Yeah, maybe I don't know about this guy.*

"You sure you're alright with splitting up?" Elkara asked while walking next to him and looked down, the sun's rays blazing from the steel.

Galahalt took a hard swallow before responding. "Oh yeah. Don't worry about me." Eyeing the dried meat in his hand, he continued. "It's only what? Less than a mile? That isn't a bad stretch, and all I have to do is follow the path, right?"

She hesitated before responding. "Yes, only..."

With a mouth full of cheese and meat, the knight looked up at her, awaiting the conclusion.

"Keep in mind that I will be hunting on foot, so don't go whipping along. Be ready to wait for me."

Galahalt saluted with his mouth still full, then swallowed. "What's the worst sort of peril I might encounter on this side of the river?" A few crumbs spilled onto his tunic, tumbling and rolling as he spoke.

"Eh," Elkara began, gathering her thoughts. "I'd say the worst would be an ogre, maybe?" She shook her head after a moment. "But, no, scratch that. I don't think any ogres have traveled this far south in a long time. Maybe a drake or an asp weaver? But I *highly* doubt you'll stumble into anything remotely dangerous. And should you encounter either of those: avoid them."

The knight's demeanor remained cool and unwavering as he listened intently with puffed cheeks.

"The last time I crossed this section," Elkara went on. "I saw some gnomes and goblins, but nothing too severe or anything that you couldn't handle." *At least, what you appear to be able to handle.*

Sparing a sidelong glance at his borrowed horse, she took in the spear attached to the saddle. Both animals were now a few paces from the waters, inhaling mouthfuls of the tender plant life that lined the shore, inches from the stony embankment.

"Ogres and gnomes, got it." Galahalt clapped his hands before standing to full height, then leaned back with a yawning stretch.

"No. No ogres."

"Whatever," Galahalt said dismissively, making for the horses.

The laif buried the last bit of the jerky into her cheeks and followed. *You only have to get him past the ward, then take him to the fort like you have done hundreds of times, then after, we turn back and head for home. You'll never need to see this knucklehead again.*

11

Lucas had shaken Nathan awake nearly an hour ago as dawn was breaking over the forest. Early rising songbirds were tittering here and there, merely a prelude before the full chorus eventually swung into motion.

Nathan had slept like a rock, not waking when the previous shift change took place only a few feet away from where he slept. Once he found a gentle pocket in the densely rooted soil, sleep overcame him and held him close like a second womb.

Even though an adequate amount of hours passed behind his shuttered eyelids, Nathan felt heavy. Not drowsy or sluggish. Heavy. Like he was sinking in an infinite puddle with a millstone fastened to his stomach, helplessly reaching for the blurry fragments above the surface.

Aside from the heaviness, he was overly alert for some reason, heart pounding at the slightest shuffle in the trees. His eyes darted from branch to branch, attempting to spot whichever bird was crying out, and the sounds that managed to break beyond the consistent rushing noise of the river made his temples pound. *Feels like I have sprouted gills under my skin.*

The gargoyle and cockatrices were at the forefront of his mind. *Clemence didn't cover either one in our training. At least, not in any sort of detail that I can recall. I am certain she would advise a swift retreat though.* He tugged on his breastplate, *One would turn you to stone and the other is practically made from stone.*

Nathan's mind wandered in the morning stillness, taking in his surroundings as the light began to spread, gelding every blade. *Will it feel different killing a man?*

He recalled an encounter with a faewolf that had somehow lost its pack, and at the time was aggressively posturing, unprovoked, as Nathan and Clemence trekked through a gorge in some hollow of Fenrirfang. They would have ignored the creature and went about their way, but it followed them in an uncomfortable manner, hardly attempting to sneak or hide its presence. It was entirely unnerving. Clemence whispered for her squire to hold still, then turned about at the rim of the basin, twirling on a heel in a flourish, drawing her blade while one hand restrained the scabbard. The faewolf drew much too close, its heavy breathing audible, and the knight could not abide that, so she engaged the beast.

Nathan had been surprised by the faewolf's nerve as it charged to meet the armoured knight with claws ready, but the crafty monster slayer was well versed in her art. She took a stuttering step to her left, feinting a cut, and when the faewolf moved to counter, it was quickly and abruptly caught unaware. Clemence brought the blade low, shifting so it sat in her grip like a dagger, then heaved upward, punching through the creature's chest and piercing its right lung on its course. It was a brilliant and violent display of swordsmanship, and the squire felt a tinge of sorrow for the out-maneuvered, out-played, and ultimately, unarmed beast. With an open palm on the foe's damp, matted chest, Clemence disengaged, sliding the blade free, passing from the silhouette gracing the curvature of its spine.

The faewolf had slumped to the ground, clutching the knight's steel vambraces before losing its grip and toppling on its tail. Laying back, its chest heaved unevenly, a faint crackling behind each gasp.

Nathan had been certain that the tunnel was closing around the fae-wolf's vision, and that it would soon pass from this plane. "Watch," Clemence had commanded as she met her squire's eyes and slowly, deliberately, drew a push blade from under her belt, gaze unwavering. "This is how you ease a faewolf's suffering. Same action works for a turned werewolf and really any other manner of bipedal beast."

She was always so disturbingly articulate during such situations. Ignoring the writhing and grasping, Clemence gripped the faewolf behind its head around the scruff, like one would an enraged cat, and jerked sideways so its muzzle was planted in the dirt, then with a surgeon's precision she slowly pressed the blade below the base of the beast's skull. She had tensed the muscles in her shoulders, drawing the blade deeper by fractions, holding fast until the faewolf gave up its ghost.

After that first lesson, Nathan was given many opportunities to practice the *swift passing*, and after the first dozen faewolves that painted his push blade, the squire felt more than confident in the procedure. *Never a human though.* And he doubted wholeheartedly that whenever they encountered Sir Galahalt, the knight would exude the same struggle as a faewolf. *A whole different beast.* Nathan had spent plenty of time sparring with his fellow squires in the tiltyards, but never faced a fellow human in mortal combat.

His mind began to hover over another memory, and he blinked, taking in his surroundings. Judging them to be serene enough, he delved back into reverie. *Sir Galahalt.* Nathan held only one remarkable interaction with the knight, back when he was an elder squire before accepting the belt. Nathan usually saw him in passing when he was performing chantry duties or other menial tasks, or otherwise in the proving grounds sparring with the much older squires.

One particular summer afternoon, beyond the stables, along some hedges lining a dense copse of pine trees, a group of squires were huddled, maybe a dozen or so, laughing and excitedly squealing at whatever they had discovered. Nathan rushed to see what the commotion was about, expecting some fun during the brief recess. Perhaps a new toy was gifted to one of his peers, lovingly sent by a parent, and they were sharing in the sport. Or maybe someone was performing a hilarious magic trick, or possibly a fellow squire was tight-rope walking good sense by accepting a really gross dare.

No. Nathan pressed his eyes tight and hung his head at the memory. Enzo and Lucas had discovered an abandoned baby goblin. It was writhing in the sharp spiny pine needles that littered the ground, glazed with slime, its mouth silently puckering around tiny sips of air. At the time, Nathan had no clue as to the age of the pathetic lump, but now that he was better versed in the creatures, he wagered it was nearly three weeks old, give or take a day or two.

At first, the young eyes widened in fascination, but once the wonder was swept clean, the children began to make suggestions, devising plots for what should be done to the lesser creature. The first few offered up were banal, the basic: "just leave it" or "let's take it to a grown-up," but when Sheila Overstrak suggested that they skewer the babe on a stick and hold it over an open flame until it blistered and melted, that was when the debate took a turn.

In the commotion, someone picked the goblin up, Nathan could not recall the lad's name, and suspended it daintily by its upraised hands, dancing it around the air like a string puppet. The cries for various types of mutilation subsided for an instant, overtaken by shrieks of laughter. As the morbid display gained attention, so did the puppeteer's jerking motions increase in fervor. And soon, as a lizard breaks free of its tail, the baby goblin broke free of its left hand, holding on with the remaining appendage, dangling pathetically as the dance abruptly came to a halt.

The squire disgustedly tossed the ripped hand aside, and spectators watched the blood pour out from the stump. It started slowly like an eyedropper, but then flowed heavily like rain from a spout.

At once, the crowd's mentality deflated. Deciding that their new toy was limp and damaged beyond repair, they tossed it aside to fend for itself. The baby rolled to a stop, picking up needles along the way, dirty and broken, but without sound. Not one audible cry escaped its lips. Terror registered on its tiny beady eyes, and Nathan found himself alone with the silently mewling creature, its dismembered limb waving frantically, perhaps searching for its lost member. Not knowing how long it would take to bleed out, he simply watched, transfixed with the theatrical horrors of reality being displayed, permanently imprinted in his mind.

Looking back, he would have sought a heavy rock to ease its passing, but at the time he thought that perhaps there was some way to save the creature. *So much blood contained in such a small body.*

A tall lean squire took notice from the stables and walked into the dispersing crowd, curious what had created such a throng. Derisive laughter and violent hand motions indicated that whatever had befallen was most likely of a sinister nature.

Nathan was standing over the dying creature, helplessly spectating, when the older squire came up beside him, and kneeling down, picked off a few needles and flung them aside, inspecting the damage. No words passed between the lads, and without a hint of malice, the older squire drew a slender knife from his purse and gracefully plunged it between the goblin's watery eyes. After a brief whimper, life ended, and the innocent creature was finally at peace.

Nathan hoped, in that moment, that when the time came and the trap was sprung, he would be able to show the knight a reflective semblance of dignity. *When the time comes.*

His surroundings were steadily creeping into focus. Only minutes ago, bushes that were nothing but lumpy shadows now appeared green and vibrant, resplendent in red berries. *A bit early in the season to be producing fruit,* he thought, raising an eyebrow. In another hour or so, he would begin preparing some sort of breakfast, and the berries bouncing on their branches were an inspiration. *Not much preparation is needed when your supplies are mainly hard tack and dried meat.*

Clemence always advised to take as much fresh fruit as possible when it was available to supplement the travel diet. *Berries with crowns are the safest bet,* Nathan reminded himself, taking his mentor's tone. He scanned for possible food options instead of painstakingly seeking enemies; intentionally drawing shallow breaths.

The morning light ushered in a reprieve and he began to breathe easier, setting himself on a task with lower stakes. As he focused his eyes on a tree appearing to be some sort of willow, tentacle vines dipping into the river mist, a dark movement stole his attention. *Gargoyle!* His throat clenched tight as the air escaped. A pale gray creature was moving east, fording the river sixty yards north, and the glistening of steel betrayed its neutrality. *That posture?* Instantly Nathan recognized the loping motion and dismissed the gargoyle entirely.

Ogres!

His feet kicked at the dirt, gaining traction after a few slides, and he pressed his back to the tree and stood, armour crunching against the bark as he slid. The first figure was not alone, and trailing behind were several more ogres, hints of polished steel reflected in and out of view as they passed behind branches and trunks. *Identify...Identify.* He commanded himself to stand his ground, unflinching, and wait for clarity.

"Creator above." *Oh, that's an alpha.* He was suddenly parched. *One.* He blinked hard, focusing. *Two...no, three juveniles.* Waiting for any stragglers to appear, he lingered far longer than his good sense desired.

When his feet could no longer hold still, and when he was nearly satisfied with the tally, he sprinted back to the camp.

"Rise! Rise!" Nathan said quickly as he fumbled with his cuirass, struggling to disentangle it. "Ogres beyond the ravine!"

Lucas and Enzo bolted upright and wrestled free of their encasements, sending blankets in all directions.

"Coming our way?" Enzo demanded, quickly untying the thread that suspended his armour on a limb.

"Did they see you?" Lucas asked with a pause after sheathing his sword.

"I don't know…" Nathan pulled the steel shell over his head and let it fall to the ground. "They were facing our direction before I cut and ran…and if they saw me? It doesn't matter. We must meet them."

Feverishly arming themselves, the squires were ready within moments. Lucas and Enzo were armed from head to foot, while Nathan had abandoned a heavy portion of his armour.

"Why aren't you wearing your arms, Nate?" Enzo asked and secured a loose strap under his armpit.

"The alpha has a dagda. My armour would only constrict if he struck true, and I do not wish to suffocate today."

"But if he strikes true without your armour on, then your bones will be dust." Enzo waved his sword, loosening his wrist.

"But he won't die of suffocation," Lucas pointed out while easing his visor open, sleep finally dissipating.

"Ah. I see."

"We must move, boys." Nathan led at a fast pace, and their stiff muscles limbered up as they jogged.

"Bleed them!" Nathan shouted, needing the volume to be heard through their helms.

"Got it." Enzo gave a single nod.

"Their veins are very soft, so cut them as often as you can. You don't have to wait for the killing blow." The claymore felt good in Nathan's hands; gripping the worn leather pommel, soft between his clenched fingers, was like greeting an old friend.

"The others are flanking!" Spit flew as Nathan shouted. A pair of bone white horns crested a tree limb thirty paces ahead. "Break left!" Enzo and Lucas did as they were commanded, and Nathan remained where he was. Setting his jaw, he held the blade with both hands and waited.

The pale gray behemoth pulled a limb from its face and strode out from under the heavy branches, all sound seemed to hone in on the invasion, and when it paused, taking the squire in, the growl that permeated was almost staggering. To the left, Nathan saw the smaller ogres rushing out, attempting a flanking run. *Knew it.* A smile curled at the corner of his mouth.

LUCAS AND ENZO CAME TO A HALT, deciding that the sparse arrangement of trees was as good as they would find. With a knowing nod to his mate, Lucas clanked his visor down and sprinted wide and to the left.

Enzo slammed his sword onto his shield and yelled, "Oi! Oi!" He could not think of anything clever in the moment, but it was still effective. It drew the ogres short on their course, and they rerouted, stumbling a few steps before rushing toward the clamor.

One of the ogres caught sight of Lucas' angled approach and split from the others, leaving a furrowed angry pair for Enzo to contend with. Fuming with rage, the ogres charged, their huffing breaths nearly as loud as their footsteps as they tore the earth, flinging clumps of dirt up into the boughs. *Why are they so upset?* Enzo wondered and ceased his clanging, holding firm.

Tossing his shield aside, Lucas lowered his stance before doubling speed, meeting the foe at a dead run. The lanky ogre stood at a man's height, but lacked the muscle and bone density of a more mature beast. Even still, he appeared to be more than a match for the squire. Each step was the equivalent of a human long jump, so the gap between them was quickly closed and only seconds before Enzo met his own battle.

Clutching the broad axe overhead, the ogre pivoted his hips to strike on a downward arc, but Lucas anticipated the move, taking a stutter step and subsequent leap to the side. He darted, avoiding the swing, and aimed his blade at the ogre's eye. Capitalizing on the creature's imbalance, Lucas punched forward, but missed, his weapon glancing off the monster's high set cheekbone.

The momentum carried the squire forward, tracing a bloody path directly into the ogre's upper ear which caught the hilt and brought him to an abrupt stop. He tiptoed awkwardly, dancing sideways and struggling to maintain balance. With no other option, Lucas released his grip for less than a heartbeat, then immediately renewed the hold with thumb pressed to the guard. A subtle gesture, unnoticed by the screeching ogre, with eyes bulging, began to swing wildly at the squire in an attempt to regain its personal space.

Lucas was unsuccessful in avoiding a blow, which impacted dead center on his chest plate, which ultimately bolstered the squire's advantage. The uppercut to the midsection helped Lucas to disengage, and he was grateful that the ogre did not wrap its arms around him in an unfriendly embrace.

It's the simple blessings, Lucas thought gratefully as he sliced downward, cutting deep into the ogre's neck, parting it into a fleshy rivulet. He firmly braced his right leg, planting the sabaton into the turf, and brought the blade level with the spindly brute's collarbone, plunging it into the depths of the hardened gray flesh.

This halted the screaming, but lengthened the bloody spraying fountain. A desperate axe swing bounced off Lucas' pauldron, and the squire brushed it aside before removing his blade from the dying beast, who still remained standing against all logic. Completely disinterested with the ogre's feeble attempts to decapitate him, Lucas turned his attention to the battle that was continuing to rage beyond the trees.

"Enzo's biding his time." Lucas grinned under his visor, eyes narrowing. "Best get going." He spoke as he rushed to his friend's aid.

Enzo remained stalwart, shield upraised to the onslaught of blows that rained down upon him. He clenched his teeth as tremors reverberated with each blow. The pair of ogres were trading strikes on the shield, taking turns as if playing a game, while they pummeled the steel with their weapons.

Any second now, old friend. Enzo thought, growing impatient. He was unsure of how much longer he could maintain this distraction.

Unaware of Lucas' victory, his eyes frantically traced paths around the edges of his shield, waiting for the foes to invade and come around for a strike. Before long they would grow weary of their sport and seek to end the trial.

A glimmer of steel passed in the periphery, and Enzo instinctively knew what was about to happen. He dropped to a knee and sliced one ogre just above the kneecap; the foe stumbled backwards, but remained on his clawed feet. One moment the ogre was regaining his composure, and the next moment was gone.

The young ogre's cudgel sailed into the air. Bereft of defense, the brute was quickly dispatched, and Enzo looked above his shield to see Lucas swatting drops of blood from a crimson drenched blade. The remaining ogre looked around for help, surrounded by enemies, and his tongue wagged helplessly between immature tusks.

There was no quarter agreement between the races. Stumbling back, the lanky ogre dropped his black iron flail and raised both palms in surrender, backpedaling out of sword reach. Enzo gave a heavy sigh as he dropped his shield. Taking a few paces toward the ogre, he sheathed his sword, then stooped and retrieved the fallen flail.

Holding the heavy weapon with both hands, he shouted, "Take it!" Raising it up, the iron striker dangled by a ten link chain, "This is yours, now take it!"

The ogre shook his head, uttering guttural sounds that seemed to rise from his chest, completely indistinguishable to the squires.

"Come on!" Enzo yelled, and swung the flail back like a pendulum then hucked the weapon into the ogre's chest. The ogre folded into the heavy iron, not wanting anything more to do with the game. With a dull thud, the flail smacked the ground, and its owner took another step back, but caught on a thick serpent root, catching his heel, sending him toppling to the ground.

"Well fuck." Enzo displayed a flat palm to his mate's opposing fist.

"Paper beats rock."

Lucas' blood was still hot, and Enzo was feeding off the tension emanating from him; the anger that had pooled was now boiling. The ogre whimpered, splayed flat, and held his hands in front of his face. Bare clawed feet kicked at the soil, but he was sliding less than a pace with each attempt. Though the squires could not understand the ogre's tongue, they recognized this.

"I offered you an honest chance," Enzo said as he snatched the flail that was partially buried in the mossy turf. "Now, let's try this again."

With no more space to retreat, the ogre rested his head against the trunk of a massive cherry, one of the many ancient trees in the orchard, and gurgled a final plea. There was no more fight left in the young ogre, and all requests for mercy were not recognized.

Enzo leaned backward, holding the flail as a fishing pole, and brought it down directly onto the ogre's forehead, scraping his nose, undershooting the target. What was meant to be a killing blow became a maiming shot, and the ogre squealed, pressing the gash with both hands, blood flowing over blinded eyes.

Winding up a return strike, Enzo whirled a bit on his heel, nearly toppling, as he aimed for the side of the weeping ogre's head. The impact was sound this time, and the foe no longer suffered.

"What the hekk, Enz." Lucas offered the discarded shield, heavy dents brightly accented.

"What?"

WITHOUT SWINGING HIS MASSIVE HAMMER, the alpha feinted several rushes, jutting his jaw, daring Nathan to be the first to die.

A pair of tusks curled to a tapered end, perhaps less than an inch from the ogre's eyes. *This one has seen many, many seasons...I think I'm in over my head here.* Panic signals radiated from his brain stem, urging his feet to fly, but his feet were not paying attention. Instead, they circled the foe, mirroring the colossus' movements in a symmetrical display for the carrion fowl impatiently hovering in the skies overhead.

The alpha's weight shifted, and Nathan noticed the slight change in stance just in time to roll from the charging swing; a tornado of solid steel conjured from a relaxed pose. As the squire rose with his claymore in both hands, he somehow managed to slice the ogre's trailing thigh, then dart back into the shadow of the treeline before the enemy could whirl for a second time.

Bleed him. They are no more than paper dolls. Clemence's voice was a hollow echo in the recesses of his racing mind. The ogre raised the dagda with hands apart, then quickly slid them together as he dropped an overhead swing that whistled on its path, striking the earth with a resounding thud. Nathan scampered to the side to avoid another killing blow, but not before scraping the ogre's forearm with his blade — nearly taking off a hefty chunk.

The ogre pressed the floppy bit of flesh to his side, blood washing down in unhealthy torrents. A growl of disgust escaped from the ogre's throat as he took notice of the wound.

Setting the mammoth sized hammer down against his hip, he tried to press the flesh back together with no result, then attempted to pick the hammer back up with greasy red fingers, but fumbled and dropped it. With another growl, the ogre wiped a crimson smear from peck to naval, effectively drying his fingers, then snatched the resting weapon and tilted his head back, cracking vertebra like hollow bones.

He's enjoying this. Nathan remarked to himself as he rolled onto the balls of his feet, waiting for the next display.

The ogre wagged his left hand then locked onto the weapon with an iron vice grip. Horns parallel to the ground, he charged, sending debris flying. Nathan rolled from the storm, his heel nearly impaled, then made to kneel, blade in one fist as he regarded the ferocious turn, and pressed chest to dirt as the dagda's breeze fluttered the back of his loose tunic. Pushing off, he tucked into another roll, desperate to be free of the ogre's reach.

No signs of slowing. I must make more cuts. His eyes darted to the left, sensing movement. *Lucas?* A suit of armour clinging to a modestly framed squire burst into the clearing, just out of the ogre's periphery. The squire was hekkbent, and the monster did not take notice. Leaning forward with blade trailing, he sliced the alpha's tendon where it connected at the calf, and renewed his pace, removing himself from retaliation.

A moment passed before the ogre crunched his eyes closed and howled, nearly dropping the dagda; the weapon slid a dozen inches in his grip before the haft struck against mossy carpet.

You beautiful bastard. Nathan thought gratefully and surged forward, anticipating the ogre's downfall. The alpha attempted to settle his weight, but found it impossible, and fell forward, the weight of his hammer directing his descent. The wounded leg collapsed from underneath, and falling to a knee, the ogre met the squire's onslaught.

With precision, Nathan pivoted his hips, focusing the full force of his body into a two handed swing that sent the nearby butterflies into a tailspin. Using every fiber of his being, the squire directed the critical blow into the ogre's neck, attempting a clean decapitation.

A smile tinged the ogre's granite lips as he tilted his chin and lowered his great tusks. Painful shockwaves reverberated into the squire's arms, sending shouts of anguish throughout his being. He had expected a softer target, and the solid revelation made his head reel. Taking a step to the side, he watched the wounded colossus rear his head back and scream peals of laughter into the vast woodlands.

*What the...*Nathan's blade suddenly felt out of balance. Holding it up, he realized with horror that the weapon was shattered. Nearly two thirds of the claymore was scattered all over the clearing. The ogre was still clutching his hammer like a mighty king with a scepter, and he turned and tilted his head to look down at the squire from behind elated cheekbones, still echoing laughter.

Nathan took an unhurried step forward and buried what remained of his blade into the alpha's throat, twisting the guard to avoid the parallel tusks. With the force of ten thousand fists, the ogre clamped his jaw shut, exploding the blade into shards like shrapnel. Several buried into Nathan's wrist and face as he jumped back and released the pommel with an open-mouthed look of terror gracing his visage.

An oddly satisfied groan escaped the horned terror as he released the dagda and fell forward, his final guffaws still ringing in the trees. Nathan watched as the alpha's face crumpled into the earth, and two heartbeats passed before his weapon followed suit.

Nathan doubled over, and mumbled to himself as Enzo and Lucas approached, creaking their visors open.

"What did he say?" Enzo asked, turning to Lucas, who shrugged in reply.

"Paper dolls," Nathan wheezed, sucking in all the air that he could.

NATHAN FLEXED HIS HAND, then waved it, shaking out the needles before attempting to unclasp the left pauldron.

A dip in the river will calm my nerves and clean the stink of ogre off of me, he thought as he dropped the armour on the ground. Rolling his eyes, he realized his lapse and scooped up the floppy steel sections, then walked to the tree and secured them with the rest of his armour.

The squire noticed his *one-handed sword* and shield, suspended with the rest of his equipment, and his anxiety soared, reaching new heights. The nearby horse sensed the unrest and briefly shied away as he approached. Raising both hands, he assured her, "My problems are not yours, old lady." Nathan slowly brought one hand onto the bridle as the mare's eyes gradually calmed. *She feels my weakness.* "Let's get you to the drink, eh?" Leading her, they walked side by side as old friends.

"Where are you off to?"

A tremor jolted Nathan at the sound, and turning his head, he spotted Lucas and Enzo traipsing toward the camp. Lucas was balancing the ogre's cudgel in his palm, vertically, rushing forward as it tilted, keeping up with its momentum. Both squires carried a piece of battlefield spoils, Enzo favoring the flail, their shields strapped to their backs.

"Getting this filth off," Nathan responded, tilting his chin at the river, breaking stride to reply.

"Ah! The stink is a good reminder!" Enzo lifted the weapon with uneven hands on the haft, the striker swinging in an oval pattern smashed into his higher fist. "Fack!" The unbalanced weapon toppled onto the ground with a dull thud, sending grasshoppers flying.

"We'll sort out the breakfast situation while you get squeaky clean down there," Lucas promised with his attention remaining focused on the cudgel.

"Aye." Nathan clicked his teeth and resumed his trek, the horse pawing the earth before stepping out of earshot.

"I'm so famished I could eat an ogre's ass." Enzo picked clumps of soil from the striker's crown.

"Eh? Well, in that case, you're in luck." Lucas watched the cudgel drop from his palm, the heavy end burying itself an inch or so into the soil.

Enzo laughed. "Nothing like a bit of slaughter first thing in the morning. Although I wish we had a feast to look forward to now. But we don't."

"Nope." Lucas raised his chin, unlacing his helm. "Only hard, salted meat and dry bread on the menu, pal."

Enzo rubbed his maille-covered fist, dreaming aloud, "Wish we had a whole boar on a spit or maybe a couple dozen hunks of venison tenderloin. Mmmm, with some duck eggs and capers and onions and a few red peppers...the meat sizzling and popping..."

"Stop with that." Lucas fanned the coals, bringing them back to life. "You're getting my mouth watering and all we have is this dry tack."

"I like the imagining." Enzo was up to his elbows in the perishable supply satchel, foraging for the breakfast lineup. "We have enough for several days in here. You think we'll go through it all, or should I set out a little victory bonus?"

"Surprise me." Placing a log on the expanding flames, Lucas continued. "I think I might catch a wink before Nate gets back." Settling back into the previous night's groove under the tree, his armour cupped his back and shoulders, which was a fairly comfortable arrangement, aside from the lack of neck support.

"I, for one, am surprised at how well our buddy Nate fared against that bloody massive monster." Enzo hugged the breakfast selections to his chest plate, and walked over to a flat stump.

"Oh, Enz," Lucas sighed, squinting at his friend. "You could have at least rinsed your armour before pressing the vittles against it."

Looking down at the cherry smears, Enzo wiped his armour with his hands, the maille scraping loudly, as he apologized. "My mistake, my mistake."

"Ugh, that sound! Get a rag, you git." Lucas shook his head, ears brushing against his stacked bundle pillow. He began to drift off, eyes closed, listening as Enzo retrieved a few rags from his armour kit and dabbed them from his canteen, mumbling concerns the entire time. The combined efforts of the crackling fire and the morning sunshine delivered an all-encompassing warmth, and Lucas accepted the benefits, lightly dozing, intermittently snoring upon inhales.

"Paper dolls!" Enzo practically shouted as he arranged breakfast, kneeling against the stump. The fire sputtered as a log shifted, sending an ashy cloud into the breeze. Choking on the dust, Lucas snorted and cursed, opening his eyes.

"What did you say?" Flexing folded arms, Lucas lifted his head an inch to peek at Enzo.

"Paper dolls," Enzo replied, speaking with an inside voice. "It's what—"

"Aye, aye, yes." Lucas tipped his head back, blinking hard at the myriad of leaf-engulfed branches, trying to clear his eyes of the murky film. "Probably some nonsense he picked up from Clem."

"Well, that nonsense worked pretty good. That was a hekk of a blow on that ogre's tooth." Enzo went back to his task of arranging breakfast portions, and Lucas closed his eyes again.

"Ya think if we woulda had an elf with us, we woulda gotten into that tussle?" Enzo asked without looking up.

So we're having a conversation now. Lucas squinted an eye and wrestled back up onto his elbows. "Maybe?" Opening both eyes, he continued, "You're really not supposed to go this far into the Fang without a guide, but we're not *that* far into the weeds."

"We're on the rim, I think. Phillip and Clem made it pretty clear not to go too far north from here."

"Aye." Lucas edged further back, and propped himself up on the trunk. "What do you imagine an elf woulda done different?"

Enzo held up a strip of meat and scrubbed it against one of the rags nearby. "I don't rightly know. It's pretty hard to think about what an elf would do. Those pointy eared blokes just have a sense about 'em that we don't have, ya know?"

"Ancestral knowledge."

"Right," Enzo agreed, waving the strip at Lucas. "But, maybe they woulda known...or maybe sensed the ogres' approaching? Or maybe they woulda known that this is a common ogre trail?"

"Or *maybe* they woulda done exactly as Nathan did, an woken us up to pitch a fight."

Enzo nodded, and began fiddling with the breakfast portions, arranging them meticulously; he was bothered by asymmetrical designs and one particular stubborn hunk of bread refused to lay upright. Even after dimpling its edges, creating a better platform, the stale prick remained insolent.

Lucas spoke with a chuckle, "I hope Nate gets back soon, not only because I'm starving, but also to avoid seeing you suffer some sorta hemorrhage over there."

"Ya ever wanna take a tumble with an elf?"

"Whoa, what?"

"You heard what I said," Enzo confirmed, speaking in a weird accent.

"Can't really say that I haven't *thought* about it. But they're not really my type, in all honesty." Lucas responded and pitched a twig into the flames.

"Oh, I think about it. I mean, I really think about it." Enzo's eyes conveyed nothing but sincerity.

"I'll bet you do."

"No. I do." Enzo's eyes were shining with fervor, matching the fire's intensity.

Lucas rummaged in his satchel, leaning further than was comfortable as he attempted to change the subject. "Now where did I put my pipe?"

"What about the ones at the orphanage?"

Lucas paused, hand still buried in his bag before replying, "That's a road that I would rather not tread with ya right now, mate."

Enzo fought back the urge to press, willfully forcing lips tight, and set about disfiguring the impudent chunk of dough.

"When Nate bumbles back here, I'll see if he can spot me another bowl of that sweet leaf." Lucas settled his pipe between his teeth and rolled his jaw, bouncing the bowl. "C'mon Nate, we're wasting away here."

A copse of trees barred the river view, so Nathan's bathing progress was entirely a mystery. Lucas' inner timetable told him that Nathan should be wrapping up soon, barring any nasty encounters. *I really can't watch this guy arrange, then rearrange our food like my touched-in-the-head cousin for much longer.* He heaved a deep sigh, rolling his eyes, then noticed a change in scenery, he rolled them back down. *Finally.*

With tunic clinging to his skin, Nathan strode into their midst, arms stretched in front of him like a zombie.

"Now that's a breakfast!" Enzo nearly toppled the meat and bread mosaic in his excitement. Clutched in Nathan's fists were a pair of river trout, wriggling and flinging droplets. The sunshine had dried the glistening rainbow sheen of their scales, leaving a sticky film. River water continued to drip from Nathan's hair as he took a step and underhanded one of the flopping fish at Enzo. Enzo tried to catch the fishy projectile, but when it made contact its smooth skin slid out and away. The squire tried to rein it in, but lost control and ended up squeezing it into the air like a slick bar of soap.

Going onto all fours, Enzo exclaimed, "Oh this is going to be so good!" He salivated as he brought the fish onto the stump, clearing a space with the back of his hand. Nathan offered the second fish to Enzo, who received it looking it in the face and sucking in his cheeks, imitating its gasping mouth.

"I need to dry off," Nathan announced, beginning to wring his long hair out like a wet towel. "The rags are still with the oil and armour supplies?"

"Aye!" Lucas shouted to the passing squire. "You mind if I dig out some more of your pipe leaf?"

"Help yourself," Nathan offered, removing his tunic and wiping himself down. "It's in the—oh, you already found it, never mind."

Lucas was already leaning into the fire lighting a long matchstick while holding an overflowing pipe that bore a strong resemblance to a hairy spider mashed in a bowl, the wooden stem clenched between his incisors. After stoking the bowl with a few gentle puffs, he reclined against the trunk before speaking. "We found something for ya." From behind him among the roots, he reached back and pulled out the pommel of Nathan's exploded claymore.

"You shouldn't have," Nathan spoke through clenched teeth, securing his chest plate with a leather strap in his mouth.

"It weren't nothing," Enzo said as he produced a pan filled with white fish flakes and approached the lapping flames. As he leaned down, Lucas tossed the pommel to Nathan, and the steel guard almost smashed into the cook on its course through the fire. "Crying in the rain!" Enzo barked. He zeroed in a death glare on Lucas.

Nathan watched as Lucas began his story, in spite of the beam of hatred focused intently upon him. "That alpha fell right on top of it as you jumped away, so me and Enz found a really rigid stick, almost a log, really, and we pried the dead oaf up just enough for Enz to slither under."

"*Slither*," Enzo cut in spitefully. He resumed his cooking activity, lowering the pan closer to the yellow center. "Such a flatterer."

Lucas continued as if there had been no interruption. "We wanted to do something with that massive dagda hammer, but we couldn't manage to move it as we were. Woulda been a shame to leave it for the gremlins, so we buried it a bit and placed some sticks and leaves atop it."

"It'll fetch some coin, to be sure," Enzo spoke, mesmerized by the gradual browning flakes, crispness overtaking the moist.

Nathan held the leather pommel in his hands, only a husk of its former glory. "Thank you, boys," he said sincerely. His stomach gurgled as the breakfast aroma reached his nostrils.

"Wish I woulda brought seasonings." A frown carved into Enzo's countenance as he muttered, "And that wine."

The look on Nathan's face as he gazed at the broken sword was remarkable to Lucas. "How are ya holdin' up over there?" he asked, blowing a smoke trail from the side of his mouth.

Shaking his head, blinking Lucas into focus, Nathan began, "Oh it's just..." The words hung in the air for a few seconds, then a crackling log shifted, tossing sparks, and the mild distraction allowed Nathan to collect his thoughts. "Honestly, it's been years since I have held a long sword. The last time was probably in the sparring yards, before I left to begin squiring. And that claymore became an extension of my body, you know? Clemence had me focus my sword training using only heavy blades. Luckily, I brought my one handed sword along, only because of the church's rule for squires and knights to have them at all times. It's been purely decorative to me, you know? I'd sooner use it as a letter opener at this point."

"Won't it be easier wielding the one-hander?" Enzo lifted a morsel to his lips, giving it a gentle blow before placing it onto his tongue.

"It'll be awkward," Lucas answered for him.

"And I've never killed a man before," Nathan added, watching Enzo gingerly shake the pan, pouring out portions onto three wooden plates, counting each flake for fairness and symmetry. "So, yeah." He wanted to express more, but his brain was growing numb from hunger.

"Wouldn't worry too much over it," Lucas said and sat up to receive his breakfast, taking a long pull on the pipe before setting it aside. "It's pretty much the same as killing anything, I'd wager. And you've killed faewolves, and they're kinda like men. Well, closer to men than a ghoul or something."

"Besides," Enzo spoke with his mouth full, a few crumbs spilling out. "As long as everything goes to plan—" He swallowed, the lump passing down his stubbled windpipe. "You won't be doing any killing." Taking another bite, he chewed vigorously. "We might only need ya to help us chop up the body, and you won't need a sword and shield for that."

12

"Alright, alright!" Sir Gwayne pressed an annoying branch out of his way. "I get it." He was following the east bank of the river, traveling north toward a gremlin village he had heard of from one of the other knights before they parted ways.

"Yeah it's there somewhere." Gwayne recalled the conversation with Sir Palomides before they abandoned him. "I think it was Gareth that shot a doe in that area, and we tracked the blood trail for a ways but never found her. Too bad too, it was—"

"Never mind the deer," Gwayne had said. "What of the gremlins? The little thieves." The last three words a growl.

"Oh, yeah." Palomides had scratched the top of his head, distracted by the other knights' departure. "I don't remember too much really. We passed by a glade filled with rusty armour, it was scattered all about, and one of the guys in the hunting party made a joke or something about it." Then Palomides mounted his horse and set off to join his companions.

Didn't even bid farewell. Gwayne had watched his brothers in arms ride away, taking along his beloved Delilah with his armour strapped to her saddle. Now he wore a hunter's tunic under a grayish-green traveling cloak. The entire ensemble had been crafted by laif spinstresses at the top of their game; the shop was found somewhere deep in some forest. Gwayne didn't know where.

He carried a satchel over his shoulder and a sword on his hip. A brilliant white sabaton adorned his left foot, an extravagantly expensive piece of laif craft, while his right bore a regular tracker's boot. The pure white enamel on this solitary fragment of his armour contained a mystery; it remained untarnished after walking miles through muddy hollows and slurping mossy bogs.

The revered blacksmith who sold him the glossy plate had *warned* him that the armour would not need to be oiled like steel, and that its patina would never fade or even favor a smudge. *Low maintenance* is what he had said, and Gwayne liked the sound of that. But his first foray into the forest had proved irksome for his companions as they found themselves traveling with a shimmering bullseye.

"You're single. I'm single. I get it," Gwayne said to himself as he vaulted a felled elm that had probably been struck by lightning, heavy splinters maintained a seemingly impossible hold on the heavy upper portion. "But it is not becoming of someone in your standing to—Ack!"

A freshly spun cobweb with the dew still imprinted sprang into being directly in front of the knight who had somehow managed to overlook its glittery existence, and smashed his entire face into it. He pulled and plucked, gagging and coughing, waving frantic hands over his hair, trying to knock loose any spiders on his head. Tugging his fingers through some knots, the knight slowed down and began to breathe normally again as he searched his body for any stragglers that had managed to remain clinging.

"Now, where were we?" Gwayne asked, straightening up. To his right was a swampy maze with hanging vines draped all over, plastered in moss, weaving in and out. It smelled like early spring over there, a biting chill lingering over the musky aroma of the newly thawed soil.

I will be avoiding that.

Gwayne opted to stay close to the river as it perpetually traveled north; the direction in which he was headed. This course held its own irritations and perils, but at least he wouldn't get sucked down by quicksand or get his shoulders ripped off by a musk troll. Most of his time was spent circumventing the jumbled mess of limbs and thorns that barred reasonable passage; veritable cobwebs unto themselves, although much less sticky. He refused to use his sword to create a path, instead opting to clamber and shimmy. Tugging free of brambles and needles, he regained his balance only to press his palm into a set of spikes inconveniently growing against some sort of spiny needle tree.

"What even the hekk are you?!" he yelled, waving his hand around and kissing the puncture wound. His hand went to the scabbard at his side instinctively, but caught himself. *Oh, no Gwayne. We mustn't do such a thing. He isn't worth it.* Casting a wicked glare at the undisturbed spike tree, he cursed it, willing the vibrant thriving plant to wither and die in its overly healthy roots.

"Blood and glory is all that Quintus feasts upon," he said, explaining his decision to the indifferent tree. "Trail blazing is for lesser blades." Tapping the pommel at his side, he sauntered past only to find himself facing hundreds of the trees, seemingly mocking him, armoured like horrible spiky—

"Arseholes," the knight muttered with a palm firmly pressed over his eyes.

GWAYNE EMERGED FROM THE NIGHTMARE ORCHARD looking as though he walked into a tornado filled with feral cats. He had sustained lacerations all over his forearms and face, yet his clothing was relatively unharmed. Hardly even a thread hung loose.

Goes to show, you can't compete with those laif spinners. Worth every brick of gold. Gwayne recalled the shop had been filled with gorgeous laives, each set upon her work, dutifully creating amazing bits of fashion all without sparing him a glance. *Very few women are out of my league.* "But those spinning laives," he said, humming like a lovestruck schoolboy. "It would take an eleven to have even the slightest chance with them."

A grackle perched above cackled derisively before setting off, leaving the branch bouncing in its wake.

"Haw, haw," Gwayne mumbled darkly as he pressed on. The terrain before him was much more docile, and through the twigs and heavy boughs he could see the semblance of a clearing. Taking an optimistic step forward, he nearly landed on his chin as his armoured foot caught a distended root. Catching himself with one arm, the knight bounded back to a stand and growled at the inanimate earthy tube. "You little prick," he cursed, wiping his chin. Upon seeing that his stumble had brought him into the clearing, he whispered, "This looks nice."

After parting the hair that had fallen over his eyes and taking a few careful strides forward, the knight stood before a serene haven. A log from an ancient tree lay at an angle against the most aromatic weeping cherry Gwayne had ever seen. The log itself appeared as a soft cushion. Covering the entire circumference, from ground to top was the most inviting mossy blanket.

Looks so soft. Running a hand over the plushy shroud confirmed his suspicion, *it is so soft.* The cherry blossoms provided a canopy, rescuing the knight from the rays of the afternoon sun. Seizing the opportunity, he set his satchel against the log and climbed on top. Leaning back against the tree, he released a sigh as he breathed in the delicate spring scents, and surrounded by pallid blossoms, the knight decided to take a nap and try to forget the ridiculous wounds all over his face and arms.

The river was not too wide, but he had no plans to ford it anyhow. As he lazily gazed at the opposite bank, he began speaking to himself again. "Where the river a-widens, it's kapreta you'll be a-findin'." Reciting the old saying, he assured himself that he was safe for the time being.

After closing his eyes and trying to sleep, the knight found his body wanted to keep moving, and sleep was elusive. *I'll take a few puffs, then set back out.* He reached down, arm dangling as it reached for his purse, then he snatched the corner clasp and brought the bag onto his lap.

Gwayne squinted, adjusting his eyes as the sun peeked from behind a bundle of cumulus, and the brilliance reflected on the rushing waters was a bit painful. The man pinched a clump of leaf and stuffed it into his briar pipe. With his other hand, he produced a flint kit and blazed a matchstick in one swipe. Soon the knight was producing tufts of smoke which tumbled from his mouth and nostrils. He buried his nose in the small leather pouch containing the pipeweed, and took a long inhale before securing the leather thong and stowing it back in his purse.

The previous night, his first night in the forest—after being forsaken by his fellow knights—Gwayne had not obtained a very fit amount of sleep. Now frustration was building as he realized that he needed to catch up on rest, but the jackass living in his brain said no.

He had always struggled with maintaining a healthy sleep state, and was easily roused by the slightest twig snap or belching snore. It came in handy when on guard duty, but gaining the strength and stamina from a healthy sleep was a delightfully rare occurrence. He usually found himself spending a portion of the morning groggy before the cobwebs dissipated, even on better days.

The mounting frustration only bolstered his body's unwillingness to relent, so Gwayne tried to relax. "Not like I have much going on anyhow." And as if his surrender to remain conscious contained some sort of magic spell, the knight soon felt his shoulders ease and his chin droop. The briar pipe tumbled into his lap, leaving behind a trail of charred remains.

Frogs burped and birds chirped, adding to the mellow chorus that hummed around the river retreat. And Gwayne was finally winning the battle, overtaking the hours of unrest, finally on a course toward victory over exhaustion.

"That has always been the problem!" A woman's voice rang out from somewhere in the lofty heights.

Gwayne's eyelids fluttered open. *Damn dream woman! Waking me up.* He squeezed a fist onto his ribcage, irritated at the disruption. Although the source transpired in his subconscious, he yawned and leaned back. *Let's try this again.*

"Whenever the time comes to act, you are always sitting on your haunches or nowhere to be found! And if by some act of *divine intervention*, you are around, then you are more than happy to spectate!"

What the—? Anger boiled in Gwayne's throat, rising like acid. The knight's eyes snapped open, as he came to the realization, *That was definitely not in my dream.* He choked back his fury, looking around to see who the shrieking harpy was *and pacify her with heavy rock.*

"The world is passing you by! And you are content just being a *spectator!*" The shrill beration emanated from somewhere above, seemingly in the tree.

"I'm no spectator," Gwayne muttered to himself, looking up, tracing a line with his optics; the plethora of blossoms and branches inhibited a complete climb.

"This is how I have always been!" said a whiny man's voice, and Gwayne nodded, his suspicions confirmed.

She isn't yelling at me.

"*This is how I have always been!*" The woman mocked.

Ouch. Gwayne winced.

"It's true!" the guy stated. "I leave the forest alone and it leaves me alone for the most part. And I don't ask for anything! And is it so wrong that I expect everyone to do the same? That's doing my duty!" Gwayne imagined the guy folding his arms.

"You do the bare minimum!"

"I do what I'm told!"

"Barely!"

"Just enough!"

"Just enough for what?!"

When you're in a hole, mate, it's best to stop digging, Gwayne silently advised the man.

There was a lull, then a woman's loud sigh.

The guy continued in a drastically softer voice. "I don't see why you're so upset? There was nothing I could do."

Gwayne stood up on the log to better eavesdrop, and his pipe fell onto the grassy floor.

"It's not just this one time!" the woman shouted. "It's every time! It's not an isolated incident! You *spectate*! You don't act!"

"What could I have done, Leandra?"

Leandra?

"Oh, I don't know! Make an effort once in awhile! This isn't just today! Oh no! It's every day! Every chance you get to make a difference for *someone* else, you sit out. Take a breather. An opportunity presents itself; gift wrapped and everything and you roll over and go back to sleep." A long-drawn feminine sigh registered through the bark. "I know this is how you have always been and I love you for that. But it would be a flat out lie if didn't say I wished that you would change. And I know that's not fair, but—wait!"

Oh shit.

"Where are you going?!"

He's hosing up.

"If you leave, Figharth, do not come back!"

There it is.

"Wh-what do you mean?" came the reply. "I mean to have children with you someday."

Little guy sounds crestfallen.

"I will bear you no children." Each syllable Leandra spoke was as ice.

Gwayne cringed and tugged at his collar.

Leandra continued. "Not unless you can prove to me that you have changed. I am giving you one last chance. After which I will be forced to seek the companionship of a more *suitable* caller."

"But how—" Figharth began.

"Stop spectating!" Leandra sounded weary. "Become a part of something. Make me proud for once in your life."

Damn. Gwayne thought, gently gliding down and feigning sleep as he tried to avoid an awkward encounter with whoever would be coming out of the hollow. *Weeping cherry. Such a clever name.* Chuckling, he closed his eyes and pulled up his hood, unaware of the fluttering creature that had emerged from a crevice over his covered head.

Thinking of his amazing destrier, Delilah, he was picturing himself in the stables again, tossing apples into her mouth as the pair shared a hearty laugh. She was his best friend. He had spotted her from a distance when she was merely an awkward foal, legs like twigs, but prancing harder than any other yearling in the meadow. *Or maybe she spotted me?* A tight lipped smile crested his face. They had imprinted on one another and their story became legendary, at least to them.

"Excuse me." Figharth's voice was suddenly much closer.

Gwayne tilted his head and opened his eyes under the cowl's shadow. *Oh man. A wisp. Shoulda known.*

"I didn't want to bother you. You looked so cozy and all—"

"Did I?" Gwayne asked. The words exited much harsher than he had intended and the wisp shuddered.

"I am sorry, yes, very sorry..." The creature trailed off, but his beak continued to move wordlessly.

The little fellow had the head of a scorch owl and the body of a proper gentleman, resplendent in a three piece suit, the overcoat un-buttoned and loosely framing the thin creature's torso. A pair of rather magnificent wings, mimicking those of a butterfly, cascaded from the creature's back and fluttered lazily, somehow managing to keep the lit-tle birdman afloat.

Dangling a hand's breadth from Gwayne's face, the creature spoke again. "But, but I noticed a rather fine looking pipe on the ground below you, and taking it upon myself, I retrieved the implement and placed it on that particularly flat patch of moss over yonder." The wisp fluttered to the right, allowing Gwayne to see. "Forgive my intrusion, but I would be remiss to sit and do – to sit by and..." his beak did that wordless movement again, and the wisp wilted like a daisy, lowering down onto Gwayne's lap, and burying his face in his little gentleman hands. White gloves and all.

The knight lifted a hand to pat the tiny creature, but refrained. "There, there, little guy. Things can't be all bad..." Gwayne attempted to sound sincere, but fell short.

The wisp's shoulders hunched and he mumbled something through his hands that was entirely indiscernible.

"I'm sorry, little friend guy, I didn't catch—"

Leaning his owl head back, he howled, "Things are *that* bad!" Then he returned his head to his hands, shoulders now shrugging violently around strangled whimpers.

If I stand up maybe... "Well, hey there now, little guy. I was actually pretty much all done with my afternoon nap, so I was planning on getting on my way..." Gwayne tentatively scooched backward.

"Oh sir!" The wisp cried, now on his knees and clinging fervently to the knight's tunic, his feathery face soaked. "Tarry a few moments? Allow me to overtake composure, please? Please? Please?"

Just stand up real quick. "Alright." Gwayne sighed, and folded his hands on his stomach. "What do you want to talk about?" *Not like I have a tight schedule today anyhow.*

The wisp sniffled heavily as he stood to his dainty fancy shoed feet. "Allow me a proper introduction," he said, wiping his wet face with the back of his tailored cuffs. "My name is Figharth, and you may have heard of my house?" He paused, tilting his head as if expecting Gwayne to applaud. "Of the Faehouse Stantowlford." He finished, and interlocked his fingers under his belly while giving a formal bow.

Gwayne was not well versed in faery and wisp culture, and responded unenthusiastically. "Oh, wow. Yeah, that's neat."

"I take it you are not familiar with the Faehouse Stantowlford?"

"You would be correct."

"I see." Figharth placed his chin in his hands, both wings moving slightly, but he remained on Gwayne's lap. "How can I put this? I am basically royalty, in certain sensibilities. Well, not *royalty* per se, but we own land and have servants, and we are quite wealthy." Looking up at the knight, he continued his explanation. "By fae standards, at least."

"So, like a duke?" Gwayne asked, squinting one eye.

"Well, yes, yes, I suppose so. Actually, my father, Tendervitch would be considered the duke. And I am next in line for succession."

"That's very neat." Gwayne displayed a toothless smile.

"And who may I have the pleasure of addressing?" Figharth's disturbingly laif-like eyes gazed up at Gwayne with a weird sort of glimmer.

"You can call me Gwayne."

The wisp stumbled back, placing one gloved hand to his forehead. "Not *the* Sir Gwayne of Camelot? Can it be?" he began, blinking a spastic shutter and his beak was moving again without any words tumbling out.

"Yep," Gwayne replied. "The very same. Have you heard of me?"

Uttering something resembling a cackle, and shaking his feathery head, Figharth managed to eke out his words. "Come now, you mustn't be jesting? *Everyone* knows who the knights of Camelot are!" The wisp let out another disturbing cackle, and with that, bent his knees and took flight. "Are you on a quest that requires such great discretion that it must be carried out by a lone knight?" His eyes swept the landscape hungrily. "Or are you not alone on this quest? Are there other bold knights accompanying you on this quest?"

"Nope, just me."

"But you're on a quest."

"Not exactly. The other night—"

Hovering inches from Gwayne's nose, resting his chin in both hands, the wisp spoke eagerly. "This is going to be good."

The knight tried to lean away but his back was already pressed as far as it could be against the tree trunk. "The other night while I was sleeping, I was set upon by—"

"Faewolves! Aspweavers! Drakes! Hobs! Strangle Death Squids!" the fae interrupted excitedly.

"No, no. Nothing like that." Gwayne inclined his head to his feet, and the wisp rotated in midair.

"Gremlins." They said in unison.

Gwayne was unimpressed with the timing, but the wisp clearly revered it as kismet, his eyes bulging and beak open in pure rapture.

"You're seeking your lost arms!" Figharth declared.

Gwayne nodded hesitantly.

"You *do* have a quest!"

Gwayne flinched, but nodded.

"Well, fortune has smiled at you, sir knight!" Figharth shouted joyfully, wings beating unevenly and causing his little feet to dangle oddly. "I am Fenrirfang's fae historian! I prefer the company of books and candles to the frivolity and nonsense of my kinsman!"

"I'm listening."

"I own maps upon maps upon maps! I can lead you to each and every gremlin village within this vast array of trees and beasts and monsters and daemons!" The wisp was desperate to show his paramour that he could be more than a spectator, and this could be his chance.

Gwayne sniffed and hardened his gaze. "These maps are probably much too small for me to—"

"I will accompany you!"

"What a lovely notion," Gwayne said dryly.

"Just indulge me merely a few seconds to retrieve—" Suddenly reality dawned on the little wisp, and his face fell, beak moving wordlessly again.

"What's the matter, Figharth?" Gwayne inquired.

The mist covering the wisp's eyes cleared after a few hard blinks, and he turned to the knight. "The maps were burned in a fire."

"Were they now?"

"Yep. Burned to priceless little cinders. Very sad. I have hardly gotten over it. See?" Figharth pointed at his left eye.

Gwayne leaned close. "What am I looking for?"

"Why, the overabundance of tears!" Figharth shouted, turning away so quickly that his coattails swung like a gown.

"Well, I guess that doesn't really help me too much so I'll just be..." Trailing off, Gwayne removed one leg at a time from the log perch, and leaned toward his pipe.

"Wait!" The wisp clutched the knight's outstretched hand. "The map is right here!" he declared, bouncing a fancy white finger against his feathered temple.

"Is it now?" Gwayne wrapped his hand around the briar bowl of his pipe and sat up. Beyond the river, he noticed shimmering movements between the trees that lined the opposite bank.

Is that—?

Sure enough, a mounted knight was riding, the sounds of a destrier pounded just above the rush of the river.

Figharth took notice of the drastic change in the knight's demeanor and turned to face the same direction.

Gwayne's eyes rested on a gap in the tree line, waiting for the rider to grace his sight. When the horse became visible, he instantly recognized the gait.

Delilah?!

Further along the bank, several more shapes with matching glimmer broke from their positions and charged at the mounted knight.

"Oh my!" Figharth gasped.

One of the ambushers held a long pike in his hands and charged the rider, catching him unaware, aiming below the saddle.

"Delilah!"

13

Elkara walked along the drastically uneven terrain on the east side of the river, her boot soles slipping over the knurled roots as she pushed aside the army of branchlets that hampered easy passage. Closer to the river, Error plodded along, maintaining a parallel course with his partner. Brambles and sharp thorns grasped her sleeves, making her twirl between the plants, stirring the branches with each move. Error simply entered the waters when a barricade barred passage.

Many of the leaves were shaped like cups, and the morning's dew had overfilled the tiny cisterns. When the laif disturbed one such piece of foliage, the pools upturned, splashing uninvited refreshment into her leather armour. She cursed and shook as the chilly liquid blasted her armpits, causing millions of goosebumps to pop up. "Fack!" she cursed. Lifting her arm, the leather pauldron dumped even more water down her collar. *Aw, come on!* Her damaged boot caught on another root, and she stumbled into a briar branch. It was the final straw. She drew her curved dagger and laid waste to all of the flora within her tornado's reach. Hardly breaking a sweat, the ranger sheathed the blade under her cloak and began to walk.

The swamplands stretching before her were all too familiar. She knew the perils, but also knew the tasty deer that wandered there to dine on the tender strips of lichen that dangled near the frothing lumps of swampy goo. Skirting the hem between bog and deciduous, the laif stalked silently along with her curved bow tightly fastened in her fist.

Her right boot sunk into the soft, mossy soil, and she needed to ease her foot out slowly to prevent the unnaturally loud puckering sound that would ensue.

Quiet as a wraith, we need not be seen today...by man or beast. Her eyes spanned all around, taking careful note of the ground for any tear drop deer tracks, as well as the clumsy steel shod prints of a certain stupid knight blundering about looking for a grifted piece of armour.

She recalled Gwayne's armour bundled to his abandoned horse as Galahalt wrestled it free and handed it on to the nearest royal knight.

What sort of knight wears ivory armour into the woods? She smirked, vaulting a felled maple, sticking the landing. Turning her head to look for Error, she quickly realized that she was much too far from the river to even catch a glimpse of the horse, but she did spot a few broken limbs. They hung haphazardly as if some clumsy brute had blustered through earlier, unaware of the trail he was leaving.

Her smirk evolved into a full smile. *Pay dirt.* The game shifted from meat to man as the laif abandoned the swamp and began to track the human. Although venison was not completely off the menu, she would rather hedge her bets on a more sure thing.

"As I suspected," she whispered. Her hands traced two foot prints, distinctly human or laif. Laives had longer toes, which tended to make the boot size for laives a bit bigger than humans, but they all wore the same sort of shoes.

Her fingers carved the indent of a pointed left boot that had left a more pronounced impression in the soil than its mate. A wayward rhino beetle tumbled into the heel portion of the print, having difficulty navigating the slight discontinuity in the earth. With a flick, Elkara corrected the bug's direction, relieving it from its upside down position. She watched it march away into the green stalks, then focused her attention on the right boot, tracing the curves. *Yep. Now who would be walking through this dangerous forest overflowing with deadly scary crea-tures with a sabaton on only one foot?*

"I know who," she said with satisfaction, as she stood and brushed off her knees. "A fool."

More and more broken branches revealed themselves before her as she followed the obvious path. Growing sick of the vegetation's over reaching and clutching arms, the laif intoned an incantation to send the more egregious offenders reeling as if they had been prodded with a hot iron. She used such workings sparingly; the disturbance it created would often manifest a wave that repelled nearby creatures.

Well, there goes any shot at taking down a stag. Oh wait, what? She beheld a stark auburn discoloration against the green backdrop of the swamp. The doe was shaking her head, as if clearing it of the magic's contamination.

The laif eased down and leaned against a nearby aspen, peering at the game a mere thirty yards distant.

Are you alone, my lady? Elkara swiveled her head, opting to wait and see if a larger candidate with a bit more meat would appear.

Although the doe in her sights was definitely no yearling, she had more than likely mothered many fawns over the years. The laif was hesitant to remove such a producer from the forest, but she was craving fresh meat, already picturing it sizzling over an open fire, savoring that first mouthful.

It would be a shame, really, she thought, especially as she was only planning on harvesting the backstrap from the animal. The rest would be donated to the carrion and scavenger population, who would no doubt be immensely grateful for the contribution. Without a care in the world, the doe resumed munching on a sumac after the foggy intrusion lifted from her brain.

The wait proved fruitless and the laif grew restless, fairly certain that a larger stag would not be arriving. She followed the doe for twenty paces, stalking her movements. As she shrugged and brought her bow up and snatched an arrow, zeroing in over the fletching with both eyes, she heard the sound of men screaming. She twisted her neck in the direction, then snapped back to the deer, discovering with mild frustration that the distinct sound of steel ringing on steel had caused her flight, and all that was waiting was a blank space.

"Aw!" Elkara cried ruefully as she lowered her bow and replaced the arrow. "Wait…"

* * *

SIR GALAHALT SAT UPON A LARGE ROCK and watched his laif guide disappear into the woods beyond. After a spell, he saw Error appear from the treeline, and slosh into the river continuing northward. *Hope she finds what she's seeking.*

He stood up and stretched, and noticing a few smooth stones along the riverbed, loped down the slight grade to investigate the stockpile. When he was a lad, he would while away many afternoons skipping pebbles in the ponds around the fields and meadows. He had perfected his sidearm, and never found an equal within his class, prevailing against all challengers. Smiling at the memory, he bent down to see what sort of rocks were available. Discarding most as inferior, he worked his fingers over the edges and corners, examining them like a prospector hovering over a sieve of gold nuggets.

Too fat. Not smooth enough. Eh, this one might do…

Pinching the smooth stone between his forefinger and middle, the knight beheld the projectile as if it was a priceless artifact. The river was too shallow for skipping, so he pocketed the stone for later.

He shifted his great helm from the pommel to the horse's haunches, then vaulted into the borrowed saddle. Twisting back to replace the helm to the pommel, the knight clicked his teeth and steered the mount forward, pressing his chest to the flat topped helm in order to avoid the branches of the willow they passed under. Under the wispy canopy, Galahalt saw from his periphery a river rat and a badger enjoying a meal against the trunk, as he rode clear.

His leather wrapped spear bounced against the back of his knee, secured parallel to the ground rather than sticking straight up like a pole. As with most of the forest he saw, this patch contained ancient trees with enormous circumferences, and some had even managed to sprout blankets of flowers on their aged bark.

He craned his neck at the canopy above, cracks of sunlight hardly penetrated, and when they did, the rays were filtered so much they lacked any sort of power. The hearty flowers that managed to exist in a culture of darkness reminded the knight of his sister. *Oh, Margot. The girl who wept when she found out that powerful gusts of wind could kill a butterfly midflight. The girl who toiled endlessly in the soil, growing impossible flowers, while I played squire for all those years. And now knight. The girl who pledged her virtue as collateral for a debt, only because she was born without a sign, and our family needed it. Forgive me.*

"Forgive me," Galahalt repeated aloud. The horse's ears twitched back. "Oh, don't mind me, old girl," he said, leaning in the saddle to deliver a reassuring pat onto the destrier's neck. "Just talking to ghosts."

He recalled the primrose path and the legions of birds latched to the tall swinging grass regarding the brother and sister, hand in hand, as they rushed to the meadow beyond. Wisps and fae fluttered their spectral dances over the heaving hillocks of manicured emerald. *We rushed there whenever we could, between the bouts of Uncle Brett's intoxicated blathering and the hours of endless chores. We did that.* It was on one of those impossibly green shoulders blanketed with soft grass that Margot and Galahalt made a promise to always be there for one another.

"You and me, Halty," Margot had said. Naïve children creating indelible pacts, its echoes reverberating as long as they lived. *Even here.*

The knight lowered his head. *They will pay.* His blood was hot, and in that moment, he wished for an adversary to emerge to pay a coward's blood debt.

An immense vulture broke from its perch, sending leafy debris raining down on the knight. Pieces bounced off his armoured shoulders, a soft ting accented the strikes, and Galahalt brushed the clingy bits away.

Peering up at the huge bird's flight path, he was able to infer its destination easily. Its scimitar beak pointed toward a strange tree unlike its neighbors; not a leaf sprouted, and the behemoth appeared dead, but Galahalt sensed otherwise. A skeletal specimen defying tree logic, yet thriving in the environment it was planted ages and ages ago. A sinister aura permeated the air around it, even from the distance, and hooded villains perched in the huge boughs all within plain sight.

Soon the vulture joined her kin, alighting on an empty space near the crown of the skeletal tree. The nearby carrion-feeding monsters reacted with squawks and open winged gesticulations that appeared to the knight as a display of camaraderie. The kettle of vultures indicated...*something.*

This is going to be good. The knight smiled grimly and rested a hand atop his helm. Without further provocation, he released the horse's bridle and lowered his other hand down to his spear, bouncing along with the trot.

A clearing spread before him, the trees surrounding seemed to indicate a pond was nestled in the center, but no, only a carpet of short grass and clusters of mushrooms were evident. He pulled the horse to a stop on the threshold and surveyed the area, searching for some sort of heavy shuffle or any sign of life that promoted an adversary. "You see anything, lady?" he asked, leaning over the helm to whisper in the horse's twitching ear. Common sounds filled the gladescape, tittering birds and buzzing insects darting to and fro, and, of course, the unchanging rush of the river.

The laif was correct, pretty smooth sailing on this side of the river. He passed the threshold. All at once the river hushed; the abrupt silence assaulted knight and horse simultaneously. Holding a hand to his ears, he pressed down and worked his jaw, afraid that he had been struck deaf. The clinking of his own armour dispelled those thoughts. *Magic!* he realized.

Then the clinking of someone else's armour invaded his ears, and Galahalt looked up as his horse shied to the left, shifting him in the saddle. An armoured knight on foot rushed from the hedges brandishing a long spear, and aimed it square at the horse's throat. Galahalt pulled the reins to avoid the thrust and moved the horse out of range, but was unsuccessful and the black steel punched into the destrier's neck. Before she toppled, Galahalt leapt free from the descent, spear in hand. Reaching back with one hand, he removed the tie that bound his hair, and released the cascading locks with a shake. When the battle horse collapsed in a tangled mess of kicking limbs and screaming lips, Galahalt's great helm tumbled free of the pommel and rolled in his direction, as if by some divine intervention. He brought it to a halt with a boot firmly placed on its crown, and greeted the tentatively approaching knight with a smile.

Perfect. With his eyes still on the adversary, Galahalt knelt and retrieved his helm, securing it to his head, leaving the chin strap to dangle. Flinging aside the shroud wrapping his spear, it seemed as if the trees surrounding the glade took a step back, and the knight tilted his head, measuring the foe before him. The pike that was buried in the destrier protruded at an angle from her dying form, the haft shook with each death spasm. The killer swiftly removed it then plunged it deeper, closer to the horse's jawline.

Real classy. Galahalt worked his neck muscles and tucked the spear under his armpit, waiting for his enemy to make a movement of consequence. The foe remained on the balls of his feet with his longsword drawn, but did not advance.

"Stick him!" a second assailant shouted.

Galahalt turned to the orator.

Even more perfect.

Not wanting to waste any more time on such a lovely day, Sir Galahalt focused his attentions on the first asshole who had decided to kill a perfectly good mount without any provocation. Striding forward while listening to the pounding boot falls of Asshole #2 behind him, a red haze seemed to settle over Galahalt's eyes. He surged forward, closing the gap like a snare to a fox.

Asshole #1 was clearly an inexperienced combatant, and barely even hefted his blade to deflect the spear tip that passed clean through his neck just above the maille collar.

Galahalt bounded a stride backward, withdrawing his weapon and flinging blood with a single violent tremor of his wrist.

Gurgling and clutching his throat, Asshole #1 stumbled back, knees buckling as his life receded rapidly.

Galahalt knew that the rush of Asshole #2, now an emotional and screeching rush, would be arriving shortly. He took a few calculated steps, ringing around the sputtering knight who was still clinging to life, remaining on quaking feet. Taking another measured step, Galahalt punched his spear into the dying knight's throat again, intersecting the first penetration, and held it there, waiting for the perfect moment.

Asshole #1 was trying to say something as he limply placed his hands on the haft protruding from his wind pipe. More gurgles emanated from under the conical helm, and the gravely wounded man began to slump.

Oh no, don't die just yet, Galahalt thought as he maintained an eye on Asshole #2.

Pounding footfalls and shrieking hysterics brought #2 within range, a sword in one hand and a shield in the other.

Quickly Galahalt pivoted his hips, slicing clean through Asshole #1's neck, spraying a bloody mist into Asshole #2's path. Thousands of tiny droplets splashed against his closed visor, penetrating the eye slits. Swatting his face, the man frantically tried to remove the filth from his vision.

Inside of two paces, Galahalt slammed the dull end of his spear against Asshole #2's breast plate, sending him on a wayward stumble and flinging his shield aside. His shrieking continued, and seemed to rise an octave when Galahalt put a boot to his chest, knocking him completely over into a heap. Crawling backwards on his elbows and kicking his feet, the man continued shrieking; the words now an articulate phrase, "Please don't, please don't, please don't..."

Galahalt plunged his spear into the man with such force that it buried itself into the soil several inches below the fallen man's backplate. Asshole #2 finally stopped his shrieking, holding onto the spear with both hands as he pleaded for a stay of execution. The blood bubbling from his throat prevented a rational conversation and Galahalt was uninterested in holding a debate.

With an upward pull, Galahalt popped the spear loose and caught it with one sweeping hand.

Asshole #2 propped his visor open. "I'm dying," he rasped faintly.

Galahalt gently eased the man's visor down with his spear. "Yes," he agreed. "You are."

* * *

NATHAN WATCHED IN HORRIFIED SILENCE as his companions were dispatched. Lucas' life was quickly fleeing, and any energy he mustered was only speeding the inevitable. He struggled on the ground, trying to open his visor again, flailing at his helm, his gauntlet bounced off without finding purchase. After another failed attempt, when his hand struck the earth, it remained where it had flopped.

Was this worth dying for? Nathan began to reason with himself as he crouched out of sight behind an overgrown thicket. Against his own sensible protests, the squire rose to meet his fate, the foreign one-handed sword clutched in his hand. A few steps into the glade and the knight took notice of him, turning his head before squaring his shoulders.

Oh shit. He's lightning and I'm the idiot standing out in the open. Fear began to overtake Nathan. *Let him come to you.* A blueprint unfurled in his mind, creating a strategy that presented the only option he could imagine. *Aside from begging for quarter.* If he could parry the strike and deflect it somehow, then maybe he could use the knight's momentum against him. If he tripped, then that would leave him exposed to a quick stab. *He's fucking lightning.*

The knight flicked his spear, splashing more blood from the blade.

Nathan gave his visor a slap, dropping it down, then brought his shield up just under his cheek. He shifted his stance to position his right foot back, cutting the angle of attack.

Holding the spear low in one hand, the knight approached slowly.

Nathan kept his eyes fixed upon the bladed tip, lowering his shield unwittingly. Without breaking stride, the knight struck from below the hip, lashing out like a serpent. Nathan curled inward and raised his shield as the wooden haft brushed along the top rim, bent for his trachea. The angled rise sped the piercing movement off its horrifying course, and Nathan watched with wide eyes as the blade passed out of his limited sight. A warming sensation spread along the side of his neck, but there was no time to reflect on simple wounds. His opponent remained where he stood, just beyond a spear's length, holding the weapon with its haft planted on the ground.

Nathan crumpled the blueprints and threw them away.

Beyond the knight, the pitiful corpses of Enzo and Lucas littered the backdrop in bloody armoured heaps, and Nathan's eyes briefly rested on the lifeless form of the magnificent destrier.

Such a waste of a fine beast.

With a prayer to anyone or anything, Nathan shifted, feeling sticky fluid cascade down his collar.

The knight readied himself, bringing his weapon up with one hand, as one might with a fencing sabre, and placing the other hand behind his back.

This chilled Nathan, in indescribable torrents.

The knight moved as if to strike directly into Nathan's eye slits, and the squire raised his shield in defense, and instantly felt immense pain explode from his left hip. When he tried to balance himself on his left foot, tremors of searing pain strangled his brain, and the squire felt an uneven collapse. *Yield! I yield!* The words formed on his lips, but he was unable to do anything. He knelt with his shield upraised as all his remaining strength drained.

With a half-hearted tap, the spear-wielding knight moved the shield aside with his outstretched weapon, ignoring the pathetic display and plunging his blade into the squire's chest.

The air in Nathan's throat suddenly burst from his quivering lips. Without fully comprehending what had happened, the spear retreated from his chest, passing along its initial course. Steel grated against steel as the blade exited the perforated chest plate. A familiar copper flavor engulfed his mouth, and he was helpless to speak though he felt that he still had so much left to say.

Nathan tried to remain upright forever, trying to shrug off the mortal wound as if it were a joke.

This is the stance I was meant to take when I became a knight.

Within moments, the young squire could no longer breathe comfortably. His lungs felt crinkly, and the ground swelled to the side of his head. The dark tunnel began to close the curtains on his short life, and all he could see beyond the armoured feet of his killer was that beautiful destrier.

Such a waste...

14

Taking a lungful of crisp air after removing the stifling helm, Sir Galahalt allowed the piece of armour to tumble from his grip. His limbs felt loose and stretched, and his mind felt sharp and clear. Scratching his chest with the knuckle of his gauntlet, he looked around the site, noticed his borrowed mount's hind legs were kicking.

I can't allow you to suffer, old gal. He walked toward the jet gray mound and placed his dagger under the unmoving snout.

No clouds. He regarded the mist-free blade then re-sheathed it and stood, grateful that she passed near instantly. *I'll have to walk to the laif's meeting point now. Not a big deal,* the knight thought to himself as he strode over to Asshole #1, leaning over the fresh corpse with arms crossed. The dead man's neck sported bloody gills; deep wounds of evisceration, and the maille sheared around it proved unable to prevent the kill stroke.

Galahalt knelt down to remove the helm from the twisted head which was cocked at an unnatural angle, and after unlacing the leather strap under the sticky chin had to be careful to leave the head attached. Placing one hand in the dead man's lower jaw for leverage, he used the other to pull up on the visor, wresting the helmet free and leaving the corpse relatively intact. A dark haired young man stared blankly at something above Galahalt, both eyes open and completely glazed over.

You were on my porch the other day, Galahalt realized with a jolt of recognition. "Explains why you died so easy," he said, speaking to the dead squire, recalling the young man's station. He looked up at the skeleton tree peppered with vultures and decided to leave the helmet off. Wiping off his bloody palms on the squire's tunic, Galahalt gave the chest plate a heavy tap and stood. *On to Asshole #2.*

Unlacing the helm on this lad proved to be much easier than the first, and the revelation underneath proved equally surprising. "You were also on my porch," Galahalt remarked, holding a one sided conversation with the dead fire haired youth. "Shoulda killed that third one slower, eh? Then maybe I could have gotten some answers to this riddle you idiots thrust at me."

As he walked toward Asshole #3 a shadow passed over him, and the knight smiled. Looking up at the vulture tree, several spaces were vacant, the toll rising as the huge birds lifted themselves into the air with heavy beating wings. *Go for the eyes first,* he mentally suggested to the beasts.

Pressing a boot to Asshole #3's shoulder, the knight shifted the corpse from side to back, steel plate clinking and chattering before coming to a rest. *What do we have here?* The dead knight was wearing basic body plate, but the helmet was a vision of majesty, not at all congruent with its neighboring components. The bloody puckering over his shoulders told him that vultures begin their feasting without much of a grace period.

Admiring the beautiful tourney helm in his hands, he inspected the immaculate craftsmanship, the meticulous details not unnoticed. He glanced at the previous owner, and determined that his face was vaguely familiar as he trotted away, leaving the carrion birds to their meal. *Three squires without a single knight? Did they abandon the cloth to pursue lives as highwaymen?* He squinted, scanning the area again, seeking any sign of movement, but there was nothing but the vultures' slurping and squawking.

"Get off her!" came a cry from the distance. Galahalt whirled at the sudden interruption, seeing a man in gray break through the hedgerow with a look of utter distress on his face.

Jester...Galahalt instantly recognized the knight, watching as the fallen horse's owner rushed into the flock of feasting birds. After the vultures bounded away, shrieking in protest, forfeiting ground, the older knight slowed his pace.

"For all that I have..." he mumbled. Falling to his knees, Gwayne wept openly, clutching the ears and neck of his fallen friend. "No, no, no," he cried, pressing his face to her snout. "Oh, Delilah."

Delilah. Good name. Giving the knight some space, Galahalt retrieved his spear, deciding to go after the rest of his belongings later.

"Greetings," a proper sounding voice said.

"What—?" Galahalt exclaimed, looking around and squinting in the afternoon sun.

"We appear to be making acquaintances during rather uncomfortable circumstances..." A thin wisp with the head of an owl spoke as he fluttered at face level. Sunlight pierced the elegant butterfly wings like stained glass.

"Appears so," Galahalt agreed.

A look of concern washed across the wisp's owl-face as he looked toward Gwayne with a serious gaze. "That's his horse."

"I gathered that," Galahalt replied, eyeing several vultures impatiently waiting for the knight to leave their meal. He idly wondered how aggressive they were toward the living, as he watched the other birds ripping and tearing at the dead flesh littered about.

"My name is Figharth of House Stantowlford," the wisp announced. The young knight was hardly listening, so the wisp spoke louder, hovering into view. "The knight over yonder is Sir Gwayne. *The* Sir Gwayne.

And he was not familiar with my house, so it stands to reason that you are equally ignorant of fae culture and customs."

"You would be correct," Galahalt murmured distractedly, peering over the wisp to keep an eye on the black tide that was slowly surrounding the grieving knight.

"Judging by the colors of your tunic, I would imagine that you are a holy knight? Am I correct?"

Galahalt nodded. "Also correct."

As they watched, Gwayne stood, straightening the twice wrapped sword belt on his hip, and ran a forearm across his nose, gathering composure.

Remarkable how his cloak now appears a shade of green... Galahalt looked back to the wisp whose beak was moving wordlessly, following Gwayne's movement.

Figharth turned his attention back to the younger knight. "For conversational purposes only, of course, may I beg an inquiry regarding your name?"

"It's Sir Galahalt."

"Oh, very fine, yes." Figharth nodded, bobbing in the air. "Do you have a suffix title? Like Sir Galahalt the Undaunted? Or Sir Galahalt the Serpent Spear? Or—"

"Or Sir Galahalt the Why in the Hekk Were You Riding My Horse?" Gwayne demanded, storming toward Galahalt.

Face to face, the younger knight regarded the elder with nothing but sympathy. "I am sorry for your loss, she was—"

"She was my best friend!" Gwayne shouted, shoving Galahalt back a few stumbling steps. "She should be in her stables far away from this place. Eating apples and hay and sweet candied chestnuts... *Not* acting as a feast for—You filthy buzzards!"

Gwayne drew his sword and turned on a heel, sprinting towards the giant vultures peeling flesh from Delilah's hide. Gwayne pointed Quintus at the central bird's bald head, and the massive creature stretched to its full height, rising above the knight's head in a terrifying daemonic display. The feasting vultures atop the squires took notice of the activity, and the sounds of flesh ripping stopped, leaving a cold silence as the knights realized that they were surrounded by foes.

Gwayne backed a few paces toward Galahalt. "Are you traveling alone?" he queried.

"No, why do you ask?" the younger knight quietly answered, and started to lower the new tourney helm over his head.

"Oh, you know. Because any extra help right now would be pretty nice."

"I have a laif with me, but she's on the opposite side of the river. Hunting deer or something."

Gwayne and Galahalt now stood back to back against the approaching horde. As the beasts began circling and sizing up the pair with hungry eyes, the older knight turned his head. "Did you say 'she?'"

Galahalt nodded. "I did."

Gwayne took an aggressive step at the closest encroaching vulture and the beast stumbled back with its wings outstretched, spewing a hiss from its beak. "What's her name?"

"Elkara," Galahalt replied.

"What a lovely name," Gwayne said reverently, clutching the pommel of his sword to his chest, the blade an inch from his face.

The circle broke as suddenly as it had formed, and from above, Figharth began to sputter incoherently. Massive wings beat the air as the vultures fled. Feathers as long as arms fluttered to the earth like an inky tidal wave, and the gruesome flock returned to the skies.

Galahalt breathed a sigh of relief when he saw Elkara, but Gwayne saw only an exceptionally attractive laif making her way toward them under the shadow of giant birds. The breeze from their wings brushed a few loose locks from her perfect face, and Gwayne slowly lowered Quintus with his mouth gaping.

She appraised the area with a deep frown, a look of grave concern apparent. "Who are these men?" she asked, stepping over Asshole #2.

Galahalt shrugged.

Gwayne extended a hand to Elkara. "Sir Gwayne, pleasure to meet you," he stated cordially.

The laif cast a brief glance at him. "I'm aware." Taking a few steps back and sweeping out her hand, she asked, "Did you kill these humans?"

Gwayne shook his head and pointed a finger at Galahalt.

"Who are these men?" Elkara asked.

"They are unknown to me," Galahalt lied, watching Figharth hastily flutter low, his little owl head staring at the circling carrion beasts. "I entered this clearing and they set upon me. Slaying this good knight's steed without reason."

"You killed them by yourself?" She crouched near Asshole #1 and cringed at the maimed face, impossible to recognize after the vultures had ravished him. "They were human, I assume?"

"They were," Galahalt replied, joining the laif. "And young."

Elkara looked up at the young knight. "There is a silencing ward set up around the perimeter of this glade."

"I know," Galahalt said with a singular nod.

Placing her hands on her thighs, she pushed off to a stand. "Your basic thief would not have access to such a powerful talisman."

"Unless they *stole* it." Gwayne entered the conversation, greeted by a heavy eye roll from Elkara.

"Nor would they be as heavily armoured and prepared," Elkara continued, walking toward Asshole #3. "And without a guide as well. Whoever they were, they were well aware of the nearest ward and did not venture too close to it. A shame that you didn't spare at least one of them for questioning."

The knights followed the laif, and Figharth perched on Gwayne's shoulder, keeping an eye on the vultures.

"Hind sight and all that," Galahalt mumbled.

"My best guess: they are holy knights, really inexperienced holy knights," Figharth chirped, placing a finger to his beak.

"I agree," said Gwayne as he turned his head to the small passenger.

"Ah!" Elkara sighed, and rose after surveying the dead man. "Makes little difference at this point, doesn't it? We can speculate all day." She paused, then looked north. "There must be a camp nearby. Maybe there will be more answers there. This makes no sense." She crossed her arms, the long bow on her back tilted with the change in posture.

"Did you sleep with a vestal, or perhaps the daughter of a cleric?" Gwayne asked, slapping Galahalt's shoulder. "Or piss off some irrelevant lord, interloping on his wife, and the bloke still holds some sway with the Church?"

"That seems oddly specific," Elkara said, tilting her head at Gwayne.

"It's not altogether far-fetched," Gwayne argued, and the wisp inclined his head in agreement.

Galahalt shook his head. "Not that I'm aware of...and no to the lord." He removed the helm from the dead man's head and tucked it under his arm as Elkara affixed Gwayne with a bewildered look.

"What?" Gwayne shrugged. "I've pissed a lot of people off, but never had a hit put out on me..." He paused, then continued with much less spirit. "At least as far as I know..."

"Very reassuring," Elkara said sarcastically, looking up to the skies. "No use in burying the bodies at this point. Whoever they are affiliated with will only find bones. A shame such things happen." Her eyes dipped down to Asshole #3. "They all died too soon."

"Died right on time to me," Galahalt mumbled.

FIGHARTH HOVERED OVER THE TRIO as they pressed north, seeking a possible camp. The sounds of the river rushing resumed, creating an auditory backdrop that was instantly noticeable.

"Now what was the reason again? Why do you want me to tag along with you?" Gwayne asked, taking a few hurried steps to catch up with the ranger.

"Our interests align." Elkara offered little else.

"So helping me get my stolen boot back will in turn help you?"

"Correct," the laif answered without turning her head.

Gwayne slowed and Elkara carried on.

Galahalt caught up to Gwayne with his belongings bouncing against the back of his knees. "I hope they have a horse at their camp."

"Odds are good." Gwayne laughed. "Look! There's one over there," he said, pointing across the river. "But I doubt you'll have any luck taming it."

Error was striding alongside the crashing rocks, water spraying his flanks, as he traveled parallel to the group.

"That one belongs to our guide," Galahalt informed him.

Gwayne whistled an escalating scale. "Impressive!" Turning back to Galahalt, he asked, "So how did you end up on Delilah?"

"Well, I sold my horse," Galahalt answered. "She was getting too old, then I didn't have the time to buy a new one." He scratched the back of his neck. "And while I was talking with our guide, some of your friends happened to pass us and—"

"And one of the saddles was empty, and you decided to ask you could borrow the mount?"

"Could have saved the gold they charged me and bought a decent plow horse instead..."

"Glad you told me that bit. I'll be sure to cash in when I get back," Gwayne said bitterly, shrugging his cowl up as the afternoon sun began its descent. "Did the prick have a stupid moustache or a cabbage neck beard?"

"Neither," Galahalt replied, steadying a step with his spear. "Most of the women I know don't have facial hair."

"Gundred," Gwayne hissed.

IT WAS NOT LONG BEFORE THEY SET FOOT in a small, tidy clearing with the sooty remnants of a fire in its center. Bent grass and shattered tree limbs clearly indicated that the site had been recently inhabited.

"This is where they camped," Gwayne announced as he placed his shoulder satchel on a flat stump.

"Is it now," Elkara muttered, looking at the massive sprouting limbs of a beech tree that burst from inside the clearing. Along one limb she noticed three large sacks suspended several arm lengths above an average man's crown. Having little desire to shimmy up the tree, she looked to Figharth. "Cut those down," she said.

The wisp dropped the pine needle he was using as a toothpick and set off at a hurried flutter.

A decent sized horse was tethered to an elm just outside the circle. Galahalt approached the animal with caution as it grazed, seemingly uninterested with the invasive new voices. He removed the gauntlet on his right hand before running his fingers over the creature's neck. Not startled in the least, the horse spared a side glance before returning to its supper.

From his vantage point above the camp, Figharth noticed some strange shapes while he was sawing away at the ropes on the beech tree. Tremors of dread trickled through the fae's body and his beak began to move wordlessly in terror. Sir Gwayne stood below, waiting to catch the falling sacks, and cleared his throat. With a shake of his head, the wisp resumed the task, but his eyes remained fixed on the shapes beyond the clearing.

"This one feels heavier than the other ones!" Figharth shouted down to Gwayne.

"Probably the pots and pans and stuff," Gwayne speculated, then turned to see what the wisp was enraptured with. As soon as his attention wavered, the rope snapped, and Figharth nearly shot off the bough at its release.

"Aw, no," Gwayne groaned, buckling as he caught the solid mass on his left shoulder. He somehow managed to get an arm under it, preventing a small avalanche. In the downward tussle, a hard edge caught the knight on the chin, sending a myriad of starbursts to invade his vision. "Yep," he concluded, rubbing the precursor lump on his face. "Pots and pans." He carried the sack over to the firelight where Galahalt was pawing through the other two bundles, rummaging for any useful items.

"You had any luck?" Gwayne asked, slinging the clanking bag onto the ground between some stumps.

"Found a leather pouch with some high end pipeleaf in it," Galahalt said, pointing with a strip of jerky before returning it to his mouth. "And a sword pommel. Pretty decent crafting too. The blade's been sheared clean off it though."

Gwayne retrieved the pouch before sitting on a stump, still rubbing his chin while inspecting the leatherwork. "Oh, this is some quality leaf." He looked at the younger knight. "Have ya stumbled upon a shovel by any chance?"

Galahalt gently placed an empty spice rack on the ground with two hands then stood up, arching his back. "Yeah, there's a shit spade leaning on that tree over there, next to an awful looking flail," he said, scowling.

"Ohhh," Gwayne breathed, his eyes fiendishly bright as he strode toward the tree.

"Wait," the younger knight interjected. "You aren't planning on burying your horse…"

Gwayne admired the trench tool, turning it over in his hands, mindful of the business end. "She deserves a proper burial…" he insisted.

"But, but," Galahalt stammered, waiting for a punch line, then continuing when he realized Gwayne was serious. "You'll be burying bones by the time we get to her."

At that moment, Elkara entered the area with one hand resting on Error's withers. "Discovered any marching orders?" she asked.

Galahalt flinched. "Not any luck with that yet."

"I found a shovel!" Gwayne announced, and raised the weathered tool, particles dropping off as he waved it around.

"Holy knights rarely travel without some sort of decree," Elkara murmured, watching Error trot over to the packhorse on the outskirts of camp. Their shadowy forms greeted one another without malice.

"And there's some fine pipeleaf on that stump!" Gwayne shouted.

Elkara closed her eyes and took a measured breath.

"The sun's nearly set, probably have another couple hours maybe. Perhaps we should set up camp here for now?" Galahalt asked, offering the suggestion to his guide who stood with her eyes firmly shut. He quickly added, "I can get this fire roaring in no time. The ashes are still pretty hot, and we have these fine skillets now, and maybe we could wrangle a few fish from the river..."

Elkara's eyes reluctantly cracked open. "Agreed."

Figharth buzzed into the clearing, gesturing and spinning in the air while frantically pointing behind him.

Gwayne approached the fae cautiously. "Where have you been, little guy?" he inquired.

The wisp's beak was moving before the words caught up. "Ogres!" he yelled.

Gwayne stood frozen, and Elkara shifted her bow into her hands, locking it instantly. A smile slowly spread across Galahalt's face, unnoticed by his companions in the commotion as they secured their weapons, preparing for an onslaught.

"Dead!" Figharth squawked. "No! They're all dead!"

They all stopped their frantic preparations and stared at the wisp lingering in the air above.

"Just bodies! Don't panic!"

"We're not panicking!" Gwayne pointed the shovel at the wisp. "You're panicking! And why are you panicking if they're all dead?!" he demanded.

"I've never seen an ogre up close." The wisp sunk his owl-head in revulsion, and whispered, "They're hideous."

"Show us," Elkara requested. She strode in the direction the little wisp had entered from, not waiting for the others. Error appeared from the shadows and Elkara squinted at him and clicked her teeth, waving her bow at the packhorse. With a huff, the laifhorse turned and loped back to the outskirts of the camp.

The trees gradually dispersed as the party worked their way north under Figharth's guidance. Gwayne led the group, and with one arm, pressed a stern branch aside, allowing the others clear passage through.

"I see you have found a mate," Elkara said, glancing at Gwayne's feet before meeting his eyes as she passed him.

"We're getting a bit ahead of ourselves…" Gwayne responded coyly.

"She's talking about your boots," Galahalt said, slapping the knight with the back of his hand.

Gwayne looked down and wiggled his mismatched armoured feet, having taken a sabaton from one of the dead men. "Gives me better balance," he reasoned before releasing the branch.

"Looks good on you!" Elkara shouted back.

Galahalt turned and grinned at the other knight, raising both eyebrows at him.

Gwayne batted a twig away from his eyes. "Haw, haw," he muttered.

"Yonder!" Figharth shrieked dramatically, more so than the situation called for.

"Settle down, guy," Gwayne cautioned, looking up as he passed under the horror-stricken wisp. "You'd think the impact would be lessened the second time around."

Figharth settled on Gwayne's shoulder and leaned close to his ear. "They're still so hideous," he whispered.

Entering the area, they came upon a lifeless mountain of an ogre laying prostrate, its horns pointing directly at their approach.

"An alpha," Elkara breathed.

Scattered among the forest debris were a few shiny shards that glimmered in the dying light, drawing Galahalt's attention. He knelt and examined a longer specimen. "This explains the broken sword," he said, scratching the edge of the shard with his thumb.

"Broken sword?" Elkara queried, laying on her side inspecting the ogre's tusks.

"Aye," Galahalt said. "Found its handle back at the camp."

Gwayne laughed. "You mean to tell me those amateurs managed to bring down an alpha ogre from...uh...what clan does he appear to be from?"

Elkara was parting the monster's lips, employing her fingers as forceps. "Not entirely sure their affiliation at the moment. Ask me a bit later, eh?"

"But, yeah, you're telling me *they* killed this guy?" Gwayne smirked at Figharth.

"There are more of them," the wisp said, his beak chattering. "Three smaller ones." His voice rose an octave as he pointed.

"I'll go check 'em out," Gwayne said. "C'mon, Fig." He sauntered in the direction that the wisp hauntingly indicated.

Elkara bent down near the ogre's wounded knee and dipped a finger in the dry paste that had congealed.

Galahalt cringed as he brushed a few leaves off his tunic. "Anything interesting?" he asked.

"They died this morning," the laif concluded. She wiped the goo back onto the ogre's granite-like flesh.

Gwayne emerged from the darkness with a quaking Figharth. "Oh yeah," he began, gesturing over his shoulder. "There are three young ogres over there in way worse shape than this chap."

"Vultures?" Galahalt guessed.

"Naw, more than likely the work of over-eager men."

"Amateurs," Elkara determined, nodding.

With a start, Galahalt noticed a pair of shimmering eyes in the dying light. Perched above the dead alpha, a great black bulk of feathers and claws stared daggers into his soul. Taking a cautionary step back, the young knight beheld a dozen more pairs of emerald eyes glistening back at him. Pointing upward, he drew his companions' attention to the committee of vultures. "Why have they not eaten these ogres yet?" he questioned.

Elkara stood behind Galahalt and regarded the birds with much less trepidation. "Ogre flesh is exceedingly tough." She looked at the terror-stricken wisp, and went on. "They are waiting for the flesh to grow soft from rot."

Gwayne had lost interest and turned back toward camp. "Who else is hungry?"

"There is a bit more work to do before we eat," Elkara said with a raised eyebrow.

"What do you mean?" Gwayne asked.

Elkara grinned. "We need to set the stage."

ERROR HEAVED AS IF HE WAS PULLING A CART laden with lead.

"Just a little further," Elkara encouraged, standing at the laifhorse's snout.

Their plan had been simple. They would decorate the clearing so that it appeared as if the squires had been set upon by ogres. Furthermore, the vultures' feasting would efface all evidence indicating the bodies had died several hours apart.

With another great heave from Error, Elkara was finally satisfied. "Excellent work, old man," she said, giving the laifhorse a pat. "The sun will be down in less than a half hour, so we don't have time to muck around."

Several dozen gremlins scattered as Gwayne and Galahalt entered the clearing with their newly acquired packhorse dragging the three juvenile ogres behind it.

"Little pricks," Gwayne growled at the gremlins as they disappeared into the hedges.

The armour had already been scattered. The vultures had chewed the leather straps and pried the plate off the flesh, so staging that particular facet was already complete. After Galahalt smashed the pieces of armour that his spear had punctured, obscuring the evidence, all that was needed was a battlefield aesthetic.

Gwayne stood at a distance, forming a square with his hands, viewing the scene as a portrait. "Tuck the alpha's arm closer to his knee," he directed. "It will make it look like he was favoring it as he expired."

"We're leaving the alpha as is," Elkara stated, sounding weary. "Error moved him enough already."

Galahalt gathered the severed rope that had been tethered to the ogres. "Are you planning on burying Delilah?" he asked Gwayne.

"No," Gwayne answered sadly.

"Well," Elkara began. "We should probably do something with her bones. Ogres don't ride horses."

"Perhaps a burial at sea?" Gwayne said wistfully. He looked toward the silent flowing river. "She loved playing in the water."

15

When the Skyrend Basilica's first cornerstone was hewn and delivered from the Vassal Mountains, he was there.

He was there when the trench was dug and that poor simpleton lost his grip and fell, his bones crushed to powder well before suffocating. He was there when the shops and villages sprung up all around the immense structure, ushering in more and more people from the surrounding countryside, flooding the streets with flesh and bone. He was there when the love of his life was taken. Stolen from him. Stripped from him. He was there. And when the dark curtain of her life fell, he was there to pass judgment. He was and is; the Arbiter.

With hands steepled over his nose, Amyr leaned forward in his throne, attempting to focus. His mind was prone to wandering as of late.

*That girl reminded me...*It was four, maybe five years ago. The seasons seem to run together in his memory.

Perhaps it was three years? Shaking his head, he recalled the first instance he had seen her. She was standing on the front stoop of a printmaker's shop, bidding farewell, *and when she turned...*his entourage of knights carving through the crowd reigned in their horses when he pulled to a stop, allowing the girl to cross. Only for a flicker did their eyes meet, but that instant echoed endlessly in his mind.

"Arbiter," a hollow sounding voice said. "Lord Amyr." The sentinel to his left tapped the throne, snapping Amyr's attention back to the present.

How long was I...

A plump young couple adorned in fineries was still standing behind the podium with blank expressions etched on their matching pallid complexions.

Beyond the podium lay the bulk of the cathedral's main hall, brimming well over capacity. A mass of people waited by the heavy doors, some of the crowd spilling out into the street. The Skyrend Basilica was relatively empty on the off days, but on judgment days, every seat was occupied. Judgment was open to all, allowing those who felt wronged or harmed to come forward and make accusations. But as of late, the majority of folk begged for a blessing to become pregnant and raise offspring; a blessing from the Arbiter being the exclusive legal avenue.

"Lord Amyr," the young man at the podium spoke, sliding his silk cap off a glistening sweaty pate. "My wife and I." He gestured at the woman next him as he nervously strangled his hat. "We have paid the church's sum and now are asking for a blessing for our unborn." Taking a heavy swallow, he continued. "Please?" The word came out weak and warbly, and when he looked to his wife for reassurance, she pressed her hands to the podium and raised her chin proudly. The man closed his eyes, valorously conjuring his next words. "Now we—"

"Refused," Amyr cut the man off.

The man recoiled, smoothing the fine silk shirt pressing tight to his chest. The woman beside him gripped the sides of the podium, wobbling in distress. The expectant people behind, waiting to hold audience with the Arbiter, began to mull and shift. A few pointed and waved nervously, beckoning others to go before them. Some stepped back allowing others to take their number in line.

"But, but, Lord Amyr," the man stammered. "If we have a child...if we have a family...but..." The audience grew silent. "But we paid the fee—an exorbitant fee!" He grew louder, throttling his hat. "If we have a child without your permission, then we will have to give it up to the orphanages and we will be thrown into the dungeons, or worse! This is something we wish to avoid. Avoid completely! And if the child we wish to have is born under a sign, then my Lord, that would change many a thing for us. I admit, I am not the most handsome or capable-looking man, but I would dedicate this child to your service. Be they born a Scholar or a Healer, or—"

"Warrior," Amyr finished the statement.

Puffing out his chest and reaching for his wife's hand, the man boldly went on. "I come from good stock, my Lord. Our coupling would produce fine offspring."

A groan swept the audience.

"This child would mirror his father's life of service and devotion?" Amyr inquired dryly.

Sweat poured down the man's face, and he raised his hat to his brow, stamping the flow. Uttering a single lie to the Arbiter, great or small, was met with instant death.

The man stuttered and fumbled as he attempted to respond. "I...I don't...understand—"

Before he could say anything else, his eyes rolled back and he collapsed into a heap, dead long before his body met the cold marble.

The woman's hand was still clasped in her husband's, and with a scream, she pulled free, nearly toppling to the floor. Straightening herself, she vehemently gripped the podium and focused her rage at the throne. "He was a good man!" she screamed, and died instantly. She crumpled downward, joining her husband.

A pair of squires struggled with the bodies, wrestling with them for several minutes while the crowd watched. Once they rolled the man onto the stretcher, their knees buckled under the weight, straining to their limits. The squires appealed to the on-lookers, requesting stronger spines, but no one stepped forward.

Amyr was oblivious to the theatrics, having lost interest long before the man had expired, not even paying attention when the woman spat her final phrase.

A new plan was formulated by the squires, they took hold of the dead man's wrists and began to unceremoniously drag his body across the floor. With mouth hanging wide and tongue draping over puffy lips, the man was escorted from the hall, leaving a trail of fluid in his wake. A church official cleared her throat and nudged an unlucky page, who scampered off to fetch a mop. The squires soon returned and gave the same treatment to the woman. As they struggled, albeit much less, her left slipper became ensnared and was pulled free, baring her foot.

The resounding sickly squeak that issued from her heel rubbing against the stone drew Amyr's attention. *Even in death...*He sneered, placing a finger into his ear.

The sound increased its shrill pitch as the squires quickened their pace, mumbling something about a "churn and burn" as they exited the hall.

Without waiting for the page to finish mopping, a deacon beckoned the next case forward. The line dwindled as the day progressed, leaving the total body count at two for the day. Amyr settled many disputes that afternoon which required very little effort.

A man was upset with a neighbor after several chickens came up missing from his coop, and the neighbor's dog was seen with a few feathers dangling from his muzzle. The mutt's owner claimed it was goblins before stepping onto the podium, but quickly changed his story when facing mortality, admitting guilt and offering compensation for the dead birds.

After this, a particularly stubborn bar patron refused to pay his outstanding tab, so Amyr told the man he had until the end of Market Days to settle, otherwise he would be sentenced to work at the pub until the debt was satisfied. The normally sour look on the proprietor's face immediately brightened at the prospect of free labor.

One man joined the line outside, stumbling into place in a state of near blackout drunkenness, bent on telling Amyr that he was a disgraceful old asshole who was no longer relevant and should step down and back off. As the day wore on, the man began to regain his senses, and when it was his turn to step forward, he simply turned left and exited the hall.

The final cases were men and women requesting blessings, all consecutive, and all rejected. A weathered man acted as a mediator for his daughter and her husband, firmly speaking on their behalf behind a great silver beard, each word carefully selected and announced with poise. Though three stood at the podium, Amyr sensed the presence of a fourth. And to his credit, the old man remained silent while his children were taken away in shackles.

The seated audience remained throughout the proceedings; rarely was a cushion vacated, and when this happened, the space was instantly filled. The spectacle of judgment day was an unceasing format of entertainment for many in the city.

After giving the church officer a nod, the next man in line extended a calloused hand, allowing his middle aged wife to walk before him. They took tentative steps on the carpeted path leading to the center stage, all in attendance were fully aware of the request soon to be made. Young couples without children were denied, so what sort of hope could this seasoned pair have? Likely they already had a brood of their own on whatever land they tilled.

Not an ounce of desperation registered in the man's voice as he spoke. "Greetings, Lord Amyr." He placidly waited for a response, knowing full well one was not coming. "You know why we're here. We want a blessing for a child."

Amyr did not raise his chin. "Granted," he said.

The rippling gasps from the chamber became a chorus of chatter and disbelief, starting discussions that would become the grounds for many speculative debates over the evening's ale.

"I will need to test the woman's quality," Amyr stated, his face a study of great disinterest.

"Test the woman...?" the man questioned, his elation draining. "You mean my Heather?"

Heather was stoic in response as she watched her husband's tears of joy trickle down a face now painted in despair. Clutching both of her shoulders before pulling her into a tight embrace, the man began to wipe his face while stroking her head, trying to regain some composure. Nodding, the woman raised her husband's hand to her lips.

"I won't be long," she promised, then walked into the midst of the waiting sentinel escort and was enveloped by the men of steel who meant no harm, but did not offer safety.

"You!" Spittle flew as the husband trembled, pointing a shaking finger at Amyr, who stood before the sentinels, his hand on the latch that led beyond the hall. All was silent, and though the day was ended, the audience remained until the last moment.

The sentinels stepped aside, avoiding the laif's gaze.

"Yes?" Amyr offered quietly, his eyes hard and focused on his accuser. The woman turned as well, shaking her head violently as the farmer tightened his jaw, knowing he would die and leave his children fatherless if he continued this discourse.

"Arbiter." The man chose the word carefully, opting for a simple truth before lowering his head, utterly defeated.

Amyr raised one eyebrow and released the latch, disappearing through the door, and in his wake the sentinels followed.

There was a significant pause, held like a sustained note, and the people shifted in their seats awaiting the formal dismissal.

With considerably less pomp, a deacon shuffled forward and addressed all in attendance. "Those that wish to claim the bodies of those determined deceitful," he began. "May do so now or before the first bells tomorrow morn." He then waved his hands as if they were wet. "You are dismissed."

***

"WHAT WOULD IT TAKE TO PROVIDE A DECENT CHAIR for those waiting in this dreary hall? I would even settle for a simpleton's bench at this point," Schroederstall complained, shifting from one foot to the other, imploring the pair of sentinels standing guard by Amyr's chamber door. "Or even a pallet...with some threadbare carpeting to prevent my bum from getting riddled with splinters."

As usual, his questions were answered with silence. He gave a deep sigh and leaned against the wall, his back uncomfortably flat against the interlacing stone pattern. *Those impatient cads leaving me to hold the bag. Now I must give the news to Amyr alone, while those two wander off to mourn their lost squires in some seedy pub.* He bounced the back of his skull against the wall restlessly. *How long will he keep that cowherd's wife in there?*

The news he was bringing was not particularly on the up and up, his sore feet only increased the tension, and the wait was approaching two hours at this point. Clemence and Phillip had abandoned the churchman after only thirty minutes or so. After finding the bone-picked corpses of their squires earlier that day, the pair were not in the mood to be pacing around a corridor waiting for the Arbiter.

Schroederstall cast another loud sigh at the ceiling and widened his stance, still leaning heavily on his throbbing upper back. "Perhaps we will be on the precipice of a volcano?" he asked the faceless sentinels who remained fixed in place. "You know the first time I visited Lord Amyr in his chambers, I was not sure what to expect. I was told that he often changes the scenery to fit his mood, like a chameleon. But yes, the very first time," he said, emphasizing his point with a wagging finger. "I walked into a dazzling night time forestscape with a brilliant canopy of stars overhead. Oh, it was magnificent, you would have loved it, I am sure. Though I did not care for the owls that stared so dreadfully at me, flourishing such malcontent behind their beady little eyes. But the last time I was in there, behind that door, I found myself in a much less accommodating environment." He paused, waiting for a response, holding a moment before continuing. "The room was entirely slate, like chalkboards in a school room, floor to ceiling and all four walls. And no furniture at all, which I feel should be noted," he said pointedly, casting a glare around the empty floors. "Sticks of chalk were strewn about, and there were intricate scribblings all over the walls, which were entirely foreign to me. And I am an educator, so that should speak volumes to you. Such immense, elaborate glyphs! They were rather magnificent, truth be told. And there was Amyr, twirling a long piece of chalk between his fingers, somehow occupying the space I strolled through when I entered. So I wonder what will I encounter this time? Any guesses? Hm? You seem to be on the edge of your seat. Oh, you are such interesting company. Just a plethora of steaming knowledge ushering forth entirely untethered. Please don't all speak at once, though I do have an ear for each of you."

The sentinels suddenly straightened, causing Schroederstall to clutch his chest in fear, but the guard nearest the latch merely reached over and swung the door wide, revealing a pitchy room, absent of any light. With the smoothest of strides the sentinels entered the darkness and closed the door behind them with such force that the mounds of dust between the cobbles of the floor wafted up and invaded Schroederstall's nostrils. The churchman began to wave at his nose and gag, trying desperately to prevent the inevitable bout of sneezes.

The door opened just in time for Schroederstall to curse and sneeze, the mist still hanging in the air as he re-issued several more. Between blinks forced by his sneezes, Schroederstall watched a group of sentinels escort a markedly dazed woman out from the chamber.

She appeared to be middle aged and completely unharmed from what he could tell. With a swift tug, the last sentinel brought the door closed, then turned to the footsore churchman. "Enter at your leisure," he said.

Schroederstall watched the escort turn a soft corner along the rather lengthy hall, flaming sconces accenting the brilliant armour, moving at an even pace before disappearing from sight around the bend.

Choose your words carefully, Schroederstall, he thought, straightening his jupon. *One poorly chosen phrase or exaggeration will be your last.*

"Thank you most kindly, gentlemen, or gentlewomen." Schroederstall nodded at the sentinels as he crossed the corridor and released the latch, then lowered his shoulder, pressing into the unknown. With his eyes squeezed tight, hoping for a serene layout, his feet pleasantly discovered a soft, spongy carpet.

Oh, this is a familiar one. He opened his eyes to see the same forest he had encountered the first time.

A mossy path lead through a sea of wavy grass, passing under the gentle waving arms of willow boughs. The stars above, punching through the darkest shroud, bathed every surface in silvery light. The crisp night air stung the back of his parched throat as he navigated the simple trail that opened into a fire lit clearing with overgrown root segments undulating from the ground.

His flat soled shoes nearly bouncing with each step, the churchman entered the clearing sensing a presence from the corner of his eye, he turned to see the ancient laif seated on one of the overly large root protrusions. A considerable tree grew behind Amyr, its trunk taking a slight horseshoe shape as it rose, creating a comfortable hollow for the laif to recline against. Within an arm's length, a tear-shaped bottle was nestled inside a hollow of the tree, its crimson contents reaching just above the orb.

*A most rare and exotic vintage, I am sure. Probably older than my grandparents' grandparents...*Schroederstall stood before the roaring fire, embers rushing upward, and squinted at the seated laif who was raising a wooden cup in welcome.

The churchman looked at the root benches despairingly. *No regard for fine furniture at all,* he thought, and selected a section with a slight depression, then brushed the rough surface with a hollow smile before hoisting up onto it. He did his best to adjust himself as his feet dangled several inches from even the tallest blade of grass.

"May I offer some wine?" Amyr asked, nodding toward the tree with a smile.

"That sounds lovely," Schroederstall replied without hesitation.

The laif swiveled on the root to retrieve the bottle and with his other hand produced another wooden cup matching his own. Lightly stepping around the blaze, Amyr's greaves shone brilliantly between the folds of his long tunic. Standing before Schroederstall, he handed the cup and began pouring, as a servant to a master. Without a drop wasted, the laif reversed the angle as the cup nearly overflowed, allowing the wine to fall back below the bubble. Not a hint of froth formed along the rim of the cup, and Schroederstall stared, mesmerized by the swirling liquid's incandescence.

"Thank you." Schroederstall looked up to see the laif once again seated on his log, the bottle back in its bole without a drop missing. Amyr gave a nod and stared over the flames, patiently waiting.

After taking a sip, Schroederstall reminded himself to select his words with care. "This wine is magnificent!" He lowered the cup into his lap with both hands wrapped around it. "I must know the vineyard."

Amyr's eyes remained fixed. "That is for another time," he stated.

Too much, too much. Stay formal. "I understand. It's delicious. Thank you again." Schroederstall brought the cup to his mouth again, trying to gather his thoughts.

"I do not punish those that tell the truth," Amyr reminded him. "That only inspires war."

Schroederstall nodded as he swallowed. "I know that you entrusted me with this delicate matter, and I must assure you that it is within the boundaries of being attainable. But we have come across a snag and I must make another request in order to obtain proper victory." He wanted to slap himself. "Well you see, the squires that we sent—"

Amyr had raised a hand. "I do not wish to be privy to any details."

Schroederstall tipped his cup so that Amyr could not see him squeeze his eyes tight. "Mmmm, such good wine." A branch overhead sounded as if it were about to snap, and he looked up to see an owl perched above gazing directly at him. *Those damn owls.* "Well, you see, the knights, Sir Clemence and Sir Phillip, wish to go deeper into the forest, and they would like to forego the necessity of employing a guide, so I would like to ask on their behalf for another type of talisman or trinket or some such magical item that would allow them to cross the wards unmolested," he blurted out quickly.

"How many wards will they be crossing?"

Schroederstall pictured the forest and began to count with his eyes in the back of his head. "It's difficult for me to say..." he said, tapping his teeth with a forefinger. "I don't really know."

"Well, then," Amyr said, eyeing his cup. "I shall play this game as safely as possible."

The churchman nodded, pretending to understand.

Amyr brought the cup to his lips and tossed his head back. "Granted."

AMYR REMAINED IN THE FOREST, WATCHING the churchman waddle away, and shook his head.

"I know that none of this will bring her back," he said as he refilled his cup. "But she reminds me of her."

16

Every fiber of Galahalt's being was crying out for sleep, and once his head hit the rolled up sack, the young knight was entirely unconscious. Gwayne fussed with the fire, trying to bring the embers back to life, while Elkara sharpened a dagger, the ensuing sparks falling harmlessly like tiny comets. Figharth trembled on a stump, hugging himself, waiting for the fire to renew its heated glory.

"There she is," Gwayne said as he settled back into his bundle of blankets and cloaks and admired the dancing flames. "Didn't take too long, did it, Fig?"

In response, the wisp took flight, and hovered a few inches from the issuing smoke, rubbing his hands and holding them out to the waves of warmth. His little eyes reflected the flames and he nodded vigorously at the knight. "Perfect." He struggled to make the comment, shivering the word from his thawing beak.

After a few minutes, the wisp could no longer contain his yawns, and looked around for a suitable place to lay his head for the night. Deciding that he could leech some warmth from Galahalt, he fluttered over to the sleeping knight and very slowly and very gently settled onto the knight's hip. Carefully he removed his overcoat and stretched it across himself, smoothing the corners, then curled up with only his feet peeping out from underneath. Not once did Galahalt stir while the fae prepared for sleep.

Elkara watched the scene take place, gazing adoringly at Figharth as his little beak began to chatter away in his sleep, clearly the chill was returning. Rummaging through her garments, the laif produced a clean woolen sock, then tiptoed around the fire and knelt down beside the sleeping wisp. With her chin just above his clicking head, she whispered, "This will serve you better." Scooping Figharth up without waking Galahalt, she popped the little gentleman into the sock.

The wisp's face beamed in appreciation, tightly wrapped in the fuzzy fabric, he nuzzled the softness as the laif set him down as gently as if he was the most fragile of glass orbs. With only his head poking out, he whispered back, "Thank you," then closed his eyes and fell asleep; the chilly tremors soundly defeated.

Elkara picked her way back to the stump and resumed the rhythmic scraping of stone to steel. Gwayne rested with his back against the sprawling beech, swaddled in a heap of blankets that he had found in one of the squires' bundles hanging from the tree.

"That was rather thoughtful," Gwayne said, looking to his left at the sleeping wisp. "I hope that's a clean one though."

Elkara smirked and continued to scratch the dagger.

"This particular neck of Fenrirfang is slightly familiar to me," the knight continued, gazing upward at the overcast skies, meager striations revealing pinhole stars glumly carrying on their nightly duties. "I think I've escorted a few young folk looking to become lampyrs at the fount further north..." He paused, squinting his eyes. "...And west of here..." he concluded, consulting his inner map.

"Yes," Elkara agreed without breaking rhythm, running a thumb across the freshly sharpened blade.

Gwayne folded his arms. "I suppose it goes without saying that you have been all over these woods and know exactly where we are and more than likely have a good bead drawn on the nearest gremlin settlement."

"I do."

"And your companion here," Gwayne said, nodding at Galahalt. "He is fine with us taking a slight detour from whatever quest he is set upon?"

Elkara nodded as she leaned down and placed the whetstone back in her satchel.

Gwayne spoke again. "Where are you guys heading anyhow?"

"Fort Navarene," Elkara replied. "And there is a gremlin village between us and the fort and another beyond the fort. I'm fairly certain your boot will be in one of those."

"If not?" Gwayne wondered.

"There are a few other villages in these *woods*," Elkara explained. "But from what I know of gremlins and how they travel and trade, it will be closer rather than farther."

"I see." Gwayne smiled. "Fort Navarene, eh? That's not too ridiculously far. And may I ask what this young knight is looking for?"

Elkara placed a finger on the dagger's tip. "*This young knight* is seeking what most young knights seek at one time or another. Or should I say young *people*, really."

Gwayne's armoured foot scraped the inside of the blankets as he stretched his legs out. "So it's a rather common quest," he guessed. "Like looking for a gorgon or a basilisk or something?"

"Or something. Yes."

"Well, that's exciting!" Gwayne said with enthusiasm. "Whatever it is that he is hunting, I wouldn't count him out. He is rather horrifying with that spear."

"It would seem so," Elkara agreed. She tilted her head, recalling the awkward young knight and had trouble piecing together the carnage left in his wake that afternoon. "Can you tell me what you saw?"

Gwayne scratched his chin with the back of his hand. "How long have you known this fellow? Just the few days you've been riding together?"

Elkara nodded.

"For me it's a bit disturbing...the more I saw today..."

"What does that mean?" the laif inquired, leaning forward.

"When I saw our friend fighting those lads from across the river, I just assumed that they had never encountered a man with a spear before. Or perhaps they were just really *green*, you know? But then we found those dead ogres clustered over there with an *alpha* among them." Gwayne raised his eyebrows significantly. "Makes me think a bit different now." Leaning back against the beech, he abruptly shifted topics. "Ooh, can I have a look at that dagger?"

Elkara tossed the blade into the midst of Gwayne's nest.

Galahalt shuddered in his sleep, but did not wake.

"Maybe we should cover him?" Gwayne whispered.

"Then Fig will suffocate," Elkara pointed out.

"Yeah, he's probably fine," Gwayne said. "Well, there really isn't too much to say. Halty just poked them all, one, two, three as if he were taking an afternoon stroll. Not much effort or strain on his part, really. Cunning. Yes, *cunning* is a good word. And he moved like liquid. Very nonchalant. But it was over so fast, I don't believe I blinked even once." He whistled as he rolled the dagger in the yellow light, taking in the intricate details enveloping the handle, all resolving into a flat steel bottom. Raising the dagger over his head, he squinted at the base, angling it toward the fire. "A dragonfly." Another whistle of admiration issued from his mouth as he gazed at the laif smith's mark.

"That blade has been in my family for centuries," Elkara revealed, folding her hands on her lap.

"Priceless." Gwayne held it in an open palm. "The balance. My, my…"

Elkara rose and approached the knight who wrestled free of his bondage to return the dagger, the blade tip in his fingers as he reached out. Accepting it handle first, the laif recoiled. "Fack!" she cursed. A static shock passed between them with an audible snap. Gwayne waved his hands as if scorched by a hot iron, although Elkara managed to maintain her hold on the knife, kissing a finger after returning the dagger to its sheath.

"So, Sir Galahalt is a capable warrior," Elkara mused, sitting back down, still nursing her fingertip. "That is comforting, I suppose."

"I *know* that he is capable," Gwayne began, producing a pipe. His next phrase was almost inaudible to the laif. "But I don't *know* if he's a…" He regarded the clouds as if waiting for something to fall, then silently mouthed the word "warrior."

Elkara's eyes widened. "You noticed too?" She pitched a furtive glance at the sleeping knight, then spoke with her mouth cupped on the side. "Maybe we should talk of this another time?" she suggested.

Gwayne nodded, dousing a spent match in the dirt.

Unable to help herself, the laif leaned closer. "He's not a red knight, you think?"

Gwayne was momentarily taken aback by the comment, a small gasp escaped before he shook his head. Elkara leaned back, wishing she could say more.

A patch of silence spread between them, but neither turned in for sleep. Gwayne wafted smoky trails and was lost in thought somewhere between Delilah and gremlins, while Elkara held centuries behind her eyes, remembering the eager young knights she had escorted bent on slaying the Questing Beast. Each knight had cast a slightly different shadow, but underneath they had all been the same. The laif nodded to herself, humming a song from the old halls while the fire crackled and shifted, completely out of rhythm.

But Galahalt... Elkara pondered. *Seems like there is more—*

"I want to know more," Gwayne interrupted the laif's thoughts. "About this quest."

"Temper your expectations," Elkara advised.

"Consider them dulled."

Elkara shifted on the stump and tried not to look in Galahalt's direction. "He's after the Questing Beast," she divulged.

"That's—" Gwayne paused, taking another draw from his pipe. "Neat." He exhaled gray, the smoke intermingling with the fire that was drifting into the sky. "So how many wards will we be crossing before we reach my gremlins?"

Elkara bit her lip. "One," she replied.

"So in order for me to return, I will need you with me." Gwayne tapped the stem of his pipe against his chin. "So effectively, we are chasing fiction."

This journey is not nearly as dumb as it sounds. Elkara wished she could speak volumes and explain to the knight that they would only be going as far as the fort, but she had to be cautious with Galahalt so near.

Squinting and cringing, the laif answered, "Basically, yes."

Gwayne blinked. "Sounds really stupid."

Elkara sighed. "Listen, if you—"

"I'm in."

17

❧

*T*here it was again.

Working his way through the thistles and thorns, Elmer could hear it all around; the sound of tripping footfalls dragging leaves with each step, silencing each time he came to halt.

He bounced on his forepaws, wrestling free of a pesky ground vine. "This is not good," he growled. Although this situation was not altogether unfamiliar, it was nonetheless very unpleasant.

Are the footsteps multiplying now?

He took another controlled step, lurching forward on all fours, pausing and holding a breath. Craning his ears, it became clearer to him. *They're converging too? Come on!*

He stopped.

They stopped.

He took a few steps.

They took a few steps.

He started again.

They started again.

He came up short, eyes darting everywhere, not moving another muscle.

They did not stop this time. A whirling torrent of leaves and earth, parting and flinging out in all directions, sent a surge of panic from Elmer's skull to his stomach. Ignoring the searing pain in his side from the wound reopening with each violent extension, the dog bolted forward.

Every direction felt equally dangerous, but the path straight ahead presented itself as the most logical option. Keeping his eyes in a tunnel, he focused on escaping from whatever horrible things were pursuing him. Thorns tried their best to cripple him, latching onto his fur and tearing the flesh underneath, and an endless supply of ground vines hampered any decent flow of momentum. His paw became entangled again, and with a vicious growl, he kicked free, but nearly tumbled on his snout.

Elmer's wound felt damp and when he staggered, he caught sight of a bristled form surging toward him at full tilt, arms pumping like a sprinter, tearing branches and leaping fallen trees without breaking stride. Instantly, he recognized what kind of beast was pursuing him.

This won't do at all. In one of his previous lives, a pack of faewolves had ravaged him into a bloody mess. Though that sensation would be entirely unwelcome on such a lovely afternoon, it was not what was currently causing his concern. If he were to be caught by the creatures, his goal would not be reached and all would come to naught.

Shelter. He could not slow for even an instant. Eyes darting, he frantically searched for a badger den or any kind of cave with a narrow opening. *Anything that will restrict a horrorbeast...oh, and there's another one joining their ranks. Hallo mate, can we please keep a respectful distance here?* Urging his muscles to their maximum, he increased his pace, leaving an obvious crimson trail behind. The familiar tang of copper had reached his tongue. *I must find shelter...*Just then he spotted a crevice created by a felled tree tilted at a deadly angle, its roots fully exposed and clinging to the earth.

We can make this happen! Tapping into a hidden reserve of energy, the prey slid to a sudden stop, causing one faewolf to overstep and tumble.

The dog pivoted ninety degrees and rushed headlong, desperately tearing at the ground. Debris showered the faewolf directly behind him, which unfortunately did not deter the beast in the slightest. Closing in on the welcoming pit of darkness, Elmer heard one of his pursuers curse as he tripped and sprawled onto the green carpet.

Did he just speak an actual word? Elmer ran through a cloud of disbelief. Behind him, he heard a brief pause in the pursuit as the faewolves leapt over their downed companion. *Or used him as a springboard.*

He was only a few yards away from safety, and decided to disregard any spatial calculations, lowering his head and charging onward. On the plus side, the roots were saturated with muddy water so they did not splinter and burst upon impact. They were, however, tethered much more securely than he had anticipated. He let out several yelps of anguish as he ricocheted between the solid bars, scraping every single rib as he passed. It was by sheer force that he gained clearance into the crevice, falling down into a hole that was deeper than he had hoped...*Not a bad thing.*

Splashing and scrambling, Elmer got to his feet and violently clung to the deepest recess of the pit, standing upright on wobbly hind legs. The faewolves crashed into the makeshift cage, peppering the opening with dirt and rocks, and sending cold splashes onto Elmer's fur.

The roots are holding them! Elmer squinted at the frothing beasts. They were tearing and grasping, reaching their filthy eldritch arms into the hole, swiping and clutching at nothing but stale air. All light was nearly blotted out by the fevered shapes, and a jumbled mess of limbs protruded out at the dog like a hideous spider demon.

Yep, they are definitely talking now.

Elmer resigned himself to his current situation as the faewolves began to riddle him with threats and insults. His body was slightly arched along the curvature of the wall with his claws buried as deeply into the mud as possible. Thankfully some of water had been absorbed since the tree fell, creating a dry rim along the rough circular base, which allowed his hind legs to gain relatively secure purchase. *Stable? Yes. Comfortable? No.*

His ears perked up when a faewolf suggested that one of them should go back and retrieve a crossbow, which garnered quite a keen response. The cheering and laughing rose to a near frenzied state.

So now they use weapons? Elmer slumped down into the water, his head resting along the dry ridge, the rest of his body partially submerged. The dog gave up attempting a head count, resigning himself to his fate. *It's too bad,* he mused, resting his head on a drenched paw. *Of all the dog bodies I've inhabited, this one is by far my favorite.*

Beyond surrender, there was not much to do to occupy time before the impending crossbow bolt. He thought about digging an escape tunnel, but it seemed it was only a matter of time before his assailants got the best of him. *Sad to admit, but I would much prefer a swift death than suffocation in tight quarters.* The damp spring soil did not inspire confidence in its ability to form a structurally sound tunnel. Besides, he was tired.

Elmer's mind began to wander into the past, long ago, before the Hold—back when he was a simple human. Shaking his head, he now lost himself in memories...

As he walked next to a shrub wall, his fingers playing between the tiny leaves, he heard screams of disorder and panic just beyond the hedgerow. A tidy hamlet, the name escaped him at the moment, was beyond the hedges.

He was virtually unarmed, so he had little motivation to get involved. Having passed through this way many times, Lannor knew the area to typically be abundantly peaceful, but the panic was now reaching a climax. The distinct sounds of a man choking on his own fluids was crystal clear from where he quietly crept, along with the unmistakable noises of flesh tearing from bone. All of this heavily accented by the puckering, chewing, and growling of a yet-to-be-determined monster.

Elmer sighed from under the tree and *Lannor sighed and he reluctantly walked through the nearest gap in the shrubbery, entering the arena of slaughter. Curiosity had gotten the best of him. He was highly doubtful in his abilities to provide any sort of meaningful aid, and he selected a path with the most obstacles that would hide his movements. A sensible chap would join the tide of those desperately retreating, but Lannor side-stepped the terror stricken folk on their path to salvation, and instead found shelter behind a bale of hay. He dropped to all fours and poked around the bottom corner, his ears got tickled by the blades of grass as he tried to see what all the fuss was about. A lone, mangy faewolf was slurping up the intestines of a farmhand, who was, gratefully, dead by that point.*

Elmer shuddered at the memory. *For reasons unknown, Lannor moved closer to the scene and made eye contact with a young maiden who was watching from a street level window. Her forehead was pressed flat to the pane and the look of panic she gave him was burned into his memory as her eyes darted from the beast, then back to him. Time stood still.*

The munching sound no longer filled the air. Lannor pressed his back against the building watching the faewolf in a reflective window as it stood upright with a hand to its neck, working out a kink. Blood and bits of entrail fell from the grinning maw as it violently shook its head, looking particularly deranged. Somehow it managed to look even more deranged than your average faewolf, which was actually rather impressive.

In an inordinately brave or exceptionally stupid move, the safely spectating girl decided to open her home's front door and beckoned Lannor enter, waving encouragingly behind a pained grimace. Lannor took the suggestion without hesitation, dashing towards the small domicile. Suddenly his integrity got the best of him, and he skidded to a stop. He had been accused of many things in his mortal life, but (A.) Coward and (B.) Selfish, had never made it onto the list.

With a wavering smile, he nodded at the pale and freckled pig-tailed girl, her mouth forming a petrified oval.

"Close the door!" he yelled, looking at the charging beast, long arms tearing at the street, claws scraping with each stride.

Regretting his previous statement, he turned back to the girl.

"Wait! Don't!"

Too late. The latch clicked.

He squared his shoulders and rose onto the balls of his feet, bracing for impact. With inhuman speed, the faewolf leapt a great distance, taking Lannor completely by surprise. He shifted low, allowing the beast to sail past, in the hopes that it would go clear over top. But he had no such luck, its trailing claw gained purchase and wrapped the two into a tumbling package of flesh and wet fur.

The faewolf scrabbled madly as if a hot prod were rammed up its ass and all Lannor could do was cover his face until the momentum died. Somehow, he had managed to pin both fore claws behind its shoulder blades, which miraculously continued to scrape and peel the skin on Lannor's back through the loose tunic. With his left forearm he held the snarling beast's snout at bay, chomping and spitting in its frantic attempts to escape. From a distance the faewolf had appeared much more menacing than it did up close, it was also surprisingly light. Its ribcage was on clear display under the mange, jutting out in near skeletal manner. Clearly this member of the pack was not receiving a fair share at the dinner table.

The dagger he kept on his hip selfishly remained in its sheath, offering no aid. With his right arm buried under the beast's neck he had no way of retrieving his weapon, it would not simply spirit itself into his fist. The girl's face was pressed against the window again, the previous impression a few inches to the left from her nose. He recalled thinking that this was quite the inappropriate scene for a child to witness, and he felt a deep sense of remorse for the role he had played. He supposed she would see something like this sooner or later, but he held little desire to be the one on display.

Driven by pure rage and a deep hunger, the faewolf tried to wriggle free and press through the iron-like force of Lannor's forearm. The mangy thing was relentless in its purpose. Spittle and bits of people violently sprinkled onto his face as the foe growled and bit at the air with no consequence. It was entirely focused, consumed by an insane drive to bite a good chunk off of his face.

Looking to the window girl, Lannor shouted, "Hey! Come out here!" He turned his mouth to prevent any faewolf spit from getting in. The girl intelligently shook her head, and he did not blame her.

"I have a good hold on his coat!" he promised. He sputtered as some foreign fleshy thing caught inside his cheek. He gagged while he worked it with his tongue before spitting it out. "Trust me!" he said with as much sincerity as he could muster.

The faewolf wretched a glob from deep in its throat and landed square on Lannor's eyelid. "You prick!" he shouted without realizing that he still held the girl's gaze. "I don't mean you!" He shook his head, deeply apologetic.

When he looked over again, the window had been vacated, his pleading seemed to have worked, and moments later the door opened and the girl stepped into the radiant daylight.

Elmer peered up at the relentless mob that was still tearing at the roots and carrying on like a bunch of possessed jackasses. "Only a matter of time," he sighed, and he lowered his gaze back down to the muddy depths.

"Quick! My dagger is on my right hip," he told the girl. "Oh, wait a moment...let me get a better grip..." Lannor corkscrewed his hand deep into the faewolf's neck scruff, summoning every ounce of his strength. "Okay, okay, go ahead and reach down now..."

The beast was not paying any attention to the little girl now that its air passage was being strangled. It gagged and coughed more lung butter onto Lannor's face.

"For crying out loud!" he sputtered, then locked eyes with the girl. "Okay, okay, nice and easy—it's just a little tie. Yeah, just untie it. Yep, pull the longer strand first. Yes, yes, very nice."

She stepped back a few paces after working the blade free, staring at it as if puzzled by its very existence.

"Okay!" Lannor felt victory surging into his veins. "All you have to do is stab the pointy end—look at me! Stab the pointy end into the base of its skull."

He articulated the next bit of instruction. "I don't think I can hold him much longer." His muscles were beginning a downward arc of exhaustion...which would lead to inevitable failure and death.

The girl shook her head vigorously in refusal, setting her braided pigtails swinging back and forth.

"Pretend you're carving a cake," Lannor pleaded, exerting a bit of extra force on the faewolf's windpipe.

The pigtails continued to swing and bounce in his periphery and the surge of victory, smooth and pure pumping from his heart, began to slow, becoming more like tar.

As if on cue, the faewolf began shifting its weight like a turtle on its back causing Lannor to scoot back a few inches in order to prevent any unnecessary eviscerations. He brought his boot up onto the beast's thigh, which afforded him some more leverage and reduced the chances of another unpleasant jostling.

"Come around behind. He won't get you." Lannor gestured with his head, indicating the spot. In that instant, the beast noticed Lannor's armed little helper. The faewolf struggled to break free, rising up as best it could under the neck restraints, aiming to lash out with its fangs. The maneuver was incon-

ceivable to Lannor, given the circumstances, but this faewolf was explicitly driven by hunger. Lannor loudly screamed, drawing the beast's focus back on himself, then he tightened his grip on its throat once more.

"Put the dagger in my mouth." Under the tree, Elmer rolled his eyes.

"I can't— I'm not going to—"

"No. Put the blade in between my teeth!" Lannor spit out another glob that had fallen into his mouth. *"Make sure the sharp side is facing out!"*

She arched her back as she knelt, very slowly, while keeping her face as far away as possible. A few rounds of spit landed on her forehead and cheek as she drew near, and her face puckered in revulsion.

"Facing out!" he instructed.

She slapped the cold steel into his waiting mouth, then sprang away like a coiled viper, her fingers scrabbling against the cobblestones as she got to her feet and sprinted home. She crossed the threshold, bashing into the door, which was thankfully still ajar, and frantically entered.

The faewolf's ears pricked at the resounding slam of the door and it was then that Lannor recalled the familiar flavor. He felt a razor's clinging, and a paper thin edge buried several layers into both corners of his mouth. To confirm his sinking suspicion, he glanced his tongue against the steel.

"Yep, not facing out."

When life throws you a backwards dagger, you just turn it and use the stabby side. Elmer chuckled, then let a heavy sigh escape.

He tried to determine a rhythm within the chomping and lunging so that he could act decisively. *"Here we go."*

When the faewolf lunged again, its weight shifted headfirst. Lannor released the hold with his left hand and kicked sharply with his boot against its thigh. The beast pitched sideways as Lannor filled his fist with the dagger and punched it into the passing throat. Blood splashed into his eye, but luckily the creature had only managed to lightly scrape him with its fangs as it fell. The dying beast frantically scratched the street, trying to get away, its *claws not gaining any progress. With a shove, Lannor rolled the faewolf over then dragged the dagger across its neck just above the collarbone.*

"With the blade facing out," Elmer said, closing his eyes.

The flailing would not stop. Lannor lowered his shoulder and rotated the dagger so the sharp side acted with the flow of gravity, and giving a violent heave, sliced so deep that the blade concluded onto stone. A sharp ting echoed across the deserted street.

Elmer wished for that dagger. And as long as he was wishing, he might as well add a pair of hands to that order. The frantic morons had not stopped cursing and digging outside and he wagered that the sun was probably beginning its gradual descent. He dipped his tongue into the foul tasting water below him, dampening his parched palate. The taste of blood was more favorable to whatever filth had seeped into the hole, but his mouth felt like a dusty fieldmouse had curled up and died in it.

How long does it take one of those stooges to retrieve a crossbow?

His question was immediately answered. A familiar metallic twang could be heard over the din of the cursing faewolves followed by a howl filled with shock and pain. Then cackling. *So much cackling.*

They just shot one of their own. Elmer shook his head, his snout carving a path in the muddy earth. The mangy tentacles that had been invading the opening all afternoon suddenly pulled back allowing dim light to enter. From between the mossy roots he could make out the shape of a clumsy looking faewolf, tongue flopping as he loaded and cocked what appeared to be a mockery of a crossbow.

Is that a crossbow?

The weapon looked stapled together and wrapped in twine, mechanisms loosely dangling with a shoulder stock bent at nearly a right angle. The dodgy looking creature had just wrenched the bolt free from a cursing and screaming mate out of Elmer's field of view, then placed the bloody quarrel into the contraption.

Those idiots only have one bolt.

Crawling into position, the surrounding faewolves laughing like drunkards, the weird faewolf made his way toward the small cavern. Elmer watched with tired disinterest, hoping that the twit was at least gifted with decent aim.

I don't want to slowly bleed out surrounded by these chuckleheads. He closed his eyes and waited for the old, familiar oblivion, praying for a swift end.

*Perhaps the Creator will allow me to return again and set out on a different path...and maybe I could take the form of something with venom or claws. Or both! Something much better equipped for protecting...*Margot flashed into his mind, an exceedingly pleasant final thought. Yet her memory triggered an urgent recollection of why he must continue. *I cannot die here! I must reach the Beast before the lad does!*

He heard the clack of the crossbow's release.

Mud splashed onto his face.

The idiot missed.

"Another! Another!" The bent faewolf howled, dancing an embarrassing jig and grabbing at the air like a child pleading for sweets. Another bolt was conjured seemingly from nowhere, and placed into its expectant claws.

Where do they keep...?

The faewolf was squealing for joy as he victoriously waved the loaded weapon, then suddenly the gleeful squealing was replaced by *just* squealing. The squealing that had been in front of the opening was abruptly somewhere overhead and far away and soon could not be heard at all. The ensuing scene fueled by panic was music to Elmer's pointy ears as the over-confident predators now found themselves locked in a game with the scales tipped against them.

What kind of creature would find these gross monsters appetizing?

The faewolves scrambled in all directions, howling and screaming, seeking shelter before the nocturnal horror decided to return.

The hours of tension had been exhausting, and as Elmer settled in for the night in the dark and damp crevice, he decided to pick up where he had left off when the sun returned to the sky. The beast that had killed the faewolf would still be out there, and if it found faewolf appealing, then a clean, well-fed dog would definitely be on its flavor palate. And his current surroundings were as good a shelter as any.

Sleep slowly crept behind his eyes with memories of warm meals haunting his pre-dream state. One meal in particular rose to the top, frothy and thick. When that pigtailed girl from long ago had welcomed him into her home, her family extended hearty hand shakes and comforting hugs, along with a table decorated with several different pies and hot cakes. He recalled that a roast mutton had been at the epicenter, tender and juicy, and his dry mouth began ache. He could almost smell that blueberry—

"Lannor." A voice woke him.

He saw nothing and closed his eyes.

Steam emanated from the crumbly desserts and even now he could taste—

"Get up, you dummy! It's me, Kiera."

Elmer squeezed his eyes tighter and shook his head. *Am I dying?*

"I'd help you out of there, but I'm too big to fit," continued the voice that *did* sound just like Kiera.

With stiff limbs and an equally stiff neck, Elmer got up and waded through the puddle. "Kiera?" he asked, gazing up at the biggest velikant owl he had ever seen.

"Yes," the owl replied with a beak coated in faewolf blood.
Elmer wagged his tail. "What does faewolf taste like?"

18

Schroederstall set his quill down and folded his hands, waiting for the aggravatingly gentle tapping to cease. He squinted at the door and placed his weary head in his hands. "Enter," he said, speaking over the arrhythmic clicks. A page eased the door slightly ajar and poked her head through.

The churchman heaved a dramatic sigh. "I *specifically* requested that you *bring the knights to me*," he reminded the girl. He could feel the tips of his ears growing hot. "Come in, for goodness sake! Come in!"

The page shyly entered, wringing her cap as if it were soaked. "They said to come to them," she said.

"Come closer, *please*." Schroederstall's features were now of a cherry coloration.

The page took a few tentative steps forward, her head peeking over the tall back of a plush cushioned chair. Holding audience with Schroederstall was not on her list of enjoyable activities. She would rather be off with her fellow pages, enjoying some well-earned free time. Earlier in the day she had been interrupted in the hall by Schroederstall. He had grabbed her by the collar and sent her on an errand. Now she was standing here while her friends were probably having loads of fun without her.

"I suppose that is close enough," Schroederstall said, rubbing the creases on his forehead. "Now *please* tell me what the knights told you. Be articulate. Posture is principal!"

The page's eyes danced all around, not settling for a moment on the man before her. "Just what I said. I told 'em you wanted to talk to 'em an' they said that you would have to come to them."

Schroederstall closed his eyes. "Where did you end up finding them?" he asked.

"I had to make a bunch of inquiries," the page replied. "It wasn't an easy job, sir." She gestured toward the door. "Lights out will be soon and if I get to the dormitory with everyone in bed, then I'll catch it from the headmistress and she don't take kindly to her young ladies coming in late. Not at all."

Schroederstall glared at the page. "Need I repeat the question?"

"Oh, sorry sir!" The page shifted onto one foot and scratched her calf with her toe. "The knights were at the Bloody Fork."

"The Bloody Fork?"

"Uh, yes sir. It's a tavern just over on—"

"I know where the Bloody Fork is." Schroederstall waved a hand. "Dismissed."

The page hesitated over an intake of breath. "Sir Clemence is in a right state, to be sure, sir." With that warning made, she secured her cap and departed the chamber.

After watching the girl struggle with the latch, opening and closing the door several times before it secured into place, Schroederstall retrieved his quill, dipped it into the inkwell, and began scratching at the parchment. The brindle feather violently jerked as he scribbled figures, applying much more pressure than was necessary.

He had been on his feet for hours waiting alone outside of Amyr's chambers as the day whittled away. The two knights, returning from Fenrirfang with murder in their eyes, were not of a mindset to stand idle. Schroederstall had instantly guessed what caused their mood and when they gave him the news, it only confirmed his suspicions. Aside from stabbing a man in the kidneys, a stiff drink or seven at the nearest pub was the logical way to end the day.

"So that's where they abandoned me to," Schroederstall grumbled, pressing down so hard that his quill nearly tore the vellum. Any conversation with Amyr, even the most banal chit-chat, was a dangerous affair, and adding extra warm bodies tended to spread the peril around a bit more evenly.

The squires and pages were all in their bunks at this point, and the closest attendant in proximity to his office was a sentinel. Asking one to serve as an errand boy was entirely out of the question. Gently blowing on the wet ink before placing his quill in its rest, he reached for his cloak and cap.

"A strong barley ale would be most appropriate," Schroederstall declared as he made for the door. "This day has proved immensely exhausting. Perhaps this unscheduled diversion will provide some semblance of comfort."

THE BLOODY FORK WAS A POPULAR DRINKING establishment for those interested in fighting and brawling, and for those interested in spectating the brawling and fighting. The room was generally split between the two, but, as with most taverns, there was usually a varied assortment of riffraff along the outskirts, along with newcomers dragged there by trusted friends. It was not dirty, neither was it *clean*.

The building had been resurrected several times before the current iteration, mostly caused by fires that had gotten out of control, but each time they secured a foundation and walls went up, it settled in the same spot. Hunched right in the apex of a busy intersection, most people believed that the moniker came from the tales of brutality going on inside, but in actuality, the original owner had intended to market the establishment with an array of hot meats from sun up until sun down.

A wall of agreeable scents greeted Schroederstall, stopping him in his tracks. The floorboards groaned as he settled in place, taking in the atmosphere. Booths ran along the wall, filled to capacity, and the open floor space before the elongated bar teemed with standing patrons, frothy drinks in hand. He pressed deeper inside, and a red meat stew smothered in gravy passed under his nose as a waitress nimbly maneuvered through the crowd, her tray somehow remaining perfectly upright. After the girl disappeared into the mass, Schroederstall's stomach grumbled loudly.

My drink must accompany dinner, eh? His calf muscles struggled as he stood on tiptoes attempting to catch a glimpse of the knights.

Onlookers smirked watching the tricorn hat pop up then unevenly dwindle back down.

Upon a rise, Schroederstall spotted one of the knights. *That looks like Phillip's proboscis!*

Sure enough, Sir Phillip was pressing through clusters of friends with a stein of ale in each fist, foam overlapping the sides and trickling down onto his fingers. Schroederstall cupped his mouth and shouted to the knight, bouncing up as best he could and trying to draw attention, but the room absorbed the sound.

"Blast it!" Schroederstall huffed. He made a note of the knight's direction and squeezed through an opening, treading carefully with his hands to his sides. One man turned to his friend, and Schroederstall's cap nearly flew from his scalp, brushing much too close to the man's elbow. Flashing his hands to the brim, he pushed it at an angle to his forehead in a desperate attempt to prevent it from being lost. He finally managed to escape the swirling mass of arms, backs, elbows, and tankards, finding himself among the seated patrons in the booths encircling the room. He plucked off his hat and placed it behind his back as he surveyed the space. Cool air passed over his head and a few strands of hair flicked and danced as a barmaid opened a door to retrieve more wood for the ovens. Slowly he rotated in a semi-circle, searching for the knights.

A laif in dark armour, seated in a booth, made eye contact with Schroederstall. The laif leaned toward his comrades without breaking his gaze from the churchman. And in that instant Schroederstall noticed the laif was sharing a booth with the very knights that he was seeking.

Shifting his weight, the churchman walked purposefully toward the trio. Apparently he had encroached upon a private conversation, and his presence went unnoticed as he awkwardly hovered next to the booth.

Without sparing another glance, the laif broke off his speech and took his leave, flashing a grin as he stood and offered his seat. He silently brushed past a blinking and gaping Schroederstall, and dissolved into the tavern.

"Was that—" Schroederstall sputtered as he slid into the seat. "Did I just see?"

The knights ignored him and continued to drink, wiping off foam moustaches after each draught.

"Was that a lampyr?" Schroederstall asked.

Without so much as a glance, Clemence replied, "Maybe." She set her drink down, her eyes red, the flesh underneath pronounced.

In truth, both knights appeared quite disheveled.

Schroederstall waited for further explanations and when none were forthcoming, he shouted out, "Well?!"

Silence was the response. The knights halted their conversation, words teetering on a precipice, just waiting for this irritating delay to pass.

"That armour he was wearing looked antiquated—" Schroederstall said.

Phillip was the first to respond. "What makes ya think he's a lampyr?" he asked.

Schroederstall swiveled his head at the notoriously quiet man, and placed a stubby finger to his upper teeth. "Fangs," he explained. "The fangs tend to be a dead giveaway."

"You're sauced," Phillip mocked with a cheerless smile.

The churchman placed a hand to his chest. "I have not had a drop, sir!" He leaned closer, jabbing the table with a finger. "I'll have you know that I waited for several hours outside of Amyr's chambers after you two louts abandoned me. Then afterwards I went back to my study to continue *our* business." His eyes scanned the room, shifting back and forth. "*Unmentionable* business," he hissed.

"*Unmentionables!*" Phillip laughed, glancing at a grinning Clemence.

Schroederstall waved their nonsense aside. "Now, who was that lampyr?" he demanded.

"I'm for another round," Phillip announced. "What say you, mate?" He wobbled to his feet, steadying himself with a hand to the table.

"Aye." Clemence threw her head back, draining her tankard. "And make sure you get one for our friend here. He knew our boys personally," she said, pointing in Phillip's vicinity. "And, and don't get into a fight."

"Got it!" Phillip belched behind a closed mouth. "The Godfrey Ale again, master?"

"That, that..." Still pointing, Clemence said, "You read my mind, good sir." Schroederstall could sense a wave of emotion coming from the knight as tears began to slowly simmer along the lower rim of Clemence's eyes. "Young Nathan...young Nathan loved those old tales about the Hinter Knight. After all, it's who we modeled his training after," she admitted. "Shhh, don't tell the church."

Schroederstall rolled his eyes, waiting for a barmaid to arrive.

Clemence continued. "Young Nathan was a goodly lad. Not the sharpest, but he worked hard at everything!" She abruptly lowered her gaze. "I remember one afternoon so clearly, so clearly, I hadn't had the boy very long, maybe a few months? Probably nine years ago or so, give or take. The boy was cross with me over some correction about his form or something, and he argued and it became more than it should have. He lacked discipline. Ah, he was young. And tall and strong for his age. He really stuck out."

Schroederstall followed along with the tale, but was drawing a complete blank on Nathan's face.

"So I decided to send him off to the vineyards," Clemence went on. "To pick grapes as a lesson. And wouldn't you *hiccup* know it, excuse me, wouldn't you know it, the lad picked nearly the entire corner patch of red echaner. You know, those sweet little black grapes that are a real bitch to pick. Nathan was so furious with me and that fueled him...And that's when I knew, that's when I knew that if I could harness that raw power, that raw emotion, and focus it into combat...Just give him a big ass sword and a heavy dose of discipline. Really focus it, you know?" She brushed away the cascading tears. "Then well, we would have a real champion on our hands. In another few years he would have had so many scarves stacked on his lance at tourneys."

Schroederstall rested his chin in his hand. "Warriors are excellent laborers, so I am told," he mused.

"Were you listening?" Clemence snarled.

"Yes, yes!" Schroederstall responded quickly. "The boy held great potential and would have no doubt garnered great renown in the lists, I am sure! A real handsome lad! Very comely, yes! But I would like to backtrack for a moment, if you will indulge me? Who was that lampyr? I never forget a face."

"It would be best if you forgot that one."

"If this concerns—"

"Leave it!" Clemence commanded, hammering her fist onto the table.

Schroederstall flinched. "Very well, very well. But I have other means of obtaining information."

"So be it," said Clemence.

"Now you were saying that your squire..." Schroederstall trailed off.

"Nathan," supplied Clemence.

"Yes, Nathan," Schroederstall began. "You stated that *Nathan* had been training with a bastard sword? That is most interesting *and* is in strict opposition to the church's laboriously clear instructions regarding the training of its squires. Do you think perhaps that is what led to—"

"Lucas and Enzo employed arming swords and shields," Clemence pointed out. "According to the church's laboriously clear instructions."

Schroederstall realized that he was venturing into sensitive territory. "But still, very interesting," he said softly.

"Oh, it was," Clemence agreed. "And he proved quite useful support in skirmishes in the forests with beasts and daemons and other nasty denizens. Things you are so well-versed in."

"Ha!" Schroederstall barked. "You know full well that my combat expertise extends to which part of the sword stabs and which part is safe to hold. My strengths lie elsewhere. Far away from your beloved battle grounds."

Clemence's brows rose upward on her forehead. "Those grounds are painted red with my sword as much as your pen," she said darkly. "Let's not kid each other."

Righteous indignation seems to have sobering properties. Schroederstall was about to argue his point further, but was interrupted by Phillip's return.

"Kill each other yet?" Phillip slid into the booth while crunching on a hand-sized cracker. "What have I missed?" he asked, digging an elbow into Schroederstall's ribcage.

Clemence followed the crumbs spilling from Phillip's mouth. "Who's playing a wafer gambit?"

"Some blokes over there," Phillip replied, gesturing in several directions.

Schroederstall's belly bumped the edge of the table as he abruptly straightened up. "Creator's claws!" he exclaimed. "That game is horrific!"

"Whoa, whoa, blasphemy. Let's try to keep it together." Phillip patted Schroederstall's hand. "Obviously, I didn't lose. Ya never dip your cracker into the clear stuff."

Somewhere across the tavern, a body struck the floor and a great commotion erupted. A woman screeched for a physician, apparently oblivious to the Bloody Fork's clientele.

From within the wave of onlookers, a middle-aged barmaid emerged. She made her way toward their booth with a tray laden with three foaming cups of ale. Schroederstall followed her with an unwavering gaze, transfixed even as she stood next to them. Holding the tray aside, one by one she placed the drinks before them.

"What is that disturbance over yonder?" Schroederstall inquired.

"Oh, that?" The barmaid's curls bounced as she turned. "Some twat chose the clear stuff."

Phillip darted a look at Clemence, and the latter covered her mouth and laughed.

"How utterly atrocious," Schroederstall said, producing a handful of coins from his purse and clinking them onto her tray.

"Eh, it's a Thursday," the barmaid said with a wink. She then turned away and dissolved into the standing area.

"That was quite the tip, churchboy," Phillip said, licking the suds on his upper lip.

Schroederstall ignored the comment and brought the ale to his mouth, sipping daintily to avoid the foam.

"So what news have you brought us?" Clemence asked Schroederstall.

"I held audience with Amyr," Schroederstall began. "And conveyed what I could—what he would allow—of what you found."

Clemence pulled a sip from her ale. "And how did he take it?"

"He is a difficult *being* to read," Schroederstall replied. "But he was not wroth, rest assured. And I would have you know what a difficult dance it is to hold communications with him. Most unpleasant!"

"You just have to tell the truth," Clemence disclosed. "That must be tough for you."

Phillip snorted. "So, is Amyr on the same page?"

"Are you inquiring as to whether you will be granted access through the wards in order to pursue Margot's brother?" Schoederstall said dryly. "Yes. Of that we are in agreement. Perhaps I have overcomplicated things with my subtleties. A mistake on my behalf that I will rectify and take responsibility for any further discrepancies."

"What does that mean?" Clemence shook her head. "We'll ride out tomorrow and sort this all out so Amyr can 'get his Linette' all over again. Do we need a talisman or a charm or something?"

"No. Nothing *physical*," Schroederstall said with a shrug. "He simply said that you are free to move about Fenrirfang. I can give you a shiny necklace if that will make you feel better?" He broke off, distracted. "Oh, will that maid be returning soon? I am ever so famished..."

"We need nothing from you," Clemence spat. "All I need is a piss."

"Nothing physical, eh?" Phillip asked, scooching closer and pressing against the churchman. "Well, a few minutes ago I started feeling this deep itch..." The knight reached for his groin.

"See now, Phillip!" Schroederstall squawked.

Clemence crowed with laughter. "See now, Phillip! You saw how that serving lass got him all bothered and hot, now he's like to burst!"

"Speaking of which," Phillip said, sliding out of the booth and standing next to Clemence. "I'm for a piss as well. And another round."

Schroederstall struggled to secure his cap. "I do believe I shall retire to my chambers," he grunted. "*Gentleman and lady*—and I use those terms loosely."

"Ouch!" Phillip staggered. "Words like that can really sting, you know."

"This has been a most fruitful engagement," Schroederstall continued, inching his departure across the bench seat. "And I must thank you for the beverage. Godfrey, was it called?"

Clemence narrowed her eyes. "It was," she replied.

Schroederstall stood and looked into the gap between the knights. "Good night," he said, tipping his hat, anxiously excusing himself.

"Men like that," Clemence began as she watched Schroederstall trundle away. "Hinder the flow of the strong."

19

*A*nother *weird dream with giant balls and familiar fictional castles.* Galahalt sighed, rolling onto his back and rubbing his eyes as he slowly transitioned into wakefulness. The mist of smoke passing over carried a pleasant aroma and the young knight sat up to investigate.

The clearing was still fairly dark; the sunlight filtering through the trees was warm, but not bright. Galahalt looked to his right where a tangled mess of blankets slowly heaved and lowered; the knight underneath still enjoying his morning repose. *I wonder what sort of dreams the Jester Knight has?* Galahalt shook his head, afraid to delve down that rabbit hole.

Drawing his knees to his chest, the young knight blinked away the remnants of sleep and nodded at his guide. Elkara sat across the flames busy shifting a skillet filled with pearly white fish flakes. Fresh logs spouted thick flames, slapping the iron all around its base, nearly kissing Elkara's knuckle as she set the skillet down.

"Woo, getting hot!" she said, waving her fingers.

"A good morning, Sir Galahalt," Figharth said from his seat on the edge of nearby stump, his feet dangling free. "Elkara snaggled a few delectable fish for us. She said I get first taste." The wisp beamed at the knight.

"That's well and good." Galahalt smiled and brought a hand up, shielding his eyes. "Would you mind dimming yourself just a touch? My eyes haven't quite adjusted."

Figharth giggled and bounced his heels against the stump. "I'm not *that* bright," he protested.

Elkara leaned over to the wisp with her hands between her knees. "Don't let anyone tell you otherwise."

"Ho! Ha!" Figharth laughed, wagging a finger.

Galahalt's armour clinked as he got to his feet. "Did you catch any sleep, Elkara?"

"No," she answered, picking up the skillet with a rolled cloth. "I didn't get bored enough, so I kept watch instead."

"Laives don't require much sleep," Figharth chimed in.

"I know that," Galahalt mumbled, tugging an arm across his chest to stretch his shoulder. "I'm just curious if anything notable happened."

Elkara placed the steaming skillet on a stump and rubbed her hands. "We should be able to eat once it cools a bit," she announced. She tossed the cloth onto her shoulder. "Now. Anything *notable*? Aside from the adorable sleep chirps from this little guy—" she paused, playfully tickling Figharth's belly.

The wisp hooted and pushed her away, residual laughs bubbling up as he rubbed the spot.

The laif settled back and continued. "Well, I spotted about three gnomes creeping around the outskirts of the firelight, but the chaps never entered the space. They fled when I stoked the fire. What else? What else?" She tapped her lower lip. "There were a handful of faeries dancing over the river when the moon was at full crest, but they were unarmed so I left them alone. And at one point I swore I heard a cockatrice clucking, but I was probably mistaken. Those monsters aren't nocturnal and it's been centuries since they crossed the wards this far south. But then again..."

Galahalt cleared his throat impatiently. The laif smiled at the interruption, and handed a chunk of fish to Figharth, who delightedly accepted the portion.

"My deepest thanks," the wisp chirped. He vigorously blew on the hot food, steam clouds dissipating almost imperceptibly with each tiny gust. His beak worked quickly once he nibbled a tan corner, tilting his head around each hurried bite.

"What an eventful night," Galahalt said sarcastically. The knight worked his way around the fire, careful not to singe his toes as he passed Gwayne's nest.

Elkara popped a mouthful of flaky meat into her mouth and spoke between chews, "I dropped a couple ogres a few hours ago near the pines."

Galahalt paused mid-stride, glancing across the fire to see the trembling wisp gaping at the laif, crumbs falling from his beak with every twitch. The knight continued his course toward the breakfast skillet, and spoke, "I'm sorry, your mouth was full. I didn't quite catch that." He squinted. "Was that something about ogres and dropping and pines? The rest was lost on me."

Shaking her head and swallowing, Elkara said, "A pair of youngish betas were clomping through the pines along the river. They were more than likely following the same trail as the dead ones we found yesterday, so I put an arrow between their eyes, and left the arrows sticking out of 'em. A bit strange, really."

"How's that?" Galahalt asked, eyeing the skillet. "Leaving the arrows as a warning seems like a sound practice."

"No, no. I mean the ogres movements," she clarified. "They don't tend to wander far like this. Well, they do sometimes, but not this far south. The four dead ogres from yesterday doesn't come across as particularly odd, just a tad out of place...but then to find another pair the following night, who I assume were scouts, that's what I find strange. It reeks of a concerted effort. Ogres need a home base for clan management, and the nearest fortification is somewhere west of Knotwithstadt, last I knew."

"Perhaps there was a division and some decided to take up residence further south?" Galahalt chewed between words, carrying a handful of breakfast back to his bedroll.

"Our travels will take us that direction, so we may find out. How experienced are you with fighting ogres?" Elkara queried.

Figharth began to quake uncontrollably, his eyes darting between the knight and the laif, unchewed morsels visible in his open beak.

"Not in the least." Galahalt shook his head. "Never encountered one." Elkara was not surprised by the response, and a smirk tinged her smile as she popped another morsel into her mouth.

Behind Galahalt, the forest was beginning to glitter as the sun began its climb. The blanket pile shifted and a muffled voice spoke, "He'll be fine." A bearded face veiled with tangles of long hair emerged. "I smell breakfast," Gwayne said, puffing a stray lock from his mouth and tucking it behind an ear.

"Help yourself." Elkara tilted her head at the skillet next to her.

With joints cracking the knight rose to his feet. "Looks to be a blessed day, eh Figgy?" Gwayne said cheerfully.

The wisp nodded enthusiastically with wings spread, allowing a gasp of the sun's light to poke through.

"I can't speak for the other two squires," Gwayne began. "But I know that Nathan was a decent fighter. And if those three managed to bring down a full grown alpha..." Gwayne reached down into the skillet. "Then our boy Gal over there should be more than up to the task." He popped a handful into his mouth and winked at the laif as he wiped his hands, grinning as he chewed.

Elkara crossed her arms. "It's true that a spear beats a longsword in nearly all contests, but I believe that Galahalt only knows men and their predictabilities. Ogres do not move like men. Their rhythm is completely different and their muscle density far outweighs even the fattest of men. And I'm talking about a lean beta. The alphas read from an entirely different script altogether."

"Ehhh, take it from me. Our young knight here is equal to a dozen betas with flails and poleaxes and bows and axes, or whatever else the knuckleheads carry around," Gwayne said confidently, looking at his little friend who was still busy munching a stack of white crumbs. "Right, Fig?"

"To be perfectly honest," Figharth said loudly, needing to speak up to be heard over the river. "I had my eyes closed." Gwayne sat down cross-legged on his pile of blankets and released a sigh.

"That is comforting," Elkara spoke flatly.

"I'll manage," Galahalt said, quickly steering the conversation elsewhere. "How much farther can we take this horse? Should we set it free before we depart or can we bring it with us?"

"The route to the fort will be fine," Elkara told him. "But some points after get a bit boggy, so we may look to abandon her if she begins to over exert herself."

Galahalt cinched a shoulder strap. "I don't mind walking."

"I want to reach the fort by evening," Elkara went on. "And if we ride then we will make it there well before sundown. The trek after will be made mostly on foot though, and I would rather not ride two deep on Error if it can't be helped."

Gwayne shook his head, a few blades of grass worked themselves loose from his hair. "I say we leave the horse, her owners will be by soon enough. Gal and I can hoof it to Navarene before dusk without a problem."

"When do you intend to head back to the kingdom?" Galahalt asked, bending over to fiddle with a buckle on his greaves.

"Whenever you do," Gwayne replied.

Figharth's feet stopped kicking. "Oh, so we will be seeing this quest through to its end?"

Gwayne nodded and flung another piece of fish into his mouth. "I must know the details!"

Elkara slapped her thighs and stood. "We can chat while we move," she declared as she strode toward Error and began organizing her supplies, loosening some bundles and securing others.

Figharth fluttered over to Galahalt and landed on his shoulder. "That fish was absolutely scrummy! Do you think that such fine cuisine will be a regular occurrence?" he asked hopefully.

Galahalt shook his head ruefully, absentmindedly watching Elkara rifle through her belongings. "I really don't think so, Fig."

"DO NOT STEP IN FRONT OF ME under any circumstance," Elkara said gravely, turning to the knights who trailed behind her, pressing through the dense undergrowth. "We will be approaching the ward soon." The laif gave the group a stern look and continued forward, bounding up a tufted knoll.

Gwayne, with Figharth perched on his shoulder, strode beside Galahalt. "She's a bit serious at times, eh?" he remarked fondly. "What do you make of—oof!" The knight was cut short by Error bashing into the small of his back with his snout.

"Alright, alright," Gwayne grumbled, jogging forward to gain a safe distance from the laifhorse.

Galahalt patted the top of Error's head, who snorted in reply, not in the greatest of spirits after being assigned pack duty. The magnificent, graceful beast had a lineage that could be traced back to the first laif war stallions. Survivor of countless skirmishes and quests, he had been victorious in most, failing in less than a handful. He had navigated swamps and mountaintops, hillocks and valleys, cobbled streets and muddy paths, and was now relegated to basic servant labor.

Error released a heavy sigh and looked away from the young knight. Galahalt, sensing the beast's irritation, decided to catch up to Gwayne, quickening his pace to get astride the knight and his cloud of smoke. "How will we know when we're at the border?" he asked.

"We won't," Gwayne said, pointing the stem of his pipe at Elkara, her cloak trailing as she swiftly moved along the indiscernible path. "That's why we have her."

"There will be another gremlin village just past the ward," Figharth revealed, rocking back and forth with each of Gwayne's steps. "Such a pity that first one yielded such disappointing results!"

"How far do those little critters travel?" Gwayne asked, exasperated. "They can't have gone far."

"It's true," Figharth replied. "It does seem like that would have been the village, seeing as it was the closest in proximity to where they took advantage of you while you slept. But gremlins are a crafty race and have developed intricate trade routes all throughout this great forest. And in other forests as well! Fenrirfang does not hold gremlin exclusivity." The wisp giggled. "If another village requests a specific armour type, then that request *must* be fulfilled, but a favorable trade must occur. As your sabaton is part of a rare and unique set, it would give whoever proffered the piece a trade advantage. It would most certainly give them a *leg* up!" Figharth finished, his head bouncing with laughter.

Gwayne pushed a thorny branch aside with his forearm and winced. "So you're saying my sabaton could be anywhere?"

"I suppose so, yes." Figharth tapped his beak. "Well, anywhere within the confines of Fenrirfang. I do not believe that the trade routes extend beyond the barriers. Gremlins do not require much sleep to function, so that lends to reason that predicting a possible location within the radius would be nigh impossible. But I do know of another village just north of the fort if the one ahead proves to be as disappointing."

THE TREES AROUND THEM WERE ANCIENT and massive in both span and stature, but ahead loomed a tree that outshone all the others.

An opening was carved at its base that would allow an average mule cart to pass under with plenty of space. When Galahalt opened his mouth to ask Elkara for the history of the gateway, the laif turned, stone faced, and began to signal wordlessly. She held up both hands, one an open palm and the other a fist. The open palm began skirting the closed fist, indicating that they should go around, then she nodded slowly, deliberately, waiting for the knights to return the nod before breaking eye contact.

Quickly bringing out her bow and nocking an arrow, the laif gave the tree a wide berth, treading lightly on her toes to dampen the sound. Ten paces past the potential threat, she signaled for the knights to follow suit. The knights carefully echoed her movements while Error trudged behind, nonchalantly chewing an uprooted fern with his eerily sharp teeth, its roots sprinkling dirt with each step. A fetid breeze passed through the giant hole, ruffling Galahalt's hair.

"That tunnel appears welcoming, but it smells like a cluster of dead feet are crammed up in there," he said, wrinkling his nose.

Gwayne nodded, covering nose and mouth. "Aspweavers," he explained.

Figharth, beak covered, looked over at Galahalt. "A most unpleasant sort of monstrosity, to be sure. And best to be avoided."

"Nightmare fuel," Gwayne added, looking back with a shiver, stepping into a soft patch of earth, his boot puckered as it left the slimy recess.

As they moved past the tree, Galahalt loosened the grip on his spear-hand, glad to be gaining more distance from the aspweavers. "Look at this," Galahalt said, holding a gloved hand out to a slender purple butterfly as it meandered by on its unpredictable course.

Gwayne and Figharth turned their heads to look, and both pairs of eyes and mouths popped open. The former was first to speak. "Careful with that!" he shouted.

Galahalt looked back to his hand and watched as the slim creature clasped onto his index finger. His glove suddenly constricted, and soon his entire hand felt strangled, pulsations throbbing in his fingertips. He watched with horror as the butterfly's proboscis pierced the leather and casually began slurping the material.

"That's a lapsucker!" Gwayne yelled. "Just swat it off!"

Galahalt dropped his spear and attempted to bat the creature from his finger, but found its body to be much more durable than he had anticipated. Frantically waving his hand, the knight stepped toward a nearby tree and bashed his hand against the trunk. "Get! Get!" he commanded. Finally taking hold of the wings, he plucked the creature off himself and the glove instantly resumed its shape. Fingers tingling like needles, he watched the butterfly shake itself off and depart for another corner of the forest, seemingly without a care.

"Little prick," Galahalt muttered to himself, striding to join the others.

They traveled on with nothing noteworthy happening until they reached a rather plain setting of the forest. The trees there appeared younger; their size not as large as the others, and the grass was a distinctly lighter shade.

Elkara slowed, raising a fist without turning and the knights took the cue and each lowered down to a knee. Gwayne drew Quintus slowly, the steel creaked out of the scabbard in fractions. As if catching an inaudible warning, Figharth leapt from Gwayne's shoulder and disappeared amongst the leaves above. The knights watched the laif gingerly place one foot in front of the other, arms outstretched and parallel to the ground as if walking a tightrope.

"What does she see?" Galahalt whispered to Gwayne, straining his eyes.

"We're at the ward," the jester knight replied with his pipe clenched in his teeth.

With perfect balance, Elkara tiptoed forward without making a sound. Each step barely registered on the soil as she silently graced the invisible trail, leaving the ground flora entirely undisturbed. Aside from a few tittering songbirds, the only sound Galahalt heard was the incessant crunching coming from Error's mouth. As the laif took a long stride, spreading to near split, she drew the dagger on her hip and tucked her chin to her chest. She drew herself to her full height, locking her legs together, knees tight, and gripped the blade within a balled fist. She raised her chin, drew a deep breath, and held it for a beat. As if trying to fool herself with the timing, the laif suddenly slashed downward drawing a bloody line on her palm before sheathing the dagger. Acting as though she was carrying a delicate moth within her fist, she held the blood-filled hand loosely, crimson trails forming over her knuckles.

Galahalt cringed as the laif squeezed her bloody fist over the ground, the blood showering the dirt with each tentative step. Her posture was reminiscent of his sister when she was sowing seeds and the resemblance flickered in his mind, causing him to blink back the darkness beginning to overtake his vision.

Bounding the final step, Elkara twirled on her heels to face the waiting men, a grin of relief spreading across her face. "It's all safe to cross now," she said, waving a hand, beckoning them to approach. Gwayne rose and sheathed Quintus, while Galahalt pulled himself up from the ground using his spear as a crutch.

Galahalt was deep in thought, distracted by thoughts of his quest. *I must press on.*

As Error brushed past him, Galahalt was struck with the sudden desire to retrieve an item from his pack. He tried to keep pace with the group while simultaneously reaching inside the sack, fishing for something while awkwardly trotting sideways, maintaining a stumbling pace alongside the laifhorse. Nearly losing his footing on a hook-shaped root, he cursed and stumbled a few paces, almost dropping his spear.

"Perhaps if he were to set the spear aside..." Gwayne whispered, leaning toward Elkara as they waited across the ward's killzone.

"Error," Elkara spoke sternly, but her face registered the opposite. She bit back a grin as she produced a thin strip of cloth and began to wrap her wounded hand. Crossing wards was simple enough, but the consequences for failure were severe and the signs of relief were still pinned to her countenance.

The laifhorse enjoyed toying with the young knight, but at his master's word he paused. Galahalt took a few unnecessary steps, tripping over his feet, and he would have toppled were he not elbow deep in his sack, anchored to something substantial. "Ah, there you are," he breathed, heaving Nathan's helm into the sparkling daylight.

"The carpet does not seem to match the tapestry," Gwayne commented dryly as the knight approached, synching his chinstrap. The elegant helm was leagues apart in craftsmanship from the meager church issued arms.

"Aye, I married up," Galahalt smirked, tapping the side of the remarkable helm.

"I'll say," Gwayne agreed, removing his pipe and blowing a generous puff into the air. Above him the familiar shape of Figharth was making an aerial escape from the boughs and the knight cordially brushed his shoulder, inviting the wisp to return to the perch.

Galahalt tilted his head at Elkara. "What manner of magic is guarding this ward?" he asked.

"You mean pillars of fire or lightning bolts from mysterious elementals? Or spectres that float invisibly along the border until a hapless traveler crosses its path, and then it materializes and violently forces itself into the poor sod's trachea, bursting him like a grape?"

Galahalt appeared at a loss. "Is that a possibility?" he asked eagerly. "I have it on good authority that all manner of guardians were put in place throughout the laif's forest kingdoms ages ago."

"True," Elkara conceded, turning away. "We need to keep moving if we're to continue making good time. Should be there right before sundown if we maintain this pace." She looked to the sky, "Hopefully the swamps haven't overflowed too much..."

Error snorted and flapped his lips.

"I know you're capable, old man," Elkara retorted. "No need to get lippy." She bonked her head against the laifhorse's snout and turned to face the knights. "Heads on a swivel, men." She extracted the bow from her shoulder and pressed on, leading the members into a more open landscape.

The trees were further apart, and the afternoon sun pierced through the canopy above, highlighting the floral arrangements, igniting gilded rims around the silhouettes. The portrait they found themselves in rose along a gentle incline; stone steps fabricated into the small hillside made the climb easier. Stumps dotted the slope and mature oaks stood on the ridgeline, preventing a clear view of what lay beyond.

The trio walked abreast, Error stomping behind, now that they were no longer confined to narrow pathways with invading branches and tangling brambles.

Galahalt glanced over at Elkara. "So what *does* guard that ward?" he asked.

The laif tugged a strip of dried meat, chewing as she answered. "Hobs."

Gwayne raised an eyebrow and smirked. "I always wondered."

"Most rangers don't like to reveal trade secrets," Elkara disclosed.

"I appreciate it," Gwayne said. "The guides I have traveled with are very tight-lipped about pretty much everything." The knight paused against an oak and tapped the remnants of his pipe against the sole of his boot.

Elkara and Galahalt continued the steady incline, their boots scuffing along the surface and Gwayne had to rush to catch up, hurriedly stuffing the pipe in his satchel. "So we're headed this way?" he asked, pointing. "I have come through here several times, but we always went that way." Gwayne swung his arm to the left, indicating a northwest direction. "It's a real maze getting to the fountain."

Figharth bent his knees and leapt from the knight's shoulder, fluttering upward and surveying the landscape with busy eyes.

"How many lampyrs have you escorted back from the fount over the years?" Galahalt asked Gwayne, admiring a lark on a low hanging branch, his head remained fixed while his feet continued.

"Less than a dozen," Gwayne estimated, scratching his neck.

Elkara swallowed then wrestled another bite of jerky. "Seeing less and less, eh?" she asked, chewing another mouthful.

"It's funny how that works." Gwayne faked a smile at the guide. "We have more Warriors than plate to cover 'em in, and yet you'd think there would be an equal number of Healers for all the bloodshed. Like it was in the past, which I am sure you are more familiar with than we are. I have been told that some lampyrs fought side-by-side with the knights battling the archenlaives, donning armour and all. Wielding blades while staunching blood," he enthused. "Rather poetic if you stop and think about it."

"With all the blood on a battlefield, you would think lampyrs would be attracted like moths to a flame," Galahalt noted, looking over at Elkara who took a hard swallow, still chewing.

"That was the case," Gwayne said. "Not so much anymore." He turned to Galahalt. "Does the church want for more Healers? There are lampyrs in service to the crown, but I am wondering how the church is faring."

"As far as *physicians* are concerned, the church seems able enough to keep up, but I'm not certain of the exact number of lampyrs they employ."

Elkara tilted her head to one side. "Dead men are dying," she stated. Picking up into a run, she left the knights behind, reaching the summit first.

An expansive view greeted the knights as they joined their guide. A discernible stone path began at the base of the overlook, worming its way toward a matching stone bridge and terminating at a wall of dense trees, picking up where the forest left off. Galahalt made to take a step forward, but his path was barred by Elkara's forearm bumping his chest.

A few chest hairs pinched in his maille. "Ouch, what?" he grunted. Following the laif's hand gesture, he noticed a trundling movement far below.

A family of griffins was crossing the cobbled path. Two mature adults led while three tender aged younglings followed behind in single file.

"They won't harm us," Elkara spoke just above a whisper, seemingly giddy. "I want to watch the hatchlings."

Sensing their presence, the mother griffin suddenly stopped and looked around. Locking eyes with the strangers above, she brought herself up and bristled. The youngling directly behind was not aware of her mother's abrupt stop, and bumped beak first into her mother's hind legs and fell back onto her rear end, looking dazed.

Elkara covered her mouth. "So cute!" she whispered.

Looking back at the little one, the mother screeched a command causing the father to instantly swing his head toward the group and raise his hackles. The mother led their ilk away at a quickened pace while the father remained still as stone, eyes locked on the knights.

The fallen griffin youngling remained on her rump as her siblings passed, and her father swiftly bent down, propping her up before returning to his vigilant watch. The little one squawked happily as she walked forward, now trailing behind the others. Her little beak was painted in a smile, her eyes taking in her father as she wobbled past. He screeched at the little griffin what could be interpreted as "Pay attention," and she bounced a pace, missing a step, then faced forward with the smile still etched across her face.

Gwayne faintly clapped as the griffins moved out of sight. A sudden flurry drew his attention to his left shoulder as Figharth gently alighted there.

"Tim says that many ogres have been passing through the ward recently," Figharth began. "Going back and forth." The wisp stood with his arms folded.

"Who?" Gwayne asked, tightening his eyes.

"Me."

"Gah!" Gwayne swiveled his head to his right shoulder, nearly sent another wisp sailing.

"Seems Tim startled ya!" the wisp tittered gleefully. The new arrival wore a peasant's frock and trousers that only reached his knees. His head was much squatter than Figharth's, resembling a chickadee. "Just as Tim's recent acquaintance here has told ya, a buncha ogres have been passing by since the thaw commenced. Sometimes they're armed and sometimes they're *really* armed...and sometimes they are really armed and pulling carts. To where?" The little fellow shrugged. "Tim does not know."

Elkara's eyes suddenly held a murderous gleam. "What is in their carts?" she questioned.

"Tim can't say." The wisp looked to the ground, abashed. "Tim covers his eyes when they pass. Supplies maybe?"

"Is this normal?" Galahalt asked, looking to his guide.

"Normal for ogres, sure," Elkara replied, her eyes fixed on their new friend. "But this close to a ward—"

"Tim doesn't fly too close!" Tim interjected.

Elkara blinked. "Thank you, Tim," she said politely. "But their proximity to the ward is not normal." She turned to Galahalt. "We will stick to the path as long as we can. It will lead us to the fort, but if I sense any ogres, we will make for the brush and avoid confrontation. There are other routes we can take if needs arise."

Galahalt nodded and looked to Gwayne's right shoulder. "Tim, you said that they were pulling carts?"

"Tim did."

"Are the ogres pulling the carts themselves or do they have brood-mares or oxen?"

"For Betsy's sake, no," the fae chuckled. "There aren't any creatures that will work with those brutes as far as Tim knows. Not even mules or donkeys. It's usually a pair of young ogres heaving the carts with a few others pushing from behind."

Elkara could summon several examples for debate, but a lengthy argument concerning race relations within Fenrirfang was not on her roster for the day. A sense of urgency was tugging at her, and she was eager to be on their way. "So, Fig, will your friend be joining us?"

The more formal wisp made to speak, but Tim broke in first.

"Oh, no, no, no. Tim has lessons to draw for the young learners this afternoon and he was only flying about, stretching his wings," he slowly fanned his wings. "Then Tim saw goodly Sir Figharth and we began our current engagement. But! Tim must be off! An educator's job is never done!" He hovered over Gwayne's head for a moment, extending a hand toward Figharth, and the pair exchanged a hearty handshake. And with that, Tim took to the skies. "Farewell!"

"Seems a decent chap," Figharth noted, smoothing the wrinkles on his trousers.

The travelers set off down the steep hill, carefully selecting their steps along the way. Error, however, went around, following a gentle sloping side trail that eventually joined the main pathway. A stone embankment greeted them at the base, creating a sheer drop, and as the knights navigated the fall, Error came trotting along the lane, stopping under Elkara.

"Thank you, kind sir," she said before dropping down with both hands pressed to the laifhorse's back, using him for stability.

Gwayne smiled sadly, recalling his faithful Delilah as he watched the laif rub her head affectionately against Error's muzzle.

The path meandered on its course, but ultimately traveled north, bisecting a meadow with ankle-high crimson tipped grass. Shrubs and vines clung to well-seasoned bulwarks, abandoned ages ago, their stones not matching those along the embankment or the path. Elkara kept a hand on Error as they walked ahead of the knights.

Faeries played and dipped all throughout the meadow, twirling around the skeletal remains of watchtowers soaked in wisteria. The faes' laughter somehow enhanced the warm breezes, imbuing them with pleasant greetings, placidly mussing any untethered lock of hair.

The river met them once again as they reached a mossy bridge that nearly matched width with length. Looking at the bridge from the side, it formed a semicircle over the waters and the stonework supports on each side were incredibly dense, tracing several feet of thickness from the bank. Vein-like cracks ran along the path where it met with the smooth rock of the bridge, and a smattering of crimson grass peeked up through the fissures. Waist high walls graced each side of the bridge, though erosion had whittled them down in places.

Using his spear, Galahalt vaulted onto one of the higher sections, both boots springing on the mossy carpet as he gained purchase.

Elkara raised a finger in warning, but before she could manage a word, Galahalt yelled out, "What the—!"

The knight nearly toppled from the wall, his startled momentum sending him onto the bridge, sticking an uneasy landing. He crept back to the wall and placed both hands on the fuzzy stone and peeked over the side. Each time the knight's head breeched the wall, a hairy face with an enormous nose would mirror his movements. When he shot an arm out, the creature below symmetrically responded, albeit with a much furrier extremity than his own.

"I was about to mention the family of trolls," Elkara said dryly, placing a hand on the perplexed knight's armoured shoulder before joining him as he looked again. A second head protruded to match the laif's movement, and she waved downward at the grinning faces. "They are completely harmless and rather friendly."

"Are they part of a ward or something?" Galahalt asked, taking a few steps from the wall.

Elkara stuck out her tongue at the bizarre reflection. "No," she replied, straightening up. "Just trolls." Without looking back, she placed a gold coin between thumb and forefinger and flipped it over the edge of the bridge.

Continuing along the route, the travelers soon found themselves in the forest again, although the cobbled path retained its integrity. As their eyes began to adjust to the fresh dimness, Gwayne blinked at his little passenger.

"What was your lady's name?" he asked, attempting to fill the silence.

"Leandra," Figharth responded warily, tipping his head back, exposing soft white feathers.

"Tell me about the lass, Fig. Cast some light on the gathering shadows." Gwayne kicked a loose pebble, and it clicked along its course, bouncing off the uneven angles of the path before darting into the tall grass growing along the edges.

If the wisp could have blushed, his little head would have been a radish. He stood and clasped his hands behind his back, facing the trail behind, plucking thoughts from the ether.

"She's the most—" he paused, the words strangled with emotion. He cleared his throat. "Ahem—Leandra is the most beautiful fae in all of Fenrirfang. But, she is the eldest princess in line of succession, you see, and it would suit her family best if she were to marry another of royal blood, or at least one with great wealth. I will not bore you with the intricacies of her royal line..."

"Oh, please do." Gwayne encouraged.

Figharth shook his head. "No, no, no. That tale would take us to the spire of Navarene and beyond. Just know that it is not uncommon for fae royalty to marry *down*, so to speak. You see, the fae hold true love above all else, but still, you cannot blame her father for disapproving of a union such as ours."

"Wait, her *father*—a king, does not approve?" Galahalt asked, lock step with Gwayne. "Go on," he prodded.

"Well, my family holds a bit of *honor,* but has never risen above its current standard. Not for generations. The house of Stantowlford stands as a pillar of knowledge, though some may jest that we are born with a roll of vellum tucked under our arms as we emerge from the womb."

"I would have thought they hatched from eggs," Galahalt whispered to Gwayne.

"I mean, that is an amusing thought," Figharth went on, completely ignoring Galahalt. "Seeing as we are born covered in writing utensils!" The wisp reached under his overcoat and winced, withdrawing a copper colored feather and holding it up to Galahalt. "See! We are equipped for our task from birth." He laughed, tossing the feather aside. The breeze grabbed hold of the feather and sent it directly into the side of Gwayne's mouth.

"That just came off your chest!" Gwayne sputtered, wiping his face with the back of his wrist.

"It was actually closer to my armpit," the wisp corrected, hunched over and emitting a few evil giggles. "But, anyhow, what Leandra sees in me? I'll never know. Last we spoke, we had a bit of a falling out. Some *things* were said." He heaved a deep sigh. "I don't—I don't know what she expects of me, you know?"

"We never do," Gwayne agreed, picking at his tongue.

"I want to hear more about this king," Galahalt said.

"In due time, in due time." Figharth waved both hands. "I'm a scholar, not a rough and tumbler. I prefer parchment and ciphers and candlewax and soft bed sheets. She knew what she was getting into when she accepted my proposal. But she calls me a *spectator*." The wisp made a sound that started as a laugh and quickly transformed into a sob. "I mean, look at me. She knew she would be marrying a—"

"Ogre!" Elkara interjected, pivoting back toward the knights.

Figharth shook his head in utter confusion as he watched Error break for the trees. "I do not believe that is an accurate description, my lady."

"Into the brush and get down," Elkara hissed. "And Galahalt, take off that helm, keep it low, and try not to allow your armour to shine too much."

Realization finally bloomed in Figharth's head, and he launched from Gwayne's shoulder, spiraling into the waiting boughs, completely immersing himself in the darkness. Elkara took point position with Gwayne at the rear as the trio abandoned the path.

"Lean against this one," Elkara commanded, tapping the bark of a generously wide oak while looking at Galahalt. The knight, who had been shadowing the laif, nodded, unlacing his helm and settling into position, pauldrons scraping as he lowered down.

Gwayne drew his sword and hunched next to Galahalt, concealing himself with his dark leaf cloak. He placed Quintus on the soil, ushering a few leaves over to cover the steel's reflection while whispering apologies.

"This will do," Elkara said, standing next to Galahalt with one arm resting on the immense tree. She shifted her feet, seeking a more comfortable stance, her eyes concentrated on the path, continually scanning, waiting for the ogre to stumble into view.

Silence filled the forest, save for the sound of scraping leaves to Galahalt's left. The young knight was listening carefully, focused on any sound that might be an approaching foe. His fingers traced a path along the helm's faceplate until a sudden rustling made his fist clench. Galahalt turned in disbelief to see Gwayne cradling Quintus with the blade nestled against his ear.

"What's that?" Gwayne whispered. "I know, Quintus. I'm bored too."

Slowly working its way along the path, a solid figure emerged between the shrubs and tangled branches. Between a gap in the foliage, Galahalt glimpsed what appeared to be an aged ogre.

"The ogre looks unarmed," he whispered to Gwayne. "And really old."

Gwayne's eyes rummaged over the knight's face. "Even better," he said, and quickly turned to his sword. "Gal says our enemy is both unarmed and decrepit."

"But the codes of chivalry prevent us from attacking the vulnerable and defenseless," Galahalt argued.

"Chivalry only concerns *armed combatants*. This guy is *unarmed* so the rules don't apply. See? It's a loophole."

Galahalt leaned back and thought for a moment. "Checks out." His pauldrons clicked when he shrugged.

"Plus, it's an ogre. So who cares?" Gwayne grinned.

Suddenly Elkara's face was between the knights and Galahalt felt the heat of her breath as she hissed at them. "Will you buffoons kindly shut your traps?" She stabbed the air with her finger to accent her words. "The ogre is *right there*." She had intended the warning as a deterrent, but Gwayne took it to be an encouragement. The knight sprang to his feet, cloak unfurling, and strode toward the path, pushing aside branches with his sword. Elkara reached out to keep the knight concealed, but she was too late and her hand caught only the breeze.

The ogre sensed the approaching knight and drew himself up, covering his chest with the tattered cloak that was draped from head to heel. With the attention focused on Gwayne, Elkara pulled at Galahalt's arm.

"Come on," she whispered urgently. She led him along a careful arc that circled the rear side of the ogre.

Once settled into their new position, Galahalt whispered, "He should be able to handle that old guy."

Elkara shrugged her bow into her hand and retrieved an arrow. "It makes little difference," she said. "Either outcome leaves a mess."

Gwayne placed his satchel on the ground and stepped onto the walkway. His hair flowed with each stride and as he came to a halt a safe distance from the foe, a few strands kicked forward and brushed his jaw. With his sword tip resting on the cobble, the lone knight leaned forward with both hands on the pommel, sizing up the monster before him.

The ogre remained fixed in place after sensing the approach, his hooded head placidly bobbing along with the knight's steps. The dozen or so heartbeats that passed felt tense for those in the thicket, but quite the opposite for the knight before them.

Gwayne clasped Quintus and casually rested the blade against his shoulder as he sauntered forward.

Suddenly a gnarled hand appeared from under the ogre's cloak, fabric cascading as the limb revealed itself further. Clasped within the grasp was what appeared to be a strange walking cane. An orb accented the handle at its peak and the monster's spindly gray fingers curled spiderlike around the polished surface.

"See!" Gwayne yelled triumphantly, pointing and looking to the forest. "He's armed!" As his head turned back, the ogre raised the cane, hovering inches from the path, then brought it down with a sharp click.

Upon contact, the orb flashed like a beacon and a white bolt seared the air, shooting out from below the ogre's hand. The working blasted Gwayne in the chest, knocking him back, doubling him over, and sending him flying. His body soared through the air like a discarded puppet, and he struck the ground at a roll, sending him out of sight.

A shuddering wave emanated from the impact site, shooting leaves and debris straight up into the air, holding for a few moments before tumbling back down.

"That's no ogre!" Elkara shouted right before a sharp ringing filled their ears.

The creature returned the cane under his shrouded cloak, and using it as a harmless walking stick, continued onward, paying no heed to the crumpled mess of a man heaped against the roots of a giant oak.

"I didn't know that ogres had mages," Galahalt said loudly, working a finger in his ear.

Elkara winced and shook her head. "Did you not hear me?"

The knight returned her pained expression and shook his head.

"That was no ogre."

20

After dragging the unconscious Sir Gwayne from the path and into the anonymity of the darkened shadows, Elkara waited impatiently for him to wake.

She sighed several times while pacing before producing a spherical capsule from her pouch. As soon as the chickpea sized item was cracked an inch from Gwayne's nostrils, the knight began to sputter and cough back to life, tears streaming down his face in torrents.

"What in the holy hekk!" he hollered, sitting up with an intake of air, and recoiling as if the air was knocked out of him once again, bouncing his head against the treebark. Frantically flinging his cloak aside, he raised the tunic underneath to reveal a massive black and yellow bruise with vein-like tentacles reaching outward from the ebon epicenter. "What the—!"

Elkara knelt down and pulled the tunic out of the knight's hands, fingering the fabric over where the magic missile had struck. "Not even a singe..." She sounded puzzled, but her expression did not match her tone.

"What does that mean?" Gwayne queried, sliding closer to the tree roots and locking eyes with the laif.

"Some serious magic," Elkara replied, accepting the discarded cloak from Galahalt, and handed it down to the perplexed knight. "We are not far from the fort. We will find shelter and get you sorted out."

Figharth joined them and was visibly relieved as he buzzed down with tears openly pouring down his feathery face, dribbling onto the overcoat below.

Apparently the concussive blast had sent the little fellow tumbling like a clumsy acrobat into the bole of a tree. Luckily, a family of amiable gliders had taken up residence inside, and the creatures were overjoyed by the sudden, unexpected company. They immediately offered a seat at their table and placed a steaming bowl of almond stew in front of him. Figharth had protested until the matriarch forced a delicious spoonful into his beak, but then the wisp relented and decided that he had a few moments to spare after all. He nearly lost all grip on time as he tittered on with the new friends in their warm little hole, and he had to raise his voice, almost rudely, before the family agreed to let him leave, bidding the wisp a tearful farewell.

The sun was still at its peak, not yet embarking upon its descent, as the group continued their trek along the path.

"There it is," Elkara announced, pointing a finger toward a gap in the treetops where a stonework spire loomed in the distance.

"Mighty tall," Gwayne commented, exhaling smoke from his nostrils, pipe in his mouth once again. "How does it keep from tipping over?"

Seeing the road entirely clear ahead, Elkara quickened her steps. "You'll see," she promised, looking back at the knight. A slight downhill gradient allowed clear optics for the laif all the way to the fort's heavy gate, though it was still a league or more in the distance. She was unexpectedly unsettled and bid Figharth to come near.

"Can you fly ahead and see if the fort is occupied?"

"'Twould be a pleasure, my lady," the wisp replied grandly, bowing before setting off with purpose, butterfly wings beating the air.

Come back with good news... She sighed and reluctantly led the knights forward, watching the wisp sail along the air currents before becoming nothing more than a speck.

"Little guy can really make time when he wants," Gwayne commented, shielding his eyes as they strained to follow the flight. "You wager there are more of those magic ogre things ahead?" Smoke billowed from the side of his mouth. "What was it that you called 'em?"

"Lichs," Elkara replied dully. She had already fielded several rounds of questions from the knights earlier on the topic and had explained all she knew about the creatures; that they were some sort of evil spirit that occupied and reanimated corpses. "And no," the laif continued. "This feels altogether different and I hope to be mistaken." Error clopped beside her, a wild radish churning in his teeth. Facing the distant gates, the laifhorse radiated hesitance, mirroring the ranger's mood.

Gwayne pointed the stem of his pipe toward the tower. "Ogres have taken residence up ahead," he stated. "Bet on it."

"Is that possible?" Galahalt asked, holding a handful of jerky and catching Elkara's eye.

The laif shook her head. "It would confirm my suspicions," she said, accepting a piece of the dried meat with her bandaged hand. "According to Tim, he has been seeing them frequently, which means the ogres are closer to the kingdom than is comfortable. Closer than they have been in centuries." Taking another bite, she added, "A rather bold move."

"A rather stupid move," Gwayne interjected, leaning against Error. "Once Elithiel catches wind, those idiots will be slaughtered like grazing cattle. That guy doesn't need any prompting."

"I may be mistaken," Elkara began. "They may be holed up elsewhere and are bypassing the fort entirely. It's an old fortification that was used as more of an outpost, and defending it is a real hassle."

"So you're saying we should be able to retake it," Galahalt stated, working his shoulder, squinting under the sun.

Elkara scowled. "That is not what I am implying," she said. "I'm merely stating that ogres are a simple race, but they are also very picky when it comes to selecting a base of operations. And I think that their elders would find Navarene not quite up to their standards. In any case, attacking a fort filled with ogres sounds dreadful and is entirely out of the question." *This simple stroll to Navarene is becoming more and more of a pain...*

"Could anything else be tripping up your senses?" Gwayne wondered.

Elkara flicked her wrist and Error moved toward her. Gwayne stumbled as his leaning wall shifted unexpectedly.

"Could be a number of things, really," Elkara replied, giving Error's muzzle a friendly shake. "Could be faewolves? Maybe crooked humans? A host of fae convening? Goblins and hobgoblins planning a spring festival? A coven of ghouls tearing a feast through the mausoleum? Or maybe it's nothing at all."

"My money's on ogres," Gwayne declared, folding his arms and flinching as a sharp pain surfaced from his bruised torso.

"Yeah, I'm thinking ogres," Galahalt agreed, rotating his spear.

Overhead, a sudden heavy panting could be heard. Before the group could discern the source, Figharth landed on Elkara's shoulder, huffing and wheezing, his face plastered with concern.

"Ogres," he gasped. The wisp doubled over, sucking in as much air as he could manage. "A whole bunch of them!"

21

"The people are rioting?" Amyr stood in his bedroom, evaluating the troubled priest before him. "How original."

The holy man rubbed his forearm, the robes barely shifting under the ill-fitting robes. "Well, it's not actually a riot, per se, but there is a great deal of unrest."

Amyr wore a handspun tunic with a full set of elegant greaves, his long hair pulled back, accentuating long ears which protruded more than the average laif. Drastically both longer and thinner.

"Is my edict the cause for such discontent?" Amyr asked, wearily rubbing his eyebrows. "I'm sorry, your name again?"

"Fluget, my lord," the priest supplied. "Yes, the edict, in part. But you see, it appears that you have been denying far more than birthrights...there was Knotwithstadt, which alone caused a lot of dismay, and all the orphans that came with that business...and the other day when you held judgment." His lower lip trembled. "When you took that farmer's wife..." Fluget trailed off, expecting the ancient laif to catch his drift.

Seemingly, Amyr did not. "Continue, Fluget," he said.

Fluget passed a dry tongue over his even dryer lips. "Well, you see my lord," he began. "That was sort of the 'leaf that collapsed the bridge,' if you catch my meaning? And now, there is quite a multitude gathered outside demanding an audience. Only your presence will satiate them."

"It is not often that men ignore survival instincts in favor of personal comfort," Amyr reflected.

"They believe they have just cause—" the priest slapped a hand over his mouth, eyes bulging in terror.

Amyr nodded at the bold, albeit risky statement. "Tell them I will hold audience on the morrow," he informed the priest. "Perhaps their anger will cool overnight."

"As you wish, lord Amyr." Fluget bowed and hurried away.

* * *

UNREAL. ELKARA POKED AT THE FIRE SENDING little red dots blossoming into the night air, batting away the embers before they latched onto her loose hair.

After a surprisingly mild debate, the knights had decided to avoid the fort altogether and skirt around it, using the forest as a curtain. Figharth had been able to make a head count while he fluttered over the ogres, which had been the deciding factor when they opted to go for the bypass.

The laif was the only one still awake, and she looked around the site at the sleeping knights who appeared almost gelatinous in the tumbling shadows. This night was not as chilly as the previous one, but Figharth had requested a spare sock anyhow, and she obliged by passing him the same sock from before, telling the wisp that she would keep it aside for his exclusive use.

"A proper adventurer's sleeping roll," she had said as she set the woolen article on a flat rock.

Gwayne slept on his back, the only position that offered any relief from the ever-present ache in his chest. Galahalt had sat up against a tree puffing his pipe, staring into the fire for hours. Elkara was uncertain for how long. One moment his eyes were open, and the next his head was back with eyes closed, the pipe resting on the ground.

"What, what, what," she whispered to herself as various scenarios played out in her mind. Occasionally thunderous noises invaded the site, originating from the distant fort, interrupting her train of thought.

Before darkness fell, they had managed to trace a circular path around the ogres, but they were not entirely clear of possible intrusions. Elkara assured the knights that she would spend another night as sentinel, forgoing sleep in favor of uninterrupted vigilance. She was happy to do so; the hours of quiet were always a welcome atmosphere for pondering moral mathematics. *I have never abided by a code of ethics, and I don't aim to start now. Those damn ogres in Navarene have created quite an obstacle for pushing the narrative that succeeding in a quest for the Questing Beast is fruitless.*

Countless knights, mostly young, but some old, had beseeched her for the glorious endeavor, each brimming with naïve optimism. It had become trade practice among the guides to take these customers to Fort Navarene and show them with their own eyes how impossible the quest was. *I have never shamed any of the crestfallen men or women when they decided to abandon hope and return home.* The whole trip usually took only four or five days, and was an easy and predictable coin source. Sometimes the ranger would even help them seek out a lesser monster as consolation. Their pride prevented them from admitting their defeat to others, so the illusion remained, which only boosted her yearly profits.

She heaved a pent up breath and looked over at Galahalt. *Sneaking into the fort would be stupid if ogres are traipsing about the spire. The whole thing would seem forced and weird. If we cut east and slink across the marshlands, avoiding gorgons—no, that won't do, the looking tree will be surrounded by smaller trees in full dress at this time of year.* Elkara tried to conjure up another place that would offer the sweeping views needed to illus-trate her point, while she chewed another strip of meat and unwound the dressing on her palm. The wound was now only a discolored crease. The ranger opened her hand, testing the range of motion, and hefted a nearby log into the fire, smiling as she realized that the cut no longer hampered her grip.

I should go for a midnight stroll. She believed that sitting in one place for too long caused the blood in her soul to pool and become stagnant, which was not good for critical thinking. *A bit of exercise will circulate fresh thoughts.*

She stood and brushed her legs, sending crusty bits from the log onto the ground. *Always be on the move and never worry about coin and numbers. The lack of one and the abundance of the other will make you weak. Weakness will not seep into these bones.*

She set off from the camp, resting her hands on the trees as she passed, trying to draw a sense of how the nearby creatures fared with the new foreign presence. Many years had passed since she had last set foot in these parts and there had been no published reports giving tes-timony of the fort's occupancy.

Perhaps the ogres moved into the fort more than a year ago, she thought as she balanced on a spongy moss coated log. *Maybe more.* Dismounting from the beam, she continued to walk forward without breaking stride. *The forest here does not seem too disrupted by their presence.*

A dark blue sloth hung from a low branch, gripping tight with all four paws. A thick moustache forked over his eyes and he twitched his neck as the laif walked into view. Off in the gloom, faeries and wisps weaved and danced, their light trails leaving glowing impressions be-hind. A sly looking fox crept past with her belly scraping the ground, and the laif smiled at the kindred spirit. She watched the hunter snake around the curvature of a broad maple, clearly in pursuit of a particularly elusive prey.

Elkara found herself where the remnants of a porch had once stood, the remains of an ancient laif home, long abandoned. A triangular stone structure that had been a modest hearth was now worn down to a jagged pulp. The house was a husk of its former existence, unrecognizable as the meticulous piece of laif craftsmanship, creating very little inspiration and only stirring a cloud of nostalgia.

This won't do. She vaulted over the crumbling wall along the perimeter, seeking another haven for ideas. Her damaged boot snagged on the torn stump of a sapling, and the laif growled a curse before recovering into full stride.

Trying to convince Gwayne or Fig to dissuade Galahalt would more than likely end up in an argument that would go nowhere. She hopped a babbling brook that transported lily pads on its tiny current, the moonlight reflecting silver along the glassy surface. *And if I'm to collect Elithiel's gold then I can't have the Jester returning without me. If I manage to work this out, I'm in for an excellent payday.*

The faint scent of decay wafted in the air, stopping the laif short. Absentmindedly she reached for her bow, but her hand found only cloth. She cursed, backing up a few paces, remembering that she had left her armour and bow back at the camp.

All I have is my dagger for defense.

Circling around, she avoided the ruins altogether, deciding that it would be best to avoid confrontation. A hushed splash in the brook drew all her attention, the color that had drained from her face gradually returning when she caught sight of a small lemon-yellow frog in the waters, struggling against the meager current.

Little bloke should have looked before he leapt. The laif jumped the brook again, holding steady gaze on the frog that was now wrestling itself up onto the bank.

What if I feigned an injury? She paused to stare up at the moon in full peak. *Then we would be forced to turn back...but I guarantee that lad will want to come right back out again, and I am doubtful the fort will be clear anytime soon. Gwayne was right, Elithiel would bring fury down on the ogres if he caught wind, but his hands are overflowing with burdens right now and I don't want to be the one to tell him...* The fox from earlier crossed her path again, the bold creature's muzzle riddled with needles from snout to brows.

"Bit off more than you could chew, eh?" The laif smirked as the defeated fox slinked toward the ruins, wounded nose to the ground.

Faking an injury is a deceptive tactic that screams desperation. I am not about to resort to such base tactics. I can do better than that.

Her footsteps led into a circular glade, the trees formed a barrier around a dense swath of bracken. The plants grew to her waist, completely concealing the floor underneath. Her feet continued to carry her forward, wading into the silky leaves, holding her elbows aloft as if entering a pond. She took a moment, standing in the center of the circle, watching the moonbeams scintillate the floating spores that drowsily floated through the air.

*I could always take him to the lake...*she thought, tucking a few loose strands behind an ear, listening intently to the nocturnal murmurings. *That is always an option, I suppose, but that would mean more days spent in the forest and I need to get back sooner than later.*

She continued to wade through the ferns, her feet plotting an unseen course, the plants nodding meekly in the wake of her departure. A pleasant passage granted before returning to the night shadows and the clingy brambles that awaited beyond the glade. *No, the lake is out of the question.* Shaking her head wordlessly, she placed a hand on the trunk of an encircling tree as she passed beyond its barrier.

Elkara paused as she came upon a cracked and withering fountain, cast long before her time, punctuating the center of another grove. Her eyes were drawn to the pallid hues of the moonlight's reflection on the smoother stones as she pressed through the low hanging branches. Vines smeared the symmetrical structure, binding it like randomly spun yarn, constricting the statue on the pedestal at the fount's center.

Pressing into the clearing, Elkara strode toward the kindred statue, admiring what was left of the detail. The female laif depicted was holding a down-turned kite shield, from which water would be flowing if the mechanism had not been destroyed by erosion. A portion of the stone laif's head had been sliced diagonally in a clean and even strike. It was just above the left eyebrow to the top of the opposite mandible, leaving a single eye to stare into the forest.

"Yaval..." Elkara reverently intoned, running her fingers over the smooth separation, leaning into the fountain and looking for the missing fragment in the empty pool. Her eyes locked on a few deceptive stones, but only useless debris and mismatched leaves inhabited the deserted ornament. *Yaval; the paragon of steadfast loyalty...If this was formed before her story ended, that would be...*She eased away with her hand resting on the stone laif's shoulder, turning away, and stepping over the pool's wall.

"...rather prophetic," she finished, whispering as she recalled the treachery surrounding the demise of Yaval. The first warrior laif had been betrayed by her own people simply for falling in love with a human. It was before her time, but Elkara was well-versed on the tale.

The laif picked a path through the trees, ducking unyielding branches and leaping over the lower, guiding the pliable stalks with an open palm.

A heaving bulk coiled around the base of a threadbare elm, giving the waning tree a startlingly diseased appearance. Slivers of moonlight revealed that whatever was hugging the trunk held life and its pulsating movements were respirations. Darker patterns gave way to lighter, from spine to belly, the beast's scales like heavy gauge ringlets of maille. Knowing the dangers that this obstacle created, the laif carefully retreated, walking backwards with eyes straining against the ebon darkness.

She held her breath, staring into the pale light, watching for any indication that the sleeping monster was aware of her presence. Once her heels nearly bumped into the fountain, she opted to travel further around; holding distance from the crumbling homestead, then pitch a line to the camp.

A tighter course would be safer, but I am not ready to backtrack through the familiar. Looking up toward the boughs of ancient trees, thick branches created tempting pathways, and as the laif contemplated taking a stroll above the earth, a parting of grass and a shuffling of feet raised the hairs on her arms. The heavy panting was a dead giveaway to the intruder's identity, and Elkara dropped to a knee and welcomed the inbound dog. With a tongue hanging loose from the side of his muzzle and bushy eyebrows topping wide, intelligent eyes, the animal closed his mouth and approached the laif as if they were old friends.

"You don't miss too many suppers, do you?" Elkara said, kneeling and cupping the hound's face in her hands. "Let's get you back home. What say you?"

If that basilisk spots you, I don't think your master will be too pleased with the stone replica you'll leave.

The stray hound guided Elkara toward a clearing with a cottage punctuating its center. Firelight from a roaring hearth poured out from its windows.

Elkara knelt along the outskirts of the clearing. "Farewell, my new friend," she said, burying her face in the hound's thick fur.

Whimpering in confusion, the hound swiveled his head between the cottage and the laif. "Come with me," his eyes seemed to plead. "We can play in the morning."

"No, go on," Elkara whispered.

Reluctantly, the hound loped away, sparing a few dozen hopeful backward glances.

The night was still young, but Elkara decided it best she return to camp. After pressing through branches and navigating the dark hillocks, she spotted the outline of a familiar laifhorse in the dim light. Error's meal of soggy grass was suddenly interrupted by her approach, his ears sharply perking up, and the laif gave her old friend a reassuring pat as she walked into the firelight. She tossed a fresh log on the fire then sat down, drawing her cowl up.

I will tell Galahalt of the routine once he wakes. She smiled as she gazed into the flames. *No more deception.*

22

Gwayne was the first to stir and wake, his sore chest accompanied by a nagging ache in his bladder. He groaned loudly as he rolled over and got to his feet, patting Error on the head and making for a tree down the nearby embankment. Hearing the disturbance, Figharth tossed inside his sock, eyelids creeping open.

"Will there be fish on the menu this morning?" the wisp asked sleepily, eyes not quite fully open.

Elkara shook her head at the fae while placing a small leaf wrapped bundle on the rock beside him. Figharth kicked free of the sock and walked over to the wisp-sized package. He pulled the leafy corner open, the sides retracting flat, revealing an even mix of berries and nuts. Shades of brown intertwined with the dark purples and reds, and the wisp could not hide his delight.

"My deepest thanks, my lady!" he chirped.

Elkara placed a hand over her heart and bowed her head. "My pleasure, Fig."

The wisp immediately sat down with his legs out in a v-shape around his breakfast, devouring it with both hands.

"Chewing is important!" the laif said emphatically, her voice directed at the knight still sprawled on the ground.

Figharth paused mid-munch, then looked up at the laif and nodded before stuffing another handful into his beak.

"So Fig, what's on the agenda today?!" Elkara asked, her volume still very loud. "Should we look to sack the fort?!"

A few crumbs rolled from Figharth's lower beak as he cocked his head to one side.

"I think I agree!" Elkara nearly shouted.

Galahalt remained asleep, despite her efforts.

"We will go around—!"

"Why are you speaking like that?" Gwayne interrupted, approaching while adjusting his belt. "I can hear you plain from all the way in the gully."

Elkara inclined her head toward Galahalt. "I'm trying to—"

"Wake the lad?" Gwayne asked. He strode over to the sleeping knight and nudged him with the toe of his boot. "Wakey, wakey."

The bedroll moved of its own volition. "I'm awake. Aye. I'm up." Bleary eyed, Galahalt sat up and ran a hand through his hair. "No fish, eh?"

"No, but I have berries!" Fig announced, crumbs and droplets sprayed from his beak.

Galahalt got to his feet and rummaged through a supply bag suspended from a branch.

"Once we are situated," Elkara began. "We can set off on a different course that will put us clear of the fort and any sort of ogre activity."

"Avoiding the stone path then?" Gwayne guessed, speaking with his tunic lifted and chin down, examining the dark wound on his sternum.

"I think that would be best," Elkara agreed, grimacing at the knight's spidery bruise. "It's been awhile since I have gone further than the fort on this side of the forest, but I don't believe the course has changed dramatically."

Gwayne gingerly lowered his tunic. "Well, aside from the ogres," he remarked.

"Aye," Elkara said. "Well, the *terrain* will be the same as I recall. The dangers, however, will always be unpredictable."

Galahalt chewed a mouthful of bread as he ambled back to the fire, Error right beside him. "Once our faithful assistant here is loaded up," he said, ruffling the hair between the laifhorse's ears. "Then we can shrug off?"

Elkara gestured for the hunk of bread in the young knight's hand. "Thanks." She tore off a bite and slowly chewed, taking a moment to reflect. "Correct. There isn't much to do this morning other than preparations for departure. But I do need a private word." She thumbed aside, away from the other three.

Gwayne sat, sharing the rock with Figharth. "By all means," he said. "I'll see to everything else."

Elkara led the knight past the fire pit and out toward a secluded spot in the trees. A pair of hedgehogs trundled in the grass toward a stone plateau, yawning as they pressed on for the sun-drenched platform. Other creatures stumbled from their hovels, eagerly shaking themselves free from the night's cold tendrils. A triumvirate of grackles posted on a limb announced the intruders' arrival.

Galahalt had foregone boots and cursed under his breath as sharp protrusions assaulted his bare feet, not enough to draw blood but enough to bring dismay.

"How far are you leading me?" he asked, leaning against a tree for balance while examining the sole of his foot, picking off stems and leaves.

The laif's head swiveled, taking in their surroundings, squinting towards the rays of daybreak.

"This'll do fine."

Galahalt groaned, slowly testing the ground with his foot before placing his weight on it.

"Now what I am about to tell you," Elkara began. "And please understand that I understand any sort of frustration you might feel."

"Understood." Galahalt picked up the theme, crossing his arms.

Elkara coughed a nervous laugh. "I have been a ranger for most of my life," she said, glancing to the boughs overhead. "Several lifetimes for a human, and you are certainly not the first to seek my help in reaching the infamous *Questing Beast* and acquiring the glory and splendor that goes along with accomplishing such an impossible feat. As warriors are still suckling, they are told about this quest and it can become an obsession for some early on. Most grow out of that phase and set their sights on more attainable goals; a hearth and land and perhaps a mate to share it all with. Or they seek glory on the field of battle, for church or crown, hunting monsters to keep their skills honed, longing for the killing fields.

"Their dreams run red, and tainted with reality...a reality that cannot include fictitious beasts, and coin vainly obtained to seek them out and drive them down with the edge of a blade. No, their heads are below the clouds where glory goes as deep as three meals with a solid roof to cover it.

"A simple life is what many really want, underneath it all, after the blades of war have grown dull and the warmth of a fire beckons. The promise of a life of consistency, free from days riddled with bloodshed where your final breath is cut short mid stride. You are young and I know that your blood runs hot, as all marked Warriors. I am telling you these things because I know. Because I have seen. This is probably when I would be showing you how futile the quest is, if we were at the top of the spire at Navarene. It's not so easy to illustrate otherwise."

Galahalt worked his jaw. "Speak plain," he demanded.

"Picture in your mind a very great distance. Alright? And beyond along the expanse is woefully dangerous terrain. And then further past that—"

"How many days?" Galahalt interrupted.

Rolling her eyes upward, Elkara mentally calculated the distance. "Four of five days," she replied. "Perhaps a week? It depends. Anyhow, beyond the manticores and a myriad of other sharp stabby things, lies Lake Humiel."

The knight's eyes tightened into slits. "Sounds like you're spinning a tale."

"It's the honest truth," Elkara said, withdrawing the drinking flask from her hip.

"I've never once heard that the Beast lives at *that* lake," Galahalt said.

"Well that's where he is and that's why—" A distant noise changed the laif's face into a mask of astonishment. "Behind the tree! Now! Get low! Don't breathe!"

The knight pivoted around the wide trunk, ignoring the painful steps getting there. Elkara leaned against the tree, sniffing the air with nostrils flared while Galahalt crouched on the other side. Like the calm before a downpour, the forest was dead silent for the space of a breath before branches began snapping in the distance, followed by violent shouts that rent the calm air. Maddened voices pierced the area in a dialect that was either foreign or grossly inarticulate, accompanied by the approach of what sounded like a small army of frenzied daemons. Something between panic and excitement began creeping into Galahalt's limbs and the knight greeted the emotions with a smile.

Elkara was the first to catch sight of the creatures, and she leaned down, her nose nearly brushing the young knight's earlobe. "Faewolves," she whispered.

"And me without my spear." Galahalt counted the faewolves as they rushed past, only a stone's throw from the tree. They moved like laives imbued with a more frantic spirit, as if a current of agitation coursed through their limbs, sending their minds on the precipice of madness.

One of the faewolves stopped and inclined its head in Galahalt's direction while the other faewolves raged onward.

Galahalt and Elkara stared at one another, neither daring to move.

At length the pounding of feet slowly dwindled into the distance. And after a stretch of silence went by, Galahalt peeked out, and to his great relief, discovered the faewolf had moved on with the rest of the pack.

Placing a hand on Galahalt's shoulder, Elkara strode from the tree, bent on inspecting the faewolve's tracks. She looked hard in the direction of the spire, traced their footprints with a thumb and forefinger.

"A siege," Elkara exhaled. "They are going to attack Fort Navarene."

She looked at Galahalt and an understanding passed between them. At full tilt they sprinted for the camp.

ELKARA AND GALAHALT REACHED THE CAMP as Gwayne loaded Error with supplies. The knight observed their approach with an arched brow. "Sounds like a bloody fight," he said, securing his sword belt with a tug. "Fig went off to see what all the fuss is about."

Galahalt looked upwards, the sounds of battle clearly ringing. "Faewolves. We saw them running for the fort."

"I know a place where we can observe," Elkara offered, looking at both the laifhorse and knight. "If you are game?"

"Of course," Gwayne replied.

Elkara scanned the skies. "Now where is that wisp? We must be off."

Galahalt tugged his armour free from a satchel on Error's sidesaddle, the pauldrons and greaves unraveling in a bundled mess.

"Your boots are on that stump," Gwayne said helpfully, pointing toward the smoking ashes, the blaze reduced to gray powder.

Particles picked up by the breeze caught in the young knight's face and hair as he wrestled with the boots, his back against the stump. He rubbed his face and spat, still seated, working to secure his armour. Elkara checked the supplies and secured the loose straps while Gwayne stooped behind Galahalt, locking the right pauldron into place with a sharp pull.

Figharth swooped down and hovered at eye level, a gloved hand held to his heart. "Faewolves!" he yelled. "Ogres! Embroiled in—"

"We know," Elkara interjected. "We are heading out now. Keep up."

"They formed a ladder!" Figharth blurted. "Climbed one on top of the other like ants!" The wisp excitedly followed overhead as the knights below ran behind their guide.

"It's not far!" Elkara turned her head to the side. "Keep up!"

The laif led the knights over several shrugging foothills that increased in grade and height as they progressed, finally reaching the base of a ridge that heaved upwards toward a lesser mountain chain.

"Just past that treeline," Elkara explained, pointing toward a hill that leveled off. Upon entering the cooler shade of the forest, Elkara slowed to a trot.

Galahalt paused to admire the view down into the valley. "Oh my." He beheld Fort Navarene, the colossal spire at its center, the outer rim encircled by dense forest with the exception of the front and rear gates where the stone path bisected.

He could hear the battle, but was unable to see it. *If I were only a couple dozen feet in the air...*

"Oi!" Elkara shouted from somewhere overhead.

Turning toward the noise, Galahalt spotted the laif waving down at them from what appeared to be a raised balcony set into a tree. Gwayne had not stopped to take in the view and was already at the base of the tree.

"There's a silk ladder hanging down!" Elkara cupped her mouth as she shouted.

Galahalt felt a sharp tingle in the tips of his fingers and toes as he watched Gwayne effortlessly scale the swinging ladder. He took a deep breath, waiting for the ladder to stop swinging.

The translucent rungs were much more pliable than your typical rope and Galahalt's steel-clad hands held fast as he hefted his weight from the ground and secured a boot on the bottom rung. His body swung parallel to the earth before he pulled himself up, advancing upward with one clasp after another. As the swinging radius tightened, he noticed the edge of the platform was within a few more extensions. Kicking his chest onto the landing, he grasped the flat surface, his shoulders registered purchase before Gwayne bent down and pulled him clear of the drop.

"That's a sheer one!" Gwayne laughed, helping the younger knight to his feet. "The view of the siege is spectacular from here."

"Who's winning?" Galahalt asked. The floor was surprisingly sturdy.

"Hard to say at the moment," Gwayne replied, swiping a heavy branch aside, allowing the pair to enter the sunlight. Elkara was leaning against the balustrade, intently fixated on the battle unfolding far below, and Figharth sat beside her.

This angle is perfect. Galahalt gripped the top rail, catching sight of the frantic display of brutality, the sort that mere men are unable to muster. The faewolves scaled walls and leapt in unpredictable gyrations at the defenders, swarming staircases and flooding courtyards. Claws like the reaper's sickle raked and gouged any undefended gray flesh and each of the vastly outnumbered ogres had incisions that wept openly.

Though the ogres were critically outnumbered, at least four attackers for each in defense, the number of slain faewolves strewn about was rather startling. A well timed swing from an alpha's great axe could easily sever three or more of the frantic beasts completely in half, and the others within the radius were left incapacitated at the very least.

As long as the fools are aligned properly. Galahalt admired the powerful rebuffs made by the overwhelmed ogres. Fortune appeared to be smiling down upon one particular alpha and Galahalt watched as the brute defended the top of a staircase leading to an upper rampart. *If such high ground was obtained, the tide of battle would shift significantly at this point.*

A stream of faewolves diverted in that direction, though the bulk seemed to spill along the main pathways on the ground level. The invading creatures overtook the stairs, leaping three steps at a time, rushing headlong into a veritable meat grinder. As if driven by madness, the beasts attempted to push through the split and decapitated corpses of their brethren at the top of the flight, who were still on their feet, essences draining and mucking up the stairs. As soon as one managed to slither through the bloody clump, either the weight of the dead or the slickness of the stone would unbalance their footing. Before a correction could be made, their lives were soundly extinguished by the waiting axe.

A stone wall barred Galahalt from clear sight of the staircase carnage, but he could infer the amount of bodies piling up in the passage as the gatekeeper pressed a heavy boot into the last culled faewolf, attempting to compress the mess.

Bodies were stacking up as both sides sustained heavy casualties, however the faewolves' number dwindled faster, creating more even odds.

"Perhaps we will stay in the fort tonight," Elkara said quietly, leaning forward so her chin rested on her knuckles wrapped around the top rail of the overlook.

"Put the survivors out of their misery," noted Figharth ominously. The normally opalescent glow around the wisp seemed to be tinged a darker shade.

"Whoa, Garth!" Gwayne eyed the little creature. "Maybe the fort will be abandoned after the dust settles. If the ogres manage to survive then they won't have the numbers for a proper garrison."

Figharth peered at the knight from slitted eyes and the corners of his beak curled into the semblance of a grin. "Even so."

Gwayne's eyes widened as his feet stole a half step from the fae, watching sideling for a moment before returning his attention to the fort.

Two ogres remained standing in the courtyard, while the faewolves were whittled to a half dozen; their stamina greatly diminished as they rallied in the center, leaning against the base of a statue. The axe wielding alpha on the ramparts rushed toward an open staircase as he looked to join the last survivors of the siege. He saw from above that his fellows were surrounded by foes at the fort's epicenter.

The haggard and torn ogres sustained more wounds than they deflected as they attempted to mount a final stand, back to back against the foes who danced in and out, flashing claws, almost toying with them.

The beta was clearly closer to the grave than his much larger partner and was nearly collapsing from blood loss and exhaustion. His life was prolonged by a pair of strong guiding arms that forbade total failure. Perhaps it was self-preservation that drove the alpha to defend the smaller of their ranks, propping him up each time he fell, prolonging the inevitable. Despite hanging like a puppet clinging to a solitary string, the alpha tried to defy the end.

Finally, feeling almost like mercy to the spectators, a pair of faewolves worked in unison to overtake the poor beta and drag him from the desperate grasping. Bellowing with rage and despair, the mighty brute brought his hammer down from an overhead arc, crushing the pair of retreating faewolves and effectively bringing his companion to an end.

The bold act prevented the agonizing dismemberment of his companion, but it exposed the alpha's blind side momentarily, which was long enough for one his foes to take advantage. In an explosion of fangs and claws, the faewolf seized onto the alpha's upper back, instantly ravaging the gray flesh into red strips. In overwhelming shock, the ogre dropped his anvil of a hammer, struggling in vain to seize the parasite, but the beast was positioned just shy of grabbing. Clawing at his own back, the ogre's hope drained alongside the rivers of blood. He surely believed that he was the last of his brothers within Navarene.

When victory seemed sure and it was only a matter of time before the feast would begin, the faewolves gathered in the courtyard to watch and wait for the fall. Exhausted with tongues draped over fangs, sucking in air with delighted gleaming eyes, and fully engrossed as their sister exacted the final strokes.

It was not to be.

The dying alpha grinned as he noticed something from the corner of his eye hurtling with total abandon toward the heckling faewolves.

Like an avenging daemon, the newly arrived alpha seemed to spread his wings before bestowing ruin upon those who had brought suffering to his kin. All that had remained of the invading horde was soon splattered all over the cobblestone yard in indiscernible masses of limbs and organs. The ogre, intent on retribution, was not interested in technique and a few swings missed completely, but he recovered each time, finding solid ground before the blade of his axe cleaved its target.

The final faewolf leapt clear of the dying alpha, and locked eyes with the embodiment of vengeance that stood before her with chest heaving, dressed in dribbling crimson from axe head to waist. She teetered on the edge of exhaustion, pure hatred driving her forward, glancing over at the ivory spinal column revealed from the torn flesh of the shuddering, dying alpha. The faewolf's eyes displayed nothing but contempt as she side-stepped the ogre's charge, avoiding the axe.

"Get him! Gut him!" Figharth drummed his lap, overly enthralled by the display. His companions were unsure to whom he was referring, only sure that the little fellow was clearly in favor of one side.

When the alpha charged and missed, his foe capitalized, tearing a gaping wound and severing his left hamstring on the trailing step. Standing proved difficult for the ogre and hefting a massive axe was a struggle. The gash poured in a deluge onto the cobblestone, red speckles splashing onto his boots.

He shifted his weight to ease the pain, groaning heavily as he tested and failed again. The faewolf crouched out of reach, tongue wagging, patiently waiting for another opening. With a final effort, the ogre mustered forward momentum, but failed pitifully, like a bird with a scorched wing. He staggered, the weapon unwieldy in his current state, and the faewolf sprung. One swipe with her left claw opened the brute's exposed throat, then rounding low, she lashed again at the leg wound, compounding the injury.

"Yes. Yes!" Figharth hissed excitedly with balled fists as he watched the dying mass crumple to the ground. The survivor staggered back, taking in her surroundings before pressing against the nearest wall. Allowing gravity to take hold, she slid to the ground, leaving a distinct impression on the brick.

Elkara laughed deep in her throat. "That played out rather well!" She backhanded Galahalt's chest as she crossed toward the ladder. "Best we head down and reclaim the battlements!"

23

"There are a few sights that I have observed in my time that cause great irritation," Amyr said to his escort, the sentinels turning at the sound of his voice. "And one of those being when a drowning man attempts to save another drowning man."

Amyr and the sentinels stood in an armoury, decorated with a vast array of ornate weapons and arms. This room was windowless, the scent of grinded steel and oil prevailed heavily in the air. The flaming sconces along the walls pierced the otherwise dark cell, casting shadows that needlessly drew the eye.

"Captain?" Amyr fixed hard eyes on the sentinel beside him. "You stated that the main hall is at capacity?"

"Yes, lord Amyr," the captain replied. "The crowds spill out into the streets beyond the Basilica."

"The doors remain open?" Amyr employed his teeth to synch a pauldron strap, then tucked it under his breastplate with a few nudges.

"They are closed, but not without struggle."

"I see," Amyr said. "Let us be off."

The ancient laif tugged his armoured collar and led the way out of his chambers into the stony corridor, his armoured retinue filling the expanse behind. Armoured feet sent reverberations out into the main hall, alerting those inside of the approach.

The captain had not exaggerated when she had given her account to Amyr. A wall of holy knights, resplendent in azure and steel, comprised a barrier from one wall to the other, bisecting the podium for the judged. Beyond the wall of steel was a sea of people standing shoulder to shoulder and elbow to elbow. No one was seated, even those within the audience section remained on their feet. The existing chairs created the only semblance of personal space, keeping chins from pressing into backs.

An angry buzz filled the air before the Arbiter entered, hundreds of voices in separate heated conversations merging into a singular wave of inarticulate disgust. A wave of pure sound rattled the sentinel's armour as they filed into the great chamber, wincing at the pitch and implied power of the common man's voice becoming an audible fist.

Holy knights shoved the overzealous back, pressing them with lowered shields, and giving more severe attention to those who were bold enough to reach over the human barrier. One woman stumbled back into a jumble of waiting arms, blood pouring from her nose after receiving a swift armoured backhand. The woman was absorbed by the crowd, dissolving out of sight, and in her absence an angry section surged forward, nearly toppling the phalanx.

Amyr ascended the dais in one step, taking his seat as if this were a regular day, regarding the scene with only mild irritation. His head turned as a statue come to life. Staring directly at the frenzy, he raised a hand, signifying silence. The angry group met his gaze, but the gesture only added fuel to their ire. Shouts renewed, they gnashed their teeth and bashed angry fists on the holy knights' unyielding armour.

As Amyr's open palm began to close, the sentinels strode in behind the holy knights, fortifying the barrier and standing in their shadows. When his hand was entirely closed into a fist, the entire chamber hushed, instantly silent. The turmoil did not decrease, only the voices were stolen. The crowd soundlessly opened their mouths in rage, veins on necks and foreheads popping as they shook their fists in defiance.

Some further back in the crowd twisted fingers into their ears, completely confused by what was transpiring.

"Enough." Amyr's voice filled the silence. "If you fail to display order, trust that I hold no qualms with reaping more than your voices." The people began to settle, and the Arbiter continued. "Select amongst yourselves a single representative, and I will give them voice. If you cannot manage this, then you will be dismissed and this matter will be considered settled, whatever it might be."

The crowd gestured and shoved, trying to exert their meaning without the use of their voices. After a few minutes of pantomimed debate, the crowd parted along the right wall and two large men headed toward the podium. The holy knights standing before Amyr stepped aside, granting him clear sight.

The two hulking men stood in front of the Arbiter with hands clasped below their bellies, anger simmering below unwavering eyes. Their peasant frocks and roughhewn garb indicated that these were marked Warriors who had sworn fealty to an unorganized combat trade.

"Which of you will be given voice?" Amyr wondered dispassionately.

The men stepped aside, revealing a smaller man adorned in fineries. He strode forward, slowly lifting a hand.

Amyr gave the man a singular nod.

"Thank you, Lord Amyr," the man began. "My name is Armand Archibald Ariento, and it appears that it has fallen upon me to be the voice for the voiceless." His eyes swam over the armoured knights. "We, the people of Camelot, are as diverse in trade as we are in standing. We possess a veritable well of skill and talent that surpasses any known kingdom in existence. We fight and reap and toil and struggle, each with our own set of adversities and trials that come with being an individual. Some are born with gifts that place them above others, marked as such, then set apart. This is the life we know. And those born without such skill and prowess, be it in trade or might of arms, are left with a divide that is a yoke unto itself. A burden that may never be shifted free. And we have accepted this."

Armand lowered his eyes, removed his satin cap. "And *we are the people* who are born below," he continued. "Having nothing but a hope that mayhaps our offspring will be born with a beneficial mark of distinction. A mark of our Creator that may usher prosperity and nourishment to a parched, pockmarked, and barren soil. But you, Lord Amyr, the Arbiter of our land, hold this seedling of hope within your hands."

Amyr glanced up at the mention of his name.

Armand smiled and went on. "A seed that you now control and are willingly withholding from these people. Not only withholding, but punishing those who continue to yearn for a future that may deepen the well of skill within the gates of Camelot."

"Twice now," Amyr began. "You have mentioned *Camelot*. But have you requested an audience with the King of Camelot in regards to this withholding of hope?"

Armand shook his head.

"Then I see you understand the proper channels."

"I believe the King is fully aware," Armand said. "The wailing of his people rarely falls upon deaf ears."

A wave seemed to pass through the people, straightening their spines.

"My name is Armand Archibald Ariento, and I ask that you rescind your law that prevents the men and women of Camelot from bearing children without your approval." He tugged at the ruffled collar of his tunic. "We tolerated the noose as it tightened around our throats, but today we say 'no more' now that we are a dangling corpse, lifelessly suspended from the boughs of an ancient guest."

Blinking back the inferno simmering behind his eyes, Amyr managed to compose himself. "Denied," he stated.

"My name is Armand Archibald Ariento," Armand repeated, returning his satin cap to his head. "My name is Armand Archibald Ariento."

In a riot of whirling fabrics, a woman surged through the crowd. From within her mantle she produced a small crossbow. Already cocked and loaded, she steadied the weapon upon Armand's cap. Then with both eyes narrowed at Amyr, she released the trigger.

A hand's breadth from Amyr's throat, the bolt froze, suspended midflight. Amyr raised his chin, glowered at the assassin.

The woman shrieked, dropped her crossbow. "Please no!" she pleaded, clutching at her shoulders as she dwindled in size, transforming into the shape of a cork dartboard.

Gasps and screams reverberated throughout the chamber.

Just like her spent quarrel, the assassin-turned-dartboard hung suspended in mid-air.

The crowd watched on, terrified.

Armand's eyes climbed upward, taking in the dartboard hovering over his head.

Calmly, Amyr plucked the bolt from the air, rolled it between his thumb and forefinger. Of a sudden the bolt departed his fingers, blurred a course over his knights, and struck the face of the dartboard.

"So close to a bullseye," Amyr said, frowning.

The dartboard wavered as if teetering before a fall, and Armand leapt from the podium. Upon its fall, the dartboard returned to its human shape.

On her stomach the assassin sprawled on the floor of the podium. She struggled to her knees, wailing in agony. With one hand she clutched at her cheek while the other sought a podium balustrade.

"Armand!" she bawled. "Why can't I see anything!"

Upon his escape from the podium, Armand had fallen on his face. At present, he sat upright, turning toward the cry of his name.

"Janessa!" he screamed, trembling at the bolt protruding beneath the woman's left eye.

From the dais, Amyr regarded Armand.

"Do you think I am here for games?"

* * *

THE SMELL WAS POWERFUL as they passed through the open gate leading into Fort Navarene. Warm dead bodies were highly attractive to vultures, and a host had already descended and was greedily tearing away. Stepping over bone shards and scattered corpses, Elkara led them to the soldier's quarters underneath the fort. *A proper tour will come later, but first we need to get situated.*

The air grew cooler as they descended the staircase, leaving the stench of death behind. An expansive, dimly lit single room stretched before them, dozens of granite bollards propping up the low ceiling on the dirt floor.

Elkara raised a hand. "There may be stragglers," she warned. Leaving the knights on the stairs, she strode into the room, dagger at the ready, and disappeared into the murky shadows. The laif soon returned with a tinder box in her hand. "We are alone," she affirmed.

"Plenty of room down here," Gwayne remarked, regarding the empty cots that filled the chamber in a symmetrical pattern.

"As I had hoped," Elkara stated, a small blaze forming in her hand. She began working her way around the perimeter, lighting sconces that held torches. The room was much deeper than Galahalt had first suspected, and the young knight placed his satchel on one of the many beds.

"A hand with the supplies before we make ourselves at home, eh?" Elkara requested, turning for the stairs. The three trudged back up the staircase, leaving Figharth behind to buzz about the space, his body glowing as he inspected the darker corners.

Above ground, Error appeared at ease among the gore, though he brightened at Elkara's approach.

After relieving the beast of his burden, Galahalt eyed the doorway leading back to the cellar. "I think Error can manage to fit through," he said. "Shouldn't we be leading him down to stay with us?"

"No way." Elkara hefted a sack onto her shoulder, passing the young knight. "He hates caves."

After the knights had secured the gates, front and rear, they decided to inspect the ramparts and various crenellations. Long ago abandoned by the laives who had built it, only the fortified buildings remained standing as a testament of their skill. Inside the abandoned armoury, a lonely anvil sat under a thinning tarpaulin surrounded by cobweb plastered shelves and hooked holders.

"Pity," Gwayne commented, wiping his hand on his tunic after running it along a dusty shelf. "Hoped there would be some relics left behind."

Galahalt drew a line with a fingertip, dust spilling over the tarpaulin. "Anything of worth is long gone, my friend."

Sunlight drenched the walkways, forcing the knights to shield their eyes as they exited the unlit armoury. The shadow cast by the spire extended far beyond the outer walls, like a colossal sundial, the days' time not nearly spent. Gwayne stepped over the crumpled body of an expired faewolf, the creature's spine contorted in a manner that left little room for speculation.

"Ya want to give it a go?" Gwayne aimed a shrug at the tower. "See what's at the top?"

"Elkara mentioned that she wanted to show me something in there," Galahalt replied. "Perhaps we'll wait."

Gwayne pitched a pebble, sending it bouncing along the walkway. "Suit yourself." The small stone skipped off an ogre's chestplate with a metallic ping, causing a nearby vulture to bristle. The pair walked into the courtyard and surveyed the carnage remaining from the last stand. The carrion-feeding birds appeared as mismatched tombstones, hunched and still when the knights entered the space.

"Please don't forego your meal on our account," Gwayne said, folding his hands as if in prayer, stepping over more bodies. "Carry on, fellows."

"I found some crates down below," Figharth announced, suddenly appearing.

"Aye?" Gwayne was clearly disinterested. After the disappointment of the armoury, he held little hope for treasure.

"Aye." The wisp nodded vigorously. "Elkara helped me pry one open."

Galahalt smirked. "You mean Elkara pried one open?"

Figharth chuckled, bobbing in the air. "Yes. That is more accurate. But what we found may prove to be of use."

Gwayne nudged a man-sized cudgel with the toe of his sabaton. "What could possibly prove to be useful locked away down there? Any weapons would rust in those cellars and useful cloth would be worm food."

"Food would be spoiled," Galahalt added.

"Not *all* food," Figharth hinted. Unable to contain his excitement any longer, the wisp nodded and blurted, "We found wine! Bottles and bottles of it!"

Gwayne rushed out of the courtyard. "Enjoy your feast, buzzards!"

The knights quickly made for the underground, leaping carcasses and side-stepping birds, and Gwayne took the last steps in a bound, skipping into the room where the laif was rummaging through crates along the far wall.

"I didn't notice them," Gwayne commented, walking between the cots toward the wine bottles. "Hidden in plain sight."

"Yep." Elkara smeared the dust from a label, inspecting the inscriptions. "Fig was hoping for treasure." She dragged the nearest cot over and began carefully laying bottles on it.

"Seeking a particular vintage?" Gwayne queried, testing the cork on a bottle.

"Each bottle holds value," Elkara said. "But yes, there is a specific brand that I am seeking, though not for profit."

"A Cedric Ransom, perhaps?" Gwayne guessed, his eyebrows jutted up.

Elkara's breath caught. "How did you know?"

"Come now," Gwayne began with a chuckle. "All laives love a good Ceddy Ran—especially females, so I'm told."

Elkara frowned. "It's tasty. Especially when it's aged a bit," she admitted, wiping the dust from her fingers. "Galahalt," she said, still scowling at Gwayne. "Would you like to join me for a proper tour?"

Galahalt glanced at Figharth perched on his shoulder. "May I bring a bottle?"

WINDING STAIRS CREPT ALONG THE WALLS of the spire, leading ever upward, encircling a magnificent tree. Galahalt leaned over and looked up, feeling a bit dizzy and tingly again.

It appeared to the young knight as if the tree was the primary support host of the structure, its branches absorbed by the wall, penetrating through the stone. The bark did not look like any bark he had ever seen before. It was an extraordinary smooth silver, as if the ancient plant were completely concealed in arming plate. Brief hints of windows, mere pin pricks by comparison, allowed only faint slivers of light to enter, and from what Galahalt could see, the tree did not have a single blemish.

The exterior is as close to perfection as possible. The young knight was astonished. "This is a wonder," he remarked as he ascended the first of many landings, pausing to gaze at the unfamiliar.

"The tree was growing in solitude—away from the forest," Elkara explained. "My ancestors found it like this, dead center between the groves. It was as tall and strong as an immortal, and it's rumored to be imbued with power directly from the Creator's breath."

"A shame it's covered up," Galahalt noted, grasping the handrail with one hand and a bottle of wine with the other.

"Yes, I suppose." The laif drew up, waiting for the knight to get closer. "It is what keeps the spire aloft and like most of creation, it garners strength from deep within, out of view for prying eyes."

The pair continued to trudge along the winding stairs that swirled upward near endlessly inside the ancient structure. Despite its age and signs of wear, the walkway was surprisingly sturdy, their footsteps hardly causing a groan.

Looking out from one of the rare oval windows, Galahalt saw that the clouds were closer to him than the ground, and with this realization, a prickly sensation rose from his stomach. *Am I a part of the horizon now?* He drew relief when he looked to the silver tree, forever anchored, barring his fall. Even still, he began to walk closer to the wall, favoring the hard stone.

At some point Galahalt had begun to count the stairs, losing count after eight hundred twenty-something. The steady incline droned on and on until they finally came upon a platform that was grafted into the very peak of the tree. The silver colossus' circumference had not diminished as it reached the skies, and Galahalt was caught off-guard when they reached the top. His legs were prepared to keep walking, but the abrupt conclusion was a welcome event.

Standing still feels very strange. His muscles twitched just above the knees as he looked at the laif. She turned around with a hand on the top rung of a short ladder secured to the wall.

"Brace yourself," Elkara warned. She looked into his eyes then released a hatch and scaled the four rungs that led up into the beyond.

Galahalt walked forward with his neck tilted back, looking where the laif had just climbed, seeing nothing but a pure and untainted blue canvas. Grasping the top rung with one hand, the knight hefted himself into the unknown atmosphere, head and shoulders breeching the surface. A creamy mist veiled what seemed like the entire world stretched out on all sides. Above and below patches of undulating clouds meandered and broke apart creating windows of clarity.

Elkara walked to the edge of the stone platform and placed a foot on the embrasure along the parapet, then reached with an open palm toward the sky. Her hand seemed to press against an invisible wall. "Old laif magic," she said, leaning all her weight against the invisible barrier. Galahalt blinked in wonder as the laif turned with her back against the sky with arms wide open, the unseen force preventing her from falling.

"I think this may have been used as a holding cell of sorts," Elkara said, stepping down onto the platform.

"Never been afraid of heights nor depths." Galahalt walked to the edge and placed his wine bottle on a merlon, the tingling coming up from the soles of his boots nearly rooting him to the stone. "Just politely wary of their dangers." He placed a tentative hand against the strangely elastic barrier, probing for distance. The knight smiled as he placed his other hand out and leaned forward. His nose connected first, with little give, then he rolled his chin down so his forehead touched, allowing him to gaze straight down into the infinite descent.

"So is this where you show me how *futile* my quest is?" Galahalt said. "Because right now, if I'm truly honest, I feel nothing but inspiration." He spoke into the barrier, eyes soaking in every hill and river.

"Galahalt," Elkara began softly. "Not many get a chance to see above the clouds and see what lies below. Now, over this way is the great lake."

Galahalt joined his guide, looking out.

Elkara raised a finger. "There," she said. "Out past that wandering copse of—"

"How can I miss it?" Galahalt bit her off. "It's a big puddle. So what? Looks to be about a week's walk, like you said."

"The path that leads there can be treacherous," Elkara advised, tracing a route with her finger. "But the true danger lies where the water meets the land. Are you aware of what Lake Humiel *is*? Like, what actually lives there? Sordid old wives' tales spin a lot of fabric, but I have stood on those shores."

"Yes, of course," Galahalt replied. "No one ventures there. It's brimming with kapreta."

"Exactly. And I'll tell you a great secret that not many humans know about the lake."

The knight fought the urge to tell her she was wasting her time. "Alright," he said dryly, stepping away from the ledge and picking at the cork on the bottle of wine.

"Allow me," Elkara said, unclasping her traveling cloak and wrapping it around the base of the bottle. "Old trick," she explained, bringing the bottle parallel to the floor and smacking the cloth end against the solid stone parapet. "And if done properly…"

After a second firm smack, the cork came free with a dull pop. Only a few drops spilled before the laif skillfully righted it. With a twirl of the wrist, she unwrapped her cloak and took a swig from the bottle.

"Excellent vintage, this one!" She passed the wine to the knight.

"That's a neat trick," Galahalt said, bringing the bottle to his mouth. "I'll have to remember that."

Elkara nodded, securing her cloak. "Now, Lake Humiel is home to many, many kapreta, hundreds of them as well as other perilous monsters, but it is also the home of the Questing Beast, in a manner of speaking. He has been *around* there for centuries."

"Wait, wait," Galahalt interrupted and passed Elkara the wine. "I know the Beast is said to be a myth and that it's said to be various things like a giant hummingbird or an overgrown basilisk. But I have never heard that it is a fish or a water beast of some fashion."

"Hear me out." Elkara lifted a finger and slugged a hit from the bottle. "This is *very* good!" she exclaimed. "Seriously. Compliments to the vintner, may he *possibly* rest in peace." She handed the bottle back to Galahalt and continued. "The Questing Beast is not a frog or a fish. He dwells on dry land. You see there is an archaic cave under the waters that is not only unspeakably dangerous to swim to, but is also imbued with a time curse."

Galahalt quirked a smile. "A time curse?"

"Or a time passage spell? Whatever you wish to call it," Elkara said, shaking her head. "If you can somehow manage to avoid the swarms of monsters and make it to the cave, time does not pass as normal once you enter. You may rise on the other side in the domain of the Beast, but beyond his realm ten days may have passed. Or ten years. The same applies for the return trip. So when you get back, there's a definite possibility that everyone you know and love will be dead and gone. You will not have aged at all and it may only be hours spent, but the cave's magic decides your fate. Coming and going. I can survive underwater for great lengths of time, but how long can you hold your breath?"

The knight was not dissuaded. "I'll hold my breath or you can revive me on the shores."

"It is not only the forest, the kapreta, and the time-grifting cave that present difficulties," Elkara began, her countenance dour. "The Questing Beast is one of the most formidable beings in all of existence. Harvesting a fang is completely out of the question. Your spear would hardly make a scratch, and attempting to steal your prize while he slept would not go over well at all. Every footstep is accounted for in his realm."

Galahalt turned away from Elkara.

"Do you have family?" Elkara wondered. "Or loved ones that are waiting for you?"

"None of consequence," Galahalt murmured.

"There must be someone," Elkara tried again. "This quest will cost *everything*. Please reconsider. Think on it overnight, at the very least."

"There is nothing to consider." Galahalt turned and met the laif's eyes. "You will take me to Lake Humiel and into that cave."

From under their feet someone fumbled with the latch, and suddenly the hatch door flew open.

"You ever notice how—" Sir Gwayne's head breached the hatchway. Each of his words came out slurred. "You ever notice how you can give somebody bad news, like, 'Hey, I accidentally poisoned your cat,' but if you go up an octave when you say it, then the news doesn't hit quite so hard." Rather unsteadily the knight pulled himself up through the opening. In one hand he clasped an empty wine bottle. "Like if you mess something up and when you go and tell your superiors, or whomever—who cares—and you explain what happened, you say it in falsetto; '*And that's what happened.*'"

"Wait, is that?" Elkara blinked, pointing at Gwayne's seemingly empty hand.

Gwayne also blinked. "Oh, yeah," he said, opening his fingers, revealing Figharth curled up sound asleep. "Little bloke can't hold his wine."

"Give him to me," Elkara demanded.

"I was afraid that I'd sober up making my way up here," Gwayne explained, obediently passing the wisp into Elkara's waiting palm. "Good thing I brought two bottles. I had to drink the first so I could carry Fig."

Elkara gently inspected Figharth's wings. "He doesn't appear harmed," she said. "What possessed you to—"

"This is all wrong!" Gwayne shouted, pressing both palms to the invisible barrier. "How am I supposed to pee from up here?"

Elkara scowled. "You climbed all those stairs just so you could spill a piss from top of the spire...?"

Gwayne whirled around, snatched his bottle from where he had left it upon the platform. "So," he began as his gaze settled on Elkara. "Have you asked the lad *about*..." He tugged at his collar, straining his neck to reveal his Warrior mark.

"We have not touched on that subject," Elkara replied.

Galahalt's shoulders rose and fell beneath a heavy sigh. "So you've noticed," he said. "Like so many others." He turned to Gwayne. "It's not a subject I like discussing."

"If you'd rather not," Elkara cut in sympathetically.

"No, it's alright," Galahalt said. "You see, I was born feet first. Which damaged my mother greatly. The attending lampyr was helpless to staunch the flow of her blood, and she died giving birth to me."

"Wait, whoa," Gwayne interjected. "So—two questions." He raised an index finger. "One—how does being born all reversed change where the mark is placed on the body? And two—why was the lampyr so use-less?" He looked at Elkara. "You were wondering this too, right?"

"I'm allowing him to explain," Elkara replied.

Galahalt sat on the parapet and began unlacing his right boot. "See," he said, pulling the boot off. "It ended up on my ankle instead of my neck because that's what met the world first."

"Ah-ha! Did you see that coming?" Gwayne asked Elkara.

The laif ignored Gwayne and narrowed her eyes at the young knight's ankle.

"And for your second question," Galahalt began, lacing his boot. "My mother ate garlic soup for breakfast that morning. My uncle still blames himself for suggesting the meal."

"How dreadful," Gwayne muttered. "Garlic is a lampyr's worst nightmare."

"You were your mother's first and only?" Elkara asked.

"Yep," Galahalt lied.

"And your father?" Elkara placed a hand to her collarbone.

"He was a red knight," Galahalt replied. "My memories of him are hazy."

Gwayne patted Galahalt's shoulder. "Not many red knights live long, storied careers," he said, rising to his feet. "Sorry for your losses, Gal. I truly am. But, I fear that I must turn in for the night."

"Good-night, Gwayne," Galahalt said without looking up.

The knight departed the platform, leaving the hatch door raised.

As soon as they were alone, Elkara rounded on Galahalt. "So you wish to carry out this quest?" she growled.

Galahalt was caught off-guard by the laif's sudden fury.

"Understand this," she continued before the knight could reply. "Fort Navarene is as far as I go. Translation: this is as far as you go."

"Hold just a moment—!"

Elkara was swift to cut him off. "Upon our return, I expect full payment!" Figharth stirred in her hand, so she continued in a whisper. "I am not swimming through that cave! Imagine your bill if we emerged fifty years from now?"

"Is that all that concerns you?" Galahalt seethed. "Coin?"

"Yes!" Elkara drew a step toward him. "Why the do you think I'm out here? Do you think I enjoy stomping under trees that I have stomped under thousands of times? This isn't fun. This is my job. Is that completely lost on you?"

Galahalt turned and strode for the open hatch. "As you wish," he said.

"What are you seeking?" Elkara pressed.

"As I told you once before," Galahalt replied. "Salvation." With that, the knight descended the ladder.

Elkara lifted her hand, gazed at the slumbering wisp. "Who is he trying to heal?"

24

If he does not stop shaking me, Margot thought with her eyes firmly closed. *I will be forced to snap his twig neck.* Uncle Brett placed a hand on her shoulder and jostled again. She had fallen asleep on the porch floor after wandering the fields for the better part of the night.

"Margot. Hey. Wake up!" he insisted, resorting to words.

She slapped his hand away. "Enough!" she growled. "Yes? Uncle, what do you want?" She propped herself up on an elbow.

"I'm not sure when you—" Brett paused, surveying the porch. "When you went to bed last night, but, oh, and speaking of which, and I don't mean to be insensitive, but do you have an idea if or when you'll be sleeping in your room again? If not, we could possibly rent it out or use it for storage?"

Forking fingers through her tangled hair, Margot held the locks away from her eyes and looked Uncle Brett in the face. "Is that what you woke me for?" she asked.

Raising both hands in surrender, Brett sat back on the stool he had pulled over. "Oh, no, no. It's just...well." He moved a hand to the back of his neck. "We haven't spoken much recently, and I just wanted to talk with you and see where my niece is at with all the things going on in our little world. Your brother and Elmer and—"

Margot rolled over and groaned into the floorboards.

"And your impending nuptials," Brett concluded, head in hands.

The groan increased in volume.

"Your groom-to-be paid us a visit yesterday," Brett went on with eyes closed. "I told him you were out dress shopping and he seemed rather pleased with that, but mentioned that the Church will provide the bridal gown. Which is nice, I suppose." He opened his eyes, observed Margot with her forehead still pressed to the floor. "But, I don't much care for lying to folks, much less church folk, but I feared the conversation we would have had. Now, I'm only bothering you today, and I have given you a great deal of space, but I think it might be a good idea if you visit the city for a change of scenery. Clear your head for a bit. Maybe find a shawl to accompany the dress? With frills and lace all kinds of flowery nonsense. I can come with you, if you'd like. We could make an afternoon of it?"

Margot clenched her jaw then buried her face into the crook of her arm.

Brett waited in silence for a response. "Well, I'll let you wash up," he said at length. "Get clean and think over my offer and let me know what you decide. It may be time to face the facts, Margot. I don't think your dog is coming back."

* * *

THROUGHOUT THE MORNING Galahalt did not make his thoughts known, silently packing his gear, preparing to break from the fort with the others. He had no interest in turning back, and the thought of conscripting another ranger seemed insurmountably irksome at the moment. *If it weren't for those damn wards, I would press on alone...*

Galahalt and Gwayne emerged from the cellar to find Elkara fully armoured and with Error laden with supplies.

"Load up," she said, side-eyeing the approaching knights. "I wish to break for the capital as soon as you're ready to move out." She then turned to Gwayne. "How is your chest? Will it hamper you?"

"It only hurts first thing in the morning," Gwayne replied, shielding his eyes from the daylight. "Once I get moving then the pain becomes merely a dull roar. My head is another matter altogether." He popped a chunk of bread into his mouth. "Ya fancy any sightseeing on the return trek?"

"No," Elkara replied flatly. "I have wasted enough time on this fool's errand."

THE CHILLY MORNING ARRIVED with a blanket of dew that soaked their boots as they made their way toward the south gate. When they stepped from the grassy path, all that remained of the fallen ogres and faewolves were skeletal remains.

Gwayne whistled, looking over at the wisp on his shoulder. "Picked 'em clean."

Figharth nodded as he surveyed the area with his keen owl eyes before suddenly bursting out, "Wait a moment!"

"You leave something, Figharth?" Elkara said, bringing Error to a stop.

"In a manner of speaking," Figharth replied excitedly. The wisp fluttered toward the laif and landed on the curve of Error's neck. "You see, if we turn around and head north and slightly east, we will come to a gremlin village that may perhaps contain noble Sir Gwayne's stolen footwear!"

Elkara remained silent, glaring at the wisp.

Figharth stepped back, hands raised. "It won't take long, I assure you!" He pointed north. "Just through the trees, the village is nestled in a shallow dale. We can rummage around, then clamber out and be back on our journey and headed toward your destination before midday. It's a short and simple jaunt, really."

Elkara was fully aware of the village's location, and the fae was correct, it was not far. With all that had transpired, her wager with Elithiel had completely slipped her mind. *To wipe that smug look from his face,* she pondered with a smile. It was early yet, and they should make good time even with all the backtracking.

She rubbed her chin and glanced at Gwayne's feet. "Eh, guess it won't hurt."

Figharth had been prepared for a dispute. His finger had been readied in the air and his beak ready for a rebuttal. "That is most generous!" he said beaming. "My thanks! Thank you very much!" He placed his hands behind his back, both wings opened to catch a passing breeze. Flapping upward, he careened back toward the knights, circled a quick landing on Galahalt's shoulder.

"About face, gentle knights! Let us beseech a gremlin regarding a parcel of absconded arming wear."

AFTER DEPARTING THE BOUNDARY of a tree line, a worn trail became evident. Elkara raised a fist, the knights halted behind her. *This wet grass is becoming a nuisance.* The squishy dampness permeated her damaged boot, which made the decision easier.

"We'll take this footpath," she said, gesturing with her chin. "May take a bit longer to get there but the terrain is more favorable."

Figharth pointed in another direction as he sat on Gwayne's shoulder, shaking his head.

"The trail loops around," Elkara stated, noticing Figharth from the corner of her eye.

"Ah, yes," the wisp said quickly, straightening. "I trust your navigation skills."

Gwayne slowed. "Well done, Fig," he hissed. "Now you've pissed her off again."

"Again?" Figharth appeared baffled.

"You didn't piss her off the first time." Gwayne gestured at Galahalt.

"Ah, regarding the quest," Figharth said. "She does seem to be in much darker spirits. I noticed the change in her demeanor this morning. I don't think she has slept at all since I've made her acquaintance, which is rather common among laives, but still, perhaps a wink or two might do her a pinch of good?"

"Maybe if you two idiots weren't ticking her off, one after the other," Gwayne whispered, inclining his head closer to the wisp. "How am I supposed to *gain the laif's favor* if she's constantly aggravated?" His nose nearly collided with Figharth's beak. "Timing is everything."

"Volume is everything," Elkara remarked, staring at the knight before flicking one ear. "They're pointy for a reason."

Figharth covered his beak with both hands as his shoulders trembled, ineffectively stifling squeaky laughter.

The path dipped inside a series of immense conifers with needles littering the ground that were long enough to pierce clean through a man's gut. Elkara kicked at the ground to avoid slipping, and the knights followed suit, creating sizable divots in their wake.

"I love this scent," Figharth exclaimed. The wisp was elevated on his tiptoes, inhaling deeply. "Fresh pine always makes my innards feel clean."

"If I spy a puddle big enough," Gwayne said with a sniff. "Perhaps we can make your outsides match your insides."

The wisp raised his arm and buried his beak in his underarm. He then withdrew his head and looked to Gwayne. "Is my odor offensive?" he asked anxiously.

"Not at all," Elkara replied ahead of Gwayne. "You're a daisy like the rest of us."

Gwayne laughed and looked at Galahalt. The young knight did not appear to be listening, his eyes were focused ahead to where the path ended. A wooden sign was staked to the ground at the intersection, teetering several inches above eye level. Galahalt squinted under his open visor, attempting to decipher the letters.

"I don't understand what she means," Figharth said. "Do I stink? This is my first excursion into the wilds, and am acutely unaware of the particular etiquette in regards to hygiene when one travels as such."

"How often do fae take baths?" Gwayne said with a laugh. "I've seen my share of naked faeries dancing over ponds on pale-lit nights."

Figharth scratched the back of his head. "Perhaps once every week? Rather depends on the amount of activity, I suppose." He cast a meaningful look at Gwayne. "I do not feel dirty."

Galahalt hurried ahead of the others, and was first to reach the trail's end. *"We'rewolves?"* he read the sign aloud.

"Werewolves, faewolves. Same thing, as far as I'm concerned," Elkara explained. "It's a very old sign, but recently some jackass added the apostrophe." Elkara gestured to her left. "If we go that way then we will meet many faewolves."

"Clever." Gwayne held a finger to his chin, admiring the painted apostrophe. "How old do you imagine this sign is? Hardly weathered at all."

"Not sure," Elkara admitted. "Locals maintain it." She waved a hand at Error, who was presently dining on a shrub. With a grunt, the laifhorse reluctantly joined her side.

Standing at the crossroads, Galahalt stared in the direction inhabited by faewolves. He narrowed his eyes, waiting for a monster to come sauntering up the trail.

Suddenly Figharth's voice sounded quite distant.

They carried on without me! Galahalt realized with a start. He bounced the heel of his spear against the ground and set off to join the others.

An unexpected breeze tossed Gwayne's hair into his face as he turned to regard the young knight's approach. A few strands splayed across Figharth, causing the wisp to sputter.

"I'm sorry," Gwayne said, looking at the struggling Figharth. "What were you saying?"

"I was saying—" the wisp coughed and spat, disentangling himself. "I was saying that the village should be in the nearby vicinity." He drew a line with his finger, indicating the forest to the right.

"We should be cutting into the tree line soon," Elkara said, regarding the overcast sky as she patted Error's neck. "I recall the gully not being far from the path we're on, although I may be wrong. It has been awhile since I've ventured into this part of the forest."

Gwayne sneezed, holding his chest and wincing.

Figharth clucked and shook his head. "Blessings, my friend," he said. "That must not feel very comfortable on your injury."

Cascading spores surrounded them, highlighted by the rays of light flooding through the leaves.

"Lots of irritants in the skies," Gwayne said, swiping his nose.

After a few glances into the forest, Elkara came to a stop. "We can enter here," she said, squinting into the trees. "Should be a straight shot to the village."

Without another word exchanged, they entered the grove. Quickly they discovered the course was rife with vines and branches that grew exceedingly thick. Midway through their passage, Gwayne asked for a halt so he could fill and tamp his pipe.

"You may want both hands free for the terrain ahead," Elkara warned, her bowstring catching in a crevice behind her spaulder.

Gwayne extinguished his match and tucked away his tinderbox. In a deliberate movement, he placed his pipe between his teeth, opened both hands wide, displaying ready palms.

Elkara rolled her eyes.

The knight pushed off from the branch that he had been leaning against, a trail of smoke followed behind.

"It's not much further," Figharth called out overhead. "Only another," he muttered, calculating the distance. "Thirty or so paces. Then it drops down into a dale. Which is rather gorgeous this time of year, I might add."

"Any life in the village?" Elkara asked, vaulting a considerable branch.

"None that I saw," Figharth replied. "There is, however, an inviting pond only a stone's throw from the dale. I do believe that I will venture there for a quick dip while you retrieve Gwayne's sabaton."

Elkara nodded, though the wisp could not see her. "Mind leading Error to the water?" she requested. "Old man could use a drink."

With both hands behind his back, the wisp fluttered in place. "Not at all, not at all," he called happily.

Error broke from Elkara's side, loped under the wisp, dauntlessly leapt the thickets, and passed from sight.

25

Figharth found the cool water quite refreshing, the cheerful surroundings invited an extended stay, but the wisp knew that time was *of the essence* this morning.

The cherry blossoms exploded with vibrancy, creating sharp contrast to the dull hardwoods along the trail, and the water lilies absorbed the morning glints of sunlight, reflecting a warm glow. Calm waters such as these often invited kapreta, or a clutch or two of hekkbenders, but luckily these monsters were entirely absent.

Must not be deep enough. The wisp spun in the air, twirling wildly to remove every last bead of moisture from his skin before donning his attire. *The pond certainly seems large enough for them...must be too shallow.* He tapped the side of his head, forcing a small stream to release from his earhole. His beak opened and closed with ease after the pressure release. The last few drops of water fell down to the pond below, and he finally felt satisfied with his level of dryness, fluttering down to the clothes fastidiously laid out on a flat rock.

"Nice and warm, nice and warm," he muttered, sliding an arm into a buttoned undershirt, careful to retract his wings. After the last button was fastened, Figharth stretched his wings and set off toward Sir Gwayne and the others, intending first to make Error aware of his departure.

Catching a breeze, he sailed along with minimal effort, leaning only a touch to manipulate the flight path. Looking down, the strikingly clear reflection of his full body in glorious flight caught his eye, and the inclination of his head caused the wisp to gradually descend. The reflection magnified, increasing in clarity. The ripples hardly distorting the image, and once he recognized his mistake, he began to furiously pump his wings. Water swirled under him, tiny aquatic tornados churned and died within the span of a breath.

These miniscule distortions drew the attention of a selkie deep under the waters that had been resting on her back lazily watching lily pads bump along on the surface far above. The sight of a clean, smartly dressed fae skimming along the water was too much for the creature's devious nature to abide. Synchronizing her tail with four clawed flippers, she crinkled her snout before surging toward the surface. Not one bubble bloomed to the surface to alert the unsuspecting gentleman before she breeched, calm waters embroiled in tumult as an arm emerged, playfully grasping for the wisp.

"Hot Daniel!" Figharth yelped as the waters erupted, soaking his entire body save his wings.

He narrowly avoided a laif-like hand, but when he reached a safer altitude, he looked down into the clear waters to see what appeared to be an otter of some sort facing the skies, a clean white belly almost cresting the residual waves.

The little fellow was completely startled—so startled that water dripped from his beak as it wordlessly moved. His breath caught in his lungs as the creature winked at him, then flicked its thick tail and corkscrewed back into the depths, disappearing into the fog of disturbed sediment.

The soaked wisp despondently sunk towards Error. "I was so dry," he lamented. The breeze carried a chill and the wet fabric began to cling. "I'm for the gully now," he said, landing atop the laifhorse's head. "Don't dally too long here, friend. I know your master would prefer a hasty exit from this particular cluster of the forest. Perhaps I shall find a tall branch in the sun far from these detrimental waters in hopes that I may return my vestments to a semblance of exsiccation."

With a markedly unenthusiastic flap of his wings, the wisp took to the skies. Gradually rising above the forest canopy, he spotted the clearing and, drawing closer, recognized the reflective shine of the steel-clad village nestled deep inside the dale. He flew the length over the treetops before settling onto a wide branch on the west side of the clearing, overlooking the gully. Lying back, Figharth bathed in the sun's drying rays.

At length the wisp checked to make sure his companions were accounted for, down below in the village, before he closed his tired eyes. He espied Galahalt traipsing along a thin stream and the other two were gawking at an immense pile of jumbled steel that appeared to have been deposited from high above.

"I have some time," said Figharth with a great yawn, moments before he nodded off.

An hour or so before...

"IT WILL BE A RELIEF to get my sabaton back," Gwayne sighed, shoving away an intruding vine. "Ya think it'll be there?"

"No idea," Elkara replied, holding a tense branch, waiting for the knights to pass before releasing it. "But this is the last village we'll be checking, so fingers crossed."

Suddenly they were overlooking a basin, and along its floor the shimmering sparkle of brilliant steel radiated. It appeared as if the sheer weight of the weapons and armour had forced the earth to descend and settle into its current locale. The walls along the gully were flat, without wrinkle, intersecting roots spread behind the wall without protrusion.

"Easy enough to get down," Elkara said with a nod. "But, not so much for the return." The laif began descending the hill with minimal effort, maintaining a hand on her bow. Gwayne's armoured feet tore into the spongy turf, forcing the knight to slowly crabwalk the steady gradient.

The gremlin village below was an organized mess of war implements and armour fastened together intricately at their seams. Maille was almost exclusively used for roofing as it was draped over many facades, and secured with heavy tethers, though some of the larger domiciles were reinforced with scale maille. The tallest structure was at the center of the discarded battlefield, and its peak nearly kissed the underside of Gwayne's chin as he ambled past, surveying the landscape for any hint of white armour. There were gauntlets for pillars and dissected greaves used as drawbridges by the homes bordering the gentle stream snaking through the center of the depression.

Cute little contraption, Galahalt mused, playing with the mechanism that controlled a drawbridge. His eyes followed the diminutive river and he decided to investigate it further, walking next to the trickle until it concluded against the far wall. Kneeling, he paused to admire the irrigation technique used by the crafty creatures. A small hole had been bored into the bedrock and a pipe was nestled inside the solid barrier. The knight could not determine how far the pipe penetrated, but the excavation lines appeared fairly fresh.

Placing a boot on the steep wall, Galahalt hefted himself up, looking over the village to the opposite side to see that the same working appeared to be present where the river entered. Lowering back down, the knight dipped a finger into the clean waters. The droplets fell back to their source, racing into the pipe and out into the beyond.

The latest pilfered armour was stacked in a pile against a portion of the angled wall, waiting for distribution; scratch marks accented the soil leading down to the stack. Elkara and Gwayne started their search at the base of the glimmering mound while Galahalt opted to explore the village scenery, fascinated by the craftsmanship.

"Give me a heads up if you spot an ivory sabaton bordered with black gold," Gwayne shouted. "It'll be quite obvious." He tapped the bowl of his pipe on the haft of a nearby poleaxe. "So where are all the gremlins? I can see that they definitely still live here." He plucked a vambrace from the pile, gave it a look, and discarded it over his shoulder.

"Gremlins are tremendously shy creatures," Elkara explained, working the visor on a round-topped helmet. "And do not like to be seen by laif or man. They scurry and hide at the faintest disturbance."

Gwayne lowered his voice and glanced sideways at Galahalt who was on his stomach in the distance inspecting an upward hinged door made from a clamshell gauntlet.

"What about the little troop of gremlins that we spooked back at Gal's massacre site?" Gwayne asked.

"Not all gremlins are as apt as others. Same can be said for pretty much *all* creatures," Elkara replied with a shrug. "I'm sure this village has look-out posts and we were spotted long before we were aware."

"You ever handle one of 'em?" Gwayne wondered. "Are they docile little blokes or as savage as imps?" He crossed his arms, resuming his scan of the pile.

"No," Elkara replied. Her left eye twitched of its own accord. "I have never really been close to a living gremlin."

"Imagine one as a pet?" Gwayne squinted as a steel backplate reflected a sharp beam of light directly into his eyes. "Their maintenance on this steel is top notch. Really, it is. I wonder how they manage to keep it all so bright and shiny?"

"Saliva," Elkara supplied the answer as she lifted the corner of a tasset and peered underneath.

"Oh, whoa, that's quite a useful asset," Gwayne said, impressed. "My squire back home is rather useless even on better days. Old lad doesn't produce anything of worth really. I think he prefers the life of a squire to—"

"Wait, wait, wait," Elkara interrupted. She leveled her gaze into the pile before her.

"You see it?" Gwayne asked, rushing to her side.

"Perhaps. Help me move the rest of this junk out of the way."

"Hey, Halty!" Gwayne cupped his mouth, shouting. "We think we found it! Come give us a hand!"

At present, Galahalt was on his hands and knees, inspecting a makeshift grain silo. He hoisted himself up with his spear, making his way to Gwayne and Elkara, managing to avoid catching his tunic on yet another balcony made of daggers. Setting his spear and helm aside to avoid losing them to the clutter, Galahalt pressed next to Gwayne and began digging shoulder deep, elbows widening the hole. Steel clinked and clattered, leathery articles bounced and rolled, and when Gwayne tugged on a stubborn hauberk an avalanche nearly claimed Elkara's pinky finger. The knight ignored the curses flung at him for his ill-timed maneuver as something more pressing drew his attention.

"Let's do this," Gwayne declared, eyes wide. With a grin, he reached into the jagged opening headfirst, pulling himself inside. Everything above his knees disappeared into the pile. Sounds of muffled laughter could be heard within the crevice and a phrase that sounded like, "null me ah," began to go on repeat. Gwayne's feet kicked and the words frantically rose in pitch.

Taking a boot in hand, Elkara and Galahalt began to pull Gwayne free.

"Gently! Ah, fack, that's sharp," Gwayne cursed as his hips became visible.

Elkara gripped Gwayne by his belt and heaved backward. Meanwhile Galahalt held Gwayne by a thigh, and had gone to a knee from the exertion.

"Like diving in a pit of vipers!" Gwayne exclaimed, nicks and cuts evident all over his face. With a mad twitch, he met Galahalt's eyes and crowed with laughter, upraising a white sabaton.

"Alright!" Elkara beamed. She looked toward the rising sun as it lurked just below the tree line. "We should still be able to make decent headway before sunset."

Gwayne seated himself on the grass, unfastened his current sabaton. "I was certain the little thieves would have set *this* aside," he remarked, admiring his found sabaton as he clamped it over his boot.

"It is rather unique," Elkara admitted, bending down to retrieve a curved bevor. "Maybe they have little use for material without a reflection?"

"That's an interesting thought," Gwayne's legs were outstretched, toes to the sky as he smiled at the matching set. "Now if you two don't mind, I'm off for Figgy's pond. Need to clean these wounds."

"We'll meet you there," Elkara promised. "Once we return this pile to a semblance of order." She then chucked an overly bent sabre onto the top of the pile.

Right behind the sabre, Gwayne underhanded his old sabaton onto the pile. "A fair trade, I say," he said, setting off for the pond. As he made his way up the dale's embankment, he discovered the climb to be much less irritating than the descent. He muscled his way to the top, and glanced furtively at Elkara down below. "So damn attractive," he muttered. "Just ain't fair."

Entering the treeline, Gwayne maintained a hand to his sternum as he listened for Figharth's voice. Unfortunately the songbirds were in full force, belting out their springtime choruses. Fortunately, Error was no bird. Gwayne heard, in the not-too-far distance, the laifhorse's distinct bray. The knight pivoted toward the sound, felt both sabatons respond, and he grinned at this return to balance.

"Feels good to have you boys back together again," Gwayne said, striding, unaware of the blood droplets that he smeared on the passing flora.

It seemed Error was the lone occupant of the pond. The laifhorse stood stark against the pink of the cherry trees, in full blossom, hemming the pond. Error spared a glance at Gwayne's arrival before returning his muzzle to the water.

Immediately Gwayne undressed, but he was wary to leave his sabatons unattended. He crossed the bank and joined Error's side, slipped the sabatons into a satchel. Cautiously the knight waded into the waters, unsure of what manner of creature inhabited the pond. He reasoned it was best not to venture deeper than the rise of his groin. Quickly, yet thoroughly, he administered a firm scrub to his hairy regions, and exited the waters.

"Fig!" Gwayne shouted into the trees as he pulled his tunic over his head. "Figharth are you here?" No response came and Gwayne turned to Error. "Just you and me, eh?"

Error heaved a sigh, inclined his head in the direction of the gremlin village. He locked eyes with the knight and released another, more aggrieved, sigh.

"Oh," Gwayne said. "Fig went that way?"

26

A short time later, Figharth was awakened by the sound of shuffled footsteps at the base of the tree.

Sir Gwayne? Blinking awake, Figharth feared that the others had departed the village without him. He bolted upright and, to his relief, espied Galahalt and Elkara conversing beneath a heap of armour.

Phew! Figharth sighed. *They haven't left me behind! Now, where might Sir Gwayne be?* The wisp crawled to the edge of the branch, peered below, expecting to see the knight's familiar colors. *There he is!* Figharth thought, elated. But then he noticed a discrepancy; the person below wore a mantle in a similar shade to the gray of Gwayne's, but this mantle displayed heavier signs of wear.

All of the forest seemed to slow to a crawl. Figharth's breath felt trapped inside his ribcage as he tried to distinguish the person's identity, but the man had pulled his cowl over his head. Markings were etched all over the longbow held firm in the stranger's grip. Figharth searched his memories, attempting to recall where he had seen comparable symbols.

It's so recent. Figharth racked his brain so hard it almost pained him. *But where?*

The man knelt just above the crest of the ridge. To those below, merely the top of his cowl would be visible. He reached within his mantle, produced a silver arrow. He then nocked the arrow and drew the bowstring to its fullest length.

Figharth watched on in horror. His mind reeled. His beak moved wordlessly as his eyes darted between his friends and the readied long-bow.

The stranger rose, selected his target.

GWAYNE ATTEMPTED TO RETRACE HIS STEPS, knowing the general direction, but each passing tree appeared less and less familiar. His internal bearings were usually correct, but this time he feared that he would overshoot the village and pass clear around, pressing beyond the nearest invisible boundary line.

"If I were a laif I'd be able to detect the twigs I snapped earlier on my way through, eh Quintus?" Gwayne said to his sword. "Plus, if I were a laif, I would be able to cross any wards that may be hunkering down, should I overstep."

As his heart rate quickened so did his feet, and vaulting a downed tree he used the momentum to carry himself forward into a controlled jog. One hand held the satchel firm to his side preventing it from catching as he dodged and weaved through the tangled branches. His face and hair were constantly snagged, fresh wounds opened anew by the clutching sticks and thorns as he dodged and weaved. The knight screwed his eyes to the left, drawn by a large splash of sunlight between the trees.

"Must be it," Gwayne mumbled. He made for the light, emerging from the tangles while holding his chest, the wound still aching. Free of the dense shadows and damp foliage, the knight's eyes quickly adjusted as he focused on Elkara and Galahalt standing by the stolen armour pile, their conversation not quite loud enough to cross the gap. He found himself on the outer crest of the dale.

The knight traversed the rim, his sabatons reflecting a brilliant glow. Then, all at once, a movement beneath a tree startled him, and he darted into the nearby thicket.

With tremendous care, Gwayne pressed toward the perceived threat, the hem of the forest granting him cover.

"Patience, Quintus," Gwayne said as his hand strayed to the pommel of his longsword. "Patience." As he peered through a sworl of vines, an ardent breeze shoved the lower tendrils aside. The knight went to a knee, perceived a hooded figure where he had first witnessed movement.

The figure crept toward the gremlin village, clutching a longbow heavily marked by glyphs. The lower half of his face was wholly concealed behind a green-gray scarf.

He moves like Elithiel, Gwayne thought. *This is not a good thing.*

A silver arrow appeared from within the man's cloak. With unthinkable speed, he set the arrow to his longbow and drew the string back.

Gwayne spared no time for thought, and he burst from the thicket.

The man angled his longbow at something in the dale.

"No!" Gwayne shouted. "Hey!" He waved his arms, failing to conjure anything clever. The wound to his chest gathered more pain, but he ran on.

The man wavered, his head twitched. At first Gwayne believed it was his own shouts that had caused the man to falter. But then, through the trees, Gwayne snatched sight of a gray beastly blur just to his right. A roar sounded off immediately afterward.

The bowman started at the sound, yet he released his arrow.

Gwayne prayed the man had missed.

The bowman quickly lowered his longbow, stuttered a step in Gwayne's direction. Above his scarf, his eyes widened with fright. But it was not Gwayne who had conjured such immediate terror. Through the branches Gwayne saw an unearthly gray lion charging a parallel route. And in a matter of moments, both knight and beast would converge on the bowman.

But that was not meant to be. In a most impressive display, the bowman scaled the tree at his back, disappearing into the boughs.

The lion, undeterred, planted his forepaws into the base of the tree, began his ascent.

From the ground, Gwayne observed the bowman only gaining distance from his pursuers, effortlessly bounding from branch to branch like a highly skilled laif.

A ribbed, pained wail emanated from the dale, and the lion froze at the sound. He craned his neck, revealing what appeared to be razors adorning his mane.

"Was that Elkara?" Gwayne said, turning.

At the mention of her name, the lion met Gwayne's eyes. The beast's face revealed nothing but dread.

The two exchanged glances and, at the same time, broke for the gremlin village.

Moments before...

DILIGENTLY RESTACKING THE DISRUPTED PILE of steel, Galahalt did not spare a glance her way. Not a single word was exchanged, and where Elkara felt there should be tension, only an icy silence existed. She was not interested in holding a conversation anyhow, but she was slightly concerned that her charge did not pout or attempt to barter. Countless upstarts had been turned down, and be they knight or potential courtier, very few, if any, had exhibited such resolve.

He might be plotting something, she thought. She observed the knight, placing her foot under a stray gauntlet and kicking the piece up onto the mound. It rotated ninety degrees, palm down before settling into place. *No, I doubt that. He'll probably just seek the service of another ranger. Now that he is aware of the old Navarene trick, he may be able to use that knowledge as leverage in order to convince another laif to help him bypass the wards to the lake.*

At present Galahalt held a conical helm. He gazed at it with pure boredom before depositing it. He turned toward his spear and helm, silently moving to retrieve them.

"I was thinking," Elkara said, cracking the silence open. "I'm assuming that once we get back to civilization you will be enlisting another ranger, but seeing as you helped me win this bet with Elithiel, I have decided to give you a discounted rate. How does that sound? These excursions can be expensive and I don't want to be responsible for holding you back too long before making another go of it. I just can't commit to a quest that can cost so much—not monetarily speaking...it's just not in me."

Galahalt had stopped to listen, but had just now resumed walking. She had hoped that her generous offer would garner a smile at the very least. Aside from the brief pause, the knight had paid her very little mind. She watched him bend down and retrieve his spear then his helm next to it, his eyes maintaining a willful barrier from her direction.

"Do you have a plan?" Elkara's words spouted freely from her thoughts.

Finally Galahalt's eyes met hers. "When I was a child," he began. "I loved crag lions. I studied every book, pamphlet, and scroll that I could get my hands on." He adjusted his helm with a thumb. "A very interesting and mysterious breed of cat."

Elkara nodded. She was well-versed on crag lion behavior, but she was unsure of where he was going with this.

"Crag lions are very powerful creatures, "Galahalt went on. "The females can scale the wall of a mountain, even if it's the smoothest obsidian. The males have very sharp manes, like razors, and they're used to tear away at any unfortunate prey. They can see in the dark, like you laives, and they make their homes far from where other large cats dare to tread. That's where they get their name. Entire prides existing in the mountain sides, overlooking dangerous peaks where exotic prey live and thrive, undisturbed throughout the centuries...until a determined crag lion became aware of their peaceful existence. I'm sure you've heard the stories," he said. "And hekk, you've probably been spectator to a few yourself, in your wanderings. I don't know.

"But the thing about these prides is that they are extraordinarily private, a detail that actually upset me when I was young. They hunt and live and share only within their pride, ignoring all others, except when mating needs arise. But that is something else entirely." He blinked a barrage and shook his head. "You see, it's in their nature to protect their interests first, no matter the needs of any other pride outside their own. If another pride is nearly wiped out by disease or an attack and a single cub survives, a nearby pride will turn a blind eye, even if the helpless cub is begging right on their doorstep. The pride will watch the cub wither away, becoming nothing but a pile of flesh and bone for the vultures. Even during the feast of a fresh kill, with plenty to spare, the foreign cub will be forcefully removed, all maternal instincts be damned if the poor thing tried to get a single scrap. And I have come to realize that it is pointless to try and change nature. Nature is a force that you must accept sometimes."

"Now that is something else entirely—" Elkara began.

From the heights above the dale, the voice of Sir Gwayne, shouting in dire urgency, interrupted the laif.

She recognized the sincerity in his voice and, as she turned, a terrific pain erupted from her right hand. She let loose an anguished cry, dropped to both knees.

Galahalt rushed to her side as the blood pooled on the soil below.

"What happened?!" he asked, frantic.

"An archer!" screamed Elkara. Her eyes had locked on a slender arrow buried in the ground a distance from her. "The arrow only cut me!"

Galahalt gripped her about the shoulders, and the laif cursed and bashed his chest with her head.

"We must find cover!" he urged. "Stop fighting me!"

The jostling only brought further agony. "No!" The laif realized this was no ordinary wound. "Leave me!"

Then Galahalt did something that caused Elkara to plead once again. But it was not for an end to her pain.

In a single shifting of feet, the knight re-positioned himself between the archer and the laif.

You stupid idiot knight! she could only voice in her head. *Why would you do this for me?*

THE LION EASILY OUTRAN GWAYNE, navigating the grade with ease, while the knight stumbled behind. Galahalt stiffened at the large creature's approach.

"Danger's passed!" shouted Gwayne. "The bowman took flight!"

"Is that a crag lion?!" Galahalt asked inside a gasp. "A *gray* crag lion?"

Elkara bolted to her feet. "Why?!" she raged at the lion. "Would you do that?!" She glanced at Galahalt, then focused narrow eyes on the lion.

The beast lowered its ears, slowing its approach.

"You know this lion?" Galahalt asked in amazement, having never seen a crag lion quite like this one before.

"You know him too." Elkara extended her wounded hand as the beast lowered his head. "This is Error."

Gwayne had finally reached them. "I'm sorry, what?"

Galahalt recognized something passing behind the beast's eyes as they looked at one another.

"Apparently Error can transform," Galahalt said. Aside from the eyes, the only other similarity was the deep gray of his coat.

"Where are your wounds?" Gwayne asked, cutting to Elkara. He took in the sight of her blood-soaked hand with a tightened jaw.

Elkara patted the soft part of Error's head. "The shot only grazed me," she began. "But it burns like it's cursed, and the blood—it won't stop." Without prompting, Gwayne tore at the tunic under his cloak, removing a length and wrapping it around the laif's hand three times over.

"Thank you," Elkara managed to say through clenched teeth. The knight then placed a steadying hand beneath her elbow. "You stupid, stupid old man!" she scolded Error. "Why did you do this?"

Error scowled, but not a hint of shame appeared on his face as he led Elkara toward a metallic gremlin cottage comprised of repurposed rabbit hutches and gardening shears.

"Hold the wound above your chest," Gwayne advised. Elkara nodded, wincing at the normally simple movement. As Gwayne and Error tended to Elkara, Galahalt retrieved the buried arrow, admiring the craftsmanship on his return to the others. The silvery surface felt odd in his hand, and the sun's partial rays reflected unevenly. The tip was partially recessed into the shaft, and when he moved to test the sharpness with a finger, Elkara leapt as one prodded by a pitchfork.

"Wait!" she shouted, appearing suddenly stricken. "Fack!" With unexpected rapidity, she unfurled the wrapping on her hand.

Gwayne's eyes narrowed with recognition. "Poisoned tip."

"Not poison," Elkara corrected. "Venom." She pressed a finger to her palm, and the area around the deep scratch did not flex as it should.

Galahalt dropped the arrow. "How do you know?"

"Basilisk venom. I can already feel the flesh hardening."

"Could be gorgon piss," Gwayne offered.

Elkara cast a withering look at Gwayne. "What difference does it make?" she asked, her tone imbued with a heady dose of incredulity. "And anyway, gorgons use their eyes."

In mirrored astonishment, Gwayne asked, "They piss from their eyes?"

"Is there a cure?" Galahalt interrupted. "In the supplies perhaps?" He looked to Error.

"No," Elkara replied as she bound her arm all the way to her bicep. "Not amongst the supplies, wherever it is that Error discarded them." She regarded Error with despondency. "This is the second time you've transformed," she told the lion. "You know what that means."

Error acknowledged her words, bowed his head.

"Do not do this again, old man," Elkara went on. "I do not care how dire you believe the situation to be." The laif bit down on the cloth, synching it tight.

"Think a lampyr can heal your petrifying wound?" Galahalt suggested. "If we can get you back quick enough? How much time until the venom—"

"Turns me to stone?" Elkara cut in. "Before I'm completely petrified? Four or five days. Maybe more. Maybe less. Hard to say." She tested the dressing on her hand with a squeeze. "And I fear the nearest lampyr would be useless. My treatment requires a skill that most lampyrs no longer possess."

Above the dale, Galahalt's eyes were drawn to a fluttering movement reluctantly drawing closer.

"Maybe there's a salve we can draw from a plant?" Gwayne pondered aloud. "Or a monster we can slay to concoct an elixir from?" His head twitched at the sound of wings flapping overhead. "Eh, there's Fig."

Galahalt stepped near the laif. "Do you know of a cure for petrification?"

Elkara's mouth formed a solid line. "There *is* a beast we can slay," she admitted, casting her eyes to the ground. "The Questing Beast."

27

Sir Phillip tucked his tinderbox into the layered pouch, observing Clemence guiding the infant flame toward maturity with a retractable battle fan. Ashes from the fire built by their squires days before still lingered, a subtle reminder of their grief. The wounds from their deaths still bled openly.

The knights had hired a laif assassin to track Sir Galahalt. At present, they awaited his return. Previously, they had given the assassin a rough idea as to where they would be setting up camp. He had interrupted their directions, assuring them that he would find them. No doubt his claim had been intended as encouragement—assuring the knights of his competence—but instead it had come across rather unsettling.

Clemence was familiar with the politics of laives, after sorting various squabbles in the past. Some resolutions had arrived more hastily than others. Phillip was much more comfortable in the city, or upon an open battlefield. In truth, he was not very keen on forests, where he was often more vulnerable than his foe. Overall, he did not trust laives. He found it difficult to trust anyone at this point in his life, but as a general rule, he approached laif deals with great skepticism.

"Did you remember to bring some of that stew from last night?" Phillip asked, rummaging for a pan as the fire lapped at the air.

Clemence nodded. "I did." She brushed the soil from her tunic as she rose to her feet. "I'll fetch it. Should be just enough for the both of us."

The knight approached her tethered horse as the last slivers of daylight passed between the trees. She raised a hand to pat the horse's muzzle, but the animal shied away, pulling at the anchored rope.

"Hey-now!" Clemence backed away.

Standing on the outskirts of the treeline, Clemence caught sight of a figure clad in grays and greens.

Meanwhile the horse's eyes rolled, bursting with panic. She kicked and reared, her left forehoof nearly connecting with Clemence's jaw.

The figure's long hair fell loose, draping his shoulders, intertwining with his cloak. As he strode toward the knight, glistening plate flashed within his cloak.

"Greetings, Elshur." Clemence saluted the approaching shadow. "Our assassin has returned."

"Well met." The laif adjusted his longbow, spared a glance at Clemence's horse. The beast had suddenly calmed. "The Arbiter and the obese churchman are all that have been made privy to our meeting, correct?"

"That's correct," Clemence replied, and plunged both her arms into a deep saddle sack. "You'll find Sir Phillip over yonder." She withdrew her arms, having found what she sought; a wax-coated box. "Shall we?" she said, beckoning the laif follow her.

Elshur nodded and followed Clemence into the clearing. They found Phillip upon his knees before the fire. He had erected a cooking grate over the flames and was attempting to shim it with a handful wooden slivers.

"Found the stew," Clemence announced, raising the box.

"That's not all you found," Phillip said, his voice devoid of humor.

Clemence retrieved the kettle from a nearby stump and upended the contents of the box into it. "If we had more, we would offer you some," she explained to Elshur. "I'm afraid there is merely a single man-sized portion here."

"I am not here for a meal," Elshur said. His arms remained hidden beneath his cloak. "I only bring news, when you are prepared to listen."

After carefully placing the kettle on the cooking stand, Phillip folded his arms. "It sure is nice to get out of the city and clear my head," he began, sounding almost wistful. "All this fresh air, far from the turmoil in the city. Folks getting denied their rights to have kids, making them all upset. Damn near rioting. Then there was that slaughter at Knotwithstadt that got them all riled up in the first place." He noticed Elshur fiddling with the handle on his longbow, clearly disinterested. "It's all such a shame," Phillip concluded, leaned forward, and stirred the kettle.

"Truly is a shame," Clemence agreed, "all those young people wishing to start families." With a shake of her head, she redirected the conversation. "Speaking of children, just what conclusions have you drawn regarding our squires? Feel free to have a seat."

Elshur yawned. "Oh?" he said, blinking. "Is it my turn already?"

The knights exchanged looks; Phillip's appeared murderous while Clemence's verged on embarrassment.

"Let's begin with the demise of your squires," Elshur continued. "It appears they engaged in more than one foray."

Phillip's spoon halted mid-scrape.

"The desecration of the three human corpses near the river was a ploy," Elshur explained. "A mere stone's throw north from that stew you're toiling over, one can find evidence of a battle between no more than eight combatants. I wager seven were engaged." The laif admired the fingernails on his sword hand. "Your three squires and some ogres."

Phillip released his spoon into the stew, handle and all. "How can you be certain?" he demanded.

"The ogre's great mallet lays there now." Elshur applied his tone evenly. "Obscured under a blanket of leaves and sticks. That is where he fell. The bodies were moved as a diversion, after the fact."

"Ah, yes," Clemence said. "So I imagine that you caught up with those who—" she paused, giving careful thought to her next words. "*Murdered* our lads?"

"*Those?*" Elshur grinned, the firelight revealing his lampyr fangs. At his back, the sun had completely set. "You're speaking in plural, knight." He withdrew a hand from his cloak, raised its index finger. "A single weapon killed your armoured squires."

Concern etched Phillip's brow. "Are you certain?" he asked, but did not await a reply, and continued. "The ambush site we selected was strategically flawless and our lads were days from being knighted. They were squires in title alone. Surely they were more than capable of handling a solitary knight?" He glanced at Clemence, then turned back to Elshur. "How's that even possible? Didn't you just tell us that our lads bested a handful of ogres despite being outnumbered?"

"I did not come here to speculate," Elshur stated. "The weapon that slew your squires, along with its bearer, are currently traveling north, towards Lake Humiel."

Phillip shifted on his stump.

"How do you know this?" Clemence inquired.

"Because I engaged them off a trail north of Fort Navarene," Elshur replied, seeming bored. "I have indicated the location on this map." From within his cloak he presented a parchment.

Clemence rose and received the scroll. She then hunched close to the flames, inspecting what had been scribbled on the sheaf.

"I regret to admit," Elshur began with a sigh. "As I leveled my bow on my target, I was met by an unforeseen *intervention.*"

"Wait!" Phillip leapt to his feet, sending his stump on a somersault. "You mean to tell us—!"

"My shot did not claim the ranger," admitted Elshur. "At least not immediately. My arrow struck her, but it was not an instant death, as you'd hoped." He turned abrupt to Clemence, gestured toward the map in her hands. "Please take note of the exaggerated lines. Those are the routes they may possibly take."

Phillip tilted his head back, gazing disdainfully at the laif. "And this unforeseen intervention?"

"The ranger travels with a mount of a dragoon," Elshur replied.

Clemence inhaled sharp while Phillip simply cocked an eyebrow.

"I don't quite catch the reference?" Phillip said.

"What isn't clear to you?" Elshur wondered. "The mount intervened, upsetting my aim—"

"That!" Phillip interjected. "Just what is a *mount of a dragoon?*"

Elshur smiled a passive sort of smile. "I fear that I haven't the time for explanations," he said. "But based on your companions' response, I wager she is fully aware, and she may fill you in later."

"I can't believe you missed," Phillip growled. "The plan was to kill the ranger, thus leaving the knight vulnerable to us." He looked up into the skies, released a sigh. "I suppose it's a good thing your arrows are doused in basilisk sauce."

Elshur's smile wavered.

"For clarity, if we follow your lines," Clemence said, tracing a finger along the surface of the map. "Then we should meet our knight somewhere between this campfire and where you took your shot?"

"Unless they decided to travel north," Elshur replied. "Either way, I am prepared to take you to where you need to be. We should arrive by midafternoon if we set out soon. Then we shall part ways."

"My squires were like sons to me." Phillip wiped his nose. "Do you have children, Elshur?"

The laif ignored Phillip and instead turned to Clemence. "I will wake you in a few hours," he said. "You will be riding hard under moonlight, then we will discard your horses and continue on foot." With that, he turned and strode in the direction of the river.

"After that, I'm sure you will be expecting payment?" Phillip called to the laif's back.

Elshur stopped. "The first kill is free."

* * *

AFTER DISCUSSING THEIR PLIGHT, the party decided it best to act fast, and once a course was set, they moved swiftly from the shimmering gremlin village, heading northwest toward the shores of Lake Humiel.

The tourniquet applied to Elkara's left arm helped slow the venom's progress, but she estimated that her entire hand would be rendered useless by morning. She consciously kept the hand as flat as possible, so that when the hardening took its final effect on the appendage, she would have a sharp implement instead of a useless cudgel. Gwayne was the only one who laughed when the laif joked about filing the fingertips down to a razor's edge. Galahalt had been lost in thought, and Figharth was sullen and completely out of sorts.

The wisp sat glumly, dejected, on Gwayne's newly armoured shoulder as they plotted the most direct course. After Elkara had revealed the horrors they may face, Gwayne had not said a word, but had walked back toward the gremlin's armour pile and selected a few choice bits. Galahalt had only spit on the ground and walked away when Elkara estimated the lake was thirty miles away.

"We should be on the shores by tomorrow afternoon," Elkara said. "If we travel through the night without stopping."

"After traveling light for the last few days," Gwayne said after nearly scraping his forehead with an armoured wrist. "I must reacquaint myself with this new armour. The scary monsters that lay ahead will be disappointed, eh Fig?"

The wisp sighed into his hands, looking at the knight from the sides of his eyes.

"What's eating you, little guy?" Gwayne asked, pushing aside a heavy branch filled with leaves resembling the rind of a pear. Elkara had discovered a deer trail, which was proving helpful, but still provided some obstacles for those a bit thicker than the slender animals. "You don't seem frightened by all that is going on. Or is this how a wisp acts when he's deeply scared?"

"I'm not afraid," revealed Figharth. "Well, not really more afraid than my standard level of anxious."

"So what's eating you?" Gwayne repeated. "If you're not abnormally afraid, then what are you feeling, Fig?"

A pause stretched between knight and wisp. Gwayne thought the wisp had forgotten to respond. The scenery was very distracting, to say the least. A vast meadow opened on their left flank, displaying a happy but small cross section. The depth appeared infinite from their standpoint, and the swirling fae beckoned the travelers enter. Dull splashing could be heard somewhere over the meadow's horizon, and a formation of ducks careened downward. The field was piped with open flowers, their petals differing shades of pinks and purples, a disorganized mosaic that attracted a thrum of insects.

Elkara abruptly signaled them all to get down, and everyone lowered their bellies to the dirt, Gwayne gently holding Figharth in his hand.

Galahalt, however, was stricken with curiosity, wondering what sort of danger barred their path. He silently crawled to Elkara's side, causing the laif to stare at the knight with muted disbelief as he mouthed the word, *"What?"*

Popping twigs and twanging undergrowth immediately vaulted their attention to the trail ahead.

Pressing his chin into the grass, Galahalt worked his jaw, eagerly sizing up whatever lay beyond while Elkara's eyes widened as the beast in front scratched at the earth. Leathery flapping noises emanated from before them, but seemed to dwindle, retreating deeper into the forest.

Elkara drew herself up on one elbow, glaring at Galahalt. "That was a chanticleer in heat, you idiot!" she whispered harshly. "I'm already turning to stone, do you wish to join me?"

"I daresay the two of you would make handsome statues," Gwayne said, placing Figharth back onto his shoulder after standing and brushing grassy particles from his knees.

Elkara ignored Gwayne. "Never make a move like that again," she warned Galahalt as the knight rose to a stand.

"Apologies." Galahalt extended a hand, aiding the laif to her feet. "I was merely curious."

From their backs, Figharth let out a grief-stricken sob. Startled, they turned to the passenger on Gwayne's shoulder.

"Guilt!" Figharth sobbed. "Shame and guilt!"

Elkara and Galahalt exchanged puzzled looks.

"In answer to your question, Gwayne, that's what I *feel*," the wisp cried. "I saw the assassin endeavoring his ghastly approach to the gully!" He coughed and wheezed, tears circled past his beak. "And I did nuh-nuh-nuh—" A bout of shuddering sobs overwhelmed him for several moments. "Nothing!" he finally spat his conclusion.

"There, there little guy, we don't—" Gwayne began.

"I am a spectator!" Figharth declared, burying his face in his hands, his protruding beak moving wordlessly.

"Easy now," Gwayne said sofly. "That cockatrice is still near." He lifted a steel-clad hand to administer a pat to the wisp's back, but thought better of it.

Elkara strode to the sorrowful fae, knelt before him. "This," she began, presenting her bandaged hand. "Is not your doing. I do not blame you, and even if I did, it wouldn't matter. We don't have the luxury of time to stand around blaming one another. The longer we dwell here, the faster I become a rock. So please, if you're truly sorry, then make amends by stiffening that beak and composing yourself." She glanced a brief smile at Gwayne. "I forgive you, Fig, so please quit your sniveling. We don't need to alert anymore monsters."

"I'm-I'm-I'm," Figharth struggled to formulate a response as the laif ruffled the top of his head.

"Let's get moving, eh?" said Elkara. "We're wasting daylight here."

"A liability!" Figharth burst, unexpectedly propelling himself from Gwayne's shoulder, and into the skies.

In disbelief, the others looked up as a handful of leaves twirled to the ground around them.

Gwayne tried to follow his flight path, but after the wisp hooked a turn behind a crooked elm, the knight lost all sight of him.

"What do you think Leandra would say?" Gwayne said, peering sadly at his vacant shoulder. "You little jerk."

* * *

IN TRUTH, IT HAD NOT BEEN SO MUCH THE INCONSISTENT pacing, nor the long stretches of jogging then walking then jogging again that had so irritated Sir Phillip. Nor the fact that they had abandoned their horses in favor of traveling through thick foliage and incessant thorns. What had really irked him was their laif guide. The pointy-eared prat only spoke when giving orders, and had never broken a sweat nor lagged in his steps.

Also, there had not been one shred of proof to validate what Elshur claimed. For all Phillip knew they were headed for some sort of deadly grinding trap. And earlier that day, he had overheard Sir Clemence apologizing for her companion's lack of etiquette, and Elshur's response had presented Phillip with the urge to bounce the laif's head off a boulder.

"I would need to value the man in order to feel offended by his speech," Elshur had said.

The phrase endlessly needled at Phillip, especially knowing that the laif had deliberately spoken loud enough for him to hear it.

When the knights had finally parted ways with the laif, Phillip did not shed a single tear. Elshur's final instructions had been given next to a weatherworn statue of a knight with long braided hair and delicate features. Females born with the Warrior's gift had a certain edge in battle due in most part to their maternal instincts, or so Phillip had been told when he was young. He had seen evidence of this firsthand, and it had sown the seeds of resentment in him early on. He never forgot when Lacamora had bested him on the training ground when they were pages, just shy of ten. Her thin frame and pretty face betrayed him as she wrestled the bow staff from his grip, nearly snapping his wrist at the thumb. She beat him continually, prevailing in tests of strength every time the knight-commander paired them together. Which had been quite often.

"That little git," Phillip muttered, the memory presently burning in his mind.

"I hear waves and water birds!" Clemence abruptly said, swiping Phillip's chest plate with a backhand. "And the smell of a beach."

Wrestling a branch from his throat, Phillip smiled. "A culling awaits," he said darkly.

"Aye," Clemence agreed, meeting Phillip's eyes. "For our lads." She stopped for a moment to free the kite shield from her back, then shrugged the longbow and quiver from her shoulder, leaning them against a nearby elm.

The pair pressed through the weeping boughs, and stepped into the radiant daylight. Phillip reached for his belt, unconsciously reassuring himself by grazing the hanging crossbow as he walked behind Clemence. To their right, standing on a sandy hillock perhaps an acre's span away was a horse and three persons.

Three?

Clemence secured her helm with the visor locked open.

"Fucking elf!" Phillip swore, and wheeled back into the shade to retrieve Clemence's discarded bow. "Elshur failed to mention a *second* knight."

* * *

"CREATOR'S BLESSING," GALAHALT SPOKE in utter exhaustion. Elkara had informed him that Lake Humiel lay just over the next crest.

The party, down to four after Figharth had made his hasty escape, had walked endlessly through the night, miraculously avoiding any incidents. The only resemblance of a threat they had encountered had been a band of goblins. Elkara, however, had heard them, or smelled them long before coming upon them. The creatures had been in the middle of a clearing seated around a fire with a roasting spit bisecting its center. The high-pitched shrieks of laughter alerted the knights, and they wordlessly gave the gleeful party a wide berth.

When they came upon a ward, Elkara instructed the knights to remain behind, and the men gladly acquiesced, as the wards prompted the only break from the endless trudging. After safely crossing the last ward, the only foe that barred their path was weariness and sore feet, enemies that could not be defeated with steel.

Elkara had urged them onward. "Just a few more steps. A few more hills. A few more knolls." She did not show any sign of fatigue, weakness completely eradicated by iron resolve. When the journey seemed unending, exhaustion flooding their mortal limbs, the unexpected squawk of a white-backed gull ushered in new life and vigor. Just beyond a rolling mound, perched on an old wooden bollard was a web-footed bird that never ventured far from water.

"I could kiss you!" Gwayne exclaimed, staring at the creature's ivory plumage as they walked past. The bird jerked its head at the sound of the knight's voice, but remained firmly rooted to the pedestal.

The final hillock before the lakeshore was thinly carpeted in grass, the soil surrendering to sand on the opposite slope. The sun was behind them, above their shoulders, streaking the lake with a golden shimmer.

Gwayne sniffed. "Smells like rotting corpses," he said, spitting on the ground, too fatigued to wipe the trail of spittle from his stubble.

"The lake is plagued with kapreta," Elkara reminded them. "We must move with greater caution. If one sees us, they all see us. The cave entrance should be directly before us." She began pulling her boots off, balancing on one foot on the apex of the sandy mound. The breeze coming from the lake swirled the hair around her face as she stood with her back to it. She pushed a few strands away with the only dexterous hand she had. "We are not downwind and I'm not interested in fooling around, so I'm going for it."

Galahalt worked feverishly to remove his pauldrons. Gwayne, taking notice, quickly moved to aid his fellow knight.

"Don't wait too long for us, Gwayne," Galahalt said, setting a hand on the other knight's shoulder. "Remember that Error can lead you back toward the safe havens, free from wards."

Gwayne nodded and extended an armoured hand and Galahalt slapped his hand into the offered gauntlet.

"It may be weeks or months..." Elkara began.

"I know, I know," Gwayne said, closing his eyes and nodding. "I got you this far. No need to thank me or anything. And I'll wait as long—"

A sharp *ting!* interrupted the knight, and Elkara's shoulders reacted to a sudden impact on her stone arm. An arrow had glanced off her solidified flesh near the wrist, sending shaved splinters into the air.

At a distance down the shoreline, two knights resplendent in armour emerged from the shadows of the treeline, azure fabric swirling about their knees. One knight lowered a longbow while the other knight leveled a longsword toward Galahalt.

"Take to the waters," Gwayne instructed as he freed Quintus from its scabbard.

Elkara tugged at Galahalt's tunic, motioning toward the waves, but the knight remained still, wanting to help Gwayne.

"Quintus and I are more than equal to these knights," Gwayne assured Galahalt from over his shoulder. "Finish what you set out to do."

Error lowered his head, eyes fixed on the enemy, his mouth curling around burgeoning fangs.

"Error!" Elkara screamed.

The laifhorse focused on the approaching knights, ignoring her cry.

"Error! Do not!" she warned. "Seek shelter! Error! No! You stupid horse!"

"Elkara, please, we must go!" Galahalt tugged at the laif's wrist. "We need to heal you!" he shouted, pulling up her hand completely cast in stone. "We must heal me!"

Elkara blinked through tears as her lifelong companion transformed into a monster. It felt like peering into a flipbook portraying the saddest of endings.

"You idiot," Elkara exhaled toward Error. "I'll never forgive you."

Galahalt gripped the laif forcefully by her tourniquet and guided her toward the shimmering waters. The sand was warm ahead of the lapping tide, but the patch they entered was considerably colder. Knight and ranger held their breath, bracing themselves for the frigid plunge.

From the shore the sound of steel smashing steel carried over the lake. To Galahalt's left the waters foamed, churning violently from a disturbance beneath the waves. Elkara drew her dagger and placed it between her teeth.

"No sense in turning back," Galahalt said, shifting his spear between a thumb.

Several kapreta emerged from the froth, drawn toward the clanging of the battle. Galahalt inhaled sharp, wishing he were invisible. The kapreta did not seem to notice neither Galahalt nor Elkara, and trudged toward the beach. Then, as Galahalt was about to release a sigh, one of the kapreta swiveled her head in his direction.

"Oh, no," Galahalt mumbled as he met the kapreta's eyes.

The kapreta then performed what Galahalt could only describe as a double-take, and squared her bony shoulders toward him.

Elkara's eyes widened. Retreat was not an option. She removed her dagger from its rest in her mouth.

"Kill it clean," she advised Galahalt. "Like hornets, they are attracted to their own dead. Kill it quickly, then we must swim like mad."

A grimace plastered the kapreta's face, wet scales refracting sunlight in all directions. Gratefully the other kapreta were wholly interested in what transpired on the beach, leaving this kapreta alone on her hunt.

Ever so slowly Galahalt lowered his spear, concealing it behind the chop of the waves. Unaware of the danger, and delirious with hunger, the kapreta only trudged faster. As Galahalt aimed his lunge for the kapreta's chest, the monster warily espied the movement. The kapreta dipped, attempting to avoid the weapon's thrust. Before she was fully submerged, Galahalt adjusted the spear's trajectory by the faintest degree, piercing the monster at her throat. With gills straining, the kapreta clutched her throat, warbling through the black ichor spilling from her mouth.

"We must go now! Before the blood—" Elkara shouted and returned her dagger to her mouth.

The kapreta flailed as she dove into the water, spewing blood in a great arc behind her. All at once, a shrieking wail sounded from the depths of the lake. Elkara covered her ears, stupidly bashing her stone hand against her head. The waters all around them began to foam, this time in greater ferocity and scope, completely barring their escape.

"Sorry," Galahalt said. "Didn't think she'd thrash like that."

Removing the dagger from her teeth, Elkara pressed her back against Galahalt. "I don't think that's a response anyone could have anticipated," she replied.

In the seeming hundreds, the kapreta emerged in an alarming array, forming a ring that could be perceived from the heavens. Seemingly blinded by their rage, the monstrous host waved frantically at the air. Violently they plucked at their scales, screaming with hatred, but refrained from approaching the knight and laif.

Galahalt swiveled his head, met Elkara's eyes. "Is this normal?"

The kapreta that had initially charged the beach were also clawing at their own flesh, backpedaling for the lake. One kapreta snagged a heel on a chunk of driftwood, and convulsed on the ground.

As Elkara observed the spasming kapreta, she recognized what was happening.

"We must swim for the cave!" she shouted, prodding Galahalt with her petrified fingertips. "And don't come up for air!"

Galahalt did not require further encouragement. *Let's hope this aelder terrapin shell lives up the rumors.* He inhaled the deepest breath of his life. *If only I could have tested it beforehand.*

Water surged through the helm's eye slits. *Really should've tested it,* he thought, holding his breath. He kicked his feet, resolving to swim as far as possible on his present lungful. He turned his head and watched Elkara swimming next to him, her stone hand proving cumbersome.

So that's why she didn't take the lead.

Suddenly she began pointing at something below and ahead of them. Bubbles escaped her mouth as she shouted indiscernibly.

Galahalt gazed downward, observed the sand running in furrows along the lakebed. Where the patterns ceased, a stone structure punctuated its center, and a dusky cave insinuated itself therein. By this point he was ravenous for air. He could feel his blood vessels readying to burst. He swam hard for the cave. *Elkara can revive me,* he assured himself. *She can revive me. I only need to get into that cave.*

From around his eye slits his vision narrowed. Though he yet neared the tunnel mouth, he already felt as though he had entered. Of a sudden, his body's nature took hold of him, forcing a gasp. He inhaled, ready to suffocate.

In the place of a frigid choke, a warm sensation flooded his mouth, coursed down his throat. He inhaled lungfuls of air, exhaled laughter.

Elkara, having already surged ahead, turned around to the noise. *If I ever doubted the lad's sanity,* she thought. *I can now lay those doubts to rest.*

28

"You want *what?* And you're going to put it *where?*" Pietr, in contrast to his outrage, gently set his stylus down upon his sketching board. He sat at his desk, currently dumbstruck by his brother Holden's previous statement.

"For the second time," Holden began. "I want you to draw for me a great red dragon quaffing a frosty flagon of ale with one arm locked around an unseemly milkmaid whilst standing upon the ashy remnants of an incinerated knight." He slammed a crumpled sheet of vellum beneath Pietr's nose. "Here, I even went through the trouble of making a rough sketch for you."

Pietr smoothed the paper with an elongated sigh. "First of all," he said. "That is a wyvern, and second—"

"Who gives a tinker's care?" Holden interrupted. "Just give it your artisan spin. And make it look amazing! I'm presenting it to Claustin, my tattoo mate, so he can render the likeness onto my back. All the other squires will be so jealous! And no doubt all the ladies will faint!" He settled his hands firmly upon the ledge of Pietr's desk, leaned forward. "Make it happen, brother."

Pietr rose abrupt, briskly approached his brother. "Holden!" The artist squished the young man's cheeks, forcing a pucker. "I love you, little brother and I will do *anything* for you. Well, almost anything. But *this?*" He arched his back, retrieved the parchment. "This, my brother, is a waste of ink. Why don't you take it to Claustin and see if he can draw it?"

"I see how it is," Holden said, snatching his drawing and tossing it over his shoulder. "Let's pretend I already asked Claustin, and he produced something eerily similar to what you've already seen..."

"For all we deign holy." Pietr's hand found his forehead as he retreated for his desk. "I want no part in this, Holden. If mother and father—"

"Mother and father will never know," Holden promised, grinning. "You're the only person I can trust with this."

Pietr raised a quill, pointed its sharp end toward the door. "No."

"Come on, big brother," Holden pleaded. "Can you at least give me a recommendation? You must know of another competent artist." He folded his arms, cocked his head. "Just direct me to the door of the second finest doodler in the kingdom and I'll be on my way."

Meanwhile, Pietr had departed his desk and had bounded for the door.

"You can at least give me a hint," Holden continued. "What might her name rhyme with?"

Without a glance at his brother, Pietr reached for the latch, opened the door. "I'll give you a hint," he growled. The invading breeze sent papers in his drawing room fluttering. "Her name rhymes with 'Get Stuffed.'"

After receiving a firm shove from his elder brother, Holden found himself deployed out onto the front stoop. "The artist is a 'she' then?" he said, quickly turning around. "Thank you brother! Your kindness will be rewarded! With such a lead no doubt I'll be able to—" The remainder of his sentence was curtly bitten short by the slam of Pietr's door.

Pietr forcefully snapped the door's latch into the locked position. "How do people believe we share a bloodline," he muttered as he crossed his shop. With disdain, he noticed the papers strewn about the floor. The moment he bent down into a crouch, his door was assailed by a series of knocks. He clenched his fist around the vellum he had presently retrieved, which just so happened to depict a wyvern clutching a heavy breasted maid.

With an even more forceful slap, Pietr released the latch upon his front door. "Come back for this?!" he snarled, heaved the door open, and thrust the drawing out into the daylight. "You entitled little—!" Suddenly he espied beneath the parchment a set of legs concluding into a pair slippers that his oaf of a brother could only dream of squeezing into.

"Is this a bad time, Pietr?"

At once Pietr recognized the voice. He quickly crumpled the parchment and tucked it behind his back.

"Oh, hullo Margot!" he exclaimed. "That sketch wasn't anything that you need to be—"

The pretty young woman in the mottled tunic peered at the artist as if he had grown antlers.

"Never you mind!" said Pietr with a sweeping bow. "Please, come in, come in!"

Margot ducked unnecessarily as she entered the foyer, stepping past Pietr before turning. "Uncle Brett is seeking pigmeat and vegetables in the other district," Margot began. Her voice arrived unusually soft. "And I thought I might pop by for a visit. I hope I'm not disturbing you."

"Not at all!" Pietr assured her. "Please have a seat. I certainly welcome your breed of distraction over the previous one." He watched the girl lower herself onto the sofa, sinking down between the two cushions. "I am thrilled to see you, but I must admit that I am relieved that you have come empty handed. You see, I have hardly touched the nectar supply from two harvest's past. While I would have kindly accepted your most generous gift, I am beyond over-stocked at the moment."

Margot's chin lowered, a look of gloom passed over her. She seemed lost in the swirl of the grains upon the wooden floor.

Pietr tapped his teeth with a fingernail. "I suppose the harvest should be soon," he said. "So this visit would be a bit earlier than usual."

"There won't be a harvest this year," Margot said despondently.

"So you took a year off to allow the soil to refresh itself?" Pietr guessed hopefully.

Margot shook her head and tucked a few strands of hair behind her ear. "My flowers are nothing but ash and cinders," she revealed, unable to lift her gaze.

"I am so sorry, Margot." Pietr knelt before the sofa and reached for her hand. "That must be a huge loss for your family."

Margot closed her eyes and nodded.

"Was it a stray spark from a nearby campfire?" Pietr asked. "Or perhaps your brother tamped his pipe near a bit of overdry straw?" He administered her hand a gentle squeeze, and she withdrew her hand and laid it atop his.

"We believe it to be foul play," Margot stated.

Pietr's features calcified. "The same men who stole your gold all those years ago?" Pietr rose, caught her nod from the corner of his eye as he strode toward his studio. "Did you catch a better glimpse this time? We can begin the sketch right now, and I will have their images all over Camelot before nightfall," he declared, settling into his desk and reaching for his quill. "Every watchman, every knight, and every eye will see it. And we will find them."

Margot remained on the couch. "I didn't get a good enough look at their faces," she whispered.

"Oh," said Pietr, deflating. "I see."

A harsh reprimand tore the air from just beyond the shop's front window. Margot started, rose on the couch, leaned toward the glass to see what was happening.

Two holy knights mounted on palfreys shielded their faces as commonfolk flung rocks at them. Some hurled insults rather than stones. The palfreys screamed as if the stones were molten.

"The poor horses," Margot said as Pietr joined her on the couch, kneeling.

By the time the knights had drawn their arming swords, the crowd had dispersed.

"It has been like this for days now," Pietr murmured, observing the knights wheeling their horses, spurring them toward the Basilica. "It's only a matter of time before they catch the wrong knight on the wrong day." He withdrew himself from the couch, grimacing. "I just don't see this ending well."

Margot could not look away from the bystanders. One concerned mother ushered her two children toward a fruit stand, her gentle hands guiding them beneath the awning. The vendor's mouth disappeared in a frown under his moustache until the woman produced a purse laden with coin. Margot then took notice of a husband and wife, perhaps thirty winters in age, still pressed to a wall having just avoided being trampled by the fleeing crowd.

"I don't believe that I will share in the people's misery," Margot said as she watched the husband take hold of his wife's hand.

"Meaning?" Pietr wondered, arching a curious eyebrow.

"In the coming week," Margot began, at last meeting Pietr's eyes. "I am to be married to a church official."

At this, Pietr's eyebrow nearly punched the ceiling. "Congratulations?" He cupped his chest with both hands. "I was not aware. I must know more." He raised a finger, backpedaling for his larder. "First, allow me to fetch us a proper drink."

Cabinets clattered and rattled upon Pietr's immediate disappearance, followed closely by the artist's outburst, "Ah! So that's where I've kept you!" He returned swiftly, sweeping across the room with a glass decanter under one arm and two wooden cups pinched between his fingers. An amber liquid sloshed around the decanter as Pietr seated himself close beside Margot.

"I won't lie," Pietr said, handing one of the cups to his guest. "This isn't the best of spirits, but it's all I have at the moment. Wouldn't want you to think I'm holding out on you."

Margot tucked her cup beneath the mouth of the bottle. "I won't lie either," she disclosed, observing the liquid's flow as Pietr tilted the bottle. "I'm not much of a snob when it comes to drinking." She lifted her cup, met Pietr's eye, and synchronized her sip with his. "My thanks," she said, pulling a deep sip. "Very tasty." She coughed, punched her chest.

Pietr swallowed and his eyes welled with tears. "Ridiculously smooth," he wheezed, fighting back a cough. "Always tastes better in memory."

"Memories are a funny thing," Margot said, and seemed as though she would go on, but instead drew another sip.

Pietr squinted. "They are. They can be," he agreed. "So, tell me about this wedding."

"Well, it's more of an arranged marriage," Margot replied. "If I'm to be perfectly honest."

"That's not very romantic," Pietr said.

"I know," Margot acknowledged. "My family is far too deep in debt, and the church agreed to wipe the slate clean on the day I marry

Schroederstall Victanctious." She brought the cup to her mouth, tossed her head back.

"How very sad," Pietr said, sullenly gazing at Margot. "I'm so sorry this is happening to you. It isn't fair, but such things happen to those not Marked." He tapped a finger to the Mark upon his neck. "And I know this falls short as consolation, but you're not the first to be given up as collateral." He tapped the heel of his cup upon Margot's knee. "You're not alone."

Margot sniffed. "You're right," she said. "It does fall rather short." She laughed and shook her head. "You're not very good at this, are you Pietr?"

"At what?" Pietr scoffed. "Comforting old friends who are about to marry someone that they hardly know, and perhaps—hold a moment!" He stiffened abruptly, his drink nearly sloshing over the rim of his cup. "At least tell me he's handsome?"

Gagging, Margot bucked forward, covered her mouth. It seemed Pietr had caught her just ahead of a swallow. "Not at all!" she replied. Her hair berated her cheekbones as she shook her head. "Schroederstall Victanctious is quite the opposite of handsome! Truth be told, he doesn't have any redeeming qualities."

Pietr shivered, tossed his head back, and drained what remained in his cup.

"On the bright side," Margot went on. "The church is providing us an estate with fertile land and livestock. And the ever-looming debt will no longer be looming anymore. Also, Schroederstall's work keeps him well-occupied, which means I will have plenty of time to myself." She bounced her cup against Pietr's kneecap. "You're the closest friend that I have, Pietr. Well, besides Isabelle. And it would mean a lot if you both came to the ceremony. Aside from my uncle, you would be the only persons attending for me."

"Of course we'll be there!" Pietr assured her. He poured more spirits into his cup, then tilted the decanter her way. "My sweet cousin Isabelle and I will be having tea the day after tomorrow, and I will most assuredly extend an invitation her way." His eyes shifted to the floor. "I take it your brother is not in favor of this arrangement? That probably goes without saying."

Margot extended her cup and Pietr refreshed it with a thin smile.

"Galahalt is being Galahalt," Margot said. "He's dealing with my marriage the only way he knows how."

"I take it he's afield somewhere?" Pietr said.

Margot nodded, downed another swig. "He's likely in the mountains skinning a dragon to buy me out of my duty," she said hoarsely.

"Does that cause worry?"

"I always worry for my brother," Margot replied, abruptly shoving off the couch with her elbow. She moved to the window rather unsteadily. After her third step she found her footing. For several moments she stood gazing out the window. The townsfolk outside had dispersed, and she heard voices shouting further down the lane, emanating from the direction of the Basilica. "And I don't fear him," she continued unhappily. "But I do fear *for* him. When he sets his mind to something, he never quits, and this brings me worry." She cleared a patch of dust from the sill with a swipe of her wrist. "You know that when a badger gets its paw caught in a trap, it will chew through bone to get free?"

Pietr leaned forward and nodded.

"My brother would certainly chew through the bone, just like the badger. But then he would hobble on his remaining leg to find whoever set the snare, and come windstorm or glacier, he would hunt that person down. And he would not stop." She raised her cup, upended it against her bottom lip, and swished the contents before swallowing. "Not until he drew his last breath."

"Oh, my," Pietr said.

Margot rounded to face the artist. "In this case, the badger's only sister was the one wounded by the trap."

"Ah, I see," Pietr said as Margot set her cup aside. "So, is it actually a dragon he is aiming to slay?"

Margot laughed dryly. "Rest assured, he'd be back by now if it were a dragon."

Deeply intrigued, Pietr cast a glance for his drawing desk. He, too, understood the drive, the responsibility, of those born Marked. "So what has brave Sir Galahalt set his sights upon?"

"The Questing Beast," Margot replied with a firm shake of her head. "The damned fool."

Pietr barked a laugh, and immediately regretted it. "Apologies, Margot. I did not mean to laugh," he said through a covered smile. "But that badger really goes for it, doesn't he?"

"He really does," Margot replied. "Brave Sir Galahalt really does."

29

Gentleness is reserved for children and lovers, Gwayne thought as he ran toward the holy knights. *Not for those hindering a man's path.*

He espied a flash of gray from the corner of his eye.

"Error," Gwayne said to himself. "Glad to have you with me for this fight."

The lion ran beside the knight, his body coiling and retracting, a measure of violence within each stride. As the distance between foes tightened, Gwayne rolled his sword wrist.

One holy knight dropped to a knee, disengaged a mechanical device.

Oh no. Gwayne recognized the weapon. *Crossbow.*

The holy knight raised the weapon, dipping his aim between lion and knight.

Error drove forward all the harder and, as he was a moment shy of ripping into the holy knight, the air was rent by the sharp crack of the crossbow's release. The weapon's recoil coursed a shudder up the holy knight's arm. The bolt found Error's shoulder, and the beast toppled, unable to maintain his weight. Mere feet from the holy knight's sabatons, the great lion's body came to a halt. He lay still, unmoving.

Gwayne bit back a scream.

As the holy knight discarded his crossbow, reached for the sword at his belt, the second holy knight stepped around the downed lion. She drew her arming sword and bashed it against her kite shield.

Using both hands, Gwayne raised Quintus, angling the longsword over his left shoulder, intending a cross-body swing. The holy knight responded, positioning her shield to assume the blow. Gwayne took notice, buried his leading leg, feinted the downward swing. The knight shifted all her weight forward, biting on Gwayne's deception. Had he so wished, Gwayne could have sundered the knight's helm into perfect halves, but instead, he skipped past her completely.

"Dead!" Gwayne screamed as the crossbow knight rose to his feet, his sword coated in Error's blood. Gwayne's eyes darted to a crimson slice at the nape of the beast's neck.

With unthinkable speed, Gwayne cut the distance between the two knights. He reared back, lifted his boot, and emplaced it square into the center of the startled knight's cuirass, sending him on a violent sprawl. Muted curses spouted from underneath the knight's helm.

Whirling around, Gwayne sought the other holy knight.

"We have no quarrel!" the holy knight shouted, planting the tip of her sword into the dirt.

"That's funny," Gwayne growled. "Because your pal put one into my friend over there."

"Please, Sir Gwayne," the holy knight pleaded, presumably having recognized the knight by his choice in sabatons. Or perhaps she knew him in passing. "We are seeking retribution for our slain squires."

"You're just full of jokes today, aren't you?" Gwayne narrowed his eyes, gestured his chin toward Error. "I'm seeking the same thing."

Meanwhile the crossbow knight had gathered his bearings behind Gwayne. Upon hearing the holy knight's groan upon his rise, Gwayne dashed for the treeline in order to prevent a cowardly attack to his hind side. Quickly turning, he espied the holy knights spanned wide from one another. Lake Humiel stretched endless at their backs.

"Don't do anything stupid, Phillip," the holy knight presently circling Gwayne's right cautioned. She had retrieved her blade from its symbolic planting of surrender. "Treat this just like we're hunting a sadhuzag."

Phillip replied with a curt nod, tightened his grip on the handle of his arming sword.

Evidently they're assembling some sort of flanking maneuver, Gwayne thought, then said aloud, "Which one should die first, Quintus?" His head swiveled back and forth between the gradual approaches. Then between the holy knights Gwayne espied a great churning upheaval transpiring in the lake waters. A mounded sand drift obscured his view of the beach.

Gwayne cocked his head. *Is that sandy knoll growling?*

Heated and raspy sounds came from the drift, sounding as hundreds of lungs sorely put to it for breath. In the clear conditions surrounding the lake, the noises carried, and suddenly Gwayne was not alone in his wonderment.

"Clemence!" Phillip yelled, craning his neck toward the lake. "We must run! Now!" The holy knight worked feverishly to unfasten his helmet strap, but the tremors proved overwhelming, and he gave up and heedlessly bolted off to Gwayne's left.

Clemence, also taking notice, departed the beach at near her partner's clip. She sprinted past Gwayne, muttering a string of curses. Her voice quaked, overwhelmed by fear. Within a matter of moments the holy knights had disappeared into the forest's encompassing shadows.

The frequency and amount of breaths overtaking the hillock presented Gwayne with a bit of concern. There was only one monster, that he knew of, that could both swim the sea and run dry land. And it did not take long for his suspicions to gain confirmation.

A trio of kapreta broke the horizon, their tongues flapping as their feet churned across the sandy knoll. In all likelihood more followed behind.

"It began as such a nice day," Gwayne said to Quintus. "But I did promise you a feast." And with that, he rushed the mound freely spilling kapreta. As soon as he achieved a blade length's distance from their outstretched claws, he slid feet first toward the centermost kapreta. His boot met the monster's kneecap with such force the tendon split from the bone. The kapreta toppled, howling. Gwayne's momentum carried him past the trio. Quickly the knight leapt to his feet, squared his shoulders at the two converging kapreta. Upon their approach, the leftmost kapreta staggered a step, whether from a dip in the sand, or the Creator's hand, Gwayne knew not. But what he did recognize was an opening. In a single horizontal sweep, Quintus claimed the head of the kapreta before she had the chance to correct her miscue. Sensing the other kapreta pouncing, as kapreta do, Gwayne ducked low, and nearly avoided the monster's claws. Kapreta, like humans and laives, were designed with opposable digits. And one such digit snagged Gwayne at his collar, which under most circumstance would be considered rather lamentable. However, Gwayne appeared unconcerned, and jolted abruptly to his feet, punching Quintus clean through the kapreta's abdomen.

Gwayne held the kapreta up by one of its spindly shoulders, making certain it had expired before he released. And through the spritzing of blood bursting from the monster's back, the knight espied the kapreta with the shattered kneecap crawling over the dune toward the lake. He let go of the kapreta's shoulder, allowing her to crumple under his stride. He made for the last kapreta, regarded the way she dragged herself onward, felt no pity. The kapreta's misery ended with a thrust to the back of her neck.

"Vile creatures," Gwayne mumbled, flicking blood from Quintus. Now standing at the peak of the mound, he was granted clear view of the lake. The knight found himself robbed of the stunning vista he felt entitled to, and instead was met by a scene torn from nightmares. Hundreds, nay, thousands of skulls emerged from the waters. From a sea bird's view, the front crescent of the lake would have appeared wholly crusted in the sickly green of kapreta flesh.

Gwayne's shoulders slumped, his sword hand dropped. "Arseholes." He knew there was no use in running. The monsters would catch him.

By this time the sun had neared its zenith, and shone down upon the lake unbarred by clouds. As Gwayne surveyed the vast kapreta host charging the beach, the pain in his chest returned. He scanned the waters, found Elkara and Galahalt escaping unnoticed. *Best of luck, friends,* Gwayne thought with a waning smile. *See you in Avalon.*

Shadows scurried over Gwayne's head. At first they trickled, dotting the sand around him as they coursed into the choppy waters. Then, quite suddenly, the entire ground around the knight was consumed in shadow. Disoriented, Gwayne shielded his eyes. Beneath his hands, the first line of kapreta were assailed by the shadows. The monsters flailed their arms in a frenzied state of panic, the foremost kapreta rendered to bone. Their screams filled the air as the lake turned black.

The shadow over Gwayne's head ended, leaving him standing in broad daylight.

A familiar pressure alighted on his shoulder.

"It's good to have friends," Figharth said.

"Are those...?" Gwayne wondered, unable to conjure the term in the moment.

"Fae," Figharth supplied. "This is what happens when we get angry." The wisp folded his arms across his chest, stared into the slaughter.

"It seems the spectator finally got involved," said Gwayne. "And not a moment too soon."

* * *

THE TUNNEL WAS EXCEEDINGLY DARK. The waters may as well have been ink. Galahalt resisted the urge to remove his helmet with its meager eye opening. Every so often the point of his spear would glance off the ceiling, and as they continued to dive, the occurrence increased. *It seems the tunnel is narrowing,* Galahalt thought.

Confined spaces had never bothered him much, and as a child he would tuck himself inside casks, hiding from his sister for hours on summer afternoons. On one such occasion Margot had asked Uncle Brett to place a millstone on top of the barrel as a joke, and still he had not been frightened. He simply used the opportunity to take a nap. The tight space had been very dark, much like the channel he found himself in, but he found that he greatly preferred the dryness of the barrel.

At this point Galahalt was completely unaware of his directional orientation. Adding further insult, the tunnel had become so tight he could no longer spread his arms, which forced him to rely on his feet to propel him.

Elkara has probably left me behind, Galahalt wagered. *She's relaxing, enjoying some exotic fruit on the island.* Clutching the spear to his chest, his knuckles sustained damage from the sharp grains on the cave floor. *Or is it the ceiling?* The air inside the helm had grown stale. It seemed the helm's magic could only do so much.

Minutes passed, but at this point according to Elkara, it could be years. And soon the back of his hands were no longer sustaining continuous trauma. To his immense relief, the tunnel began to widen. He cupped his empty hand, shoveling water backwards, pulling his body forward as best he could, when abruptly he felt a harsh tapping on his helm. It was Elkara, she had not abandoned him after all. She was tugging him forward, guiding him firmly towards murky waters. Light was growing, the total dark giving way, and he could see particles floating freely all around them.

They were unexpectedly free of the cave and all its mysteries, the sun appearing gelatinous from under the waves. Swimming upward through a brilliant light beam, Elkara released Galahalt's wrist several strokes before reaching the surface. The breeze that greeted them felt much colder than the waters. As they waded waist high striding toward an empty beach, a moment of panic gripped the young knight.

"Did we get turned around?!" Galahalt stopped and raised his face-plate. "Is this where we started?"

Elkara continued to slog through the shallows and without breaking stride answered, "Of course not." She lifted a finger toward the trees. "Don't recall all those things decorating the shoreline."

Galahalt's eyes traced what Elkara pointed at, and noticed large steel enclosures suspended from the ground, spherical in shape, like bird cages scattered amongst the trees. Torn cloth dangled between the bars of the closest sun-bleached cage, and from where he stood, the knight could not tell if it was inhabited. Directly under the small swinging prison was a scattering of bones in differing sizes, dissipating any hopes that these enclosures were benevolent in any way.

"You didn't think we were going to a safe place, did you?" Elkara said. "This mission is suicide, but it beats waiting for total petrification." She raised her hand, the curse now working its way past her wrist. "I offer you nothing less than a horror story. Keep that spear ready. Let us get this done."

The sliding sand gradually gave way to firm soil, their bare feet crunching the dry grass before entering a lush, yet eerily silent grove of trees.

"Do we have a plan?" Galahalt asked, peering up at another cage.

Elkara smiled and shook her head.

Galahalt drew close to her side and whispered, "Anywhere in your laif lore mention where the beast's lair is?"

"You don't need to whisper," Elkara replied, still smiling. "And no, you don't find the beast. The beast finds you."

Nervously Galahalt tightened his grip on his spear. "That's delightful."

With no specific direction in mind, Elkara found she was of little use as a guide, and sought the knight's advice.

"What makes you think we should go this way?" Elkara inquired, standing at the base of a rocky outcropping.

"For one thing," Galahalt replied. "There's far less of those awful swinging cages."

The laif smirked, satisfied with that line of logic.

An elevated field of rock and stone and scorched earth lay to their right as they walked along the path. Laif and knight favored the left, opting to remain under the shade of the forest's edge, the cloudless sky offering little respite from the blazing sun. The empty island made Fenrirfang seem a bustling metropolis in comparison. Every turn of the head had yielded at least one or more creature in the forest they had abandoned for this one. In contrast, the soil on the island was rich and the plant life throbbed with health and vibrancy, although the trees in Fenrirfang seemed to outdate the island's trees.

Great amethyst flowers grew in clusters, their pastel petals forming small basins filled with rainwater. Instinct warned Galahalt to give these pretty plants a wide berth, but before he could take a cautious step, Elkara placed a hand on his shoulder. "Let's be clear of these ladies," she advised. They veered into the forest, passing well away from the ominous arrangement.

"What are your feelings on crossbows?" Galahalt asked, looking over his shoulder at the laif.

Elkara took hold of the vine the knight had held for her and passed under it before letting it drop. "They come in handy for cowards."

Galahalt released a chuckle that bounded all throughout the empty trees. "So an archer with a crossbow would be the most craven of creatures?"

"I don't share the same disdain for archers as you noble knights, with your codes and silly rules and—" Elkara abruptly cut herself short.

They had entered a clearing devoid of shrub or shroom, a shallow carpet of red-colored grass gripped the dirt, and through the trees a slender draconic form could be seen navigating the boughs like silk passing over a wrist. The creature was quickly moving in their direction and it grew rapidly in size.

"Creator hold us," Elkara breathed. With mind reeling, the laif summoned an instant of clarity and gripped the young knight's shoulder, pushing him toward a row of boulders just shy of the clearing. Somehow they slipped from sight without creating a disturbance.

With backs pressed to the solid stone, Galahalt turned to the horrified laif. "What is that?" he whispered, trying to meet her darting eyes.

"A sovereign," she replied, her lips trembling. "A pej'asa."

Galahalt flinched. "You just said two different things?"

Elkara's eyes came to a rest on something in the distance. "You can't kill it," she said firmly.

"Have you ever before encountered whatever you just said that thing is?"

Slowly Elkara shook her head back and forth.

Galahalt only grew more confused. "Aren't you like 950 years old?" he asked, tapping the head of his spear on the soil. "I thought you'd seen it all." Looking at the laif's face, it finally dawned on Galahalt that Elkara was well and truly frightened.

"Do you think it saw us?" Elkara whimpered, her lower lip quaking as she faced the knight, clearly out of her element on this island.

"This will not be our end," Galahalt assured her. The knight shifted his weight in an effort to rise, and the laif nearly tackled him, forcing him back to the ground.

"We must stay hidden!" Elkara hissed.

"That thing should have passed us by now," Galahalt wagered. "I just want to take a quick peek."

"We wait," Elkara commanded, not allowing further argument.

The trees around them seemed to be holding their breath. Not one sound escaped from the forest. There was a complete stillness, yet an aura of terror thrummed in the breeze. Fear gripped the laif while her counterpart sat unaffected with fingers interlaced on his lap, balancing his spear across his thighs.

A sudden shifting noise drew the knight's attention to his right. Elkara had turned around to bring herself up to the crest of the rock, her face still stricken, and moving as if she were placing her neck in the hangman's noose. The laif's hesitancy seemed very wrong to Gala-halt, and he was growing weary of waiting. Having been awake all night and running, navigating an underwater cavern, and trudging through a strange forest, to now be hiding from a flying serpent when his body was groaning for sleep was nearly unbearable. If the pej'asa was still out there waiting, then they had only two options, and neither one contained an escape hatch.

With a sharp intake of air, Elkara shot back down to a slouch, forehead pressed to the rock. "It's just waiting for us," she lamented. "Just hovering there."

Let's get this over with. Galahalt unlaced his helm and set it aside. He pressed off the ground, surging into a stand. An indiscernible warning came from Elkara, but the knight paid no heed.

The undulating dragon, scales coursing peristaltic with the glimmer of the sun, grew rigid at the sudden appearance of the man. Its reptilian face glared at the knight, and it opened its mouth, revealing a tiny flame. The lethal potential instantly became apparent when the beast snapped its snout shut, and exhaled a thick smoke in two separate trails. And whatever the smoke touched, be it tree or creature, wilted and crumbled into dust.

"That's...well, that's something," Galahalt murmured.

Elkara knelt with her hands folded in prayer as she pled for the knight to get behind shelter. "Please, please," she begged.

Galahalt spared her a glance, breathing out through his nostrils, though not quite as impressively as the dragon, and tossed a reassuring smirk at the laif before darting off. The despair on Elkara's face immediately dissolved from his mind as he rushed through the clearing.

In an unanticipated maneuver, the pej'asa lifted higher into the air, and glared down at the knight. The creature did not seem interested in combat, though he clearly deemed the knight's encroachment to be entirely unwelcome.

Elkara watched from her knees, head poking out from the side of the boulders as the knight stopped short in the center of the open space. The pej'asa suspended high above and Galahalt was standing below. The adversaries locked on one another, but neither was willing to make a move before the other.

"Why doesn't it just scorch him?" Elkara wondered. "What is it waiting for?" The laif got to her feet and looked around, noticing the parting of reeds and taller grasses a short distance from the clearing. It was the only movement in the vicinity, aside from the wavy pattern of the dragon treading air well out of spear range.

"Galahalt!" she shouted, recognizing what approached. The knight regarded her over his shoulder with a look of concern. She began punching the air in the direction of the brush filled with encroaching bodies that were making their way toward the knight. "Hobgoblins! Hobgoblins in the thicket!"

Galahalt spun around as a small projectile whistled past his cheek. It had originated from somewhere amidst the shivering plants. He spared a glance at the pej'asa then rolled in the direction of the boulders, having no option other than to create a harder target to strike. Another projectile struck the ground behind him, and he saw a crudely sculpted dart protruding from the soil. He moved quickly as more projectiles hissed and struck around him, but none made contact with flesh. *At some point they must run out*, Galahalt guessed, hoping the hobgoblins' stock was finite.

Elkara shouted something again and when Galahalt wheeled to her voice, a dart bounced off the rock just beneath her chin, scattering chips of stone. A hobgoblin, a creature much like a goblin in stature, but more like a laif in physique, had scuttled into the open to retrieve a dart, confirming to Galahalt that their supply was low.

Galahalt sneered. *Come and get them.*

Before the hobgoblin had a chance to tumble away, the knight lashed out with one hand at the base of the spear's haft, the striking distance perfectly calculated. As the creature stood after snatching the dart, it was greeted by a quick stab to its trachea and missed a backwards step, falling onto its back with a pained look of shock. The dart was flung into the air in a harmless arc before falling to the ground. Galahalt only allowed a second to pass before he somersaulted again, picking up the projectile along the way.

A loud huff issued from the pej'asa, clearly not impressed with the events playing out below. More hobgoblins ambled into the clearing looking to scavenge their missed shots. Naked from the waist up, most of the creatures appeared well fed and not as lithe as their goblin cousins. Galahalt's neck felt ready to snap as he continually looked to the skies, down to the hobgoblins, and back up again, waiting for the pej'asa to tire of the dance and blast him to cinders.

One hobgoblin twirled in place while surveying the vicinity, sure that its dart had settled there. Galahalt, no longer interested in playing games, quickly dispatched the confused creature by adding an eighth hole to its head. The knight's heel dug into the earth and he sprang back from the strike, keen for the next invader. He never stopped moving, not for an instant, sure it was only a matter of time before he either was nuked from above or struck by a dart. Four hobgoblin bodies lay motionless in the clearing and the knight was not slowing in his assault. The hobgoblins had backed off into cover, scouring the boundary for any darts that passed over and missed their mark.

On her knees, Elkara pressed her arms against the boulder, her dagger clutched tightly in one fist. Too afraid to move, her mind screamed at her to help the knight in his final stand, but her body vehemently dismissed the calls.

Springing from cover, the clutch of hobgoblins burst forward in a concerted effort to bring Galahalt down. With a flick of his wrist, the knight flung a dart at the center of the rushing creatures. It buried itself just below the collar of a hobgoblin who instantly crumpled to the ground upon impact, creating a stumbling block for its brethren.

The first wave was dead before they could even gain enough momentum for a proper charge, becoming only a jumbled mass of limbs flailing and stumbling at the rim of the tree line. With surgical precision, Galahalt dispatched the foes effortlessly, not giving any a chance to rise.

"Like liquid," Elkara breathed, recalling Gwayne's words.

The few remaining hobgoblins retreated into the shuddering bracken, some squealing with dismay and gesturing to the dragon who was fixated on something beyond them. The pej'asa seemed to shrug and smirk with mild amusement before whirling around and setting off, its long serpentine body rising and falling, rippling a path through the treetops before disappearing out of view.

This turn of events distracted Galahalt just long enough for a well-placed dart to strike the side of his neck. Elkara scrambled to her feet and vaulted the lowest of the boulders, moving to intercept the hobgoblins before they could overwhelm the swooning knight. The hobgoblins, however, were tracing the same line of retreat as the pej'asa. Elkara heaved a sigh of relief as she watched the grass parting around the fleeing survivors.

"There was something that you said a little while ago that I have been wondering about," Galahalt said as the laif cradled his head in her lap. He swallowed a gasp while his eyelids fluttered.

Elkara hunched close to the knight. "What's that?"

"Dead men are dying," came his labored reply.

The laif placed her hand on the knight's cheek. "It's just," she began. "It's just something that lampyrs once said on battlefields when—"

"Oh," Galahalt's eyes flashed open. "Here comes another dragon."

Elkara turned around, espied a tremendous shape slipping through the trees with immaculate precision.

The shape hurtled closer, and Elkara lowered her chin.

"Creator release us," she whispered.

30

❧

Sir Galahalt tried to sit up, but the slight upward shift brought a spanning siren of pain to the hollows of his eye sockets.

"My head," he moaned. He brought a hand to his forehead and warily poked an eye open, fearful the throbbing would intensify. The memory of the dragons, hobgoblins, and bloody red grass suddenly bloomed in his mind and he sat up with a groan.

Elkara, seated on a chair next to the bed, straightened abruptly. "You're awake!" Her face lit up.

"How?" Galahalt murmured. With a slight start, discovered he had been dressed in a clean tunic that smelled of hyacinth. "How did I get here?"

The laif appeared as if she had recently bathed. Her hair had been tied into glistening plaits, which assembled neatly upon a pristine emerald gown.

"You need more rest." Elkara leaned over, glanced a dampened cloth across the knight's forehead. "We're safe for now."

"What of that other dragon?" Galahalt asked, scanning the room. To his relief, discovered his armour and spear bundled in a corner.

"There was no other dragon," Elkara replied, dropping the cloth into a basin. "What you saw in your haze was the Questing Beast."

Galahalt surged further upright. "What?!" His throbbing head began to swim.

"You should rest more." Elkara placed a hand to his chest, attempting to coax him back down.

"I'll rest once you explain how we got here," Galahalt said, glaring at her hand. "I'm wide awake now!"

"Fine," Elkara agreed. Though she relieved the pressure to his chest, she did not withdraw her hand. "If you lay down, I will tell you what happened after you succumbed to the hobgoblin poison. And then you must rest."

With a nod, Galahalt obediently reclined. The moment his head contacted the pillow, he fixed the laif with an expectant gaze.

Elkara retrieved her hand, punched her chest to clear it. "After you fell unconscious," she began. "The Questing Beast rushed to the clearing, which might explain the hasty retreat of the pej'asa and the hobgoblins. And I thought we were dead. But, as fate would have it, the Beast somehow knew of our existence, although he mentioned something about a dog 'being correct' before he introduced himself."

"A dog?" Galahalt said. "And what does the Questing Beast look like? You said it talks?"

"Well, there is a bit of truth to the rumored depictions," Elkara replied. Her feet scuffed the floor as she adjusted her seat. "He has the body of a mighty stag, but much, much greater than any stag I have ever encountered. And he has the head of a serpent that is proportional in size to his massive body. The head closely resembled a cobra with a hood that opens and closes and all that. He never explained the dog though, but honestly I didn't dare to ask in the moment."

"Odd," Galahalt noted.

"Agreed," Elkara said, and continued. "Once I managed to wrestle your deadweight onto his back, he led me to an abandoned laif kingdom, which is where we are now. We're currently inside a quaint hovel along the main street that leads to a wonderful coliseum created by my ancestors." Her face softened wistfully. "We stood on an overlook before we entered the gates, and the sun beat down on the majestic structures and intricate buildings that were built right into the forest like a proper laif city. Unlike humans who feel the need to decimate spaces in order to build. The kingdom that we are now in was abandoned long ago, and from what I can tell, we are the only occupants. Aside from the Beast, of course."

Galahalt arched an eyebrow, studiously appraised Elkara's raiment. "Which explains how you got away with raiding someone's closet unnoticed."

Elkara laughed and passed a hand down her sleeve. "I'll admit that I experienced very little resistance," she said, tugging the cuff to conceal her petrified flesh. "The Beast did not say much on the way here, but did say that once you are ready, he will be waiting to hold audience in the coliseum's amphitheatre."

"What are we waiting for?" Galahalt wondered, rising upright.

"You aren't ready for that," Elkara said. "The poison hasn't completely left your body. Once you can wake without a headache, then we will meet the Beast."

With little effort, Elkara managed to push Galahalt back down. This time, the knight did not put up a fight.

"Dead men are dying," Galahalt mumbled as he nestled his cheek into the pillow. "Tell me what that means. You started to explain, but I can't remember."

Elkara scratched the stone of her petrified hand. "Humans are mortal," she began. "And to laives, you are all dead men." Her fingernails stopped, and she settled her hand atop the cursed one. "It's something that lampyrs on the battlefields would say to one another when they set off to heal yet another of your kind. To them it was merely prolonging the inevitable, which was an absurdity, yet they continued, snatching fools like you from the jaws of oblivion. Or the shores of Avalon, depending on your perspective." She noticed Galahalt's eyes had closed, and his breathing had slowed.

Settling back in her chair, Elkara smirked a glance at the spear at rest against the wall.

"Now get some sleep," she said, returning glad eyes to the slumbering knight. "You fool."

GALAHALT WOKE TO AN EMPTY CHAMBER, promptly discovered the shooting pain in his head had seemingly retreated to his nether regions. While discreetly relieving himself out a nearby window, he wondered if he should wear his church tunic when meeting the Questing Beast for the first time. He understood how crucial first impressions were, and after a moment spent in quiet deliberation, he decided to take a page from Elkara's playbook. He observed the conclusion of his stream, and quickly set off in search of any available garb the hovel had on offer.

For the better part of an hour the knight rummaged through dressers and closets before an article at last caught his eye; a powder blue tunic that had been left upon a hook.

"This will do," Galahalt remarked, taking the tunic into his hands. After several moments spent in admiration, he decided it was time to meet his fate. He snatched his spear upon his departure, but left his armour behind. Striding out the front door, the knight found himself on a quiet promenade beneath a silvered moon.

Alone the knight made his way toward the citadel. Only for a moment did he stop to gaze at the celestial ribbons lazing across the star-dusted sky.

"Even the stars seem foreign in this city," he remarked.

The thrum of insects was markedly absent, and his bare feet slapping against the flagged stone was all he heard. He winced as a sharp pain drew his attention to the big toe on his right foot. "Must have smashed it when I was tumbling in that clearing." A bruise had developed from his big toe to the middle of his foot. But it appeared diminished, displaying a very non-threatening shade of yellow.

As Galahalt continued on, he could not help but wonder at the scenery; unlit lampposts—presumably centuries since their last use, fountains in gardens overwhelmed by vegetation, and benches longing for company. He walked by dozens of abandoned storefronts, and spared a thought for the clerks, wondering what had become of them. Turning back time was not possible, but for a moment, he wished that he could go back for just a brief spell.

"Would they welcome me or slay me?" he wondered aloud. An unaccompanied human traipsing their thoroughfare would have, without a doubt, caused some sort of stir.

"Aye!" A voice shouted from the lofts above.

Galahalt lifted his eyes, saw Elkara perched on a balcony. "Hold a moment!" she called to him, waving. "I will be down in a second." She disappeared into the doorway behind her, and almost immediately reappeared at a ground-level stoop further down the lane.

"Isn't this place amazing?" Elkara enthused. A delicate fragrance struck the knight as she drew up before him. "I've heard tales and rumors," she went on. "And read old crummy scrolls about the city on Lake Humiel, but had dismissed them as horseshit." At present she wore a formal-looking tunic, this one a deep shade of red. The cut of its collar rose to her jawline, nearly cradled her face.

Galahalt also noticed the tunic did not present sleeves. "Your arm," he exhaled. "The curse has spread." Her tourniquet, on full display, was cinched above her deltoid, from armpit to clavicle.

"It has," she confirmed, momentarily dour. Then she suddenly perked. "Glad to see you awake!"

"How long was I asleep?"

Elkara closed an eye and peered up at the moon. "Two days," she replied, then a look of concern flashed behind her eyes. "When did you last have a drink of water? You must be parched! There is a spring with fresh water just over—"

"Water can wait," Galahalt interrupted. The heel of his spear stirred the cobbles beneath him. "I just want to meet the Questing Beast."

Glancing at the weapon in the knight's hand, Elkara nodded, waved for him to follow. "Then I'll take you there."

In shared silence, the laif led the knight deeper into the city. Along the way, Elkara beheld sights she never thought she would ever witness. In her eyes the long-forgotten structures retained their majesty, though heavily blemished by the passage of time. Statues of warriors—in varying arms and raiment—maintaining a slight westward lean, having been abraded by wind for centuries, still brought a thrill of pride to her chest. She discovered, to her further delight, that the trees had retained their splendor. Elms, oaks, and even a few cedars scattered the lawn of an estate she passed by in the present. She wished to regale Galahalt about the wonders, but she refrained. He did not have the eyes of a laif that pierced darkness. For all the while, the knight's countenance had hardened. He plodded along beside her, employing his spear as a walking staff.

At length they approached the citadel's entry gate. Defensive towers, connected by parapets, hemmed their remaining steps.

Upon entering a palatial amphitheatre, a vast auditorium greeted them inside. Its seats swelled like an organized tide, encircling a flat field of earth. At this, Galahalt's face softened with awe. He gazed around, taking in the sights. There in the rafters above, perched like a gargoyle, a velikant owl of startlingly huge proportions observed their arrival. Galahalt believed it was a statue until the bird tilted its head.

From the far opposite end of the field, a tremendous creature with the head of a serpent and the body of a stag entered under a raised portcullis.

Elkara's breath hitched. Galahalt froze.

The roofless amphitheatre was lit by the moon and its surrounding constellations, which played ominous shadows all over the beast's flowing movements. Cantering to the Beast's left was what appeared to be a common dog. The four met in the center of the expanse, the serpent's gaze falling on Galahalt, his eyes running the length of the spear.

"Let us retire to my lair," the Beast said, his voice oddly human. "I have food and drink."

Galahalt struggled to maintain his composure, and somehow offered a solemn nod. When his eyes fell upon the Beast's canine friend, he balked. "Elmer?" The word escaped before he could harness the thought.

The dog nodded at the knight.

Immediately Galahalt went a knee, opened his arms. Elmer rushed into the knight's arms and nuzzled his chest. "How?" Galahalt asked. "Just *how?*"

"It is a tale," replied the Questing Beast as a glimmer of mischief came to his cat-like pupils. "But perhaps you noticed the velikant owl when you entered?" The Beast turned. "They're known to have quite the carrying capacity."

Elmer wriggled from Galahalt's embrace and hustled to join the Beast's side. Without further said, both creatures padded quietly toward the portcullis.

A stone stairway brought the laif and knight down into a massive room that may have served as a holding area. The room had been completely cleared of any dividing walls, and against the back corner was a pile of grass suitable for a beast the size of a mammoth. The hearth was clearly in need of maintenance, stones and mortar flaking and falling away after centuries of disuse. Along the opposite wall, five stone faces were mounted like trophies, fresh streams of water flowing out of their mouths, cascading into an elongated basin running along the wall before terminating out of sight. Galahalt, not waiting for an invitation, immediately began to drink from the beak of a gaunt-looking eagle.

"I cannot provide meat," the Beast apologized from behind a table heavily laden with a variety of fruit. "But you are welcome to partake of this recent harvest. I trust the venom from the hobgoblin's dart no longer hinders you?"

Galahalt nodded, splashing water on his face, rubbing handfuls onto the back of his neck.

"The pej'asa is quite a fickle dragon," the Questing Beast continued. "Does not like to eat its prey while the prey is awake and afraid, fear making the meat tough and unattractive. It employs hobgoblins on the island to render the prey unconscious before it begins feasting. And I assume you saw the cages when you arrived? Well, aside from being a picky eater, the pej'asa is also quite forgetful and easily distracted, leaving its meals in cages to eat later, but rarely returning."

Elkara picked through a bowl of prickly orbs, sniffing one at a time before placing them back as Galahalt joined her. The Beast and Elmer sat watching the hungry travelers greedily chew and swallow. Galahalt took bites from several different fruits, the flavors mixing in his mouth. Juice dribbled down from his chin onto his tunic creating dark purple stains.

The Beast lowered himself onto a cushion, placidly waiting for their full attention. Galahalt sensed the urging and hurriedly filled his arms with an assortment of berries, and sat down on the provided couch. Elkara snatched two inordinately large fruits from a basket and sat down beside Galahalt. In anticipation of their feasting, a table had been placed before the couch.

"Allow me to properly introduce myself," the Beast began. "In another life, in another time, I was known as Famyl."

Elkara whispered in amazement through a mouthful, "The first Healer."

"I was counted among the First Laives," said the Beast. "At that time we were called 'elves,' but that term has become quite an insult as of late, has it not?" The Beast grumbled from deep in his chest. "I was there right after the dawning of time, given the gift of immortality like my brothers and sisters. And as I am sure you are aware, as time eroded, my fellow laives gave up, or lost, their immortality." It was barely noticeable, but the Beast's shoulders sank. "Except for the Arbiter." The grumble in his chest came and went. "Many, many centuries ago, the Creator came to me early in the morning to make an offer. I was bone weary of the battlefields, of healing dying men and watching those beyond my scope suffer and wilt and die.

"It was all beginning to take its toll. Though my flesh was safe from the withering hold of death, my mind and spirit could be broken and the Creator knew this too well. As I had found favor in His eyes, He took me away from this world and we passed into a new one of His making, set aside from mortals. He and I worked side-by-side to construct a place outside of time known as the Hold."

Elkara leaned forward. "Unreal," she breathed, resting her cursed hand on the table.

"After its completion," the Beast went on. "The Creator tasked me with retrieving those among the living who displayed unparalleled resolve and courage in the face of insurmountable odds, selected to receive His favor." He turned his head toward the dog taking up a corner of his cushion. "Lannor, or Elmer—as you referred to him—is an example of one such being. And the owl that spirited him here is also among their ranks." The Beast made a noise akin to clearing his throat. "It was my task to pass between the worlds as an emissary, making offers to the chosen ones. If they had perished before I reached them, I would reverse time, and revive their bodies before escorting them to the Hold, should they accept. I was given a clear view of all things, toggling between situations and climates. I watched many triumphs, failures, and desecrations. Never once did I intervene when I could have easily stepped in to avoid an atrocity.

"Over time, I began to feel responsible. The weary poison from ages past began to seep into my bones. Foolish emotions brought on by fatigue at the post." The Beast's eyes focused on the grit scattered on the floor. "But one day as I was awash in self-loathing, an idea struck me. An unexpected revelation that would lead to my salvation...or perhaps, in the end, it led to my downfall. I began to seek those who were just and kind and far from horrible. Focusing on them, I hoped that they would make warm blood once again flow through my tired veins. One may think that finding such folk would be a simple task. But one would most assuredly be wrong.

"My attention was drawn to a young maid. A lovely young human." The Beast's focus drifted to Galahalt. "She lived with her father on a small farm. She was strikingly beautiful, kind, and demure. Having lived as long as I had, I had enjoyed many carnal acts with human and laif, but the emotions that surged in me were not that sort at all. They were..." he trailed off for but a moment. "Different. Paternal. Though that term hardly encapsulates my true feelings, but you gather my meaning? And soon I began to focus upon her, not splitting my time as I should have. All I watched was her.

"Now at this time the Hold contained nearly a dozen souls, not over-flowing in the least, and certainly not at the capacity that I am sure it is at now." Elmer shifted and The Beast continued. "At first I covered my dereliction of duty, but the Creator knew what I was doing and soon I ceased caring and stopped hiding altogether.

"I begged Him to indulge me and allow me to enter the world again so that I could protect this woman who held all my attentions. Grant me access, as he did the others in the Hold. For I knew she would need protection. I knew it. They all needed protection..." The Beast's eyes seemed to lose focus, as old men often do. Then with a shake of his head, his acuity returned. "But He denied my request the first time. And He denied the second and the third and the fourth, and so on.

"Now the son of a lord began to take notice of this girl, having recently lost his new bride to another. And nearly simultaneously, Amyr, the first and only Arbiter, though he has been known by many names, took notice of her as well. Their intentions converging at once and the scene unfolding before me was all too familiar. When mortals squabble over love, it only leads to fighting, and then the blood begins to flow. It always flows. Always."

With a growl, the Beast clambered to a stand. His hooves clacked on the floor as he worked through this unbidden arrival anger.

"Wait," Galahalt said. "Is this the tale of Amyr and Linette?"

The Beast's serpent hood pulsated as though it would fling open. "Amyr and Linette?" he hissed, droplets of venom fell. "Is that how they tell it? *Amyr and Linette?*"

"Yes," Galahalt replied. "Everyone knows it. The evil Lord Ancel used daemonic means to ensorcell the fair Linette. Once Amyr overcame the evil powers, winning his true love back, Ancel came in the dark of night and strangled Linette to death by hanging her with a rope. Amyr still mourns her to this day."

A screeching wheeze pierced the air. The Beast rounded on Galahalt, his hood belting open.

"He *mourns* her?" The Beast exhaled another wheeze, seeming pained. "The yarn you weave is deeply tainted in lies." The Beast drew back, and all the shadows seemed to scurry for cover. "When I perceived those seeds of jealousy being sowed, well before they sprouted, and thusly yielded the inevitable fruit of murder, I disobeyed the Creator and eventually overtook a mature field dog, stealing his form. Such practice was frowned upon, but I deemed it necessary. I stripped the animal's identity and assumed control of its mortal form without permission or warning. A brutal and shameful act, I know, and to this day that detail haunts me."

With a soft growl, Elmer seemed to punctuate the statement.

"May what we seek this day serve as adequate penance," said the Beast to Elmer. He then lifted his eyes to his guests. "As Linette's protector, I attempted to intervene as best I could, perpetuating the best possible outcome for all. Not just for her. I was still so worn from suffering. The time spent constructing the Hold are some of the most peaceful memories I have aside from the fleeting time spent with Linette. I will never forget her. And when Amyr's sentinels came, I managed to cull two or three of them before they pierced my vitals and left me to crawl onward alone to Avalon's shores, a pathetic bloody mess. An utter failure.

"The Creator stood over my dying, stolen body, reading my mind as the air escaped my lungs. I whimpered pleas, begging Him to cast me into another body, far from the Hold and all of humanity. A place so desolate I would never encounter suffering or tragedy or desolation or treachery. Or even love, I recall pleading into the soil, gravity holding me like a boulder. Both He and I knew that such a place existed.

"After exhaling my final breath, enveloped in prayer, I inhaled my first breath as this form before you. A creature of myth whose bite contains a circle of unending pain. The Creator is kind, but he also boasts a dark sense of irony. My disobedience came at a price. My venom can heal. Oh yes, a more effective antidote one will never find. But my fangs deal considerable pain, and their value could overthrow the greatest of kingdoms. Toppling dynasties painstakingly built over centuries. And many have tried, and they all have failed. Some lost their lives outright, while others returned to find that their life had passed them by. Everything comes with a price."

With eyes bored deep into Galahalt, the Beast spoke as though they were alone.

"And now, young Sir Galahalt," began the Beast. "You must know that not one soul has made it this far. Not one has been entertained at my table."

"May I ask why?" Galahalt spoke before thinking and covered his mouth.

"Simple," the Beast answered. "Your blood."

Elmer's tail thumped.

"It smells of her."

Without provocation, the Beast's serpent head struck Elkara's cursed arm at rest on the table.

The laif shrieked, tried to pull away, but the single embedded fang held her fast at the bend of her wrist. She fought and struggled, screaming through tears. And yet the Beast did not withdraw.

"I am sorry, young one," said the Beast mournfully. "It only gets worse."

Then, with a violence Galahalt had never before witnessed, the Beast rolled his head forward, and with a snap that turned the knight's stomach, the Beast thrust himself backward, leaving his fang buried in Elkara's arm.

Leaping up, Elkara strained to leverage her arm free. Tears poured over her gritted teeth, and flowed down onto the fang.

"I am afraid my fang is equipped with a small barb at its sharpest point," the Beast revealed to Galahalt. "So your friend requires your aid."

Galahalt's eyes widened. The fang had pierced clean through Elkara's arm and had concluded through the table.

Elkara wrenched backward, her hand throttling the bend at her elbow.

Galahalt leaned into her periphery. "Pull?" he asked. "Or push?"

She screamed incoherently, her face drenched in sweat and tears.

Hesitantly, Galahalt reached for the fang, merely glanced its surface. This was met by an immediate explosion of anguish.

Elkara rotated her hips, attempting to deflect the knight's hand. "Stay back!" she screamed. "Don't you dare push!"

"So be it," Galahalt said, insinuating a shoulder between the laif and the fang. "Pull it is."

Elkara shrieked and lashed out at the knight's eye. He assumed the strike without shying.

In similar fashion to the way in which the Beast had struck, Galahalt latched his hands to the fang. Another clawing swipe came to his cheek, and with a grated scream, the knight heaved backward with all the might he could summon. The fang snapped free of its grip on the underside of the table, passed through the oak, and lodged its barb into Elkara's flesh.

The knight wagered the laif had to be near black-out by this point. Her screams had reached a pitch that only Elmer perceived.

"I'm sorry!" Galahalt cried, gathered another pull, and twisted the fang back through Elkara's arm.

Expecting blood to flow in torrents from the scope of the wound, Galahalt quickly moved to cover it.

Meanwhile Elkara's mouth gaped significantly, without sound. The stone had fully receded, her flesh made whole.

"No blood," Galahalt said, sounding disillusioned. He looked up, met the Beast's woeful smile. "There's no blood," he repeated, swept his eyes to the wound, found it already scarred.

"This is my gift." The Questing Beast bent his forelimbs, sank to floor. "Use it to reap vengeance. Slay those who intend harm upon your sister." His chin met the cushion, and the Beast exhaled ruefully. "Do not fail as we did. Promise me, there will be no peace for them."

"Of this," began Galahalt, his eyes unwavering from the Beast's gift. "You have my solemn oath."

31

The setting stole Margot's breath as the horse led carriage lurched to a stop. She placed her hand on the holy knight escort's hand and carefully descended, trying not to ensnare her gown.

The holy knight stood with hands clasped under his radiant chest plate. The man was freshly shaved, his long hair damp and smoothed back exposing some scars of various lengths. The holy knight was not particularly ugly, but she certainly preferred his features over the fat troll she would soon be joined with.

"My lady," the holy knight said. "Once the music plays, that will be your cue to walk down the jeweled aisle all the way to the dais."

"How very whimsical," Margot said, taking in the landscape. An ancient, yet well maintained onyx pavilion sat upon a recess on a gentle overlook, and beyond it the ivory shores of a pond glistened. Weeping, flowering trees tightly encircled the small body of water, their blossoms creating a mosaic of reds and yellows along the calm water's surface. Rich tapestries of gold, ebony, and azure created fragile barriers for those in attendance, the breeze brushing along the surfaces created a spectacle of light. Every holy knight in attendance wore a fine tunic, pauldrons, and white leggings. Strapped to their black leather belts, ceremonial arming swords lay at rest inside golden scabbards.

"I must leave you now." The holy knight performed a courtly bow and strode to join the others presently hemming the aisle.

Margot nodded vaguely, her attention straying back to the scenery.

The guests stood before the pavilion, divided by the aisle. Those with the church had been situated to the left, and the right had been designated for all others. The church side severely outnumbered the opposite side. From where she stood, she spotted only three familiar faces.

"This is all meant for me," she whispered. The lustrous beauty dazzled the eye, but deep pangs of disappointment rattled her core. "All of this feels so wasted."

A jeweled pathway, flanked by holy knights on both sides, led to where she would exchange vows with Schroederstall. Her eyes traced to the journey's end, falling abruptly upon the groom; the man who had brokered a deal nearly a decade ago for her hand. He stood empty handed wearing an extraordinary officer's mantle, expertly tailored, and somehow buttoned from waist to neck without appearing on the verge of bursting. What he wore on his lower half, she could not see, as the lectern impeded her view.

A hand clasped her elbow, forced her to start. She turned and met the sad eyes of her uncle.

"I am so sorry, Margot," Uncle Brett began. "I did not mean for this to get where we are. I sold nearly everything." He tugged the shoulder of his frayed tunic. "Aside from the essentials. But that hardly matters now, I'm afraid."

Margot set hard eyes on the dais. "This is the path the Creator has set for me," she said, and looked back to her uncle. He appeared frail. "Know that I harbor you no ill-will. This is my burden to carry alone."

Uncle Brett hung his head. "And here I am as your only family," he said. "What a sad showing indeed."

Margot gently touched his shoulder. "I count it a blessing that Galahalt is not here."

Whistles escaped Brett's chest as he laughed. "If he were," he said, moustache twitching. "I doubt the lad would be dolled in elegant fineries."

"Nor would he endorse the marriage," Margot added.

"He'd miss the ceremony," Brett wagered. "But he'd be sure to be on the lists for the tourney after the ceremony."

Margot beamed, recalling her brother's nature.

Brett took a step back, surveyed his niece. "You do look beautiful," he admitted warmly. "Just like your mother." He shook his head, fighting back the sudden arrival of tears.

"Thank you, uncle," Margot said. "I wish she were here, but in an odd sort of way, I'm also glad she is not here to witness this."

The crunch of pebbles interrupted their conversation as the carriages departed, leaving Margot and Brett as the only silhouettes on the hill. A quartet of stringed musicians assumed their place to the left of the pavilion, stepping onto a knee-high platform draped with blue trim.

"So it begins," Margot said, upraising her chin as the foremost musician tucked hers over the lower bout of her instrument. "If ever you were to arrive, Halty, now would be the time."

The processional's opening notes descended upon the audience, and all heads turned toward Margot. The holy knights drew their swords and raised them, creating an archway.

Placing her hand within the crease of her uncle's arm, the two set off down the gentle slope.

Margot's slippered feet experienced every gem and jewel inlaid upon the aisle. She ignored the discomfort, maintaining her composure as she entered the passage of swords. Uncle Brett ducked under the first blade, and sheepishly straightened up.

The onyx stone of the pavilion appeared without seam or joint, as if it had been heated and poured upon its formation. The lectern rose from the floor, uninterrupted by hard angles. Every surface was impossibly smooth, and the black of the onyx seemed otherworldly, taking in all the light and forgetting to give any back.

Margot departed Brett's escort with a kiss to his cheek, and slowly mounted the pavilion steps. As she took her place opposite the groom, until this point, she had avoided meeting his eyes. She scanned the attendees, first the church side, and did not recognize a single face. She looked to other side, saw the only occupants; Pietr and Isabelle. The artist caught her eye, withdrew a flask from under his coat and jiggled it slyly. Isabelle appeared as per usual, a bundle of vibrating energy. She flashed Margot an excited smile, and waved at Uncle Brett as he settled into the seat beside her.

By this time the processional's final refrain concluded. A stilled silence pervaded. Schroederstall adjusted his feet, staring off into the audience. His hands remained clasped behind his back. Unsure of ceremonial etiquette, Margot did not move from where she had been instructed to stand. She assumed, at this point, the groom should at least face her.

The musicians picked up into song.

A tall silhouette adorned the horizon at the top of the hill, where earlier Margot had been left by the carriages. For but a moment, Margot held the hope that it was Galahalt standing there. Once the silhouette initiated his walk, she realized the frame was not that of her brother.

This new song sounded as a processional, but the notes felt ominous, the chords diminished.

One by one the audience took notice of this new arrival, turning collective shoulders his way. Presently the man strode down the aisle, cutting past the holy knights whose blades remained sheathed. The man was donned in the most exquisite plate that Margot had ever seen. The steel glistened in shades of both jade and sapphire, depending on where the sun graced its surface. An azure tabard billowed at his ankles, exposing leg armour set in the same impossible coloration.

Schroederstall stiffened as one readying a salute.

Margot beheld the man blankly. Of a sudden, she recognized him.

"The Arbiter?" she whispered, glancing at Schroederstall for confirmation.

The churchman discreetly nodded.

"Lord Amyr is officiating our ceremony?"

Sweat beaded Schroederstall's forehead. "Not exactly."

Amyr ascended the pavilion steps, took Margot's hands into his own.

"Let us begin, my bride."

32

The trees of Fenrirfang held nothing but shadow.

Freeing themselves at long last, knight and laif appeared from the hedgerow. Together they entered a field beneath foreboding skies. Fertile land stretched all around, as corn shoots rose up from the soil to brush their shins.

Over their heads, clouds gathered into a solid roiling mass.

The air smelled of a fast-arriving downpour, and from the city ahead, the clanging of bells sounded clear into the trees at their backs.

"Wedding bells at midday," Elkara said warily. "You cannot think this means—" She turned abruptly to her companion.

Hundreds of bells raised their voices from all around the kingdom.

The laif watched the knight's shoulders fall as the bells tolled.

"What do we do now?" she asked.

Galahalt looked down at the fang of the Questing Beast clenched in his fist. He raised his face and cast his eyes upward, over and beyond the laif.

"There is much blood to be spilled."

Epilogue

"That's simply not possible," Lucien said, his elbow digging into a crevice on the worn tabletop. He observed the barmaid's retreat with a suspicious look. "She must be lying. There's no way he'd visit a pub like *this* one."

"Oh whoa! What're you implying?" Sir Jaufre leaned back in the booth the two men shared. "The Bloody Fork doesn't meet his standards?"

More patrons rushed into the tavern, shaking water from their cloaks and hats, shivering and wiping their faces. Overhead raindrops pummeled the roof. It did not seem as if the rainstorm would be letting up anytime soon. At present, the *Bloody Fork* had neared its capacity as folks bumped elbows and spilled foam from their tankards. Lucien and Jaufre had arrived just after the marriage bells had sounded across the kingdom earlier. The establishment, at that time, had been near empty. But as the evening wore on, the numbers swelled.

"I'm glad they didn't book a minstrel tonight," Lucien said, his voice just beneath a shout. "Or else this would be utterly insufferable."

"Absolutely," Jaufre agreed as their barmaid returned. He shifted his attention her way. "Have you confirmed that's actually Sir Percival over at the bar?"

The barmaid first set a tankard before Jaufre. "E'eryone is too afeard to ask," she replied, smiling as she placed Lucien's tankard on the table. "I'd point him out, but there's too many people in the way." She batted a stray curl of hair away from her eye. "His hood's all drawn, and he's wearing rusty armour. The barkeep was the only one to catch a good look, and he's the one who told me. Now e'eryone is giving the rusty knight some space."

"Oh, that's interesting," Lucien muttered. "What's he drinking?"

"Milk," the barmaid replied. The same curl rebounded over her eye. "Is there anything else I can bring you gentlemen?"

Jaufre thoughtfully twirled his moustache. "We're good for now," he replied. "Thank you kindly."

"Don't mention it." She bestowed Lucien a coy smile, turned a heel, and disappeared into the thick of the patrons.

A particularly intoxicated man stumbled loose from the crowd, catching Lucien's eye. Aside from being rather obese, the only other remarkable detail about the man was his choice in raiment. He wore the colors of the church, and walked with the lean of one traipsing a ship assailed by a storm.

"Milk?" Jaufre remarked. "What kind of werewolf drinks milk?"

"He's coming right toward us," Lucien advised, placing both palms to the tabletop, preparing an abrupt rise.

"Percival is—?" Jaufre turned in time to see the drunken churchman clip the outer edge of their table as he trundled past. "Watch where you're going, eh?"

The churchman rounded, eyes bloodshot and wandering. "You watch where you're going!" he shouted, leaned toward Jaufre. "Eh!" He bumped the table, spilling more of their ale.

"Be off," said Lucien, lifting his tankard, preserving what remained.

"You be off!" the churchman hissed. "Do you know who I am?"

"No," Lucien replied. "Should I?"

The churchman ogled Lucien, his jowls shivering.

Jaufre stood, placed a hand to the churchman's shoulder. "Look," he stated calmly. "We don't know you, guy. And we don't want to know you."

The churchman swatted Jaufre's hand, which as a direct result caused him to stumble backward. He teetered on one foot, nearly falling onto his back, behaving as if the floor had sharply slanted behind his heels. Then, quite suddenly, he uprighted himself, straightened his tunic, and clomped away as if nothing had happened.

"What did we just witness?" Lucien said.

Jaufre regarded the churchman's departure with a flat stare. "No clue," he replied. "For his sake, I hope we're the last he bothers tonight."

***

A DRUNKEN SCHROEDERSTALL WORMED his way through the patrons of the *Bloody Fork*.

"Such illustrious clientele," the churchman murmured, shouldering his way to the tavern's serving counter, his recent confrontation with the two men at their table quickly forgotten. Through his clotted web of a haze, he espied a vacant stool situated beneath the counter. His hurried path to the stool was filled with lurching and groping and aggravated swats, but he eventually achieved his goal. "She was supposed to be my bride!" he blurted, drawing the barkeep's wary notice. Schroederstall summoned the man toward him with a snap of his finger. "But, instead, I officiated their blasted ceremony!"

"Sounds downright unfortunate," remarked the barkeep, settling his feet opposite Schroederstall. "What's your poison?"

"An ale," replied Schroederstall. "If you please."

The barkeep swept a hand at the kegs lined at his back. "I'm afraid you'll need to be a bit more specific, friend," he said. "We offer a variety of ale."

Schroederstall took notice of the patron seated to his left. The man, perhaps a knight—based on the fact he wore armour—sat alone, his head bowed. His drenched hair fell along the sides of his head, curtaining his face and the beverage he sipped.

"I'll have whatever he's having," Schroederstall said, gesturing to the man beside him.

The barkeep spent a moment blinking. "You'd like a milk?"

"A what?" Schroederstall bristled, sat upright. His chins wagged as he turned abruptly toward the man apparently consuming milk. "Are you a child?!"

The man drew another sip from his cup, the churchman's question ignored.

"What sort of knight," Schroederstall began. "If that's what you claim to be—in that rusty set of armour—doesn't drink a proper ale?" He rose, steadying himself with a hand to the counter.

"Easy now, friend," the barkeep cautioned as the churchman unsteadily approached the man. "What's the problem? Just sit down and I'll fetch you an ale on the house, if—"

Schroederstall slapped the bartop. "I asked this lout a simple question," he seethed. Were he not so inebriated, he may have realized he had miscounted. "And I demand an answer!" Presently, Schroederstall loomed beside the man. "Are you only just weaned from your mother's teat?" He leaned close. "I'll ask again. What kind of knight are you?"

"What kind of holy man stands by as innocent children are slaughtered?" the man replied, drew another sip of milk.

A shock of sobriety came to Schroederstall. His head twitched uncontrollably, seeming of its own accord. "Do you know who I am?!" he screamed, his wrath arriving. "Answer me!" He batted the cup from the man's hand. Milk fanned the air, narrowly missing the barkeep. Then a different fluid invaded the air. This time, the barkeep was not so agile to avoid.

Schroederstall gurgled, sputtering blood, flailing his arms. From beneath his chins, the hilt of a dagger protruded. His panicked eyes were locked onto the man in rusty plate who had just buried a dagger into the base of his chin. With his tongue pinned to the roof of his mouth, the churchman was unable to plead. From the back of his throat he tried to form words. The dagger did not have the length to reach his brainpan, and because of this, Schroederstall felt a glimmer of hope.

"I do know who you are," the man said. He regarded Schroederstall with disdain as he guided the churchman's head toward the bartop. Then, swiftly, he brought the base of the dagger to the counter surface.

Schoederstall squealed as the weapon found firm rooting. The man's grip was that of iron. Inside his mouth, blood poured down the blade, funneled over his teeth, the pain terrific.

In rapid succession the man withdrew his hand from the dagger, drove his elbow down onto the top of Schroederstall's head.

"What kind of knight am I?" the man finally gave his answer, watching the churchman's body slough to the floor. "I am King Arthur's knight."

Acknowledgments

My thanks to all the readers of this book in its various stages of
development for their input and feedback.

I would like to extend my deepest gratitude to
Tom Kent, Susan Kent, Jonathan Myers, Beth Foster,
Scott Telle, Ryan Krebs, and Michael Oehlbeck.

I also need to thank my wife for her gratuitous amount
of support, wisdom, and encouragement.

About the Author

M. Warren Askins lives with his family in
the Northeastern United States.

Scan the following code to check out his current list of works.

Here is a peek at the first chapter of **Orphan's Rite**,
a companion novel in the *Dead Men are Dying* Universe.

Chapter 1

The Orphan

Care to repeat that?" the shopkeep requested, placing his hands on the counter and leaning forward to better hear the laif girl. She had rushed in alone a few minutes prior, setting the bell above the door tinkling wildly, and her meanderings through the three aisles filled with curios had eventually led her to the counter. She had mumbled to him as she tucked her chin into the sizable scarf wrapped around her neck. Her hands were empty and the shopkeep wagered that she didn't have any money to spend, however her eyes held an intensity that she was attempting to express. She mumbled what seemed to be the same phrase again, but frustratingly at the same volume and timbre as before.

"Where are your parents, sweetling?" the man asked with a tinge of concern. The child's only response was to narrow her eyes and critically scan his face. The older man appeared friendly, his round face perfectly shaped for the graying moustache perched atop his upper lip. A wooden plate of game hen and potatoes sat next to the man's elbow, the steam long gone from the meal and most of the bones were picked clean, though it was not entirely apparent as to whether he had finished with the meal yet. A thin coat of coagulated gravy was swirled around the plate where the man had used his spoon to try and snag the three remaining lumps of potato, but had been interrupted when she had entered.

"Listen, you have got to speak up. I can't help you if I can't understand you," the man said, waiting for some sort of intelligent response, working his jaw impatiently. "If you're looking to get warm, feel free to stand over by the stove, but once that's done if you aren't aiming to make a purchase, I'd be grateful if you scuttled off elsewhere." The laif girl appeared completely focused on his half eaten dinner and was not paying attention to him in the least. The shopkeep had developed a keen sense for detecting a grift after several experiences with scoundrels in the past, and while this girl did not have that type of air, it was possible she was involved in a scheme using her as some kind of distraction.

"If you don't tell me what it is that you want..." he trailed off as he noticed a pair of Church guardsmen passing by his front windows, intently tracking footprints in the recently fallen snow.

Much like most of the populace, the man was not heavily in favor of the Church at the moment, especially after that unreasonable edict and the ensuing slaughter at Knotwithstadt. And the way the Church was treating all the orphans from that brutal business, the ones that survived...*Orphans!* The shopkeep hurriedly turned back to the girl, but she was not where he had last seen her.

One of the guards peered into the window and the shopkeep met his gaze with a reassuring nod, hoping to indicate "good morning" not "please enter." Apparently nodding etiquette was not a learned skill amongst current law enforcement, as the guard immediately pressed inside under the tinkling bell.

"Lots of junk in here," the guard sneered, passing a shelf and gingerly lifting a stuffed gremlin with a monocle on its eye and a lantern in its hand.

"Well, it's a curio shop, friend," the clerk replied politely, absentmindedly reaching for his dinner plate, which like the girl, was not where he last saw it.

"Curio?" the guard queried, placing the gremlin onto the counter.

"Curiosity shop," the clerk stated. "Knick-knacks and nonsense. Some things of great value to some and utterly worthless to others," he elaborated as the bell tinkled again, ushering in the second guard. "For instance, this jeweled blade." The man reached below the counter and produced a dagger with what appeared to be a crude depiction of a bumblebee as its scabbard.

He held it out to the guard who glanced at it with less than mild amusement. "Looks splendid," the guard said dryly. His face seemed perpetually locked in a sneer as he surveyed the items beyond the counter while his companion was lurking around the aisles, lifting pots and rummaging through chests.

"We seem to have lost a mutt from our kennels," the guard began. "Have you seen one sniffing around this..." he paused, raising an eyebrow to look at the ogre head mounted on the wall with a lit smoking pipe protruding from its mouth. A tendril of smoke swirled from the bowl and the guard wrinkled his face and shook his head. "This," he continued, waving a hand, "Whatever you called this foul store."

"A curiosity shop."

"Yes, well, the mongrel's prints appear to lead to your doorstep," the guard said. He lifted his hand waist high. "The creature stands about this tall with a scarf wrapped nearly up to its pointy ears. More than likely looks like any other pathetic stray."

"Oh, well," the shopkeep murmured uncomfortably, scratching the back of his neck, "you two are the first customers to darken my doorway all afternoon. And to be perfectly honest, we don't allow animals into the shop, so I would be grateful..."

"Don't," The guard cut him off. "Do not waste our time. This particular whelp bit the hand that fed it, and anyone suspected of harboring such a creature will answer to the Arbiter." The man watched his words register as the clerk suddenly became tense and nervous. "I didn't catch your name?" the guard continued, his sneer growing more pronounced.

"Neil," the shopkeep replied apprehensively, tucking the dagger away. He chose his next words carefully, knowing that a lie could land him in front of the Judge. "I haven't entertained any strays, mutts, or whelps all day."

"You won't mind if we take a peek then?" the guard queried, obviously dissatisfied with the response. "We'll need to check your stock room as well." He flicked the gremlin's nose and stared nastily at the keeper. Neil opened his hands in surrender and nodded his head with a forced smile.

"Good," the guard said, hastily skirting the counter and making for the back room. The other guard had finally wound her way to the last aisle and was standing before the multitudes of books in front of the window. Neil was unsure as to whether she was admiring the expansive collection of manuscripts or if she was peering outside, monitoring for a possible escape.

He took a few strides toward her and followed her gaze down the row of books.

"They're all originals," he said proudly, tapping a dusty shelf. "Every last one of them. Each one is absolutely priceless." He rubbed his fingertips together, working the grime off.

"I do enjoy a good tale," she murmured with reverence, her eyes sweeping side to side. "Perhaps I will venture back here on another day."

Neil gave her a nod and walked back to the counter. "I hear that we are to be receiving a sheriff soon?" he asked at length, attempting to fill the silence.

He heard an exasperated groan in reply, and he took that as a sign to continue. "It has been generations since this district has had any formal law. I don't believe even my great grandfather would be able to recall the last one."

"It is utter foolishness," the female guard grumbled with disdain, holding a leather-bound tome and thumbing through the pages. "The Church has been overseeing the enforcement of laws for ages and has been doing a pretty decent job of it, if you ask me." She regarded the pages of the tome for a few more seconds before slamming the bindings shut with a satisfying thud, sending a cloud of dust upward and tainting the air where the sunlight poured in.

"I was pondering what it will mean for people such as yourself and your accomplice back there," Neil said, gesturing to the back stockroom, the door left ajar.

"It means some dipshit is going to serve a term as *sheriff*, and apparently nothing much else will change for us," she scoffed, approaching the clerk. "Instead of the Church giving orders we will be taking our orders from her. Well, those of us who decide to remain as guards at least."

"Oh, is service voluntary? I mean— " his words were cut short by a shriek from behind. The clerk and guard briefly locked eyes, then both wheeled around to face the stockroom. Standing at the threshold was the sneering guard, a chunk of the laif girl's hair clenched in his fist, painfully hoisting her up on tiptoes. The female guard pushed past the shopkeep and began clapping her hands in delight.

"Looky what I found!" the male guard crowed, his sneer evolving into a wicked grin. "Seems like our evening hunt has been cut short, Briel," he remarked while roughly shaking his quarry. Tears trickled down the girl's face as she sucked in air through her clenched teeth while half-heartedly swinging both fists at the man's groin. One fist nearly connected causing the guard to yank up and violently twist the locks of hair in his grip, forcing out another shriek from the child.

"She was back there in a corner eating table scraps like the wretched little mutt that she is." The guard fixed a hard gaze on Neil, tossing the dinner plate in his direction. "So it was chicken and potatoes on the menu tonight, eh? You can lie to me all you want, you bloody clown, but try and pull that with the Judge and see what happens," he threatened. "I'll be sure to make a special notation for you in my report," the guard finished with a wink, the words tinged with malice.

Neil raised his hands in submission. "Listen, listen," he said, trying to avoid the girl's desperate stare. "She came in only five minutes before you did. I don't even know her name. I thought she was cold and offered her warmth by my stove. That's all! I swear! We don't need to involve Amyr in this!" he pleaded anxiously, taking a step toward the guard. "Let's be reasonable here."

"Get back to your shop," Briel stated, placing a hand on the man's chest. "This no longer concerns you."

"I just…" the clerk began, unsure of what to say. "Alright," he acquiesced, sending the girl an apologetic shrug before turning back to his duties.

Neil heard the sneering guard order the horses brought around. In short order, the rear door to the loading docks creaked open amidst a myriad of whimpering and begging. Briel brushed past him on her way out and Neil firmly closed the stock room door, effectively muting the pitiful sounds. His emotions were a confusing cloud of guilt and fear that entered his lungs, pervading his soul, causing him to endure a spell of panicked suffocation. The tinkling bell indicated that Briel had left the building, but he hardly took notice as he gripped his chest. His eyes were drawn to the yellow and black rings on the ridiculous bumblebee dagger tucked on a shelf below the counter.

The man was unsure how long he stood there debating if he should become the violent man that he never had been nor wanted to be. The horses passed the front windows as he stood locked in indecision, and the group would be long gone if he waited much longer.

"Just hold out a few more minutes, old man," he whispered to himself. "You're no hero." He could not dispel the image of the helpless laif struggling against the iron grip of that cruel guard. Deep in thought, he pounded his fist on his thigh, hardly noticing when he snatched up the blade and whirled to the back door.

What are you doing, you fool? His good sense tried to hold him back as he hurried through the stock room. He had not noticed the slick patch of gravy on the floor and suddenly his world was sailing upward. As soon as the back of his skull bounced off the floor, he spiraled into unconsciousness.

HOW LONG? NEIL SAT UP SLOWLY and raised a hand to touch the back of his head, immediately regretting the decision once his fingertip grazed an elevated lump that caused his teeth to rattle in a shiver of agony. He looked around through bleary eyes, the meager light dribbling through the windows indicating that he had been out cold for at least an hour, if not longer. With a few curses and loud groans, the man gradually reached a standing position.

"Just how hard did you crack your noodle, old man?" he muttered to himself, walking to the exit. Neil could hear voices very clearly coming from behind the store, but questioned his senses. The back alley was not a popular place for folk to meet and typically was silent at this time of the day. As he cautiously approached, it became clear that he was not imagining things. There was definitely more than one voice, and as he congratulated himself on not losing his mind, he heaved the dock door open.

To his surprise, the walls were illuminated by flickering torchlight revealing a startling scene. A man pressing a kerchief over his mouth drew the curio clerk's attention to what appeared to be a dead body slumped against the wall. The street beyond the dock was congested with onlookers and busybodies peering over a handful of Church guards in varying stages of investigation.

One guardsman held his torch aloft while vomiting at the base of the dock staircase, just below Neil's feet. Once the man was finished with the last dry heave, he looked up and bashfully apologized before getting back to the matter at hand. "Did you see anything suspicious tonight, friend?" the guard inquired, wiping his mouth with the back of his vambrace.

All Neil could think to reply was that he had just awoken from a nap, which was not altogether false. After being threatened with judgment earlier, he was not too keen on discussing the details of his day with those who enforced the law.

"Ah," the guard replied, bobbing his head in what appeared to be an exaggerated nod, but then his shoulders heaved and he doubled over renewing the disposal of his most recent meal. Neil gave the man a reassuring pat on the back as he tiptoed past to gain a closer look at the scene. He was still a bit unsteady from his fall, and he stumbled on the cobbles, drawing the attention of several surrounding guards.

"Careful, friend," one guard cautioned, suddenly appearing with a gentle hand to the clerk's chest, urging him back. "I'm not too sure you want to see this."

Neil thumbed toward the shop as he began his reply, "This is my..." he stopped abruptly when he recognized the face of the corpse propped up like a discarded doll. *Briel.* Two symmetrical weeping wounds were apparent on her azure tunic, exactly an inch from each armpit, right below her spaulders. Painful, but likely not lethal. A moment later Neil identified the killing strike. A third equal sized puncture bisected the bridge of the guard's nose, between the eyes. Judging by the stains on the brick facade, she had been standing upright when the weapon had perforated her skull. The eye could easily trace a triangle with the wounds, the locations placed methodically and executed with swift precision.

The guard removed his hand, realizing that it was too late to prevent the shopkeep from witnessing the disturbing mess. "It appears that one was killed by a surgeon," the guard said with a shrug, indicating Briel.

"And that one," he paused, rubbing his sternum, clearly uncomfortable, "looks to have been set upon by a pack of faewolves," he finished, tilting his head toward the opposite wall.

Neil gasped and slapped a hand over his mouth when his gaze fell upon the other corpse.

In the fluttering torchlight he recognized the sneer-faced guard now crumpled in a heap. What remained of his head jutted at an awkward angle from the rest of his body. His jaw had been completely torn off and the rest of his face was an exposed crimson skull. The unblinking eyes had been left intact and were somehow completely untarnished by blood, creating a particularly disturbing contrast. It was not possible to even discern which limbs were attached, and which had been simply collected and piled atop the corpse.